MISS FEATHERTON'S Christmas Kiss

Meg gave a shiver of delight as she reached out and plucked a burning raisin from the bowl. Hawksworth got two of them, handing one to her. Then she did the same.

"You're very good at this." His voice was warm with praise.

"So are you."

Shrieks of laughter filled the room as he leaned close to her. "A passionate game."

"We have already had this discussion." Easing herself out of the circle, she murmured, "I need some air."

Hawksworth caught up to Meg at the end of the long terrace. "What is it about passion you do not like?"

She closed her eyes and counted to ten before turning to face him. "What has passion to do with anything?"

He prowled slowly toward her. The torches reflected the fire lurking in his eyes, making him more dangerous than ever before. She took a step back toward the wall, and before she knew it her back had hit the cold stone.

"If you do not want love, you must at least have passion." Bracing his hand on the wall next to her cheek, he leaned forward until his breath caressed her face. It was sweet with raisins and brandy.

Before she knew it, his lips were next to hers. The tip of his tongue trailed languidly along her bottom lip, and her knees began to turn to marmalade. "Will you lie in your cold bed with your nightgown on while your husband ruts?" His wicked tongue moved from her mouth to her ear as he whispered, "Or do you want to scream as he takes you to heaven and back?"

Books by Ella Quinn

THE SEDUCTION OF LADY PHOEBE

THE SECRET LIFE OF MISS ANNA MARSH

THE TEMPTATION OF LADY SERENA

DESIRING LADY CARO

ENTICING MISS EUGÉNIE VILLARET

A KISS FOR LADY MARY

LADY BERESFORD'S LOVER

MISS FEATHERTON'S CHRISTMAS PRINCE

Novellas

MADELEINE'S CHRISTMAS WISH

Published by Kensington Publishing Corporation

Miss Featherton's Christmas Prince

Ella Quinn

LYRICAL PRESS
Kensington Publishing Corp.
www.kensingtonbooks.com

To the extent that the image or images on the cover of this book depict a person or persons, such person or persons are merely models, and are not intended to portray any character or characters featured in the book.

LYRICAL PRESS BOOKS are published by

Kensington Publishing Corp.
119 West 40th Street
New York, NY 10018

Copyright © 2015 by Ella Quinn

All rights reserved. No part of this book may be reproduced in any form or by any means without the prior written consent of the Publisher, excepting brief quotes used in reviews.

All Kensington titles, imprints, and distributed lines are available at special quantity discounts for bulk purchases for sales promotion, premiums, fund-raising, educational, or institutional use.

Special book excerpts or customized printings can also be created to fit specific needs. For details, write or phone the office of the Kensington Sales Manager: Kensington Publishing Corp., 119 West 40th Street, New York, NY 10018. Attn. Sales Department. Phone: 1-800-221-2647.

Lyrical and the L logo are trademarks of Kensington Publishing Corp.

First Electronic Edition: November 2015
eISBN-13: 978-1-60183-460-7
eISBN-10: 1-60183-460-8

First Print Edition: November 2015
ISBN-13: 978-1-60183-461-4
ISBN-10: 1-60183-461-6

Printed in the United States of America

This book is dedicated to my lovely granddaughter, may you find your happily ever after, and to my husband who has been my hero for over thirty years.

ACKNOWLEDGMENTS

There are always so many people who help make a book. Thank you to my husband who has had to take on a lot more of the boat work, allowing me to write. To my beta readers, Doreen, Margaret, and Jenna: you ladies always give me such fantastic advice and guidance. To my lovely agent, Elizabeth Pomada, and my wonderful editor, John Scognamiglio. To the Kensington team, Jane, Alex, Vida, and Lauren for all their hard work promoting my book. To the fabulous authors in The Beau Monde for answering my questions quickly and accurately. And last, but not least, to my fantastic readers. I have no words to express how much your support means to me.

CHAPTER ONE

Featherton House, London, Late Autumn 1817

Miss Margaret Elizabeth Lucinda Featherton, second daughter of Viscount Featherton, glanced down at the missive in her lap. The letters were rounded, much like a child's would be, but the spelling and grammar were correct.

> *Dear Miss Featherton,*
> *I pray this letter arrives in time to save you from making a horrible mistake. Lord Tarlington is not what you think him. I do not expect you to take my word for it. However, if you go to number Twenty-Three Basil Street in the neighborhood of Hans Crescent around seven in the morning, you will find the evidence for yourself.*
> *A Friend*

The first time she had received such a letter, the warning had concerned her last suitor, the Earl of Swindon. She shuddered at how close she had come to marrying such a monstrous man. A heaviness lodged in her chest, making it hard to breathe. What would she discover about Tarlington?

The following morning at half past six, Meg and her maid, Hendricks, sallied forth as if taking their usual early stroll in Hyde Park. However, instead of walking down Charles Street toward the Park they headed in the opposite direction to Hay Hill, then on to Bond Street and hailed a hackney.

The day was cool but sunny. A clean, crisp scent, which reminded her of newly-harvested apples, unusual for London, filled the air. Trees were showing off their brilliant autumn colors. It was altogether too pretty a day for their mission. Meg was tempted to go back and hide in her chamber as if she had never received the missive. Yet if she did, she could end up wed to a man as bad as or worse than Swindon.

Twenty minutes later, she and her maid were situated two houses down from Twenty-Three Basil Street. The town house consisted of three stories and a cellar area. Flowers in pots stood on either side of the well-maintained front door. The brass knocker gleamed as if polished regularly.

Hendricks drew back the leather shade in the hackney, keeping watch on the house as Meg pressed back against the thin, poorly cushioned squabs. She resisted the urge to pleat her skirts, which would surely draw a rebuke from her maid, and waited.

Wondering if, yet again, she had fallen in love with a fiend.

After several minutes, she shifted on the hard bench. Two women carrying baskets hurried past the coach, staring at the vehicle as they went. If Meg and Hendricks remained here much longer, they would begin attracting attention.

Frustrated with waiting, Meg blew out a puff of air. "Do you see anything yet?"

"No." Her maid started to shake her head, then stopped. "Oh, wait. The door is opening."

Finally. She slid to the other side of the hackney and glanced out the window. A handsome gentleman with curling dark blond hair stepped out of the town house holding an infant. Lord Tarlington smiled down at the woman standing next to him, who clutched the hand of a small child still in skirts. For a moment the smile appeared to be the same as the ones he had given Meg on numerous occasions. Then his smile deepened and his face lit with love as he embraced the woman before kissing her and handing her the baby. As the woman's hand rose, a glint of gold on the third finger of her left hand appeared.

Married! The cur was already wed!

Fury swept through her. The pain in her breast deepened as her heart broke into sharp shards. How could she have been so gullible to fall in love with a man who so obviously did not return her affections and was not even free to give them?

Unable to watch any longer, she slid back to the other side of the coach. Lord Tarlington might not be the ogre Swindon was, but he had lied to her and had deceived her, and, worst of all, he had pretended to love her. For that she would never forgive him.

"That snake!" Hendricks's outraged gasp broke the silence. "And he just spoke to your father yesterday."

"It would appear"—Meg's throat closed painfully, but she refused to give in to the tears threatening to fall—"that he has a previous commitment. One he has kept well hidden." Reaching up, she knocked on the roof of the carriage. "Take us to Gunter's."

The famous ice cream shop was located at the other end of Berkeley Square from her house. They would leave the hackney there, thus disguising the direction they'd come from anyone at her house.

A deep line formed between her maid's brows. "What will you do now, miss?"

Take the only action she could under the circumstances. "I shall write to him, refusing his offer, and instruct Benson that I am not at home to his lordship."

"Mark my words, miss. He'll try to see you."

"I do not think he will." Despite the fact that unmarried ladies were not supposed to be aware of secret wives, or lovers, she had every intention of telling him she knew of his.

Then again, she had been receiving quite an education. Her "friend" seemed to be extraordinarily conversant with Meg's suitors. It was as if she had a real guardian angel.

Last Season, she had discovered Lord Swindon had whipped his mistress almost to death. She could never even have imagined such a thing was possible. Then her friend had written with an offer for Meg to meet the woman, Rose. She had turned out to be younger than Meg, with red hair and green eyes. Rose had dropped her robe. Scars covered her back and buttocks. If Meg had not seen the damage done to the young woman, she most likely would not have believed it. Her stomach twisted into a knot as she thought of the hell her life would have been if she had wed Swindon.

She applied herself to her current dilemma. The hard part would be explaining to her parents why she was turning down yet another offer. One she had initially received with enthusiasm. As when she had visited the courtesan, Meg would never be able to disclose her trip to the Basil Street house. Even her fairly liberal parents would certainly not approve of her conduct.

A half hour later, she and Hendricks completed a brisk stroll around the square before arriving home. As Meg and her maid made their way up the front steps, the door opened, and her father's butler bowed. "A good walk, miss?"

"Very good indeed, Benson." She removed her bonnet. "If Lord Tarlington calls, I am not at home."

Meg was quite sure that the entire household down to the newest tweenie knew of the proposal, but Benson did not reveal his surprise by even a twitch of his eyelashes. "Very well, miss."

Upon entering her chamber, she handed Hendricks her gloves and bonnet, then went straight to her desk, pulling out a piece of pressed paper before sitting to write her letter to his lordship.

Meg held her hand steady, being careful not to leave smudges or any other indication of her distress.

> Lord Tarlington,
> *I find I cannot accept your offer of marriage. It has become clear to me that you have given your heart to another. Please do not attempt to convince me that she and the children are not important. If that was the case*—Meg brushed angrily at the tears blurring her eyes—*I still could not wed you, as I would never trust a man who could leave his lover and children.*
> *Do not attempt to speak to me or approach me. The dances you requested will be given to another.*
> M. Featherton

She sanded the letter, reading it over again before applying her seal. It was better that she had used the term *lover* rather than *wife*. She did not want to leave him room to argue. That ought to do it. "Hendricks, please arrange to have this delivered to Lord Tarlington."

"Yes, miss. I'll ring for tea."

Tea, the answer to all ills. "Thank you."

The door clicked shut, and Meg clutched her handkerchief, waiting for the tears she had been keeping at bay to come, but after one lone drop rolled down her cheek, her eyes dried. Perhaps she had become used to betrayal. She supposed she should be grateful that her guardian angel was watching over her. For some reason she seemed to attract the wrong type of gentleman. If only she did not wish to marry. The problem was that being a spinster held no lure for her. Yet, perhaps it was time to give up on love in a marriage. She could search for an amiable, undemanding gentleman to wed, have her children, and live a comfortable, if unexciting, life.

The tears finally came, streaming down her face in a torrent as her heart crumbled into dust.

The following morning, Lucinda, Dowager Viscountess Featherton, sat in her favorite chair directly in front of the fireplace in the Featherton House breakfast room. "Did you tell Meg she could not accept Tarlington?"

Her son David, the current Viscount Featherton, glanced up from his newspaper. "It wasn't necessary. She sent a note to me first thing this morning, informing me that she had decided that she and Tarlington wouldn't suit."

Lucinda raised her brows so that she would appear surprised, and in an innocent voice said, "How fortuitous. No doubt she felt something was wrong."

"I would take her home," her daughter-in-law Helena said, "but if she leaves on the heels of Tarlington departing Town, it is bound to appear odd."

Lucinda carefully spread apricot marmalade on her toast so that it completely covered the small piece of bread she held. "Indeed it would. You are correct. It is much better for her to remain in Town for another week or so." That would also give the match she wished for Meg time to bloom. "Poor girl. Perhaps next Season she will finally meet the gentleman for her."

Last spring, at the prompting of her good friend Constance, Dowager Duchess of Bridgewater, Lucinda had hired a Bow Street runner. Constance's nephew had made a cryptic remark about the Earl of Swindon, which caused her suspicions to rise. What they discovered prompted them to warn her granddaughter. Then this autumn, when Meg appeared to be forming an attachment to Tarlington, Lucinda had hired the same runner, simply to ensure that there was nothing wrong with the man. Unfortunately, it appeared he had either contracted a marriage with an ineligible woman, or allowed his mistress to pretend to be his wife. In either case, he clearly would not do for Meg. Lucinda sighed. She wished she could have simply told Meg, but what young lady in love would listen? And her daughter-in-law would not have appreciated that Meg knew of such depravities.

"*Without* your assistance." Helena's tone was dry and a bit hard.

"Oh yes. I have learned my lesson," Lucinda lied.

Last spring she, Constance, and their dear friend Almeria Bellamny, had arranged a match between Lucinda's grandson Kit and Constance's granddaughter Lady Mary.

Although successful in the end, there had been problems, and Helena had not been best pleased with Lucinda or her friends. That was just before Constance had told them about Lord Swindon. Thankfully, no one had traced the notes Lucinda had sent to her son or granddaughter back to her. Not that she had written the letters herself.

After the Swindon debacle, Lucinda, Constance, and Almeria made a list of eligible gentlemen, and had found the very man to win Meg's heart: Damon, Marquis of Hawksworth, heir to the Duke of Somerset. He was handsome, honorable, had a good fortune of his own, and in need of a wife. All Lucinda and her friends had to do was throw them together for a long enough period of time and the two young people would realize they were made for each other. The only problem was that Meg had fallen in love with Tarlington before Hawksworth had had time to fix his attentions with her. It was not until later that Lucinda had discovered Meg had met Tarlington during a visit to her maternal grandmother in Bath. Lucinda hoped that Hawksworth would now have his chance to win her heart.

Later that day, she waited in her carriage while one of her footmen knocked on the door of Bridgewater House. Within a few short minutes, Lucinda was bowed into a warm parlor and was pleased to find Almeria, Lady Bellamny, already present. "Well, the deed is done."

"Excellent." Almeria's remaining chin juggled as she nodded. She had been on a reducing diet, and it appeared to be working. "I sent the invitation to Hawksworth before I came here."

"How did Meg take the news?" Constance asked.

"Badly." The sobbing Lucinda had heard coming from her granddaughter's chamber had broken her heart.

When she and her friends had hatched this plan, she had not realized Meg would be dealing with double betrayals, nor how hard she would take this latest matter. Lucinda was very much afraid that her granddaughter would be much more difficult to coax into marriage than Hawksworth. Nevertheless, both of them needed to be settled before his father decided to take the matter of Hawksworth's marriage in hand, and so they would be.

Damon Hawksworth lounged against a convenient pillar in Lady Cowper's crowded ballroom. A glass of wine dangled from his fingers. Directly across from him, another brittle smile appeared on Miss Margaret Featherton's normally happy countenance. Her latest suitor, the Earl of Tarlington, was nowhere to be seen and had not been for the past two days or so. Rumor had it that he had gone to the Continent. The only question Damon had was whether she had given the man his congé or if it had been the other way around. He rather thought something had occurred to cause her to break it off with Tarlington. His godmother would know. If anyone knew the inner workings of the *ton*, it was Almeria Bellamny.

Ever since Rupert, Earl of Stanstead's wedding, when she had introduced him to Miss Featherton, he had developed a fascination for the lady. Her intelligence was sharp, and several times he had seen her hold back a witty retort. Her beauty was not at all in the usual mode. Her mouth was too wide for the current fashion, yet it complemented her high cheekbones and finely arched black brows. Her thick, dark chestnut hair almost begged him to run his fingers through her tresses as they tumbled down. Yet for some reason, the feature he was most fond of was her completely straight nose with a rounded tip. More importantly, she was poised beyond her years. He doubted she had ever been a missish young lady. Even when they had argued over an interpretation of poetry, she had always appeared in complete control and secure in her knowledge.

Now, her polite smile belied the look of despair in her blue eyes. It was as if she was slightly adrift and was only going through the motions until she could retire to the country. Well, with Tarlington gone, Damon wasn't fool enough to wait until some other gentleman snatched her up. He would gladly rescue her and help her on the path he wished for them. Dancing was a start. She would have held the best sets for Tarlington, and now they would be Damon's.

Pushing himself off the pillar, he handed his glass to a passing footman and crossed the room.

"Miss Featherton?" He bowed. "Would you by chance have a free dance?"

Her beautiful eyes, the color of a mountain lake, were shadowed, as if she hadn't slept much recently. "You may have the supper dance, my lord."

"I am honored." He bowed again before taking his leave.

This was worse than he'd thought. Whatever had happened between Tarlington and Miss Featherton, she was not unaffected, and that was an unwanted dilemma. Damon would have to see how the set went before he formulated his strategy for winning her. Glancing around, he saw an old school friend. "Throughgood, I thought you were still touring Europe."

"Just got back." He held out his hand. "You heard about my uncle and cousin?"

"I did, and I'm sorry for your loss." The deaths had raised his father to the Earl of Grantville, and Throughgood to the courtesy title of viscount.

"Good men, both of them. What the devil made them decide to get in one of those blasted hot air balloons together, I'll never know. In any event, m'father decided I needed to come home and learn estate management. Makes my head ache, so I bolted to Town for a week or so before the Season ends."

Although Damon had studied estate management with his father's steward, he had never been given the opportunity to put any of his ideas into practice. His father had made it very clear he did not want him meddling, and had in fact made Damon's oldest half-brother, Frank, factor. The old man had probably hoped that Damon would never return from the war. Then his brother would be the heir.

At this rate, he would inherit the dukedom and have no idea what to do. He could well imagine how Throughgood, having been raised all over the world, felt. But he was lucky to have such a farsighted father. "You'll soon get the knack of it."

"I suppose it can't be harder than Russian." Chuffy's tone was doleful, then he brightened. "By the way, I wanted to tell you that I got to Greece and gave the letter of introduction you gave to me to your cousin—capital fellow, by the way. Why is it you never tell anyone you're a prince?"

Because his father always said an heir to an English dukedom was more important than a foreign prince, and he had only just discovered it a year or so ago. His mother used to call him her little prince, but it had never entered his mind it was more than an endearment. "There are far fewer British dukes than there are Greek princes. I would appreciate it if you wouldn't mention it to anyone."

Throughgood tapped his nose. "My lips are sealed." He took out his quizzing glass and focused on the jewel-embedded heels of Damon's dress shoes. "That is an interesting conceit. Are they real or paste?"

He glanced down. "Paste."

"I have a bit of trouble thinking of you as a Dandy."

"Apparently I cannot fool my oldest friends. Nick Beresford said the same thing. To be honest, I am bored to death. So I decided to see how much havoc I could cause among the Dandy set. I am pleased to say I have become a leader."

Throughgood rolled his eyes, then suddenly glanced around. "Speaking of sets, what set is this?"

"I don't know." Damn, how did he forget to keep count? "There is a young lady glaring in this direction."

"Oh, that's m'sister. It must be the supper dance. Mother won't allow her to waltz with anyone but family yet. In exchange, she promised to have me introduced to Miss Hiller. Friend of a friend or some such thing."

"Miss Hiller?" Damon was fairly sure he had been made known to all the single ladies, but did not remember the name.

"She is the blond lady in the pink gown."

Damon followed the direction his friend indicated to a plump young lady. "I do not believe I know her."

"No?" Throughgood grinned again. "I shall count myself fortunate. You're a much more dashing fellow than I."

"She squints."

"Probably needs eyeglasses." His brows drew together, meeting in the middle. "No reason to hold it against her. My eldest sister used to go around without them, and she squinted. Besides"—he glanced her way again—"I like a lady in eyeglasses."

"In that case, I wish you luck." As his friend sauntered off, Damon strode to Miss Featherton. She, however, was so distracted she appeared not to notice he was late. "Miss Featherton."

She gave him a polite smile that did not meet her eyes. "My lord."

He wanted to hold her, and kiss her, and tell her he could take away her pain. Instead he led her to where the other couples were taking their places, placed his hand on her waist, and stopped.

This would never do. They would be struggling for conversation, and she clearly did not care if she danced or not. "Why do we not take the air instead?"

This time her smile was warmer. "Thank you."

Damon sent a footman for her shawl, and they strolled to the French windows. A few moments later, he draped the fine blend of wool and silk over her shoulders, once again wishing he could hold her in his arms. "You look as if you have a bit of a headache."

"I do, a little."

Placing her fingers on his arm, he opened the window. The air was brisk, but not uncomfortable, as they stepped out and ambled along the narrow terrace. "How much longer will you remain in Town?"

"This is our last week. All the major entertainments are already over, and there is no reason to stay any longer."

"Do you have plans for Christmas?" If only he could get Miss Featherton to tell him everything that was bothering her, he would know how to approach his courtship.

She glanced up at him, but it was too dark to read her look. "I have not yet decided. I have been invited to a house party."

Damon wondered if he had the resources to discover to whose estate she had been invited, then procure an invitation for himself. "I've been told that I am a good listener. If there is anything that is bothering you, I would be happy to assist."

Unsurprisingly, she shook her head. "I am merely ready for the Season to be over."

Well, what had he expected? That she would throw herself into his arms and tell him all her problems? Not Miss Featherton. He kept up a steady stream of inane conversation so that she would not have to exert herself. There must be some way to win her hand and her heart. Damon was sure of only one thing: He would not stop trying until he did both. He could be a patient man. If the siege of Badajoz hadn't cracked his reserve, neither would Miss Featherton.

CHAPTER TWO

Meg listened to Lord Hawksworth's conversation, nodding or giving the expected answer when she was called to do so. He was a prominent member of the Dandy set, which did not recommend him to her. She found them much more interested in their fashions, valets, and tailors than anything else. She remembered the argument they had had over one of Shakespeare's sonnets, at a wedding they had attended not long ago. He had a keen mind, yet it appeared he rarely exercised it, except when it came to his clothing.

Still, aside from that, there was something about the man that was off. As if he was pretending to be something he was not. That alone caused her to keep even more distance between them. She would like to think that kindness had made him ask if she simply wished to talk, except he appeared to be holding the conversation without much help from her. She stifled a sigh; men always wanted to talk about themselves, and he was no different. She would be glad when the evening ended, and she could retreat to her room.

The following day was her mother's at home. Normally Meg enjoyed being able to visit without going from house to house. To-day, however, the atmosphere was thick with unspoken questions regarding Lord Tarlington and her, and she couldn't wait until it was over. What made all this worse was that she could not even tell her closest friend, Miss Amanda Hiller, the reason she had refused his lordship. An unmarried lady's ears were not to be sullied with words such as *secret wife*, *mistress*, or, heaven forfend, *sadist*. If Meg said anything, her friend was sure to tell Mrs. Hiller, and she would never allow Amanda to speak with Meg again. Worse, the woman would tell Mama, then Meg would have to explain how *she* knew about those things. Still, she wished she could confide in someone.

It was pure luck that Amanda had never cared for Lord Swindon and had been relieved when Meg broke the connection. However, Tarlington seemed to embody Amanda's ideal of the perfect gentleman, and she would want to know how Meg could have rejected him. She would have to think of something close to the truth yet vague enough not to invite any questions.

After being announced, Mrs. Hiller entered the drawing room followed by Amanda, who immediately came over to Meg and sat on the window seat next to her. "Would your mother mind if we went for our walk now? Mama wants to take me to the modiste."

Meg glanced around. The only guests in the room were close friends of her mother's. "I think it will be all right." She caught Mama's eye, and her mother nodded. Meg tugged the bell-pull and asked to have her spencer and bonnet sent down. A few minutes later, their arms linked, she and Amanda descended the steps to the pavement, then continued on to the square across the street.

Amanda glanced around, lost.

"You should really wear your spectacles."

"You know I cannot. Gentlemen do not like them. Meg"—Amanda squeezed Meg's arm—"you must tell me what happened with Lord Tarlington. I was sure he was about to offer for you."

For a moment, Meg's mind went completely blank. She'd had no time to come up with a suitable story. A version of the actual truth might be the best plan. "I did as well, but it appeared that his heart was already engaged."

Amanda's eyes rounded in surprise. "Is she anyone we know? Why was he so particular in his attentions to you?"

"I don't know who she is or why he paid so much attention to me." Which was completely true. She had not wanted to know. The betrayal was bad enough.

"I am so sorry." Amanda's voice quivered, and for a moment Meg thought her friend would begin to weep. "It is taking more time than you would like, but you will find true love. I know you will."

This next part would be the hardest for Amanda to accept. Years ago, after they had found and read one of Meg's eldest sister's novels, they had sworn a pact to marry only for love. "I have decided I do not wish to have a love match after all. The heartbreak is simply too painful to endure again."

Amanda's face fell. "But we have always sworn we would never wed without love."

"I know." It had not occurred to Meg that Amanda would think she should give up on her own dreams because of Meg's decision. Although ever since they were young girls, they *had* always done everything together. She stopped and turned to face her friend. "I hope you still do. I want that for you more than anything, but the fact remains that I shall not." Amanda looked doubtful, so Meg lied. "And I am happy about my decision."

"I must say"—Amanda smiled, clearly relieved not to have to sacrifice her happiness—"that is extremely generous of you. I shall, of course, support your decision, even though I cannot enter into your feelings on this matter."

"And I would never ask you to do something so totally against your nature. I have faith that you will meet the perfect gentleman. I, however, shall choose a husband for his good nature and be quite content." Meg prayed she was taking the right course. "Someone such as Viscount Throughgood should suit. He appears to be undemanding."

"Viscount Throughgood?" Amanda's voice was slightly faint. "Has he been introduced to you?"

"Yesterday evening. I thought he was a very pleasant gentleman."

"Oh, how—how nice," Amanda said. "Have you met Lord Hawksworth? He is so clever and handsome, in a dark sort of way."

A darkness he was trying to hide for some reason, and she'd had enough of secrets. "No." Meg shook her head. "He is too . . . Oh, I don't know. *Fashionable* doesn't seem to be the right word." The man acted like a fribble, but his eyes were too intelligent for her to think he actually was one. "Lord Throughgood is much less complicated than Lord Hawksworth, and that is what I want."

"But you *do* think Lord Hawksworth is handsome, do you not?"

"Yes, of course. How could one not?" Too handsome and too dangerous.

They had begun strolling again, and Amanda smiled as she increased her pace. "Other than his hair and eyes, I do not think he is dark at all. In fact, I think he would make a perfect husband." She glanced at her pin watch. "I must go back to Mama now. We have so much to accomplish."

"Will you be home for Christmas?"

"I am not quite sure," Amanda replied. "I think Mama said something about a house party."

Something was going on. Amanda was not usually so evasive. She had not wished to discuss Lord Throughgood at all. Did she know something about Lord Throughgood that would make him ineligible? Surely not. Amanda told Meg everything. If her friend had even met his lordship, she would have heard all about it. Unfortunately, Lord Hawksworth was the type Amanda usually pined after, *and* she had smiled happily when Meg agreed he was good-looking, refusing to see the man's darker side. He would gobble up poor, innocent Amanda like a piece of French pastry. Not only that: He was hiding something. Meg knew it. She would not for the world have her dearest friend suffer the heartbreak she was experiencing. That would not do at all.

Thank heaven the Season would be over soon. Until then, she would do all she could to stop her friend from making a grave mistake with Lord Hawksworth.

A knock came on the door to the study Damon was using in Somerset House.

"Come."

A footman dressed in blue, red, and gold livery opened the door. Damon raised one brow as his father's butler, Caudray, entered.

"The flowers were sent?"

"Indeed, my lord. However, the lady was not at home."

Trusting in Miss Featherton's curiosity to discover the sender, Damon had written a note but not signed it. Researching the livery would, he hoped, take her mind off her problems. "No matter."

The door closed, and he was left alone to sort out his invitations, five of which were to house parties over Christmas. He fanned them out as he would playing cards and selected the one from Lady Bellamny. The other four had all been accompanied by letters promising scintillating company. Three of them came from ladies who had eligible unmarried daughters. One was from a gentleman whose parties were of the type no innocent lady would attend. Indeed, he would be surprised if any *lady* attended. Then there was his godmother, who promised nothing but a warm welcome and an unacknowledged escape from his father's house during Christmas. The woman scared him to death in Town, but at home with her husband she was the loving person to whom he owed so much. Damon stared at the invitation. He would be lucky to find anyone of his own generation there, but that also meant he would not be hunted by young ladies. He would be able to spend time with Lord Bellamny, who was more of a father to him than his own.

After adding the other invitations to the pile for his secretary to reject, he wondered which party Miss Featherton would attend. If she went anywhere. She had younger brothers and sisters, and from the way her oldest brother, Kit Featherton, talked, they were a close family.

A knock sounded on the door and without waiting for permission, Caudray entered. "My lord, a letter for you from his grace. You are to open it immediately."

"Thank you." Damon reached out for the heavy pressed-paper packet. "Is he expecting an answer?"

"No, my lord. The instructions were only for you to read it."

He waited until the butler left before sliding his penknife under the seal, and shaking it open. The writing covered three pages, mostly written by his step-mother, Catherine, concerning the children and the goings-on in the area. Damon finally got to the last page where the duke had written a short note.

> *Hawksworth,*
> *I am aware that you either have or will receive several invitations to house parties with eligible young ladies in attendance. I have given you sufficient time to re-enter the ton and find a wife. It is past time you marry. If you do not select a bride over Christmas, I shall have Catherine invite several ladies I believe are eligible . . .*

Damon did not bother finishing the letter. He selected a pen and wrote his acceptance to Lady Bellamny. Damn if he would wed simply because his father ordered him to.

Once he'd sent the reply by messenger, he turned his mind back to the problem of Miss Featherton and how to cajole her out of her blue devils. If the bouquet did not pique her interest, he would have to think of something else. Her brother Kit, another old schoolmate, was in town with his new bride. Perhaps Damon could manage to coax an invitation to Lord Featherton's estate for a few days before traveling on to Lady Bellamny's primary estate in the Midlands. What better way to command Miss Featherton's attention than to be at the same house with her?

He smiled to himself. His father wanted him to marry, and he would. But to a bride of his choosing.

After spending over four hours at her mother's modiste, Amanda rushed through the door of her home, still trying to decide how she was going to convince Meg to end her pursuit of Viscount Throughgood. Meg was beautiful and vivacious and everything Amanda was not. If Meg set her cap at his lordship, she would surely catch him. It was not that Amanda did not wish her friend happiness; she wanted nothing more. Yet despite what her friend had said about giving up on love, she still believed Meg would find the right gentleman for her, and Amanda did not believe it would be Lord Throughgood. He had been so kind to her last evening, even going so far as to request a dance at the next entertainment, and he had made an appointment to take her riding in the Park to-day. For which she must change immediately if she was not to be late. She smiled as she remembered how easily they had conversed, as if they had known each other forever and not merely a few hours.

As she entered the hall she almost ran into the round hall table. A large bouquet of hot-house roses stood in a vase in the center. "Where did these come from?"

"They are for you, miss." The butler directed her attention to the smallish piece of white paper. "The card is next to them."

Amanda donned her glasses and read the words, hardly able to believe them.

> *My dear Miss Hiller,*
> *Please accept this small token of my regard. I saw them this morning and their loveliness reminded me of you.*
> *Yr servant,*
> *C, Viscount Throughgood*

From the moment she first saw him, he had struck her as the most handsome gentleman at the ball. His lovely brown hair curled softly.

His blue eyes, with just a hint of gray, had smiled at her. He was not very tall, but more than tall enough for her. The fact that he was a little plump appealed as well. After all, she was no sylph. When they had danced together there had been no awkwardness at all. They just seemed to fit together.

She clutched the note to her bosom and buried her nose in the blooms. She could happily remain there for a life-time. There must be some way to preserve the roses. "Oh my," she mumbled into the flowers. "No one has ever called me lovely!"

"I'm quite sure that is not true," her mother said prosaically. "Just the other day your father said you were a beautiful girl and one day some gentleman would recognize it." Amanda lifted her head. Mama had stopped and glanced at the flowers as if seeing them for the first time. "Who are those from?"

"Lord Throughgood." Amanda reverently breathed the words. She felt as if she had died and gone to heaven. *No one* had ever sent her flowers before. "I hope you do not mind that I already opened the card. It is perfectly unexceptionable."

"Well." Her mother was still staring at the bouquet as if it might disappear at any moment. "What a nice young man. We must invite him to dinner."

Still clutching the card, she threw her arms around her mother. "Oh, could we?"

Mama patted Amanda's back. "Now, do not be such a goose. Naturally, I shall send him an invitation."

Mama held out her hand, and Amanda dutifully gave the missive to her mother. After a few moments, Mama said, "Very unexceptionable. I shall look forward to meeting his lordship. Now you must change, or have you forgot he is taking you for a ride today?"

The moment she had read the missive, she had forgot. "No, I'm on my way to my room now." Amanda practically floated to her chamber, then fell on her bed. "Oh, Jubie, I think I am falling in love."

Her maid had received the flowers from a footman who had brought them up, and placed them on Amanda's dressing table. "There, you see. There was nothing to worry about. How many times have I told you that the right gentleman would come along? Stand up and let me get you out of your gown."

Amanda stood, allowing her maid to take charge. She was the happiest lady in the world, except for one small problem. What was she going to say to Meg? She had just recovered from Lord Swindon when Lord Tarlington broke her heart. If Amanda was truly the good friend she thought she was, she would step aside for Meg to have Lord Throughgood. Then again, gentlemen regularly fell in love with Meg. This might be Amanda's only chance at love and happiness. She re-read the note and sighed.

The next time she saw Lord Throughgood she would mention Meg and watch how he responded. If he appeared interested, Amanda could not deny Meg an opportunity for true love.

Yet what would happen if he wished to court Amanda instead? One could not, after all, force a gentleman to prefer one lady over another. Would she have to make a choice between a possible husband and her closest friend?

Fate could not be so cruel. She shook her head. No, love must find both of them. Even though Meg had said she did not wish for a love match. Surely that was only her broken heart speaking. In any event, Lord Hawksworth might be a much better husband for Meg. Not only would they be a striking couple, but she liked puzzles, and he was certainly that.

Amanda had seen Lords Hawksworth and Throughgood speaking, and they appeared to be on good terms. Perhaps Lord Throughgood could tell her more about Lord Hawksworth. That way Amanda could be certain he was right for Meg.

Amanda straightened her shoulders. All their lives, Meg had been the leader. For once Amanda would take the lead. If Lord Throughgood truly did prefer her, she would find a way to ensure Meg's future, either with Lord Hawksworth or another gentleman. Amanda would begin this evening. One way or another, there would be a path to happiness for her and Meg.

CHAPTER THREE

"A big bouquet of flowers was delivered to you, Meg." Miss Sarah Featherton, Meg's youngest sister, who was seventeen and chafing at still being in the schoolroom, waltzed into the room. "The note wasn't signed."

Was there no privacy in this house? "And how would you know that?"

"Papa looked."

"Ah." Not that she blamed him. Unmarried ladies were not allowed correspondence with unrelated gentlemen. Solely due to her eldest sister's behavior, she had had to recite that many times before coming out. "Where are they?"

"On their way up to you."

Several minutes later, a massive arrangement of red roses that had already been placed in a vase were carried in by Jimmy, one of the newer running footmen.

Meg pointed to the low table in front of her sofa. "Put them there, if you would."

Nestled in the blooms was a card. She plucked it from its nesting place.

> *My dear Miss Featherton,*
> *It is my fondest wish that these blooms bring you the happiness you deserve.*
> *An Admirer*

The author's hand was firm and slanting. Obviously a man's, but what gentleman did she know who would not sign the card? Lord Throughgood? He *had* appeared to be a little shy. Yet how to be certain? She turned to Jimmy, who was still waiting to be dismissed. "How were the flowers delivered?"

"By a footman, miss."

"Did anyone happen to notice the colors of his livery?"

"I saw him, miss. They were blue and green."

"Thank you, you may go now."

He bowed and left.

Sarah wrinkled her brow. "Do you know who sent them?"

"Not yet, but I can easily look up who has blue and green colors." Meg sniffed the roses before strolling to the door.

"That is a wonderful idea," Sarah said as she followed Meg. "I hope some gentleman sends me flowers."

Her sister shared the family traits of dark hair and blue eyes, and, although they were considered an attractive family, Sarah resembled their grandmother Featherton and was truly beautiful. "When you come out, the house will be so full of flowers we'll have to set them outside."

"I hope so." She beamed. "If you need help searching, I can help."

Meg glanced at the clock. "Do you not have studies?"

Her sister scrunched up her face. "German."

"You'd better get back to it."

Once she had attained the library, it was only a matter of minutes before she had a list of houses having blue and green as their colors. She had been correct. Only the earldom of Grantville, however, had a family member in Town of the right age to send her flowers. The flowers must have come from Lord Throughgood.

Glancing at the book again, she tried to bring up a vision of Lord Throughgood. He was a good-looking enough man, albeit fairly nondescript. His light brown curls were cut fashionably, and his eyes hovered somewhere between blue and gray. She tried to imagine herself with him, when an image interfered, of raven-black hair and sultry brown eyes set above a classically straight Greek nose with a slight bump.

No!

Lord Hawksworth was not the type of gentleman she wished to wed. He was complicated, and roguish, and hiding something. Meg gave herself a shake. What she needed was an innocuous, if pudgy, gentleman who would not break her heart. Lord Throughgood would be perfect.

She considered briefly walking to Amanda's home to share her news, but thought better of it. During the whole of the past three Seasons, the only flowers Amanda had received were from her father and brothers. Meg did not know which was worse, having horrible suitors or having none at all. At least Amanda had never had to live through a broken heart. As soon as Meg was married, she would be in a better position to find a husband for her friend.

"Do you know now who they're from?"

She had forgot her sister was still with her. "Yes. Lord Throughgood."

"Sarah, return to the schoolroom this moment." Mama stood next to the open door, her arm pointing toward the corridor.

"Yes, Mama." Switching suddenly from a mature young lady to a schoolgirl, Sarah skipped out, grinning, and said, "I know who sent the flowers."

"There is a reason I have made all of you wait until you are eighteen to come out." Mama shook her head and closed the door. "Well?"

"I believe it was Lord Throughgood." Meg placed the book carefully back on the shelf. "I based that on the livery colors."

"Who was it that told you the colors?" Her mother's tone was only mildly curious.

"The new footman, Jimmy. He said he saw the bouquet delivered."

"Did he indeed? That is interesting." Before Meg could ask what was so out of the ordinary, Mama continued. "I received a visit from Mrs. Hiller today. She and Amanda have been invited to Lady Bellamny's house party over Christmas. We received an invitation as well, but, as you know, I do not like to leave the younger children. However, Mrs. Hiller suggested that you be allowed to accompany them, and I agreed. Do you wish to attend?"

Meg wondered who else was invited, but it really did not matter. She and Amanda always managed to have a good time together, and Lady Bellamny had been a family friend for more years than Meg had been alive. "I would love to."

"Good, it is settled then. We will leave Town in a few days. I suggest you finish any shopping you wish to do." Mama moved to the shelf where Meg had placed their most recent copy of *Debrett's*. "You may go now. Take the town coach. It looks like rain."

At first Meg wondered what her mother was looking for, but it was probably to glean more information about Lord Throughgood. His line of the family had recently come into the title, and he was, after all, her chosen mate, not that Mama knew of Meg's decision.

Shortly before tea, Lucinda entered the library to find Helena studying a large tome. "What are you looking for, dear?"

"Liveries in blue and red." She raised her head, a slight line creasing her brow. "There are quite a lot of them."

"Yes, but how many are in Town? That is the question."

Her attention was drawn back to the book.

"What is the significance of the livery?"

"Jimmy," Helena answered distractedly, "our youngest footman, told Meg the flowers were delivered by a footman wearing blue and green. But he is forever mixing up red and green. The other day I asked him to bring down some green embroidery thread. My dresser showed him where the basket was, and he brought the wrong color."

Lucinda sat on a chair at the table. "Was there no card?"

"It was not signed." Her daughter-in-law looked up. "Poor Meg has had such bad luck in suitors, I am concerned."

"As you should be, my dear." Lucinda closed her eyes as she pictured the liveries of all the great houses. "Somerset uses red and blue." And his son, Hawksworth, was in Town. "Have you found anyone else?"

"Several, but no one who would send Meg flowers." Suddenly Helena fixed her bright blue gaze on Lucinda. "Tell me you are not matchmaking again."

Lucinda held up her hands with her palms out. "Of course not, my dear. If indeed Hawksworth is interested in Meg, that would be a very good match." Lucinda rose. "His life is an open book." At least to those who made it their business to know. "I merely came by to tell you that I will join you at Granby Abbey before traveling on to a house party I have been invited to, and wished to know if you would mind if I brought a guest with me."

The dower house at Granby was still occupied by a great-aunt of Lucinda's late husband. Not wanting to remove the lady, and at the invitation of her son and daughter-in-law, Lucinda had an apartment in one wing of the main house.

"Of course not." Helena smiled warmly. "It is still your home. Forgive me for being so quick to accuse you of matchmaking."

Lucinda leaned down and bussed her daughter-in-law's cheek. "I thank you for that. I know a great deal about Hawksworth. He is Almeria Bellamny's godson. She would have told me if there is anything amiss with him."

"Thank you," Helena said. "I shall keep that in mind. At the moment, though, Meg must allow her heart to mend. It is too soon to think about another match."

Lucinda left the library and climbed the stairs to her chambers. So, Hawksworth had decided to distract Meg with a puzzle. Lucinda paused for a moment. Yet who, she wondered, did Meg think the flowers were from? This could turn out to be a very interesting Christmas indeed.

Later that afternoon, Chuffy entered his rooms on Jermyn Street to find a stack of cards that his valet, Manning, had sorted by the type of entertainment. Most of them were for balls, several for house parties, but one was from Mrs. Hiller, inviting him to join the family for dinner the next evening.

He smiled to himself, pleased to have such an indication of success. After having spent two years traveling in countries where most of the ladies had dark hair and eyes, he had immediately been drawn to Miss Hiller's fair and purely English appearance. With her light blond hair and pale blue eyes, as well as a perfectly creamy complexion, she was his ideal of a beautiful woman. During their dance, he had been enchanted by her slight shyness, and later by her common sense. Granted, it was early days, but he was fairly certain she was the type of lady he was looking to wed. He would know more after their carriage ride in the Park to-day and dinner the next evening. If he could manage to stand up with her at the party to-night, that would be even better.

Forty minutes later, he pulled his pair of matched grays to a halt outside of the Hiller town house. As he ascended the steps, the butler opened the door and bowed. "Lord Throughgood?"

For a moment Chuffy wondered what the servant would say if he said no, but those days of foolishness were behind him. "I am. Is Miss Hiller available?"

"I shall send word that you have arrived." He spoke softly to a footman, who scurried up the stairs.

All in all a well-run household, Chuffy thought. Much different than his father's, which was inclined to have a number of servants Papa had brought with him from abroad, some of whom did not speak the same language and believed in relaying messages in the loudest voice possible. Those were mixed in with old retainers who disapproved of the foreign servants' behaviors and lack of English manners. In short, most of the time the staff was involved in full-out war. Chuffy wondered how Miss Hiller would like his family's new home, and what she would make of the disorder that ruled there.

As he was finishing the thought, his attention was drawn to her, standing on the top step of the main staircase. Her hand was on the rail. She smiled and wiggled her fingers at him. As she squinted down at the next tread, he surged forward, taking the stairs two at a time, catching her just as her foot missed the step. "Are you all right?"

She sucked in a shaky breath and nodded. "I do not normally remove my hand from the rail."

Using a funning tone, he said, "You should wear your glasses."

She wrinkled her adorable nose. "But they make one appear so ugly."

Where ladies got that idea he had not a clue. "I don't think so at all. I find spectacles enhance the eyes."

"Do you truly?" Her own eyes grew wide.

"Of course. I wouldn't have said so otherwise. Have you a pair?" He fervently hoped she did. So much was lost without the ability to see. Although it was his considered opinion that his brother-in-law had most likely benefited from his eldest sister refusing to wear hers. He wasn't the handsomest of men.

A clear pink blush rose in her cheeks. "Yes, yet I never go out with them on."

"But you must. I shall enjoy your eyes, and you will enjoy seeing things better. I'll wait here while you fetch them." He glanced around, spying a footman. "Better yet, send for them. We may remain here and chat until they arrive."

"Very well." She gave him a grateful smile.

He nodded to the servant, who set off smartly down the corridor.

"What is all this?" A gentleman who must be Mr. Hiller said from the bottom of the stairs.

"Oh, Papa. Lord Throughgood kept me from falling, and now I am waiting for my eyeglasses." She blushed again. "I am truly a peagoose. My lord, please meet my father, Mr. Hiller. Papa, this is Viscount Throughgood. We are going for a ride in the Park."

"Pleased to meet you, my lord." Mr. Hiller nodded and Chuffy did the same, not letting go of the man's daughter. "Glad she's finally decided to wear her glasses. Keeps bumping into things without them."

Miss Hiller's blush deepened to a lovely rose. *"Papa!"*

"It is amazing," Chuffy said in a low tone, "how easily one's parents are able to embarrass one and without even trying." Situated one step down from her, he was distracted by her very fine bosom, which rose as she took a breath.

"I am so glad you understand."

"None better. My father was a diplomat, but tactfulness did not extend to his family. Plain speaking is what he prefers with us less fortunate beings."

Her spectacles arrived and soon a pretty pair of gold-rimmed glasses adorned her upturned nose. He held out his arm. "Shall we?"

Miss Hiller's smile was as warm as a summer day. "I would like that very much."

He escorted her down the stairs and out to his phaeton. He helped her up to the seat before going around to the other side. Several minutes later they were entering the Park. "Is it always so crowded?"

"Do you not know?" She laughed lightly. "I would have thought you had been here often."

"Ah, I am recently returned from abroad. I went directly to my father's estate before coming to Town."

"I hadn't realized you had just arrived." Her finely arched brows drew together. "How strange this must be for you after seeing foreign countries. Did you miss England?"

"I missed the idea of England. The only time I lived here was to attend school. Still, I have always thought of England as home." He cut her a quick grin. "I must rely on you to guide me."

She blushed charmingly. "To answer your question, the Park is normally much more crowded. We are at the end of the Season. I shall do my best to show you around."

"How much longer are you fixed in Town?"

"For at least another few weeks."

That was exactly what Chuffy had hoped for. He settled back to enjoy the ride and his companion. He should know soon if they would suit and where she was spending Christmas. If things went well and her plans were not set, he would write to his mother and ask her to issue an invitation to the Hiller family.

CHAPTER FOUR

Damon rode his horse, Mentor, at a sedate pace in the Park. On the first day of the Battle of Salamanca, his last horse had been shot out from under him. That night, he had won the beast in a card game.

Mentor pranced and tossed his head at a pretty mare that appeared to want to flirt. "Did I forget to mention that you've been gelded?"

The horse ignored him, casting his head toward the mare. Damon set him to a walk as he searched the carriages and those strolling, hoping to see Miss Featherton. Surely she was here somewhere. The rest of the *ton* who were still in Town had managed to show themselves.

He had not been able to tolerate not knowing what her reaction to his flowers had been. Had Miss Featherton liked his flowers? Had she ascertained they had come from him? How many houses had blue and red as their colors?

Bloody hell. He should have researched it before deciding to leave the blasted note unsigned. Not knowing what his reception would be, he was hesitant to go to her house. Then he had hit on the idea to find her in a public place, and he'd not been having any luck. He had been too clever by half, and now he was going to suffer for it.

His horse snorted.

"You're not the only one disgusted by this outing." As he glanced around, a phaeton painted bright yellow came into view.

Throughgood—and it appeared he had Miss Hiller with him. He had been correct. Her appearance was greatly improved by eyeglasses. She might know where Miss Featherton was.

Damon urged Mentor forward. "Throughgood, well met."

His friend pulled up onto the verge as his pair of matched grays nervously eyed Mentor. "Still in Town, I see. Miss Hiller, may I introduce Lord Hawksworth? Hawksworth, Miss Hiller."

She smiled and inclined her head. "A pleasure, my lord." She glanced at Chuffy and her smile deepened. "I believe you know my friend Miss Featherton?"

"I do." He debated an attempt at subtlety, but the last time he had not received the desired result. "Have you seen her recently? I thought she might be in the Park."

"I believe Lady Featherton has her busy shopping for last minute items before they return home in a day or two."

Hell and damnation. Did that mean he would be forced to haunt Bond Street looking for Miss Featherton? "I suppose she will remain there until next Season."

"Not at all. She is joining my mother and me at Lady Bellamny's estate for Christmas."

Now that was a piece of good news. "Then I shall meet you both there."

"You will see her this evening if you plan to attend Lady Torrey's ball." Miss Hiller had cut a quick glance at Throughgood before turning her wide blue eyes back to Damon.

"Yes, of course I shall attend." At least he had received an invitation, although he had not answered it. On the other hand, he had discovered last Season that unwed heirs to wealthy dukedoms were never turned away. "Throughgood, I assume you will be present as well?"

"I wouldn't miss it." His friend gave Miss Hiller a lingering look, and Damon began to feel as if he was missing out on something important.

He held up his crop in a salute. "Until this evening."

Chuffy drove off, and Damon headed toward home. There was no reason to be in the Park if Miss Featherton was absent.

He sent a prayer to the Deity that he had chosen the right house party to attend. The real question was how long would it take for her to recover from Tarlington, and what could Damon do to help her along?

"My lord." Amanda watched as Lord Hawksworth rode away. This was the perfect time to discover how Lord Throughgood felt about Meg. "What do you think about Lord Hawksworth's interest in Miss Featherton?"

Lord Throughgood was quiet for a few moments. "It is my belief that he has serious intentions." He glanced at Amanda. "You are her friend. Do you like the possibility of a match?"

She wished she could have been as direct as Lord Hawksworth had been, but uncertainty over Lord Throughgood's feelings toward her made her parry. "Can you think of anyone better suited?"

He grinned. "Not at present. Are you of a matchmaking disposition, Miss Hiller?"

"Oh no." Flustered, she pleated her skirts. "I mean, not usually. It is only that Miss Featherton is so sad right now, and I do want her to be happy. What do you know of him?"

"We are old school friends and have not seen much of each other in recent years. That said, we have kept in touch . . ." He gave Amanda a glowing report of his friend. Then his lordship's much larger hand covered hers, stopping the destruction of her gown. "I am of a mind to leave Hawksworth to the business of making your friend happy. What *I* would like to know is how you would feel if I were to visit you while you are attending Lady Bellamny's house party. My father's estate is only a few miles from it."

Her hands stilled completely, and tears of happiness rushed to her eyes. She blinked rapidly before gazing at him. "I would very much like to see you there."

"In that case, the moment I return to my rooms, I shall write to my mother and ask her to arrange invitations to some of the parties."

"How much longer are you in Town?" Suddenly, Christmas seemed very far off, and she wanted to spend as much time getting to know him as possible.

"I have no plans to leave much before Christmas."

That was good. She glanced up from beneath her eyelashes. "Will I see you tomorrow evening?"

"I sent my response immediately. I would not miss the opportunity to dine with you *en famille*. Will you grant me the supper dance at the ball? If you are not already spoken for, that is."

This was all Amanda had hoped for. She was sorry that he had lost his uncle and cousin, but glad the circumstances had brought Lord Throughgood home. She might never have met him otherwise.

She felt as if the sun was shining directly over her, brightening and warming everything. "The dance is yours, my lord."

He grinned at her, completing her happiness. "Thank you. I will hope that the time between your leaving Town and the house party goes quickly."

"As will I." Amanda counted the days and wondered how many of them she could spend with Lord Throughgood.

Then she remembered poor Meg. Yet today had solidified Amanda's conviction that Lord Hawksworth was the right gentleman for her friend. And that Lord Throughgood might very well be the perfect man for her. Now all she had to do was find a way to bring Meg around.

Meg would never have believed there were still so many people in Town, but the ballroom could not possibly hold another person. She had seen Amanda descend the stairs, but had been unable to catch even a glimpse of her since. Actually, Meg had not seen much of Amanda recently. Well, that would change once they were back at home.

Meg glanced at her dance card. Only two sets did not have a name next to them. She supposed she should be glad, but instead she felt as if she'd been set adrift. She had always thought gentlemen were essentially good at heart, but now knew that with the exception of her father and brothers, they could not be trusted.

She stole a glance, hoping to find Lord Throughgood, but her view was blocked by a tall man with a large ruby nestled in his cravat. Really, what kind of gentleman wore such a large jewel? She continued to look up until she met the deep brown gaze of Lord Hawksworth.

Warmth lurked in his eyes, disturbing the serene mien she was attempting to project. Ah well, at least he was not wearing the pink and white striped neckcloth he had worn earlier to-day when she'd seen him on Bruton Street. And she had to admit, with a chest as broad as his, the ruby did not look out of place or overly showy.

He bowed. "Miss Featherton, would it be too much to hope that you have a set for which you are not engaged?"

She wanted to say her card was full, but then she would be caught in a lie. Meg was certain that she could convince her mother to leave before the last waltz, but not before the supper dance. "I am free for the first waltz."

"Thank you."

He bowed, and for the first time she noticed the restless restraint with which he held himself. Forcibly reminding her of one of the caged lions in the Royal Menagerie. Then he turned, and as he walked away the heels of his shoes glittered. Jewels? Meg let out the breath she'd been holding. He was nothing more than a Dandy, and she had been concerned. More fool she. It really was time to go home when she saw danger in every gentleman. Still, she had never before met a Dandy who reminded her of a dangerous beast. Even now, he seemed to prowl around the ballroom. No, she was correct in her first assessment of his lordship: He was not to be trusted.

"Meg?" Kit and his wife, Mary, had strolled up. "Did Hawksworth say anything to upset you?"

"No, of course not." He did not have to say anything at all. His mere presence troubled her. "He merely asked for a dance."

"You were looking at him as if he . . ." Her brother shook his head. "Never mind. How are you?"

Kit and Mary had been in Town for a week, but had opted to reside at the Pulteney Hotel until their apartments were ready at Featherton House. Meg had recently discovered their father had received the same information about Tarlington that Meg had, and Papa would have told Kit. "I am well. How long have you known Lord Hawksworth?"

"I knew him in school, then he went off to the army. Strange thing for an heir to do. After that, I didn't see him again until last Season. He's a bruising rider, handles a team well, and he recently won a wager at Angelo's, betting on himself."

That did not fit in at all with his silk neckcloth and jeweled heels. What was the man playing at? It was as if he was trying to be all things to all people.

She had been right to be distrustful of him. Fortunately, the Season was ending in a couple of days. And Amanda would not have a chance to fall in love with the devil.

A half hour before midnight, Damon collected Miss Featherton for his dance with her, which happened to be not only the first waltz but the supper dance. Yet unlike the last time he had arranged to stand up with her, she had a militant cast to her eyes. Had he done something to upset her, or was this a result of her recent heartbreak?

They took their places on the floor. When he put his palm on her waist, he had the urge to tug her a bit closer, yet she stood perfectly still, as if she felt nothing. Was she now afraid to get close to a man? That would make his courting of her much more difficult.

Damn Tarlington to hell. Damon had almost decided to tell her he was attending Lady Bellamny's house party, but now that didn't seem like a good idea at all.

The music began and he was not surprised at how gracefully she followed his lead, or how well she performed the steps. They were silent for several moments. He must say something, but what? Miss Featherton was definitely not encouraging conversation. "I suppose Lady Torrey is happy this is such a crush."

Although she glanced up at him, he could glean nothing from her shuttered expression. "Naturally, she will be pleased. I did not think there would be so many present."

"Will you depart for the country soon?"

"Mama and I will leave the day after to-morrow. My father still has some issues to settle before he joins us. And you, my lord?"

"I shall remain a while longer." Damon would have liked to learn more about her, but obviously she was not in the mood to disclose or invite confidences. "After that, a round of house parties awaits me." Not exactly the truth, but close enough. "I suppose you will remain with your family."

"For the most part."

This was the most excruciatingly tortured conversation he had ever had with a woman. "In that case, I shall wish you a Happy Christmas."

Her countenance seemed to soften for a moment before she replied, "I wish you the same."

Damon gave up attempting to converse and settled in to enjoy having Miss Featherton in his arms, envisioning a time when she would be in his bed. Her long dark hair spread on a snowy white pillow, her ruby lips swollen with his kisses, and her porcelain skin flushed with passion. Unfortunately, it would not be tonight or any night in the immediate future. Knowing what a vibrant lady she was, it was disconcerting and heartrending to see her so guarded and subdued.

When the dance ended, he returned Miss Featherton to her mother.

The lady's sharp eyes studied her daughter. "Are you not feeling well, my dear?"

"I have a headache. It must be the heat."

She turned to him, obviously wishing to beg off having his escort to supper. Before she could speak, he said, "It is rather warm in here."

Or it had been when they'd been dancing. "Perhaps you should retire."

"I think that is a very good idea." Lady Featherton nodded approvingly.

He watched as they made their way out of the room. To-night had not gone as he had wished. Still, he had the house party to look forward to. Perhaps she would be in better spirits by then.

Without saying good-night to his hostess, Damon slipped into the hall and called for his town coach. Several minutes later he was home, a glass of brandy warming in his palms. Somehow he would find a way to break through the barrier Miss Featherton had erected around her and the path to her heart. Yet first, he needed to know how badly she had been hurt. Before Tarlington left the country, the gossip was that an offer from the man had been imminent. Speculation had flared for a few days, but when the Feathertons behaved as if nothing untoward had occurred, it died down. What had happened between them, and who could Damon ask?

The next afternoon Damon plied the knocker on the front door of Lady Bellamny's town house. The old lady terrorized most of the *ton*, including him when he was in Town. But she was his godmother and had always been kind to him. While he'd been in the army, she had maintained a steady correspondence. Not that he would let anyone know it. The information might ruin her reputation as a Fury.

A few minutes later, he was shown into an upstairs parlor and announced. "Godmamma."

"Hawksworth." She presented her powdered cheek for him to kiss. "What brings you here at such an ungodly hour?"

"It is past one o'clock in the afternoon." Stifling a grin, he lowered himself onto one of her delicate chairs. "I require information, and I believe you are the best person to ask."

She reached over and tugged the bell-pull. "We shall have tea, and you will tell me what you have been up to. By then I will be in the correct frame of mind to answer your questions."

"Yes, ma'am." He folded his hands on his lap, chastised.

The tea tray arrived filled with sandwiches and biscuits. Damon took several of the sandwiches. He would not want her to think he didn't appreciate the offer of food, and he was hungry.

"I hear that you visited your mother's family before returning home?"

He hid his surprise by draining his tea-cup. He had thought only his step-mother knew about that. "Yes, to my father's infinite displeasure."

"One would suppose"—Lady Bellamny's tone was supercilious—"that after sending you off to war, your father would have better sense than to think he could demand your obedience. I have never found military men to be particularly disposed to take orders from civilians."

"He *is* a duke," Damon replied in his driest tone. He did not like to discuss his father, even with her.

"And you, my dear, are a Greek prince."

She refilled his cup, and he saluted her with it. "Has no one ever told you that Greek princes are thick on the ground? It is true, actually."

"They might be, but not all of them are in the succession," she retorted. "Your father's stance might make more sense if you did not own any property in Greece. However, I am well aware of not only your holdings but the funds that made up your mother's estate. All of which went to you upon her death."

"And about which my father neglected to inform me until two years ago when I was facing a battle the next day."

"In fairness"—she grimaced, giving him the impression that she would rather not be fair to his father—"he could hardly *know* you were about to go into battle when you received the news." He opened his mouth, and she held up her hand. "Although you were at war, and being in a battle is not unexpected."

"Precisely." At the time, Damon had been so angry he would have gladly throttled his father. By his mother's settlement agreements, he had come into the properties when she died, and the trust had ended when he was one and twenty. Yet his father had kept the information from him until one of his Greek relatives contacted a solicitor who threatened to send him the news if the duke did not. Disappointment and bitterness still burned in him over his father's deception. He had been made to memorize every piece of property down to the smallest item he would receive if he lived to become duke, but what he inherited from his mother had been kept secret. Even though he had been very young, Damon had never had the impression that his father hated his mother so much as to deny him any part of her. Yet that seemed to be the case.

"Now." Lady Bellamny placed her tea-cup on the low table between them. "What can I help you with?"

He gave himself an inner shake before answering. "Miss Featherton. I wish to know how close she actually was to receiving an offer from Tarlington."

"Why do you want to know?"

"Is there a reason you ask?"

"Her grandmother is a dear friend of mine. I consider it my duty to keep an eye on her."

Fair enough. "As you know, I lurked through most of last Season, and I have been actively looking for a possible wife most of this Season. Yet by the time you introduced us, Tarlington was courting her. I am interested in her and would like to know what I'm up against."

Lady Bellamny fixed Damon with a basilisk gaze. "He had spoken to her father."

Damon fought down the strong urge to swear long and fluently in several languages, but his godmother would probably box his ears, and he needed her assistance. "What happened?"

"Sometime before Tarlington was to propose to Miss Featherton, she was given information about his mistress and children. He will never marry the woman, but neither would he have cut the connection with her. He is now in Paris pursuing an American heiress. The plain fact of the matter is that his pockets are to let. His father and grandfather ran the estates down, and he must find a way to build them back up. Under the circumstances, marrying an heiress is his best choice."

Bloody hell. "I understand."

"That is not all." Her lips had thinned to the point of disappearing.

"Isn't that enough?" What else could the man have done?

"Last spring, Swindon was courting her."

"I'm not familiar with him."

"Doesn't run in your circles. He is violent with women."

"He beats them?"

"He is a flagellant and almost killed his last mistress."

Bloody, bloody hell! "I gather she discovered that as well?"

Lady Bellamny gave one short nod. "Yes."

His blood began to boil. "Did he touch her?"

"No. He is not stupid enough to do anything before marriage. When Featherton found out what the man was, he made it clear that if Swindon ever attempted to court another gently bred lady, his reputation would be destroyed."

Thank God for that. No wonder Miss Featherton didn't trust Damon or men in general. He demolished the last biscuit, then rose. "Thank you."

His godmother looked up at him. "What do you intend to do?"

"Win her trust. It will be hard, but at least now I know what I'm up against."

After a few moments she said, "I would not object to the match. She will be at my house party."

"So I have been given to understand." He leaned down and bussed her cheek. "Thank you, Godmamma. Be assured that no matter what happens, I will never hurt her in any fashion."

Lady Bellamny patted his cheek as she had when he was a boy. "I'll see you in a few weeks."

Damon strode out of the house, wondering how to approach a lady who had been betrayed in two such brutal ways in a matter of months. Well, he had just over thirty days to formulate a plan of attack. Something was bound to come to him.

CHAPTER FIVE

The next afternoon, Almeria poured tea, passing the cups to Constance and Lucinda. "I have sent an invitation to Lady Grantville and her family for most of the outings and events I have planned. They live so close there is no reason for them to stay with me. Their oldest son, Throughgood, is such a nice young man. I am sure he will get on well with the younger people."

"What a wonderful idea." Lucinda selected a cake from the plate. "It will also allow the Grantvilles to start meeting people. It is a shame they did not come for the Season, but I understand trying to accustom oneself to a new life." A gleam entered her eyes. "I believe Throughgood is interested in Miss Hiller. At least, I saw him with her in the Park a few times. I do wish my daughter-in-law had not decided to hie off to the country so soon. Getting out around Town would have done Meg more good than sitting at home licking her wounds."

"A shame she is taking the business about Tarlington so hard." Constance's tone was gruffer than usual. They had all been affected by Meg's disappointments. "I thought she might come around more quickly than she is."

Since last Season, Lucinda had favored Hawksworth for Meg. But until Almeria and her friends had discovered that Tarlington was almost bankrupt and had a longtime mistress, Lucinda was content to allow her granddaughter to select her own husband. "There was no help for it, and we were obliged to warn Meg. She would never have simply accepted her father's decree that she not wed the man." Lucinda's lips thinned and anger flashed in her fine blue eyes. "It is Swindon I'd like to run through."

"Indeed." Constance thumped her silver-headed malacca cane on the carpet. "Men such as he should not look for wives, or not innocent ones. However, I believe Hawksworth will do splendidly for her."

"I have thought so since he returned to England. If we had not been so busy with Kit and Mary, Meg would have been settled by now. Hawksworth is up to her weight and will make an excellent husband. Almeria, are you not some sort of relation to Somerset?"

"A third cousin once removed, but we do not get on. Despite his animosity toward me, the boy's mother insisted I stand as one of his godmothers." Almeria agreed that Meg needed a strong man, and Hawksworth was just that. "Hawksworth stopped by to visit me yesterday, and I told him about Swindon and Tarlington. This will finally give him something to do other than visit his tailor and attend sporting events. I believe he is bored to death."

"Not unheard of for military men." Lucinda reached for another biscuit. "It is a shame his father cannot give up the reins even a little. Having an estate to manage would be good for him."

Constance, who had been listening for the most part, finally asked, "Who else have you invited?"

"Miss Riverton and her betrothed, Lord Darby, the Fotheringales, Lord and Lady Smithson . . ." She rattled off several other couples, and ended triumphantly with her greatest coup. "And the Marquis and Marchioness of Merton."

"Smithsons?" Constance frowned. "Why would you invite them?"

"As a favor to Smithson's great-aunt."

"Other than the Smithsons, the guests are unexceptional." Lucinda clapped her hands. "But, Almeria, how did you convince the Mertons? They never leave their estate during the Christmas holidays."

"They will only be there for the first week. Then, of course, they have duties at home, but I am praying that is long enough. They will bring their son, and you know how the presence of a young child will turn a lady's mind toward marriage."

"Yes, of course," Constance said, nodding. "A brilliant scheme."

Even though Almeria had assisted in her friends' other matchmaking efforts, for her this one was more important than all the others. Since Hawksworth's mother's death, it appeared as if the Duke of Somerset had lost interest in his firstborn and heir at best, or was actively hostile to the boy at worst. She wished she knew what had got into the man.

If she fell in love with him, Meg Featherton would be the perfect wife for Damon. She and her family would provide him the familial stability he did not have at his own home.

The problem would be bringing Meg around. Having the Mertons there would help, but Almeria was counting on the magic of Christmas to assist as well.

The past month at home at Granby Abbey had been torture for Meg. Even though none of her sisters, brothers, or parents had said a word, she could feel their pity that yet another gentleman had turned out to be a cur. Meg pulled on her gloves before taking the large ermine muff from a maid. Hendricks had left earlier so that she would be at Lady Bellamny's when Meg arrived.

If only Kit and Mary had decided to stay at home for a while longer, but they had traveled almost immediately to Northumberland from London.

Nevertheless, Meg, now dressed in a new Pompeian red cashmere gown with an ermine-lined red velvet cloak, was more than ready to depart.

Having stated that the coach was comfortable, and she wanted the door opened as infrequently as possible, Mrs. Hiller and Amanda were waiting in the carriage for the journey.

When Meg entered the coach, the first thing she noticed was the joy in her friend's eyes. Amanda too must be glad for a break, but Meg sensed it was something more. Amanda had been in a very good mood since she and her family had returned from Town a little over a week ago. Every time Meg queried her, Amanda would only shake her head and say it was early days. Ever since Tarlington, it seemed as if she had grown more distant to Meg. If only she knew how to bring back their closeness. Maybe being together for Christmas would help mend whatever rift there was between them.

The door closed, and Mrs. Hiller gave the order to start. "We should arrive late this afternoon. I have brought books and games to entertain you girls."

Although cold, the day was sunny, and as neither Amanda nor Meg had been on this particular route before, they spent the first hour or so watching the countryside and commenting on the towns and villages. After that palled, they chose books over board games. Other than the sound of the horses and wheels, silence descended on the coach.

The time at home had served to make Meg more certain than ever that marriage with a quiet and undemanding gentleman would be the best thing for her. She would never be able to give her heart away again. Even now, unbidden tears sprung to her eyes at odd moments, and the ache in her chest threatened to stop her breath. Surely one did not truly die of a broken heart.

It was a shame she had not had an opportunity to present her proposal to Lord Throughgood before leaving Town. Other than the flowers she had received, she had not heard from him again. However, she had given it careful thought. She must be truthful with him. It would not do to have him fall in love with her when she could not return his affections.

She stared at the page, reading the same lines over again, and against her will, Lord Hawksworth's visage invaded her thoughts. In some ways he reminded her of Tarlington and, to some extent, Swindon. Both had been dashing and worldly.

Yet Lord Hawksworth was worse. He was a confusing enigma, which was the very last thing she needed in her life. His flights of fancy in fashion were not as extreme as some, and what he wore was copied by many gentlemen aspiring to be Dandies. Yet he also appeared to be a notable Corinthian. Generally, the two groups did not get on well at all, but he managed to be successful at both. Not to mention that he was dangerously handsome. There must be a flaw somewhere, and it was bound to be a huge one. Every gentleman she knew who was too perfect turned out to have the worst failings.

Meg turned to the window and blew out a breath. No, Lord Throughgood would be much better. It was too bad her mother had an aversion to a parent's arranging matches. Her father contacting his father would have made life a great deal easier. As it was, Meg was going to have to approach his lordship herself. If he was as conventional as she hoped he was, he could think she was much too bold, and that wouldn't do at all. Well, fiddlesticks. She had to do something, or she would end up a spinster.

Although there was no snow on the roads, the weather had turned increasingly bitter and low dark clouds hid the sun and hung overhead as if they would fall on them at any moment, and the scent of the air had changed.

Mrs. Hiller had arranged a luncheon along the way, but after her coachman began predicting snow before long, she hurried them through the meal, anxious to arrive before they were caught in a storm.

They arrived at Bellsville Court, the Bellamnys' principal estate, as the first fat, wet flakes began to fall, blurring her view of the old red-brick manor house. Despite the hour being only shortly after two o'-clock, candles gleamed through the mullioned glass windows of one room. The old Elizabethan house had four floors, cellars, and two wings, but cozy was the description that came to Meg when she gazed at it.

Lady Bellamny greeted them as the coach drew up. "Come in and have something warm to drink. We are in the drawing room."

After they removed their outer garments, she led them to a long rectangular room. Windows flanked one side, fireplaces anchored each end of the room, and thick carpets muffled their feet as they entered.

"We" included a youngish couple with a child of about three years who was currently knocking down the blocks of the structure his father built for him. Meg had never seen the Mertons in such an informal setting before. Lord Merton swooped his son up in his arms and bowed. "A pleasure to see you ladies."

"You as well, my lord." Meg curtseyed, as did Amanda and Mrs. Hiller.

Meg moved over to the closest fireplace, stretching her hands out to warm them. Lady Merton was at the other end of the room in close conversation with a tall, scholarly looking man.

"Mama," Amanda said, "do you know who is with Lady Merton?"

"That is Lord Bellamny, my dear."

"I've never seen him before."

Neither had Meg, and she had been to Lady Bellamny's townhome many times. "Why does he not come to Town?"

"He chooses to remain here or on one of their other estates. When I came out they were held up as the perfect example of an arranged match between people with contrary interests. They had been wed several years at that time. My mother told me that he was fascinated with Lady Bellamny and did attempt a Season or two, but truly disliked London. She was such a social being that he would not refuse his wife her pleasure."

"How selfless of him." Where, Meg wondered, were gentlemen such as Lord Bellamny now?

"Yes, it is, but you mustn't think she has all the benefit. She is quite devoted to him and spends a great deal of time in Town advancing his scientific ideas through her political entertainments."

The echoing of a carriage coming up the drive, then the front door opening, reached the drawing room. A few minutes later the Marquis of Hawksworth was announced.

Meg froze, not daring to turn around. This could not be happening to her. The one gentleman she wished to avoid was here and would be living in the same house for weeks!

Oh God. Could fate be any more contrary?

Miss Hiller nudged Meg's elbow, and she turned to curtsey, but her gaze was glued to the extremely broad smile on Amanda's face. Had she known he would be present? Was this the reason for her happiness? Meg could not allow her friend to fall for a man such as Hawksworth. A man who must have dangerous secrets he was hiding.

Hawksworth leaned down, whispered in Amanda's ear, and she giggled. Had it been possible, Meg would have dragged her friend out by the ear. She glanced around, wondering why Mrs. Hiller didn't do something, yet the lady barely appeared to notice his entrance. Well, someone needed to stop Amanda from making the mistake of her life.

Meg straightened, marched forward, and curtseyed. "My lord."

Damon's gaze had immediately been drawn to Miss Featherton; however, Miss Hiller had reached him first, and he had a message for her from Throughgood. Damon squeezed Miss Hiller's fingers, handing her the note that had been folded into a triangle. Throughgood and his family had been invited to dine with Lady Bellamny, and he had wanted Miss Hiller to meet him early in the drawing room. Damon had agreed to pass the message. After flashing Damon a shy smile, she moved out of the way, grasping the precious message in her closed hand.

After the Feathertons had left Town, he, Throughgood, and Miss Hiller had become more than merely good friends. After seeing them together, Damon apologized to Throughgood for not thinking that Miss Hiller was a good choice for him. The two complemented one another perfectly. They had also pledged their help in bringing Miss Featherton around.

Now here she was before him, and looking extremely militant. For the life of him, he could not think what he had done to get on her bad side.

He bowed. "Miss Featherton, it is always a pleasure to meet you again."

"Thank you." Her lips moved twice or three times, as if she would say something more, but as Lady Bellamny was almost upon them, Miss Featherton made a strategic retreat back to the fireplace.

She was obviously not going to make getting close to her easy, and he had not been able to formulate a scheme to approach her. Nevertheless, he'd always loved a challenge, and when he won her, this one would be exceptionally sweet.

His godmother embraced him, kissing him on both cheeks. "I'm glad you arrived before the weather got any worse." Linking her arm in his, she led him to a table where drinks and food had been set up. "I have brandy, or you might prefer the spiced wine. My chef is from France and makes it in their style."

"The wine, please." He'd been partial to hot spiced wine since he'd first tried it in northern Spain. Taking the glass, he thanked her. "You are keeping country hours, I trust."

"Naturally. As you should know, my husband would cavil loudly and long if I made him wait for his dinner. How was your drive here?"

"Not bad. Dry until the last bit. I stopped at home to see my stepmother and the children. Fortunately, my father was away for a few days."

Her black eyes lost their good humor. "Still on the outs, I see. Well, the right wife will go a long way to settling that."

"I only wish that was true. Something gives me the unsettling feeling that he would like to arrange my wife for me."

"Old fool." Her lips pressed together. "There can be no objection to Miss Featherton—if you can manage to bring her up to scratch, that is."

"While we're on the subject, if you have any ideas, you perceive me all ears."

"What was the paper you passed to Miss Hiller?"

Damon didn't know and did not wish to know how Lady Bellamny saw everything. "It was from Throughgood, telling her his family would dine here this evening."

She nodded. "Excellent." She gave him a second glass of wine. "Take that to Miss Featherton. She looks cold and rather peaked."

A glass in each hand, Damon ambled over to the fireplace, then stood off to the side of his quarry. "I brought you some warm wine."

She glanced at him, startled. "Thank you. That was very kind."

Pressing the glass into her hand, he replied, "It was Lady B's idea. She said you looked cold."

"Yes." As if to add effect to the words, she shivered. "I do not know why I'm so chilly. I am normally not such a poor creature."

"It is a very old house and tends to be drafty." Which was only a partial lie. The house was old. It had been in the Bellamny family since Queen Elizabeth's time, but it was also extremely well maintained. "I am feeling a bit chilled as well," he said, continuing to malign his hosts. He lifted his glass in a toast. "If Lady Bellamny is to be believed, this will warm us."

Miss Featherton raised her glass as well. "I suppose it cannot hurt." She sipped, and a faint smile appeared on her lips. "It is very good. Nothing at all like the mulled wine I've had before."

He bent his head toward her as if he were about to impart a great secret. "French chef."

"Oh." A small burble of laughter escaped her. "That explains it."

This might be easier than he had thought. Apparently, she *had* had time to recover. "This is excellent, but the best hot spiced wine I've ever had was in the north of Spain. Although, come to think of it, we might have been in southern France."

"Were you making your Grand Tour?" She took a larger sip of the wine.

"After a fashion. If you consider Wellington a proper bear leader."

Her jaw dropped for only a moment, but it was long enough for him to begin to imagine what her lips would feel like, and how she would taste.

"You were in the army. I did not know."

Holding his arm out, he gave a mocking bow, and said jokingly, "You perceive before you a man of many talents."

Her countenance shuttered as if she had slammed a door. That had obviously been the wrong thing to say. Perhaps he needed to learn more about her former suitors' public personas. How had they presented themselves and what had they done for her to fall in love with them? His heart ached for her. No one, especially a lady like Miss Featherton, should be made to suffer such pain.

He drained his glass. "I beg your leave. I must change for dinner."

"Yes, of course," she said in a distracted tone. "As should I."

Damon took her wineglass, taking the opportunity to kiss her hand. "I look forward to seeing you at dinner."

She gazed at their hands. "Thank you again for the wine."

As he released her fingers he wished he were a gypsy and could read her mind. This was much worse than he had ever thought it would be. No one he knew had been betrayed to such an extent. No one to whom he could turn for advice on the matter, who had suffered such betrayal. Except perhaps himself, with regard to his father. The only difficulty with that was Damon had not yet resolved his feelings concerning the matter.

As he left the drawing room, he asked a footman to escort him to his chambers, and found himself being led to the rooms he had occupied since he left Eton.

He had been through a war. Surely he could find a way to break through Miss Featherton's defenses, as they had breached the walls at the siege of Badajoz. The images of fire and blood rushed back to him and he fought the memories. The success of the Forlorn Hope, the rape of the city. Even Wellesley, now the Duke of Wellington, had trouble controlling the soldiers. Officers had been ordered to shoot misfeasors on sight.

Damon shook himself. He did not need those memories to haunt him here. Miss Featherton would have nothing to fear from him. When he won his siege of her, she would finally be free of her enemies.

CHAPTER SIX

Amanda snoodled toward the center of the drawing room's wall of windows, took out the note from Lord Throughgood, and read it.

> *My dearest Miss Hiller,*
> *Please meet me in the drawing room. I shall arrive no later than half past four.*
> *Your humble servant,*
> *C. Throughgood*

It was only an hour until he arrived, but it seemed like a lifetime. Except that she had to wash off the dust from the road, and dress. Oh goodness. Would she have enough time?

She glanced at her mother, who appeared to be unaware she had received an illicit message. Not that it mattered. Her father had given her permission to receive letters from Lord Throughgood, and respond to him, after he had read them of course. In Papa's absence, Mama was to read them. Amanda caught her mother's eye and indicated she was leaving.

As she made her way to the door, her happiness dimmed. The air between Meg and Lord Hawksworth seemed alive, shimmering, but neither of them was acting as if anything was going on. There had to be something other than mere politeness between them. Perhaps Meg needed a reason to spend time with his lordship. If only Amanda could think of some scheme to throw them at one another. Unfortunately, nothing came immediately to mind. Perhaps Lord Throughgood would have an idea. The more she had come to know him, the more she respected his commonsensical approach to problems. When she was concerned about their families getting along, he had the idea for his mother to invite her and her parents to stay a few days at Grantville so that their parents would feel comfortable together. Lady Bellamny had agreed to take over chaperoning Meg.

Happily, her ladyship's house had enough chambers to allow Meg and Amanda to have their own rooms. Normally they would have shared a room, but under the circumstances, that did not appeal to Amanda. Not that she planned a secret assignation, nothing of the sort, but she and her family would be spending time with the Grantvilles. Sharing a room would make that difficult. Not to mention that Meg was so dour right now, and Amanda did not wish to have her spirits lowered.

She pinched herself until it hurt. That was not being fair to Meg. Perhaps Amanda and Lord Throughgood could be an example of how a couple in love should be.

Amanda's maid, Lucy, was already laying out the pale pink velvet gown she would wear to dinner. "I must hurry."

"Yes, miss. Your wash water is coming."

Amanda wanted to pace, which was not at all like her. Just as she was about to fetch the water herself, a light tapping sounded, and Lucy opened the door, then stood aside while a young woman went directly to the bowl and filled it.

Once the maid left, Lucy helped Amanda out of her gown, and she washed her face and hands.

"I thought you were not due down until quarter to five?" Lucy asked as she laced Amanda's gown.

"Lord Throughgood will be here at half four."

Her maid's eyes widened. "You'd better hurry."

She shrugged off the temptation to tell her maid that was what she was trying to do. Lucy was the daughter of a senior maid and had been raised around the estate. Although she was terribly clever with Amanda's clothing and hair, Lucy could be rather slow in other areas. Amanda had always thought it might be because her maid cared only about fashion, which was no bad trait in a lady's maid.

"I'll have your hair done in no time."

Minutes later, she began to rush toward the stairs, but a voice from Meg's room brought Amanda to a halt. Her friend was engaging in an angry tirade about Lord Hawksworth and her. *What could that be about?*

She took a step toward the door. After a few moments, her friend stopped talking, and Amanda continued to her meeting with Lord Throughgood. As she entered the drawing room next to the dining room, he turned and smiled. She would have to discuss what she had heard Meg say, but it could wait.

She walked forward, meeting him half-way. When he took her hands and kissed them, she almost cried with happiness.

His deep blue gaze captured hers. "I have missed you."

"I missed you as well."

He squeezed her fingers, but the feeling was much different than when Lord Hawksworth had done the same. This time warmth filled her hands and heart. "I hope you do not mind, but I met with your father before leaving Town and asked permission to court you."

"Did you?" He nodded, and a heat that had nothing to do with the fires or her shawl surged through her, and even though it was dark outside, the sun shone over her. "Perhaps it is time that you call me Amanda when we are in private."

"Only if you call me Chuffy."

"Chuffy?" She couldn't help giggling a bit. "Is that your real name or a nickname?"

He grinned ruefully. "Charles is my true name, but my father is Charles, so I've always been Chuffy."

She twined her fingers with his. "I think it is a wonderful nickname. It fits you somehow." She paused, thinking about their courtship. "Does my mother know?"

"I haven't given it any thought. I would assume your father informed her. Naturally, I told my parents. My mother is planning to have you visit our home even more times than we had thought. I believe arrangements have been made with Lady Bellamny."

Amanda's brow had creased, but it cleared when Chuffy explained what was planned. He was sure she was the right lady for him, and had not wanted the delay. But as she had suspected, Mr. Hiller had insisted that Mrs. Hiller and Amanda meet Chuffy's parents before a final agreement to wed was made. He found himself chafing under the delay, but was not so rash as to oppose his future father-in-law, and therefore presented the proposal they had discussed before Amanda had left Town.

"Yes, that will do nicely—if they get along, that is." The crease on her forehead had returned.

He led her to a small sofa. "Having been out of the country for so long, my family is a bit unusual. They are not ones to stand on ceremony at home and among friends." He began to wonder if their families would like one another. "Will your mother mind?"

Amanda tilted her head to the side. "I do not believe so. However, the only way to find out is when they meet." She gazed into his eyes and smiled. "In any event, I do not believe they will need to be the best of friends in order for us to make our decision." That was exactly what he had wished to hear. "I do hope they get on well. It will make our lives easier."

"As do I, but my mother and grandmother could barely stand the sight of one another. Then again, they were a continent apart."

Amanda's hand covered her lips as she choked. "Oh dear. I do hope your mother and I will like each other."

He drew her into his arms. "How she could fail to love you is beyond me." Chuffy touched his lips to hers in a chaste kiss. "I love you."

Her lips had puckered and moved beneath his. "And I love you."

Grinning, he held her, savoring her warm, soft body. "Perhaps by Twelfth Night we will be able to announce our wedding."

"That is my wish as well."

Her arms had crept cautiously around his neck, and they remained there until he heard steps outside the door. "I believe we shall shortly have company."

As she drew back, her cheeks turned the color of a damask rose he had seen in Persia. "I had almost forgot."

The door opened and Lady Hiller strolled into the room with his mother. Both were so engrossed in their conversation that he didn't think they had noticed Amanda and him until they stopped.

"Chuffy," Mama said. "I would like very much to be introduced to Miss Hiller."

In short order the introductions were made.

His mother held out her hand to Amanda. "It is my pleasure to finally meet the lady who has commanded my son's attention."

His beloved sank gracefully into a curtsey. "Thank you, my lady. Lord Throughgood and I have much in common."

Mama glanced at him over Amanda's head and nodded her satisfaction. "Did I not tell you, Mother? She is a jewel among ladies."

"Indeed you did."

Although he did not feel as if he needed his mother's approval, it was welcome and would smooth the path to marriage. He only hoped her mother approved of his family. Which, considering the servants, might be a problem.

Meg made her way to the drawing room and was surprised but glad that Lord Throughgood was present. However, before she could approach him, Lady Bellamny drew her off to meet another couple who had arrived.

Lord and Lady Smithson were the epitome of a fashionable couple who seemed out of place in the country. Lady Smithson's gown was more suited to a London ball, and Lord Smithson aped the most extravagant garb of the Dandy set, with shirt points so high he could not turn his head. He had worn a spotted silk neckcloth, and his waist was unnaturally nipped. He must be wearing a corset.

Meg dropped a slight curtsey. "How nice to meet you."

Lady Smithson, Meg was sure, gauged her graceful curtsey to the precise point for the daughter of a viscount, and curled her lips into a smile. "A pleasure, Miss Featherton. I have heard a great deal about your family."

That in itself was not surprising. Her family and the original title dated back to King William I. Suddenly she felt as if she had to protect her family from this woman. "Indeed."

Lord Smithson blatantly surveyed Meg's body before bowing and taking her hand. "A singular pleasure, Miss Featherton."

He kissed her hand and Meg wanted to wash it immediately. "My lord."

Before she knew what was happening, a warm presence loomed behind her. "Smithson, my lady." Lord Hawksworth's deep voice would have startled her if she had not already felt his presence. "How was your journey?"

Lady Smithson simpered, and Meg had the strong urge to roll her eyes in disgust.

"Long and cold, my lord." The lady gave a dramatic shiver and stepped closer to Lord Hawksworth.

If these were the types of people with whom he normally socialized, it was all the more reason to keep Amanda away from him.

"As it has been for all of us." He turned his attention to Lord Smithson. "I would have thought this type of party a bit dull for you."

The man flushed. "Not at all. I understand Lady Bellamny is an excellent hostess."

"She is." Lord Hawksworth's words were curt and dismissive.

Apparently he did not want anything to do with the couple. His face held no humor, and for a moment it appeared as if he might make another remark. Yet, any setdown he gave the couple would reflect badly on Lady Bellamny. They were, after all, her guests. Which raised the question of why the Smithsons had been invited. They did not fit in with the rest of the party. But Lord Hawksworth's presence was distracting her too much to give them any further consideration.

She was used to large men. Her brother's friends, as well as her father, were all tall with broad shoulders, yet there was something different about Lord Hawksworth. A force that sizzled beneath the Dandy façade. She had sensed it in both Lord Swindon and Lord Tarlington, but not to the same extent. Another reason to guard herself around the man.

Lord Hawksworth placed her hand on his arm. "You will excuse us."

Not a question but a statement. She wanted to shake the cobwebs from her mind, but his strong arm and the determination with which he led her away confused her. Wasn't he planning to court Amanda? When she glanced to where Lord Throughgood had been, Meg saw another woman and Mrs. Hiller talking. Meg was still trying to find her friend when dinner was announced.

"I believe I have been instructed to escort you." Lord Hawksworth steered her toward the door to the hall.

She tried, briefly, to recall everyone's rank and who they should be matched with, then gave it up. If Lady Bellamny had told him to escort Meg, then that was the end of it. She quickly glanced around and saw Amanda with Lord Throughgood. Hopefully, Meg would have the opportunity to speak with him later. Yet how was she to do that and keep Lord Hawksworth away from Amanda at the same time? Dear Lord, this was becoming complicated. She shrugged. If she could not discuss a possible future with Lord Throughgood this evening, Meg would ask Lady Bellamny when next he would be present.

Damon noted with approval that Miss Hiller seemed to be getting on well with Throughgood's parents. His father, mother, and the lady were having a lively discussion as the four of them strolled toward the dining room. Lord Smithson and his wife approached the dining room with two of the more elderly guests. Damon wondered what the devil Lady Bellamny was about inviting that pair of loose fish. He would warn Throughgood to keep an eye out for Miss Hiller when Smithson was around, and Damon would protect Miss Featherton. Although she seemed to sense there was something repellent about the couple.

When all the guests were in the dining room, Lady Bellamny stood by her chair and announced, "As you can see, I have decided to break with tradition. After this evening, you shall choose your own dining partners." She gave her husband a fond but stern look, most likely reminding him not to keep the gentlemen too long. "While we are having tea, I shall discuss with you a few of the entertainments I have planned."

She took her seat, indicating that everyone else should do the same.

Damon held the chair for Miss Featherton. "I wonder what she has in mind."

"I wish I knew." Her words were slightly breathless, as if she had been walking too fast, and worry infused her tone.

If only he could take her in his arms. He would never allow anyone to harm her again. When it came to his godmother's planning, he might have a reason to be concerned as well. It would take time to court Miss Featherton, and he did not need to have it taken up with too many other activities.

Dinner, as he had expected, was excellent. As the courses were being served, he had asked which dishes she would prefer and had done his best to draw her into conversation. Yet that had been the work of Sisyphus. Her answers were desultory at best, and by the time the ladies left, Damon felt as if he'd been pushing a boulder up a hill. Perhaps he should have a conversation with Miss Hiller. She had seemed pleased that he was interested in Miss Featherton. Perhaps Miss Hiller would help him.

The bottles of port and brandy had been passed around the table only once when Lord Bellamny rose. "Gentlemen, I have been given strict instructions not to keep you long. It is time we joined the ladies."

So Damon had been right about what Lady Bellamny's earlier look had meant. Needing no further prompting, he rose. Someday he hoped that he and Miss Featherton would come to the point where no words were needed for such communications.

Smithson quickly drained his glass and reached for the bottle, but the other gentlemen abandoned their seats, making it impossible for the man to have another drink. As it was, his nose was already red.

Sir Randolph Culpepper, the elderly man who had escorted Mrs. Smithson into dinner, grinned. "Always happy to join my lady. She makes more sense than most people I know."

Smithson had frowned, but Damon now had another goal for his marriage. Miss Featherton was one of the most intelligent and clever people he had met. He could easily envision wishing to spend all his time with her.

Already at the dining room door, Throughgood caught Damon's eye and waited for him. "Miss Hiller has something she wishes to say to us concerning Miss Featherton. We won't have an opportunity before Lady Bellamny's announcement, but afterward we should meet somewhere."

The music room was next to the drawing room. "I hope Miss Hiller is musical, as I shall suggest to Lady Bellamny that she give us a few minutes to look over the music before she opens the connecting doors. I sincerely hope you either play or sing?"

Throughgood grinned. "I do both, but my voice is not as good as I recall yours being." A sly expression appeared on his face. "We should discover if Miss Featherton is of a musical bent as well."

"Excellent idea." Throughgood and Damon began to stroll out of the dining room. "Do you know if we are the only younger guests?"

"There are four others, but they might have been held up by the weather, in which case they will not arrive until to-morrow."

Damon nodded. The only question that interested him was whether or not that would help him with Miss Featherton. If any of the guests were single gentlemen, he would find a way to deal with them.

After the guests had gathered in the drawing room and been served tea, Lady Bellamny tapped her spoon against her cup. "We have a few more guests arriving to-morrow, but that need not stop us from visiting the local fair. I believe you will be impressed by the offerings."

A fair sounded interesting. Shopping was an activity designed to interest females of all sorts, and there would be sufficient time for Damon to court Miss Featherton.

A few minutes later, he approached Lady Bellamny with his musical idea.

"If you can talk the young ladies into performing, I shall agree. Having never been able to carry a note myself, I will not force them."

"Miss Hiller is willing. Perhaps if she finds some music that Miss Featherton knows, she will be able to convince her to join us. Throughgood and I shall perform as well."

"Excellent. I'll leave you to it. Open the doors when you are ready."

Damon hid his smile. "I shall."

CHAPTER SEVEN

Damon gathered Throughgood, and thus Miss Hiller, with a glance. They left the drawing room by way of the terrace and re-entered the house through the music room.

Miss Hiller's color was high, and she looked as if she would burst with her news.

"My love." Throughgood drew Miss Hiller protectively into his arms. "Have you been shocked by someone? If it is Smithson, I shall ensure he is removed—"

"No, no, nothing like that, I assure you." She focused her gaze on Damon. "Earlier this evening, I was passing Miss Featherton's chamber. Although it would not normally occur to me to eavesdrop, I heard my name and thought she was calling me. After a few moments, it became clear that she was speaking to herself. What she said gave me an idea!" She beamed with satisfaction. "I have a scheme that will help you win Miss Featherton."

He had been absently thumbing through the music, but at Miss Hiller's last words, stopped. "What kind of scheme?"

"A good one." She pressed her lips in a prim manner, reminding him of his sisters' governess. "Do I mistake the matter, or are you still interested in courting Miss Featherton?"

"My love!" Throughgood uttered in a shocked tone. "You can't ask a man something like that."

"Indeed I can. I think he cares very much about her. Yet she has been hurt so badly she doesn't believe she is able to love anyone ever again." She gazed up at Throughgood. "And I must warn you not to—"

"Your instincts are correct, Miss Hiller," Damon interrupted before the conversation could ramble off in other directions. "I am very much interested in Miss Featherton."

How Miss Hiller's smile could have become broader, he didn't know, but it did. "I knew it. Well, she thinks that I am interested in you." A low growl emanated from Throughgood. "Of course, I am not at all." She took Throughgood's hand twining her fingers with his. "But she said she will do anything to protect me from a rogue such as Lord Hawksworth."

Damon wasn't sure he liked what he was hearing, but . . . "This is what caused you to develop your plan?"

"Yes." She said the word with all the aplomb of having made a great discovery. "She is going to save me from you by allowing you to pay her attentions."

He found himself staring at Miss Hiller, not quite understanding how this would help him.

Fortunately, Throughgood echoed Damon's doubts. "But how will that help Hawksworth?"

She glanced from him to Throughgood as if they were lacking in intellect. "Meg and Lord Hawksworth will have to spend a great deal of time together, and she will come to know him. Before long, she will see that he is just the right gentleman for her."

Damon considered the idea. Be that as it may, he was not sure that in protecting Miss Hiller from him, Miss Featherton would open herself up to him. On the other hand, he didn't have a better idea, and it might work. Lowering as it was, somehow Miss Featherton had come to the conclusion he was not to be trusted. He was not so stupid as to believe that he could succeed with her as long as she was set against him. On the other hand, Miss Hiller had a point. If he was able to spend time with Miss Featherton, he could put her mind at ease. Not immediately. That would defeat his purpose, but over the course of several days. "I think it will work. No matter her misgivings, if she believes she is saving you, she must spend time with me."

"Precisely," Miss Hiller said in a tone that reminded him of his tutor when he gave the correct response.

Throughgood kissed her lightly on the lips. "You are brilliant, my love."

"I agree, Miss Hiller. Your idea is splendid."

"Now," Throughgood said to her, "what were you going to warn me about?"

"I had almost forgot." She colored a little. "Meg thinks that she would like to wed a man who is undemanding and easy to please. Someone with whom she will not fall in love."

"A dead bore," Damon said, not at all pleased. "She would be leading him around by his nose and not enjoying it at all."

Miss Hiller nodded. "I believe you are right. But the thing is that"—she looked at Throughgood—"she thinks Chuffy would do for her."

Throughgood's mouth dropped open. "I—I am almost speechless. I know I have put on some weight, but . . ." He pulled a comical face, then the full ramifications of what Miss Hiller had said seemed to dawn on him. "Good Lord. I must not be around her at all. The embarrassment she would suffer when she discovered the truth would devastate her. Amanda, cannot you tell her about us now?"

"No, my love. That would not do at all. If I did that, she would have no reason to be in Lord Hawksworth's company."

"Ah yes." Throughgood grimaced. "Hawksworth, I sincerely trust you appreciate my sacrifice. I must convince my mother to change some of her plans for being here."

Miss Hiller glanced at the door. "Now that that is settled, we had better look at the music."

In a few short moments, they had found several pieces they all knew. Miss Hiller left by the door to the corridor to find Miss Featherton. Damon hoped Miss Hiller's plan would work. If not, he might have worse problems with his lady than he had originally thought.

He was certain Throughgood would never fall in with Miss Featherton's scheme. But another gentleman might very well see it as the perfect solution.

Damnation! He had precisely fourteen days to change her mind.

Meg glanced at the drawing room door as it opened. Amanda looked around for a moment, then focused on Meg and beckoned. When had her friend started wearing her eyeglasses in public? Perhaps now she would discover what else had been going on. She made her way to the door, following Amanda into the corridor.

"Lord Hawksworth thought we might entertain ourselves with some music. Please join us. It will be so much fun!"

"You were in the music room with him alone!" This was much worse than Meg had thought. Anyone could have found them, and Amanda would be compromised and have to marry the man.

"No, Lord Throughgood is there as well, and the door was open. Lady Bellamny knew we were there. I would have asked you to join us immediately, but I—um, did not see you." Amanda tugged on Meg's hand. "Please say you will. You have a much better voice than I do. I shall accompany you."

Meg nodded. This might be her opportunity to approach Lord Throughgood. "Very well."

As they entered the room, Lord Hawksworth looked up and smiled. Her feet slowed as the full force of his charm hit her. No man had a right to be so handsome. Something should be wrong with him, but he even seemed to have a full set of white teeth. No wonder Amanda was smitten.

"Excellent." He set down the sheet of music he had been holding. "I am delighted you wished to join us, Miss Featherton."

Wished was not precisely the word she would have used. Forced to defend her friend would be more accurate. "Right, then," she said, determined not to respond to his allure. "What do we have?"

"Yes, thank you for joining us." Throughgood jumped into the conversation. "There is a duet here that Miss Hiller thinks would be just the thing."

Lord Hawksworth handed Meg the sheet he had been holding. While she glanced over the music, he slid open the doors to the drawing room. Now that was an intriguing arrangement. Paneled as they were, they had appeared to be part of the wall.

In the other room, Lady Bellamny rose and began motioning the others toward the music room. "Marvelous. The young people are going to sing for us."

When he returned, Meg handed him the words to "Barbara Allan," an old folk song that most everyone should know. "What about this one?"

"It will do. You begin and I shall join in on the second verse."

Amanda and Lord Throughgood took their places at the piano, and they waited until Lady Bellamny signaled for them to begin.

Amanda played the introduction, then Meg began to sing.

> *"It was in and about the Martinmas time,*
> *When the green leaves were a falling,*
> *That Sir John Graeme in the West Country*
> *Fell in love with Barbara Allan.*
> *He sent his man down through the town,*

> *To the place where she was dwelling:*
> *'O haste and come to my master dear,*
> *Gin ye be Barbara Allan.'"*

Lord Hawksworth joined her. His strong baritone harmonized easily with her contralto. It had been so long since Meg had sung a duet with anyone. Neither of her last two suitors had enjoyed singing, and she was of an age where it was no longer required of her.

> *"O holy, holy rose she up,*
> *To the place where he was lying,*
> *And when she drew the curtain by,*
> *'Young man, I think you're dying.'*
> *'O I'm sick, and very, very sick,*
> *And 'tis all for Barbara Allan.'"*

When they came to the last verse, he stopped singing as she began the lament. Tears pricked her eyes as she thought of the young woman dying after having rejected love.

> *"It cried, Woe to Barbara Allan!*
> *'O mother, mother make my bed!*
> *O make it soft and narrow!*
> *Since my love died for me to-day,*
> *I'll die for him to-morrow.'"*

As she finished, Lady Culpepper dabbed her eyes. "I always think it is such a sad song, but you did it beautifully, Miss Featherton. You as well, Lord Hawksworth. I do not think I have heard it sung with more feeling."

"Perhaps something more spritely?" Sir Randolph asked, patting his wife's hand. "Mustn't leave the ladies weeping."

Amanda placed another sheet of music on the piano and Lord Hawksworth handed Meg "Child Waters," a bawdy song that always made her blush. Yet she and Amanda had performed it many times over the years.

Lord Hawksworth glanced at the music. "That will certainly liven things up." A wicked gleam appeared in his eyes. "Why don't you sing Margaret's part, and I'll sing the other?"

"Very well," Meg agreed, only because she had never been able to sing the last line.

He nodded to Amanda, who began to play.

Lord Hawksworth put his fists on his hips as if he were actually arguing with Meg.

> *"I beg you bide at home, Margaret,*
> *And sew your silken seam;*
> *If ye were in wide Highlands,*
> *You would be over far from home."*

Despite how low she had been feeling lately, his playacting appealed to her. She tossed her head and laughed, getting into the part.

> *"I will not bide at home, she said,*
> *Nor sew my silken seam;*
> *For if I were in the wide Highlands,*
> *I would not be far from home.*
>
> *"My steed shall drink the blood-red wine,*
> *And you the water wan;*
> *I'll make you sigh, and say alas*
> *That ever I loved a man!"*

At the end of the last verse she gave her head an emphatic nod. He leaned slightly toward her and jutted his chin, making her want to break out in whoops. Hawksworth was really very good at this.

> *"My hounds shall eat the bread of wheat,*
> *And you the bread of bran;*
> *I'll make you sigh, and say, alas,*
> *That ever you loved Lord John!"*

The next part was hers, so she raised her chin, challenging him.

> *"Though your hounds do eat the bread of wheat,*
> *And me the bread of bran,*
> *Yet will I sing, and merry be,*
> *That ever I loved Lord John."*

For the last verse, he took both her hands in one of his and gazed down at her.

"But cheer up your heart now, Fair Margaret,
For, be it as it may,
Your kirken and your fair wedding
Shall both be on one day."

Even though he had used the Scottish word for churching, making it more acceptable, Meg could not imagine anything worse than having a child before being married. Unbidden, her face warmed, and she couldn't stop herself from blushing. Then she began to laugh, and he chuckled.

Everyone in the room joined them. Hawksworth bowed, while she curtseyed. Someone called for another song, but Lady Bellamny rose. "It has been a long day for many of us. We shall have other evenings to enjoy the talents of our guests."

She led the others back into the drawing room, while Amanda, Lord Throughgood, Lord Hawksworth, and Meg put away the music.

Glancing at Lord Throughgood, who was speaking with Amanda, Meg decided to speak with him and present her proposal. One way or the other, she wanted the matter to be settled. If he did not wish to marry her, she would make a list of gentlemen who would probably agree to her conditions. Some of the happiness she'd felt while she was singing leached away as she edged her way around the piano. She stiffened her spine. Better marriage with someone who was nice, than remain single. She wanted to take her place in Polite Society, and she wanted children.

"Throughgood." Lord Hawksworth's deep voice commanded the other man's attention. "Introduce me to your parents, if you would. I think we might have some friends in common."

She opened her mouth and shut it again. She could have screamed with frustration. *The misbegotten, interfering slibberslabber. Drat and blast him!*

Meg made herself count to ten. In all fairness, she could not blame Hawksworth. After all, he could not have known of her plan.

For a moment, Lord Throughgood stared at Hawksworth, then he blinked. "Of course. Love to. You'll like them. Everyone does." He bowed to Amanda. "This evening was a pleasure. I don't know when I've had such a good time of it."

She gave him her usual shy smile. "Nor do I, my lord."

After the men had left the room, she linked arms with Meg. "Do not deny that you had fun as well. I heard you laugh."

"I did. Music always makes me feel better."

"I know what you mean." She lowered her voice. "Lord Hawksworth has a lovely voice."

Just how far has Amanda fallen under the man's spell? Meg prayed that her friend did not realize that she was trying to keep her away from him. "He does. Perhaps he plays piano as well."

"I do not think so," Amanda said slowly. "Otherwise I am sure he would have said something."

"You are probably right. He is not a man to hide his talents under a bushel."

Amanda brought her hand to her mouth and yawned. "I am for my bed."

It was only ten o'clock, but the travel might have tired her. "Good night. I'll be up later."

After she left, Meg decided to approach Lord Throughgood. He and his family would most likely be here a while longer.

Entering the drawing room, she glanced around. Lord Hawksworth was standing with Lord and Lady Grantville, but their son was nowhere to be seen.

CHAPTER EIGHT

Damon slid a glance to where Miss Featherton stood. She closed her eyes for a moment, and her hands were clenched. Finally she let out a huff.

It was a damned good thing Throughgood wasn't staying here. As determined as she was, she would have tracked him down to his room. As it was, keeping her away from him would be a challenge. She was exceedingly clever. If she discovered what he, Throughgood, and Miss Hiller were about, their whole scheme would come tumbling down.

One of the other guests joined the conversation, and Damon made his way to Miss Featherton. Over the years, he had sung many duets, but none with a lady so perfectly matched to his voice and style. It was as if they had been singing together for years. She had been happy and relaxed during their songs and had even allowed him to hold her hands. Unfortunately, once their performance ended, she returned to her wary self. If only he knew how to break through the wall she had built around herself. To make matters worse, she wasn't even confiding in her closest friend. Although he had to admit that would be far too much to hope for, since she thought Miss Hiller was interested in him, and Meg wanted to arrange a marriage with Throughgood.

Flowers, romantic words, and tokens of his affection were not going to work with her. No doubt she had received too many of them to count. Damon would have to show her how he felt. Convince her that he could be trusted with her heart. What he truly required was a scoundrel from whom he could rescue her. Not a likely scenario in their present location. Then again, his luck had always been good; perhaps someone would come along.

He intercepted her as she approached the door to the corridor. "Miss Featherton, I greatly enjoyed our duets. Your voice is enchanting."

As she glanced up at him an irritated look briefly appeared before she masked her feelings with a polite smile. "It was quite enjoyable, and your voice is equally charming. I had wanted a word with Lord Throughgood, but I do not see him."

He should have expected that, but it still hurt. He matched her smile with one of his own. "He arrived separately from his parents. I believe he has already departed." Not precisely a lie. He was somewhere with Miss Hiller, most likely teaching her the finer points of kissing. Which was exactly what he would like to be doing with Miss Featherton.

Her face fell, and he wanted to hit something. He looked at Smithson, willing the rascal to do something that would require Damon to take action. Unfortunately, the man seemed to be on his best behavior. "If it is important, perhaps I can help you."

Finally her lush lips relaxed into a small, but true, grin. "Thank you, but I merely wished to ask him a question. I have had a long day and should seek my couch."

Frustration curled through him, yet he maintained his countenance as he lifted her fingers to his lips. "I wish you a good night."

She stared at her hand for a moment. "A pleasant night to you as well."

A few moments later the door closed behind her, and Damon let out a breath. Then Smithson headed for the door. Damon slipped out through the music room, catching up to the rake as he was about to climb the stairs. "Going somewhere?"

Smithson seemed to straighten. "To my chamber, not that it is any business of yours."

Damon was in no mood to play games. "Let me make myself clear. If you bother Miss Featherton, or any other lady here, I will take great pleasure in seeing you on your way home."

"That, my lord, is for Lady Bellamny to say."

In a voice that braver men than Smithson feared to challenge, Damon said, "I do not make idle threats, sir."

Smithson patted his waistcoat. "I seem to have forgot something."

He returned to the drawing room, but Damon did not believe for a minute that he had given up. Though amusing, it may have been a mistake for him to pretend to be a Dandy. He smiled to himself. On the other hand, there might be a way to put Smithson to good use.

* * *

The stable was warm, and the soft snorting of the horses surrounded Amanda and Chuffy. She had always loved the stables, and now she had even more reason to like them.

They had only a few minutes together while his carriage was being readied. She nestled her head against his jacket as he stroked her back, sending streaks of heat where his hand touched her. "Your parents are very nice."

"They are." His lips nuzzled her hair. "I knew you would all get along."

She slid her palms up over his shoulders. "My father will be here soon."

"Excellent." He lowered his lips to the corner of hers, pressing softly, until he reached the middle and caught her bottom lip gently between his teeth. "I wish to propose to you."

She trailed her tongue along the seam of his mouth like he had taught her.

Kissing lessons were ever so agreeable. "Then we would have to keep it a secret from my mother. She would not understand why she could not tell the world. I would like to give Lord Hawksworth some more time."

"If you wish." Chuffy opened his lips and began to languidly stroke his tongue against hers. "But it will all come out when your father arrives."

She flattened her body against his and claimed his mouth again, tilting her head to deepen the kiss. They did not have much time and practice was important. After a few moments she broke the kiss. "Christmas Day."

Chuffy held her tightly, ravaging her mouth. Amanda could barely catch a breath, but had never enjoyed a kiss more. She had never dreamed kissing could be this lovely. She wiggled against him, needing to be closer, and sensations she had never experienced before took control of her body. She gasped as his palm covered her derrière and squeezed.

"Forgive me." His voice was ragged. "I should not have done that."

Placing her fingers over his lips, she said, "I liked it. We'll be married soon."

"Not soon enough. I—"

"My lord." His groom's voice pierced the gentle sounds of the stable and the door opened a crack, letting the winter air rush in. "Your carriage is ready, and you don't want to leave the horses standing in this cold."

"I love you." He kissed her hard just as the door began to open.

"I love you too." Amanda hugged him tightly, not wanting to let him go. "I must go in before Mama misses me."

"I'll see you to the side door."

They left the warmth of the stable, and she shivered in the icy air. The night was clear, and stars filled the sky. She pointed to the brightest one. "I have always thought that was the star the Wise Men followed."

"I had never thought of it, but you might be right. I remember seeing the North Star from Palestine. One has a very good view of Orion from there."

She scrunched her nose up. "Is that a constellation? I must have constellations pointed out to me. They seem terribly vague. It is as if one must know what one is seeing before one can actually see it."

He cleared his throat. "I can understand how that could be. Come, let me get you inside." They strode quickly to the small door near the stables, his arm wrapped around her. "To-morrow seems a long way away."

Amanda cupped Chuffy's strong jaw, stroking his cheek with her thumb. "I will dream of you."

He turned his head into her palm and kissed it. "I shall dream of the day we do not have to part."

"My lord!"

"I must go." He kissed her one last time. "Until morning."

She entered the door, climbed the stairs to the first window, and watched as he jumped fluidly into his curricle. She said a short prayer that he would arrive home safely. Creeping softly past Meg's chamber, Amanda arrived at her room feeling like she had run a race. As usual her maid was waiting for her.

Lucy kept up a steady stream of talk while she unlaced Amanda's gown. "Your mother said to tell you that you're invited for tea with Lady Grantville. After that you'll go with her to the fair in the town."

Amanda practically burst with happiness. That meant that she would not have to think of an excuse to be with Chuffy. Surely it would not be difficult to avoid Meg if they arrived at the fair separately. Amanda immediately berated herself. That type of thinking was not fair to her friend. She would also have to make a point of telling Lord Hawksworth he had until Christmas Day to fix Meg's attentions.

Chuffy waited until Amanda was safely in the house. He had barely let her leave him this evening. If he could have, he would have taken her home with him. Perhaps his mother would invite them to stay at Grantville. Having his beloved at his house would also settle the problem of Miss Featherton. When Hawksworth had called Chuffy away from the lady, it had taken him a few moments to remember he was not to speak with her.

Yes. Having Amanda at his house would be much safer. On the other hand, if she would simply tell Miss Featherton that he and Amanda wished to wed, that would be the end of this farce. But part of what he loved about her was her kind heart and loyalty. He supposed he could go along with it for a while longer. At least he had a commitment that they would announce their betrothal on Christmas Day. Hawksworth had better work fast. Poor devil. Chuffy had better warn him.

He was about to give his horses their office when he was hailed.

"Throughgood." Hawksworth's long steps quickly ate up the distance from the front door. "What are your plans for to-morrow?"

"I shall be escorting Miss Hiller to the fair. I am not exactly sure how that will come about. I have decided to ask my mother to invite her and her family to Grantville. I was just coming to tell you, though, that we will announce our decision to wed on Christmas Day."

"Blast it to hell." He mumbled a string of curses in various languages, before saying, "I'll come about. I always do."

"Perhaps once I am no longer eligible, she will be easier to convince."

"Or find some other gentleman to wed."

"Not here. M'mother told me that all the guests are either married or betrothed."

Hawksworth paused, frowning for a moment. "Now that *is* interesting." He backed away from the carriage. "Have a safe journey home."

"It is not even a mile and the roads are well kept." Chuffy snorted. "Our house is at the far north end of the property. One could walk there faster. Apparently the fourth viscountess wished to be closer to the town and her family."

"Family?" Hawksworth raised his brows. "Don't tell me Lady Bellamny is a connection of yours?"

"By marriage at least. I have always had the feeling she was connected to pretty much all of the great houses in England."

"That does not surprise me. She's related to my father as well." He grinned. "Although the last time her name was mentioned around him, he called her an interfering old besom. I shall attempt to avoid you to-morrow."

"Please do. Miss Hiller is feeling very guilty about Miss Featherton."

Hawksworth barked a laugh. "But not guilty enough to turn you down."

Chuffy grinned. "No. She is a loyal friend, not a sacrificial lamb." Now, though, the thought stuck in his head. "Must ensure she doesn't do anything like that."

"Good idea." His friend saluted him. "I suppose I'll see you soon."

"No offense, but not if I can help it. Better for me to stay away from here." He gave his horses the office to start.

There were enough stars to see the well-maintained road clearly, and as he'd told Hawksworth, the houses were not far apart. He would have to remember to have a conversation with his father about the marriage settlements and ask Amanda's mother if she could discover when Mr. Hiller was due to arrive. There would also need to be a special license for the wedding; he wished to be wed sooner rather than later.

Could he manage to have Amanda stay at Grantville until they were wed, then he need not be in Miss Featherton's orbit at all. No. That wouldn't work. His mother was hosting a dinner and some other entertainments to which Lady Bellamny's guests were invited. Not for the first time, he prayed that their ill-run house would meet with Amanda's approval.

Chuffy reached home to find his parents had not yet arrived. He was just about to retire when he decided to write missives to them about his concerns. It was only right to give them a warning. Especially Papa. He was just now coming to understand the earldom's assets and liabilities, and he would need to be conversant in order for the settlement agreements to be drafted.

After Chuffy dismissed his valet, he poured a brandy. He should not borrow trouble, but he couldn't rid himself of the thought that as much as Amanda loved him, she might defer to her friend. Then what would he do?

Damn the devil. He had to do something to ensure she never gave him up.

Meg awoke heavy eyed to the weak winter sun shining onto her face. She was tempted to roll over and go back to sleep. But Hendricks obviously wanted Meg up as soon as possible. Hence the reason for the open curtains.

"Time you were awake, miss." Her maid's cheerful voice broke the silence.

Meg wanted to complain that the room was too cold to rise, yet the one hand outside of the covers was not at all chilly. The banked fire had probably been stoked hours ago. "I do not understand the rush."

"The other ladies and some of the gentlemen are going into the village soon."

"I thought that was not planned until this afternoon." Silence greeted her statement. What time was it? She never slept past nine o'clock. She rose, casting a glance at the mantel clock.

Noon? Impossible.

"That cannot be correct. I was in bed by eleven o'clock, as you well know."

"What I know, miss, is that you haven't been sleeping well for weeks now. It was bound to catch up with you. I have your breakfast coming. Some of the ladies broke their fast in their chambers, so it won't look strange that you did as well." Hendricks threw the covers off Meg. "What will look odd is if you don't go with them to the town. Unless you're coming down with something. Are you?"

Meg wished she could claim a headache, but that would only draw attention to herself. "No. I am getting up."

An hour later she was in the morning room where the others were gathering. In addition to Lord Hawksworth were Sir Randolph and Lady Culpepper, the Smithsons, Miss Riverton—a lively lady of about nineteen with brown curls—and her betrothed, Lord Darby. The latter was several years older than she, and had arrived late last night. He was clearly infatuated with her. His mother, Lady Darby, was also present, although she did not look as if she wanted to join their excursion.

Lady Darby's face puckered as if she had eaten a lemon. "Are you sure a *village*"—she said the word as if it disgusted her—"fair will not be too dull?"

Lady Bellamny's eyes narrowed. "You must not be aware, my lady, that Grantville is a market town. Each year before Christmas Day, there is a fair to help the town. This year it is to raise funds for a new roof on the church."

"You see, Mother"—Lord Darby's tone did not hide his irritation with her—"it is for a good cause."

"You should be looking to the welfare of your betrothed," she retorted. "I am sure Susan is fatigued from the travel."

Lord Darby glanced at Miss Riverton, who appeared anything but tired. "My dear?"

"I am quite well and excited about the treat." She turned to Lady Bellamny. "I was raised in London and have never attended a town fair. I am greatly looking forward to it."

Lady Bellamny nodded her head approvingly. "I am sure you will have a wonderful time." She addressed Lady Darby. "I am certain you will feel better with a rest."

Knowing she had been dismissed, Lady Darby paled. "Yes, that is most likely it. Thank you."

Again Meg wondered at someone such as Lady Darby being invited. Most likely she was only here to chaperone Miss Riverton.

Meg glanced around and did not see either Amanda or her mother. "How long until we depart?"

"Immediately," Lady Bellamny answered.

"Are Mrs. Hiller and Miss Hiller not joining us?"

"They will meet us there," Lady Bellamny said in a matter-of-fact tone before turning and ordering a nearby footman to have the coaches brought around.

Meg did not understand why Amanda and her mother were not coming with them, but before she could ask, she sensed Lord Hawksworth next to her. "Good afternoon, my lord."

"Good afternoon, Miss Featherton." The corners of his lips curled up as he inclined his head. "Allow me to escort you around the fair." He held his arm out, not giving her a choice.

"It would be my pleasure."

Placing his mouth next to her ear, he whispered, "I doubt that, but I can assure you it *will* be *my* pleasure."

She had no answer for that piece of impudence, and placed her hand on his arm. "Thank you."

"Life is not always just, Miss Featherton," he said as he led her to the hall. "However, if one prevails, one can conquer one's demons."

"Is that a lesson you learned during the war?" She tried to mask her interest, but the more she spent around him, the more he intrigued her. She really must not allow that to happen. She was only suffering his attention to save Amanda.

Even in the bright light cast from the long mullioned windows his eyes were shaded. "One of many."

"And are all your demons vanquished?"

"Many of them." He was quiet for a moment. "Most of them. There are times when I dream of battle and wake up believing I am still in the fight. Yet those times are rare now."

Despite her concerns about Lord Hawksworth, she was drawn to comfort him. "I would that you had not had them at all."

He flashed her a brief grin. "I was fortunate, unlike many of my fellow soldiers."

"My father is extremely active in helping the plight of those who fought in the war."

"You are lucky to have a family that cares not only about you, but the world at large."

Did that mean that his family did not?

Meg's maid appeared with her outer clothing. After she had donned her bonnet and gloves, she was shocked to feel a tremor of pleasure snake down her spine as Hawksworth's long, warm, and gloveless fingers brushed her neck as he gently placed her cloak on her shoulders. Meg sucked in a breath, but did not trust her voice to respond. How could she feel anything for him when she knew he was dangerous? He was not what she wanted. From now on, she would simply have to steel herself not to respond.

To make matters worse, when they got out to the carriages, Meg was put into the same one as Lord Hawksworth and the dratted man had to sit right next to her. Not that anything would happen. Lady Bellamny was with them, but she had commanded the whole of the forward-facing seat. Still, Meg didn't want to feel his shoulder brushing the side of her cheek when he moved or his hard thigh as it touched her leg when the coach hit a rut, and she definitely did not want to hear his deep, seductive laughter as he responded to a quip Lady Bellamny made.

She turned her head, looking out the window and praying not to be affected by the rogue.

"Miss Featherton?" Lady Bellamny asked.

"Yes, my lady?"

"Are you feeling quite the thing?"

Once again she considered pleading a headache. Yet then she would be sent back to the house, and she so enjoyed country fairs that she did not wish to miss it merely because Hawksworth was so distracting. "I'm well. The countryside has caught my attention." Not that anyone would believe that faradiddle. "I thought I saw a deer."

"Possibly. Although I would rather you keep that information to yourself. I do not wish the gentlemen to begin organizing a hunt and interfering with my arrangements." She shifted her black gaze to Lord Hawksworth. "I know you will not say a word."

He placed his hand on his heart. "Far be it from me to excite the other gentlemen to blood sport." Humor lurked in his voice. "If anyone is to provide venison for the table, it should be your gamekeeper, but I beg it not be the deer Miss Featherton saw."

Meg almost rolled her eyes, but instead pursed her lips and said primly, "I am quite fond of venison. However, I would not wish to upset his lordship's delicate sensibilities."

He turned his head toward her, raising his brows. "My delicate . . . ?"

"Ha! She got the better of you there, my boy." Lady Bellamny chuckled. "Serves you right for pretending to be what you are not."

Meg had almost giggled, but her ladyship's last statement sobered her. No matter how handsome and charming he was, Lord Hawksworth was not for her.

If fate was with her, she would see Lord Throughgood at the fair and be able to discuss her proposition with him.

Damon could have howled with frustration. For a brief moment, Miss Featherton had come out of her shell. Then, like a tortoise, she'd stuck her head back in again. What had happened?

He reviewed the short exchange. She had been on the verge of smiling when his godmother said that bit about being what he was not.

Hell and damnation. That was it. Swindon and Tarlington had shown her false faces and broken her heart. She must think he was following their lead. And, of course, Damon had been playing a game with Polite Society since reentering it. But his intent had never been to harm anyone, even if he had made some of the more ridiculous Dandies appear even more so. Earlier this past Season, his friend Nick Beresford had told Damon his pretense would come back to bite him, and it had. Just not in the way he thought it might.

He glanced at Miss Featherton, who was applying herself to the barren scenery. She probably had not seen a deer at all. He slid a look to his godmother. Her brows were raised, and her expression said as clearly as if she'd spoken, *Now you know what she is afraid of.*

He pressed his lips tightly together, acknowledging her message.

At the first opportunity, Damon must show Miss Featherton his true self and pray she believed him.

The ride to the market town was mercifully short, and in what seemed like seconds they were pulling up in the yard of a tavern.

Once they had all alighted from their vehicles, Lady Bellamny announced, "I have reserved a parlor for anyone who is cold or in need of nourishment other than what the fair has to offer. We will meet back here at four. Dinner will be delayed by an hour."

Damon appropriated Miss Featherton's arm again. Not that there was anyone available around, except Smithson, who was looking none too happy to be with his wife, nor was the lady smiling.

The fair took up the entire market place, spreading down the main street through the town. Even in a town this large, many of the booths must be from outside peddlers.

He and Miss Featherton strolled around for a few minutes, before he stopped in front of a stall displaying an assortment of ribbons, lace, and other furbelows. "I promised my sisters presents, as I am missing Christmas with them. Would you help me select some appropriate gifts?"

Miss Featherton appeared to study the merchandise. "How many sisters do you have and what are their ages?"

"I have four. They are sixteen, twelve, nine, and five. All of them have their mother's blond hair and blue eyes."

She cut a swift glance at him, her brows drawn together. "Your mother died?"

"When I was seven. My father remarried several months later, but my step-mother has always made me feel like I was one of her children."

"Do you have brothers as well?" She fingered a piece of lace. "This would make a lovely fichu or trim for a gown. I take it the older one will make her come out next Season."

"I have twelve brothers. All but the first have been given Latin numbers as names. Eight through twelve are at home, but they would much rather I take them out than buy them things."

"Twelve?" Her eyes rounded.

"My step-mother says my father has only to look at her and she begins to breed. Fortunately, she has an easy time birthing them."

A shudder ran through Miss Featherton's arm. "Still, that is a lot of children to provide for."

"My father is committed only to the eldest and the girls. The others must make their own way. A few of them do not bother with their titles as it makes for an awkward situation with their employers." He pointed out a brightly colored ribbon in a pinkish color. "What do you think of this?"

"Not with blond hair." She selected two ribbons, one blue and the other bright red. "How do you like these? Your brothers' decisions are very unusual."

"The ribbons are perfect. They are. Fortunately, my father didn't cut up stiff over it. What about something for my youngest sister?"

"What is she like?"

He paid for the purchases and took Miss Featherton's arm again. "A minx. She fights my brothers for the tin soldiers and can climb a tree better than some of the boys."

She led him to a booth with wooden swords and scabbards. "I would encourage her independence."

He picked up one of the swords, testing it for weight. The varnished wood was as smooth as metal. The hilt was wrapped in leather. "I'll take this one and a scabbard to go with it."

"Very good choice, sir. Your son will enjoy it." The trader beamed at Damon and Miss Featherton, who blushed charmingly. "I'll wrap it up for you."

"Don't bother," he said, counting out the coins, and wondering what his and Miss Featherton's children would look like. His stomach rumbled. "Are you hungry?"

"A little. Would you like to go back to the inn?"

"Not particularly. The malingerers are probably there. Shall we see what we can find here?"

"Malingerers?" she asked, this time taking his arm instead of waiting for him to take hers. Was that progress?

"In the army, malingerers are those soldiers who attempt to avoid their duty by faking illness or injury. In this case I refer to those guests who fear a country fair beneath them or think they are too frail to be out in mildly chilly weather."

"Hmm. It has warmed up quite a bit since yesterday, and it is hurtful for a landlord not to pay attention to his dependents. Most wealth is still derived from the land, after all. Is the army hard on malingerers?"

Damon was rapidly falling in love. "It is a hanging offense, but usually other methods are found to make them rethink their maladies before it gets to that point."

"It is a shame civilians cannot use harsher measures." Her tone was so low, he did not know if it was meant for him to hear.

"Although, Lady Bellamny's punishment of Lady Darby was efficiently accomplished."

"Ah yes. The threat of social annihilation can work wonders."

"But, Miss Featherton, how could you deprive the physician and watering places of their income?"

"Yes, of course." Her voice shook with laughter. "How horrible of me to forget the income they provide."

"Indeed." He used a supercilious tone. "Quite careless of you."

Her head snapped around to look at him, and he gave her his best boyish grin.

"You, sir, are teasing."

"Am I not allowed to?"

"Yes, of course—you are doing it again," she said, frowning sternly.

"My dear Miss Featherton. Naturally I must, if you rise so easily to the bait."

"Wretch." Her tone was severe, but her eyes danced.

Damon's hope rose. He wanted her to laugh and be happy. He wished to be the one to make her happy. "Clearly, I have fallen in your estimation."

She opened her full red lips, then closed them. Would she admit she thought him as false as her other suitors?

"I had hardly formed an opinion." Her tone was noncommittal and prim. Worst of all, she stiffened.

"Had you not?" he whispered in her ear.

"No. Now I must select gifts for my brothers and sisters."

She started in one direction, but he caught a glimpse of Throughgood. "I think I saw a booth down this way." Damon turned her deftly in another direction. He knew Kit, but did not know how many other brothers and sisters she had. "It is your turn to tell me about your family."

Damon reveled as she took his arm and her stride relaxed. "I believe you know Kit, my eldest brother. I have two more who are younger. Gideon is at Oxford. I truly have no idea what he would like, so I will buy handkerchiefs for him and Kit. Alan, my youngest brother, is still at Eton, and very bookish. I have already ordered him several volumes in a series he wished to read. I shall see what there is in the way of silk flowers for my sisters, or perhaps some trinkets."

"A much more easily managed family."

She looked surprised. "Because of our size? Every family has its problems. My father was ready to order Kit to find a wife when he met Mary. My youngest brother will never follow the family tradition of going into the army. He'll go to the church. My father has several livings, so that is not a problem. My youngest sister has decided to be an explorer, and my next oldest sister is almost old enough to make her come out, but not nearly mature enough yet."

"I can see why Featherton wishes his father a long and healthy life."

"Did he tell you that?" This time she did smile.

"More than once."

"Not surprising. He did not even remain home for Christmas this year. He and his wife have escaped to their home in Northumberland."

Damon would like to escape now with Miss Featherton; then she could not be hurt by the news that her good friend was marrying the man she had decided to wed. God only knew how she would take what might very well be another betrayal.

Meg was astonished how much she was enjoying her time with Lord Hawksworth. He appeared much more natural than before. She had trouble believing his father had numbered his sons and was so hardhearted about their welfare. Although many younger sons were required to make their own way. His voice when he had told her was hard, as if he disapproved of his father's decisions in some way. That, of course, raised a question. "Why was the heir to a dukedom allowed to join the army?"

"I did tell you that my father believed in everyone making their own way? That held for me as well." They walked a bit farther until she spied a stand with artificial flowers, and turned them toward it. "The only one who has been allowed to remain at home is the second son." He gave her a travesty of a smile, and his bitterness was clear in his tone. "Are those flowers I see?"

"They are. Let us see what they have. After that, my lord, you may find something to eat." Had he turned the subject? "What does your brother at home do?"

"I had almost forgot about eating. Strange, I do not normally ignore my stomach. He is learning to manage the estates."

Meg almost gasped in shock. Her father would never allow one of her other brothers to supplant Kit's role as his heir. "Nor do my brothers. If one is not quick, they will demolish the tea tray before I have even one biscuit."

Was it bad that he now seemed so much less harmful than before? She had considered asking Lady Merton about men. She and the lady were not too far apart in age and knew one another. But the Mertons' little boy was not feeling well, and it was probable that they would have left for their home before the shopping party returned. Before she had discovered that Lady Bellamny was Hawksworth's godmother, Meg would have asked her ladyship's advice. Amanda was not a possibility, as she was interested in Lord Hawksworth.

Oh no! What had Meg been thinking? If he was not as dangerous as she had thought, then she had no right to keep him from her friend, and absolutely no right to want to be in his company. What a muddle she had made of things in attempting to help Amanda.

There was only one thing to do. Meg would enjoy his company today, and then tell Amanda what she had been up to and leave him to her.

"Miss Featherton?"

His voice brought her out of her musings. "Yes?"

"We are at the flower stand." His tone gently prodded her to attend to business.

The counter was full of brightly colored silk flowers, as well as some in pastels more suited to young ladies. They were all exceedingly well made, complete with pistils and stamens. "They are lovely." Thinking of the short time she had left with Hawksworth as an escort, she lost her taste for shopping. "Which ones would you pick?"

"You are being vastly trusting." He appeared to study the selection carefully. "I take it their coloring is much like your own?"

"It is."

He held up a bunch of white flowers to her face, then one by one, several others. "I would pick the white and this purple."

"They will work well. Thank you." She pulled her purse out of her reticule. "I appreciate your help." Taking a deep breath, she smiled. His stomach grumbled, and it struck her as so funny, she lost her ability to pretend she was not having a pleasant time in his company. "Now we must search for food before you expire from hunger."

He placed the back of his hand against his brow, exclaiming dramatically, "I cannot last much longer."

"You, sir, are a fake," she said, but laughed at him because this time it was obvious he was acting.

He raised his brows and captured her gaze. "Am I? How long can a person go without food?"

"I do not know, yet I must assume you ate this morning."

His shapely lips formed a pout and he glanced down at his body. "But I am a large man. Surely that makes a difference."

Meg took his arm and headed toward a succulent aroma. "My mistake. You must be truly in need of sustenance."

In the next row of stalls they found meat pies and cider.

"Here you go, sir, madam. The best pies in all of Nottinghamshire. You'll not find better."

Lord Hawksworth licked his lips, and she wondered what they would feel like on hers.

Stop that. If he is a good man, Amanda deserves him!

"What have you got?" His stomach rumbled again.

"Pork, steak and kidney, and pheasant."

He turned to her. "Which do you prefer?"

"I am very partial to pork." The tempting scent of it curled around her nose, making her mouth water.

"I will take two pork pies, one pheasant, and a steak and kidney."

CHAPTER NINE

Meg was amazed. Hawksworth surely could not believe that she could eat two of the pies. Granted they were small, just large enough to fill one's hand, but still, one would suffice.

He handed her one of the pies, and she realized that he must be planning to eat the rest. "Thank you."

He wolfed down one before she had a chance to take a bite.

"You really were hungry."

"During the war, I learned to eat my fill at every opportunity, as there may not be another for many days. It is a hard habit to break."

Meg began to consider what else he had endured during the war. Most of the men she had met, including the grooms her father had hired, did not speak of their time in the army, or at least they did not talk about it to her. If she watched them would she notice the same thing, or would anyone who had been deprived of food act in the same manner?

Lady Bellamny had said that this parish was generous to the poor. Perhaps it was Meg's duty to spend as much money as possible at the fair, and eating pies was thirsty work. "We would like two ciders as well."

She watched as Lord Hawksworth demolished the other two pies and asked for a fourth. Once he had consumed that one and two glasses of cider, she linked her arm with his. "Let us find some sweets for dessert."

"A wonderful idea." He glanced around, then almost towed her in the opposite direction.

Fortunately, not far along the row, they found sweet buns, treacle pie, and fruitcake. He was so tall, he had probably seen them when she could not.

"Do you have stirring day at your house?" he asked, referring to the day that the Christmas pudding was made and everyone stirred the batter for good luck.

"We do. Even my father stirs."

"I did not know about it until my step-mother's first Christmas season. My mother was Greek, you see, and my father, I am quite sure, has never been below-stairs. Catherine, my step-mother, took me down to stir for the first time."

Meg's throat closed as tears battled to appear in her eyes. "She must be a very special lady."

"Yes, she is." He swallowed, and she wondered if he was close to tears himself.

"The treacle pie is my favorite. Although sweet buns are very nice as well."

He ordered two of each to be wrapped up. "Perhaps we should save one of each kind and eat them at night."

Meg found herself laughing again. "Sneaking food as if we were children."

"Why not? I seem to remember the food we had hidden tasted better than any other."

She did as well. "But from whom would we be hiding it?"

His dark brows drew together. "At times, being an adult is not a great deal of fun."

"That is the absolute truth." And to think she had wished for all the problems and heartache she had now. Well, not that. If she had known, she would have not come out at all.

Lord Hawksworth handed her a piece of treacle pie, while he bit into the bun. "Enjoy it anyway."

Meg bit into the rich, syrupy pie with a hint of tartness. "Excellent."

This day was the first in a very long time she had not been reminded of her failures. If only it could have been spent with someone she trusted completely, whom her friend did not wish to marry. She gave herself a shake. No matter how nice he was, she did not need the sort of fiery responses he provoked in her.

An ancient and stern-looking butler bowed Amanda and her mother into the massive hall of Grantville Manor. "Mrs. Hiller, Miss Hiller, her ladyship will be with you directly."

He took their cloaks and gloves before handing the clothing to a man with skin the color of highly polished mahogany, who was also dressed as a butler, with the addition of a black turban adorning his head. The old butler arranged the items so that he did not touch the other man's fingers at all. What a strange thing to do. They were both wearing gloves. The foreign butler rolled his eyes, making Amanda want to giggle.

When she glanced around the hall, which was shaped like a horseshoe, her mouth almost dropped open. Unlike the chilly but elegant marble and white halls of many homes, colorful artifacts the likes of which she had never seen adorned the walls and stood in niches. They must be from all the countries the family had visited. They certainly were not English, but one of the statues might be Roman.

Lady Grantville, a tallish woman with a stout build, much like her son, came forward. "I am so glad you could join us. I wished to come to know you better." She had addressed Amanda and her mother equally; now her ladyship smiled and held Amanda's hand. "Chuffy will escort you to the fair later this afternoon. I am told it is not to be missed."

Amanda curtseyed. "Thank you, my lady."

"Allow me to introduce you to the house." She waved her arm around. "These, as you might suspect, are items we have picked up along the way." A loud crash sounded from somewhere below and muffled bellowing followed. She paused for a moment, then continued on. "Nothing major. Our staff have not quite sorted themselves out."

Not understanding precisely what her ladyship meant, Amanda glanced at her mother, who lightly shrugged one shoulder.

The sound of booted feet on the stairs further halted their progress out of the hall.

"Mother, I am going to—Amanda—I mean Miss Hiller... Mother, is there a reason you did not inform me we were to have guests?" Chuffy's normally jovial countenance wore a frown. Oh dear. He must not have wanted her here.

Another crash from downstairs, this one louder than before, broke the awkward silence. Suddenly the green baize door flew open, and a rotund woman with silver hair escaping from her mobcap appeared, wielding a wooden spoon as if it was a weapon.

Chuffy winced and a flush infused his face.

Amanda decided that discretion was the better part of valor, and she hated seeing him so embarrassed. "Perhaps it is better if Mama and I return later."

He finished his descent and came to Amanda. "I'm sorry. I meant to have warned you."

"Do not be ridiculous, Chuffy." His mother turned to the servant. "Mrs. Maynard, what is the meaning of this intrusion?"

"I'll not work with that heathen any longer." Mrs. Maynard put her fists on her hips. "I've been running the Grantville kitchen for over thirty years and never had a complaint."

"Only because my uncle and cousin were terrified of her," Chuffy said in an under-tone.

The cook gave him a sharp look, but he had quickly assumed an innocent mien. "I don't see any reason to have foreigners in my kitchen trying to change the way we do things here."

Lady Grantville's bosom rose and fell slowly as if she was having difficulty maintaining her temper. "Mrs. Maynard, as his lordship and I explained to you when we arrived, although we know you have served this house and family with honor for many years, we also have servants who have served us for a very long time . . ."

Chuffy took Amanda's arm and led her and her mother to a cozy, sunny room in the back of the house. "Forgive me for not telling you of our domestic problems. It cannot have been comfortable for you."

It was certainly odd to have a servant confront the mistress of the house in that manner. "I take it that the older servants do not appreciate the ones your parents brought with them."

"There is a great deal of bitterness among the senior staff that was in place when we arrived. However, to my parents' credit, they offered a generous retirement to anyone who wished to leave. After all, some of our family's servants have been with us longer than my uncle's servants were with him." He held his arms out then dropped them. "Despite the obvious antagonism from the Grantville servants, our servants are doing their best to fit in. Except for Gerard. He is our French chef, and will not put up with Mrs. Maynard's cutting remarks. She lost two sons in the war, but he lost most of his family to the guillotine, and has no love for Napoleon. She cannot see past his accent, and he refuses to be cast in with the enemy, or referred to as a heathen."

"I admire your parents for attempting to meld the two sets of servants. Even had they all been English there would have been difficulties. I suppose that the butler in the turban came with you?"

Chuffy nodded.

"Do we have to live here?"

"No." He grinned. "My father has several other estates, and there is the house in London."

"Then I foresee no difficulty." Amanda was determined to help her beloved escape what was clearly a difficult situation for him. "Your parents appear healthy, and I have every expectation that the problem will resolve itself before we are required to take up residence."

"Thank God. I was sure you would turn and run."

She pressed the palm of his hand against her cheek. "I love you too much to abandon you."

"You are truly a treasure among women." He bent to kiss her and her mother cleared her throat.

A moment later the door opened, and Lady Grantville entered as if nothing had occurred to upset her day. The turbaned butler followed carrying a tray with an array of china cups, some that reminded Amanda of a doll's set she used to have. Except that these had the deep color of gemstones and were gilded.

Lady Grantville waved her hand toward the sofas. "Please have a seat. Chuffy, dear, you may join us."

"Mother, what did you do with Mrs. Maynard?"

Amanda was glad he had asked. She would not have dared to, and she was curious.

Lady Grantville arranged the tray that had been placed on a low table inlaid with a carving and covered with glass. "She has decided to take a holiday and visit her daughter for several weeks. The poor woman was overtired. She also seemed not to have understood how generous the bequest was that your uncle left her."

Mama nodded with approval. "I hope she will enjoy an extended holiday."

"I trust she shall. Now, I have English and Moroccan teas, as well as Turkish coffee."

"Miss Hiller," Chuffy said, "I believe you would enjoy the Moroccan tea."

She nodded her assent. Her mother chose the coffee, as did Lady Grantville.

Amanda had just taken a sip when her ladyship said, "We really must discuss the settlements and where the two of you will live."

Covering her mouth, she swallowed quickly.

"Mother"—Chuffy looked to be at the end of his patience—"Amanda has not given me permission to ask for her hand as yet."

Her ladyship's eyes widened. "What on earth are you waiting for?"

"I would like to know the same thing," Mama added.

They were both staring at Amanda as if she had grown horns. She could not tell them about Meg. "I wanted to wait until Christmas Day."

"Oh." Lady Grantville smiled softly. "Vastly romantic. Very well. Make your announcement when you wish. In the meantime, his lordship has informed me that your father will arrive later today to discuss the settlements."

Less than an hour later, Amanda and Chuffy escaped to the fair, leaving their mothers in the throes of planning their wedding.

"Are you sure that was wise?" Chuffy helped her down from the coach.

"I sincerely do not think they would have listened to any of our opinions or objections."

"True enough. At least they have allowed us to determine how to make our announcement."

"That is something to be thankful for." Somehow she had to find a way to tell her friend that she was marrying Chuffy, and prayed that Meg would understand. The situation however, was proving more difficult than Amanda had thought. Try as she might, she could not bring herself to add to Meg's troubles.

Damon was sure he had made progress with Miss Featherton. She had not shut him out as she had before, and she had laughed several times at his comments. Still, there was an underlying melancholy. He tried to put himself in her place and understand what she must be feeling. Unfortunately, he was not a tenderhearted young woman. He would have run the curs through. Now that he thought of it, she might have felt much better if she had maimed the villains. If the subject arose, he would suggest it.

He and Miss Featherton had reached the inn where they were to meet the rest of their party. Surprised to see only one coach was left, he glanced around the yard before steering her back around to the front and in the door.

He addressed a young man carrying a tray. "I am looking for Lady Bellamny."

"She went back to her house. There's a Sir Randolph and his lady in the parlor."

Naturally, they would be left with chaperones. "Thank you. Please have the coach readied. We'll only be a few moments."

The lad pulled a face. "Doubt that, sir. The gentleman just ordered dinner."

"Dinner?" Miss Featherton's tone expressed all the astonishment that Damon felt.

"Yes, miss." The servant tugged his forelock before running down the corridor, clearly not willing to stay and debate the matter.

"I do not believe it. Surely they must know Lady Bellamny has put back dinner." She glanced at a partially open door.

Damon hadn't decided if dinner at the tavern was helpful to him or not. Nevertheless, he followed Miss Featherton as she opened the door to the parlor. "Sir Randolph, Miss Featherton and I were just informed that you have ordered dinner."

"Yes, yes, please join us." He smiled, bidding them to enter. "I have had the best bottle of claret I ever drank, and Lady Bellamny has assured us that the food is even better."

"Lady Bellamny?" Meg said faintly, as if the impossible had occurred.

Damon could scarcely believe it himself. Before she could recover herself or come up with a plan to thwart whatever scheme his godmother had in mind, he propelled her forward toward the table. After he removed her cloak and his, she was sufficiently recovered to take off her bonnet and gloves. Eventually, they were ensconced at the table with the Culpeppers, partaking of the claret. Or Damon was. Miss Featherton sipped slowly.

Not long after they arrived, the landlord knocked on the door. "I was told there would be two more." He focused on Damon and his companion. "Sir Randolph has ordered the haunch of venison, French beans..."

After the innkeeper had finished, Damon understood Sir Randolph's wish to dine here. "Miss Featherton, are there any dishes you wish to add?"

"No, thank you. That will be fine." Her voice was firm, but Damon sensed a hesitance.

"I should like to have the oyster pie, as well as the parsnips and carrots."

"Very good, my lord."

The other couple he figured to be in their late fifties or sixties, and appeared to be very devoted to one another. Perhaps they were supposed to be an inspiration for Miss Featherton.

The topics of the fair and town took up much of the conversation before the soup was served.

"Sir Randolph, how did you and Lady Culpepper meet?"

She was plump with white curls. Instead of covering her hair with a cap, she wore a very small but charming velvet hat with a feather.

Sir Randolph glanced at her, covering her hand with his. "I was at Cambridge with my lady's brother. They are twins, and she kept up a lively correspondence with him. My wife did not think it was fair that her brother got to attend university and she could not."

"You must admit," the lady cut in, "I was as qualified as he."

"Indeed I do. More so." The look Sir Randolph gave her reflected the deep love they shared. "Her brother invited me to spend Christmas with his family and I finally met the sister who had written such interesting letters."

"He has left out that my brother and I carried on debates about what he was studying."

"I believe that was the only way he got through school," Sir Randolph said fondly. "As I was saying, I arrived with her brother, and she wanted nothing to do with me."

"That is not true!" She rapped his knuckles with her lorgnette. "I merely needed to know how you felt." She glanced at Damon and Miss Featherton. "You see, my brother had written to me about Sir Randolph, and I was monstrously amused by the fact that he could earn such good notes and manage to get into so much trouble at the same time."

Damon gave a sidelong look at Miss Featherton and was surprised to see her head propped on her hands, engrossed in the conversation. "I must say, I found doing the same to be quite easy."

"There, you see!" Sir Randolph exclaimed with approval. "If one is a clever fellow, one's studies do not take as long, thus providing more than enough time to engage in antics."

Lady Culpepper shook her head and smiled. "Fribbles, the both of you. Suffice it to say that my father was sure I would find a suitable older gentleman more to my taste and took me off to London for the Season. I thought they were all prosy bores." Miss Featherton's hand covered her lips. "Laugh if you wish, my dear. It was the truth. None of them had a scintilla of sense, and of what use was that to me?"

"I was nineteen and she eighteen when we met. Our parents made us wait until I was one and twenty before we could marry."

The lady's eyes had misted.

"Was it hard to wait?" Miss Featherton asked.

"Oh my, yes." Lady Culpepper gazed at her husband. "There were times when we thought we would be able to force the issue."

Damon glanced at Miss Featherton, wondering if she understood that the older lady was saying they had anticipated their vows and hoped a child might hurry things along.

She pulled her bottom lip with her teeth. "Do you have many children?"

Lady Culpepper shook her head. "No. We were not blessed in that way." Her fingers covered her husband's hand, and he turned his so that they were each clasping the other's fingers. "But we have many nieces and nephews. Sir Randolph's brother died, but his eldest son lived with us and is more than ready to step in when it is time."

"Not that I think he is looking forward to it," Sir Randolph added hastily. "We get on as if he were our son."

The evening had been pleasant, but Damon was beginning to wonder what the point had been, when Miss Featherton said, "You are so comfortable with one another. I would like a marriage such as yours."

"Comfort comes with time." The older lady grinned. "Oh, the fights we had when we were younger would curl your toes. I once threw a porcelain figurine at his head and hit him."

Her husband rubbed the side of his head. "It hurt like the devil. I think there is still a bump, but the making up was worth the pain."

"Indeed it was." Her ladyship smiled gently.

Damon wouldn't mind things thrown at him if making up was involved. Particularly with Miss Featherton.

Unfortunately, the lady's lips were pressed together. "I shall not have a grand passion."

Just then servants entered to clear dinner and bring several desserts, ending the conversation for a while. The Culpeppers gave her a sympathetic look, but said nothing.

Although Miss Featherton tried to hide it behind an outwardly calm countenance, her fingers pleated the skirts of her gown, and her jaw had developed a hard edge. It was as if a black cloud had descended over her again.

He could understand her hesitance, after a fashion. Love had deceived her twice. What need had she to court it again? Yet he knew for a certainty that if she could trust him enough to give her heart to him, she would have all the passion, love, and respect she could ever wish for and was now afraid to grasp.

CHAPTER TEN

Meg did not think she could stand being around the Culpeppers for a moment longer. The only problem was that she had no way to leave. They represented what she had thought—no, believed—for years that she must have to be happy. What she had dreamed her life would be like. Until Tarlington's betrayal, she had not understood why a lady would not wed for love, or remain single. If only she did not want children so badly. Yet the sight of Lady Merton with her child had only served to reinforce Meg's desire.

Where devil was Lord Throughgood? Every time she had been about to approach him, he seemed to disappear. If not him, then she had no one left to consider.

A small cheesecake was placed on her plate. She picked up a fork and ate it without paying much attention to the taste. Perhaps she should wait. There was bound to be someone she had not met before whom she could bear to wed. She stifled a sigh.

You have met everyone. Maybe a widower. Surely they were more interested in marrying for convenience.

"Miss Featherton?"

Meg glanced up at Lord Hawksworth.

He held out his hand. "We are leaving now. The Culpeppers have gone out to the coach."

"Thank you." She stood as he placed her cloak on her shoulders.

Good Lord! How could she have been so engrossed in her own thoughts that she had not noticed the couple had left? Her problems were making her rude. She did not want to think of how often she had mentally berated other people for allowing their difficulties to overwhelm them. This unlooked-for lesson in humility did not sit well.

"You appear distracted." Lord Hawksworth's warm voice washed over her. "I am a good listener, and I do not gossip. Anything you tell me will go no further."

For a moment she couldn't even think of a response. Confide in *him*? He must be out of his mind. One pleasant day did not mean they knew one another as well as *that*. She sucked in a shallow breath. He did have sisters. Perhaps he thought of her in that light. Nevertheless, it was impossible. "I appreciate your offer, but it is nothing, really."

It would not be accurate to say he frowned, but it was clear her answer had not pleased him. "Very well. My offer stands."

"You are very kind." Not the word she would ever have thought to describe him, yet it was the truth.

The moment she returned to Lady Bellamny's house, Meg must remember to tell Amanda that Hawksworth was not the ogre she had thought him to be. Yet another lesson in humility.

A clock on the fireplace mantel struck the hour, and she glanced at it. "That must need to be adjusted. It cannot possibly be so late."

"No, it is accurate. We have spent several hours here. I suppose we might arrive in time for tea."

"Oh."

That one word spoke volumes. Damon simply wished he knew what she meant. He forced himself to smile. She was an expert at masking her feelings, but he had always been good at reading people. Right now, though, he would give a fortune to be able to divine what Miss Featherton was thinking.

That she was not as hostile to him as she had been in the past was clear. Yet he could not figure out how she viewed him. Not as a friend—at least, not yet. Given a few more days like to-day, he might be able to convince her he meant no harm. Not for the first time, he cursed his dark looks. They made him appear more forbidding than he thought he was. Tarlington and Swindon had been fair. Perhaps the contrast between them and him might work to his advantage, eventually.

As he escorted Miss Featherton to the coach, he considered the letter he had received from his step-mother. Father was not at all happy that he had chosen to attend this house party over the others. As he had threatened, Catherine was in the middle of getting ready for the duke's own house party full of eligible young ladies.

She warned Damon he must attend. He would have, in any event. Even though they did not get along, he had never openly defied his father. To do that would make life difficult for his entire family.

He assisted Miss Featherton into the carriage and gave the coachman permission to start. As the vehicle jerked forward, he wondered what would happen if he arrived home with his new bride in tow. The only problem was that part of his marriage settlements should involve the dukedom, and Lord Featherton would expect that to be in the agreements. On the other hand, Damon had a great deal of personal wealth through his mother and none of it was entailed. That had to be better than being tied to the dukedom. And he did not want his father to deny Meg anything.

Meg? He settled back against the squabs. Maybe if he thought of her by her given name, he might make more progress. In his own mind they would be closer.

"My lord?"

He glanced at Miss Featherton—no, Meg. "Yes?"

The coach lights swayed, but he could see a small smile on her lips. "You were frowning."

"Was I?" He glanced at the Culpeppers, but they were both snoring softly.

"You were."

"It bothers me that I cannot assist you. What, I ask, is the good of having a title if I cannot rescue damsels in distress?"

"I would not have thought a courtesy title counted." Her tone was not arch, but searching.

"I will leave you to consider if the courtesy title of an English marquis is greater than that of a prince."

She shook her head. "You are speaking in riddles."

Damon raised a brow. "Am I?"

"I was right." Her bosom heaved under her thick cloak. "You are hiding something."

"Not I." He raised his hands, palms toward her in surrender. "For those who matter and care to ask, I am an open book."

"And you would answer any question put to you?" she asked doubtfully.

"Word of a Trevor."

"I may take you up on that." Her chin had risen, and her lips were set.

"Please do. There is nothing I would like better." He had spoken lightly, but meant every word.

Damon could tell she didn't believe him, but she would. Somehow, he must make her understand that he had no secrets from her and he never would. All she had to do was ask.

Chuffy quickly turned Amanda down yet another row of displays at the fair. "Miss Featherton and Hawksworth."

"I detest dodging them." Her head swiveled in the opposite direction. "I will have to tell her before our announcement."

Discussing their betrothal made him feel better, less haunted. He spied a stall with trinkets, and led her to it. "I agree. After we decorate the house to-morrow or before you retire to-morrow evening."

"You are right. It must be after the party. What pretty gewgaws." Amanda was already looking through the collection.

"Thought you might like them." Chuffy was quite proud of himself for having thought to bring her here.

He would have loved to have Amanda and her parents stay at Grantville, and had mentioned it to his mother. Unfortunately, the troubles with the servants were making his wishes impossible. The only thing to do was carry on, and finding a way for Amanda to tell Miss Featherton about their betrothal was essential. If only she would fall in love with Hawksworth, the quandary would be settled.

Nevertheless, the sooner she was told, the more quickly Chuffy could wed Amanda.

He did hope Hawksworth was making headway. Amanda would feel much better if her friend had found a husband as well.

Once he returned to his house, he would discuss with his father which estate was the most suitable for him and Amanda to live on. His beloved, a home, and peace were all he wanted.

Before he knew it, she had selected a bracelet and a few other trinkets and was about to pay for them. He had to cease woolgathering. "No no. You must allow me."

Her giggle was enchanting. In fact, just about everything about her was enthralling. Chuffy could hardly wait until she was his. Paying for her purchase made him feel all was right with the world. But no sooner had they headed one way than his soon-to-be betrothed was tugging him in a different direction. "There they are again."

Blast this all to hell. "I almost think that my home would be better than this."

She scrunched up her face. "I hate to say it, but I believe you are right."

"When the staff problem has ended, we shall visit my parents and come to the fair again." Chuffy led her to an inn at the other end of the town, from where Lady Bellamny had left her carriages. "Can you bear to be around them for a while longer? My mother wishes you and your family to join us for dinner."

Amanda's smile was all he could have asked for. "As long as I am with you, nothing else really matters."

In less than twenty minutes, they were back at Grantville. The door was opened by Benje, their Indian butler, whose real name everyone had given up trying to pronounce correctly. "My lord, miss, your parents are in the library."

"Thank you, Benje."

They were half-way down the corridor when Amanda asked, "He seems very competent."

"Yes, he is." This was the first time his uncle's butler had not been at the door. They entered the library. His father and Mr. Hiller were engrossed in a stack of documents. Their mothers were sitting on a sofa drinking Russian tea. Chuffy could tell from the cups. His mother believed in drinking every beverage from the correct container. "Mother, what happened to what's-his-name?"

"Dibble." His mother had a devilish look in her eye. "He found that he could not support life here after the cook left. Naturally, he also had a generous pension and required a holiday."

Paid for by his father, Chuffy was sure. He cocked his head, straining to listen, but there was no yelling or loud noises coming from below. "Have we peace at last?"

"I hope so." She smiled at Amanda's mother. "Thanks to Mrs. Hiller. I have discovered that I am much too softhearted for English servants. Once Dibble began to complain, she suggested he would be happier if he left our service. It has all worked out for the best."

Amanda glanced at him, an anxious look in her face.

"I must say I agree. All that fighting was too much to bear on a daily basis." Chuffy bowed to his future mother-in-law. "Madam, my thanks."

"Mama, how do you do it?" His beloved beamed. "She always

knows just what to do to rid us of unwanted servants, and they are content to leave."

"I merely suggested a course of action that would make everyone happier." Mrs. Hiller shrugged. "After all, one cannot be comfortable if one's servants are at odds. It was clear to me that the Grantvilles were much attached to their own staff. Therefore, the others must be resettled."

"Indeed," his mother added. "Once Dibble and the cook left, the house felt different. I believe they were the ones creating the problems."

Papa and Mr. Hiller rose, documents in hand. "We have worked out the settlements. They must be sent to our solicitors, of course, but we believe we have come up with an equitable plan."

"The only thing to concern you now is your wedding trip," Amanda's father said, as he wiped his glasses. "Perhaps somewhere warm."

Suddenly Chuffy knew exactly where he an Amanda should go. "Athens. It's much warmer than here."

"Greece?" Her eyes were round with what he hoped was wonder.

"We have a villa there. It won't be warm enough to swim until March, but I think you will like it."

"Like it? Chuffy, I have never even dreamed of going to Athens. I would love it above all things."

"It's settled then." As long as they got through the next few days, and Miss Featherton.

Damon breathed a sigh of relief when they entered the drawing room. Throughgood and Miss Hiller were not present. That could only mean that all was well at Grantville. Now if the couple would remain there, some of their problems would be solved.

"Miss Featherton?" A young matron smiled as she rushed up to Meg. "I haven't seen you since the wedding. How wonderful that you are here!" The woman hugged her. "I didn't dare call you Meg in front of so many people I do not know."

A gentleman, Damon supposed to be around his age, strolled up, placing his hand possessively on the woman's waist. "Miss Featherton, I am glad to see a familiar face."

"Daphne, you look well, as do you, Fotheringale." Damon could tell from the set of her jaw that Meg's smile was forced. "Daphne, allow me to introduce Lord Hawksworth. My lord, Mrs. Fotheringale and her husband."

The lady curtseyed, as Damon bowed. "Mrs. Fotheringale, it is a pleasure to meet any friend of Miss Featherton's. Fotheringale, I believe we have friends in common."

"We most certainly do." He shook Damon's hand. "I've heard a great deal of you. It is good to finally meet you."

While Meg was listening to her friend chatter, Fotheringale glanced at Meg and back to Damon, who gave a curt nod. It was time he started letting other people know he was interested in her.

After a few minutes, the other man took his wife's arm. "If you are to be tramping around outside to-morrow, you should probably get some rest."

Mrs. Fotheringale leaned on her husband. "You are right, of course." With her free hand, she lightly touched her stomach. "We are expecting an interesting event next spring."

"I am very happy for you." This time Meg's smile was genuine.

Damon wished he knew why she had not been happy to see the couple earlier.

A few moments later, Lady Bellamny hailed them. "As you are aware, the gathering of the greenery will begin in the morning; it is bad luck to do it before Christmas Eve. Hawksworth, I know you would rather be cutting the Yule log, but we need strong men to help the ladies, and I have decided you shall be one of them."

All he could do was bow, assent, and keep his grin to himself. "Wherever I can be of service."

"Breakfast will be served at eight o'clock. There will be no breaking one's fast in one's chamber."

That was unusual. He wondered how many complaints he would hear to-morrow. Even though he never took breakfast in his room, he felt he must respond. "Yes, my lady."

Meg nodded. "I understand."

Ah, he remembered. She had breakfasted in her chamber this morning. "How long do we have to gather?"

"Until noon. After that, the servants will assist in decorating, but it is the tradition here that the guests do most of the work."

He wanted to ask about mistletoe, but didn't dare. Not while Meg was present. His step-mother had it brought in from an estate in the south of England. He wondered if Lady Bellamny had any, or if it would have had to be imported as well.

"Gathering the greenery is one of my favorite tasks," Meg offered. "As is deciding where the greens should go."

Damon had a vision of his house being decorated by her—if he had one. "It is one of my favorite activities as well."

Or it had been when he was younger. Cook always made sure there was plenty of hot chocolate and food waiting when they came in. He had resented it when he'd been made to find the Yule log instead. The company was never as pleasant.

Lady Bellamny clapped her hands. "Excellent. The two of you will be in charge of the group."

That was not what he had wanted. "Perhaps someone with more experience?"

"Nonsense. You are used to command, and Miss Featherton has a great deal of experience. Together, you will be perfect."

Meg had colored a little, but replied, "I'm sure we will not disappoint you, my lady."

His admiration for her grew far beyond what he thought it could be. As upset as she was, she had managed to give the impression all was in order.

CHAPTER ELEVEN

Meg kept a smile pasted on her face as she introduced Daphne and Fotheringale to Hawksworth. Fotheringale had begun to court her friend Daphne when Meg had rejected him for Swindon. Yet as her friend chattered on, she began to realize how much in love Daphne was, and for good reason it seemed. He had been her champion against his overly domineering mother. Then he had forced his father to increase his allowance, thus allowing the couple to set up their own household.

Meg would never have believed he would stand up to his mother the way he had. Daphne, however, had trusted his assertions that he would take care of her.

Yet another example of Meg's inability to choose a husband. Still, she had not loved him, and, at the time, love had been an important consideration. Now all she wanted was companionship. While Lord Throughgood was proving a difficult man to find, Hawksworth—she really should not think of him in such a familiar fashion—was all too present. But not for her. Where were Amanda and her mother? Surely they must be in the house somewhere. Maybe in her chamber. Still, it was unusual that neither of them were present. Meg started toward the door.

"Miss Featherton," Lady Bellamny called. "Lady Culpepper has agreed to accompany you on the piano if you and Lord Hawksworth will sing a ballad for us before we retire."

Hawksworth, blast him, was already at the piano looking over the music. "I'd be happy to."

However, when he showed her the music, it was an old Christmas carol. "I believe," he said in a subtle tone that sent pleasant shivers down her back, "this might be more appropriate this evening, and it will help provide the mood for to-morrow." He glanced down at Meg. "Shall we sing it together?"

"We must change the key. My voice is too low for the higher part."

"As you wish." They agreed on a key that would complement both their voices, and after Lady Culpepper played the introduction, began to sing.

> *"While shepherds watched*
> *Their flocks by night*
> *All seated on the ground*
> *The angel of the Lord came down*
> *And glory shone around*
> *And glory shone around."*

By the time they reached the last verse, the other guests were yawning.

"Not that I like putting my audience to sleep." His breath caressed her cheek.

"But in this case . . ."

He grinned. "It is necessary."

Meg smiled back at him. He had not had the chance to shave before dinner, and now the short hairs of his beard made him appear even more handsome. She wanted to reach up and run her palm over his cheek. She had never touched a man's cheek before. What would the stubble feel like? She stepped back before she could act on her desire.

Meg must tell her friend as soon as possible that Hawksworth would be safe. No, never that, he had too much energy, too much charm, to be called safe, but he would not hurt her.

The clock chimed eleven. She would do it first thing in the morning.

Lady Bellamny was rousing the others and ringing for servants.

Hawksworth claimed Meg's arm. "May I escort you up the stairs?"

If he had said to her chamber, she would have been immediately suspicious, but up the stairs to the landing that connected the two wings was unexceptional. "Thank you."

"We should discuss how to punish those who would attempt to neglect their duties to-morrow."

"Neglect . . . ?" She was tempted to laugh, but his countenance was severe. Unable to decide whether or not he was joking, she retorted, "Flogging, to be sure."

One corner of his lips tipped up. "I should have realized you would be harsh. I was thinking more along the lines of making them wait for their hot chocolate or mulled cider."

"That *would* be cruel. Perhaps you should flirt with the ladies whenever they take too long a rest."

His black brows drew together, but in a funning way. "You have an exaggerated opinion of my skills when it comes to ladies."

"I think you are too modest, my lord." How could any gentleman who was so handsome think women would not fall at his feet? Well, most women.

They had paused for a moment in the hall, but began to climb the stairs. "I can assure you that I am not in the . . ." He rubbed his chin. "How can I put this? I do not trifle with women."

She could hardly believe she had insulted him, but she must have. "Forgive me. I—"

"No." He captured her gaze with his dark eyes. "It was a reasonable assumption. Many gentlemen do."

Meg wanted to search his face, try to divine if there was more behind what he had said; instead she dropped her gaze. "I think perhaps we have become too serious for this party."

Not nearly as serious as he would like to be. Yet she was like a skittish horse. Pushing her would only make her baulk. If only he had more time. The last thing he wanted was to see her hurt. "I believe you are correct." They had reached the top of the stairs, where he turned to face her. "I shall leave you here. Have pleasant dreams."

Perhaps of him.

"To you as well, my lord."

Damon remained where he was until she disappeared down the corridor. To-morrow he would renew his siege of her walls.

That night he dreamed of Badajoz, yet once they had broken through the city's battlements, instead of bloody mayhem, he saw Meg. Standing in the midst of the crumbled stone, smiling at him and holding out her hands.

The next morning, Damon swung his legs over the side of the bed and rubbed his face. Love and war were frequently joined together in literature and verse. Still, there must be another reason he so often thought of Meg in relation to the battles he had fought.

During the war he had needed to save his life as well as his men's, yet perhaps having Meg in his life was just as necessary. There was something between them he had never felt before, and once she gave herself to him, she would be by his side forever. His heart swelled with hope. Surely his dreams must be a sign that he was close to finding the key to winning her affections.

The fire had been built up, warming the chamber. Damon rose and crossed to the window. The sky was crystal blue. The moon, not yet set, shone on the grounds, making them sparkle as if some careless god had scattered diamonds around.

A heavy frost, but no snow. Although pretty, maneuvering in the stuff was slow, hard work, and not something he wanted to deal with while out with a gaggle of women. The snow could come later, and he would welcome it.

He was about to tug on the long braided-silk cord next to his bed when noises from the dressing room informed him that Hartwell was already preparing Damon's garb for the day.

"The water is warm, my lord. You have less than an hour to dress."

More than enough time to don country kit, but he wanted to be in the breakfast room before Meg. He made short work of cleaning his teeth and shaving. He entered the breakfast room well before the appointed time, startling two young footmen. "I'll eat when everything is ready, but I'd appreciate a pot of tea now, and two cups."

One of the footmen left, and Damon claimed chairs for Meg and himself at the long cherry table.

He had just poured his tea, when she gracefully strolled into the room and stopped. "Oh, I did not expect to see you here so early."

"Morning is my favorite time of day." Mainly because no matter how late he went to sleep, he was up earlier than the sun. The army was probably to blame for that. "How do you like your tea?"

After glancing around the room, she apparently decided to take him up on his offer. "With milk and two sugars."

Damon prepared her cup, then stood, pulled out the chair, and waited. Somehow this all seemed like a finely choreographed dance. One in which he was not sure of the steps. "Did you hear anyone else stirring?"

She gracefully lowered herself into the seat, and he pushed it in before taking the chair next to hers. "There was a great deal of rushing around. Has Miss Hiller been down yet?"

"Not that I have seen." He slid the tea-cup closer to Meg.

Her finely arched black brows drew together, creating a line between her eyes. He wanted nothing more than to smooth her brow, and remove her concerns. "I knocked on her door, but there was no answer."

"I'm sure she will be here soon." He wished he had heard from Throughgood as to the status of his pending announcement. "She dare not miss Lady Bellamny's house decorating."

As if he had called forth the devil, the lady herself appeared.

"Well, I am glad to see the two of you up. I'll have to send strong words of encouragement to the slugabeds." She tugged the bell-pull and her butler appeared almost immediately. "Send word around that breakfast is being served, and that it will not be available after I have left to ensure all is in readiness for the outings." She glanced at Damon. "Why are you not eating?"

He swung his head toward the side table, now groaning with dishes. Apparently his keen sense of what went on around him was eroded by the light scent of lavender and lemon. An enemy platoon could have marched in and he would not have noticed. "Distracted."

Just then Sir Randolph, Lady Culpepper, Miss Riverton, and Lord Darby entered the room, chattering good-naturedly about the best way to find the best greenery.

Lord Darby assisted his betrothed to sit, then turned to Lady Bellamny. "My mother begs to be excused from to-day's activities. She has a headache and would prefer to break her fast alone."

From the tone of his voice and the disapproval on his face it was clear the lady was merely attempting to circumvent Lady Bellamny's edict.

The Culpeppers and Miss Riverton ceased speaking, and the room fell silent.

Lady Bellamny poured a cup of tea. "I am vastly sorry to hear that she is not well. Naturally she would prefer to eat later in the day. I shall send up some herbal compresses."

The man's lips twitched. "Very kind of you, my lady. I am quite sure that will be all she requires."

The drama ended, Damon rose. He turned to assist Meg, who had made a choking sound which he strongly suspected was laughter. "Miss Featherton?"

She stood so that her back was to the rest of the table and gazed up at him. Her eyes were so full of laughter he could have gone into whoops himself. He had not seen that look since the beginning of the Little Season.

"Ma..." Her voice trembled. "Malingerers," she whispered, quickly putting her hand over her mouth.

"Yes, indeed." It was amusing that in seeking to remain in bed, Lady Darby would be denied her breakfast. Yet he didn't dare say more. Meg's mirth was infectious, and he did not wish to betray himself to his godmother, who obviously took the infraction seriously.

It was enough that his love was happy. All he need do now was ensure she would be his.

By the time Meg and Hawksworth were on the other side of the table, and she was responding to his queries about her choices, she had got herself under control. Under normal circumstances, the humor in the exchange might not have seemed so funny. Yet with Lord Darby practically choking on the excuse he had to give Lady Bellamny, her response, and he not being at all upset but pleased his mother had been caught, Meg could not help wanting to laugh until she wept. It had been so long since she had been truly happy. So long since she had felt anything. It was as if she had been shrouded in a gray fog that was now lifting.

"Kippers?" Hawksworth held a fork over the small fish.

"Yes, please." She refused to think of her last two suitors as they had selected morsels of food for her at suppers. That would only cast her back into the gloom.

He speared three of the small fish, placing them on her plate, then took several for himself. By the time they had worked their way through the dishes, she had added a baked egg and some ham. His plate was full of everything on offer. She did not think her brothers ate that much, but Hawksworth was even larger than Kit. Perhaps his need for sustenance was greater.

Suddenly, Meg looked at him again and saw a very different man than she usually did. Dressed as he was in buckskin breeches and a loose jacket, he was no longer the Dandy. Instead he was more primal, more real, and vastly more male. She had had a chance to feel the hard muscle under his jacket. The breeches encased his shapely thighs in a way even the pantaloons he wore had not.

She hoped Amanda would appreciate all of Hawksworth.

As he placed Meg's plate on the table, she glanced around. The Smithsons and Fotheringales had arrived. Mr. Fotheringale was steering his wife away from Lord Smithson. She wondered if he had said something he should not have. Meg always tried to give the man a wide berth. But where were Amanda and her mother?

She was just about to ask when Lord Smithson's lips twisted into a snarl. "I don't see Mrs. and Miss Hiller here."

Lady Bellamny raised one brow. "They left early this morning, but will return in time for dinner. Mr. Hiller arrived last night, and they have matters to attend to. I instructed them that they must come back with either greenery or a decoration made from it."

"Right you are, my lady," Sir Randolph said in a genial tone. "As always, everyone must contribute."

Meg had hardly seen her friend or her mother since they arrived. Not that she was worried about a chaperone. She was of age, and Lady Bellamny was perfectly capable of watching over her if she required it, which she didn't. She had managed to rid herself of two unwanted men without repercussions. She simply wished to know what was going on.

Several minutes later, Lady Bellamny rose, and they all followed suit. "We shall meet in the hall in ten minutes."

Once again, Hawksworth escorted her up the stairs. "From what Sir Randolph said, I take it this occurs every year. It amazes me that anyone comes. They must not know what they are in for."

"On the contrary, her house parties are extremely select, and no one would dare refuse an invitation."

Hawksworth grunted. "I shall see you in the hall."

"I must hurry if I am to be on time."

Once in her room, she donned her fur-lined gloves as Hendricks placed Meg's bonnet on her head. Next came the mantle and a warm wool cloak, also lined with fur.

A knock sounded on the door. A few moments later, Hendricks handed Meg a small paper folded over and sealed.

She quickly opened it and scanned the lines.

Meg dearest,
I have such wonderful news, but I cannot share it as yet!!
Please forgive me for being so mysterious, I shall tell you all about it soon.
Your friend forever,
Amanda Hiller

How very strange. What on earth could be going on? They had never before kept secrets from each other. Well, almost never. Meg could not tell her friend that she was attempting to save her from Hawksworth. Although that had turned into a fool's mission.

She'd had a wonderful time in his company yesterday at the fair. But when she thought back, there were times when he had suddenly redirected them down a different row of stands from where they were headed.

Perhaps it was a good thing Amanda was not here. He was definitely hiding something, and Meg had no use for secrecy.

CHAPTER TWELVE

Early on Christmas Eve morning, Amanda walked softly on tip-toes down the corridor to the main staircase. When she reached the bottom, she let out the breath she had been holding. One more day and she and Chuffy would announce their betrothal. She did not know how much longer she could avoid Meg, and desperately wished she knew how Lord Hawksworth was coming along with her friend.

From the brief glimpses of them Amanda had seen yesterday, the couple appeared to be enjoying themselves. She hoped Meg had not noticed the sudden turns his lordship had made at times when they were at the fair. Otherwise, she would be suspicious.

Amanda glanced at the clock just before it chimed the hour, and began to panic. Her parents must not be late. All would be ruined if Meg arrived to break her fast before they left. Mama would tell her everything.

The door opened, letting in a rush of cold air. "Amanda," her father said, "if we do not depart, we shall be late."

A footman came running in. "Sorry, miss. I was to have told you your parents were outside."

Papa took her arm. "Come along."

A short time later, they arrived at Grantville. Yesterday it had been decided that they would help decorate Chuffy's home. None of the Throughgoods had participated in a purely English celebration in many years and had wanted the Hillers to remind them how to do it.

Chuffy assisted her down from the coach. "Happy Christmas, my love."

"Happy Christmas to you." She reached up, cupping his cheek. Enjoying how good it felt to belong to him and know he was hers as well. "How did all this come about?"

When she and her parents had left Grantville last evening, nothing had been said about returning in the morning.

He twined her arm with his. "My mother was not pleased that she had failed to invite you and your parents to Grantville for Christmas. While she will not completely poach Lady Bellamny's guests, she will borrow you as much as she is able. Do you mind?"

Amanda knew that if she were any happier, she would expire on the spot. "Not at all. I suppose we will spend many Christmases here."

"Only if you wish." He let go of her arm and slid his around her waist. "You might enjoy Vienna or Florence at Christmas."

She tilted her head so that it touched his arm. "Are they superior to England?"

Chuffy gazed down at her and grinned. "Anywhere you are is superior to anywhere you are not. They are to be experienced and appreciated."

"Do you think me provincial for having traveled less than you have?" Amanda said, voicing the only concern she had about marrying him.

"Of course not." The surprise in his voice was genuine. "Most people have not, particularly with the long war." They entered the hall, where a servant took her cloak, hat, and gloves; then they continued down the corridor to the breakfast room. Chuffy took her in his arms. "I merely wish to show you the places I like the best. However, if you would rather not—"

She placed her fingers over his mouth. "I would like nothing better than to travel with you."

Chuffy maneuvered Amanda under a kissing ball. His mother had made them, complete with mistletoe. Fortunately, the plant grew in vast amounts here.

He touched his lips to hers, and she sighed. Reaching behind his back, he opened the door and coaxed her inside one of the parlors. "Amanda, my dearest love."

Her small white teeth nibbled his lower lip. "Yes, my only love."

"May I propose?"

She broke off, startled. "Now I remember what was missing."

Touching his forehead to hers, he chuckled. "I must confess to feeling very strange about making wedding plans when I had not actually been allowed to ask for your hand."

She wrinkled her adorable nose. "I should have let you continue before."

"No, you were right. Your mother would have told the entire house. However, once my mother was certain of our affections, she was like a runaway horse."

Amanda nodded. "Very true. It is no wonder that our mothers have become close so quickly."

"As well as our fathers. They worked out the settlement agreements in short order."

"Hmm, all of them seem to be ahead of us." She straightened her shoulders. "How would you like to do this?"

"If you do not mind, I shall take you in my arms like this." Chuffy circled her waist with his arms, drawing her up against him. "Kiss you." Leaning down, he pressed his lips to hers. "And say, my beloved Miss Hiller, will you do me the immense honor of being my wife?"

Her creamy complexion turned pink, and all of her exuded a joy he hoped she would retain their whole lives. "My adored Lord Throughgood, it would be my pleasure to have you as my husband."

Chuffy kissed her again. "Minx."

"Am I truly?" Her eyes twinkled with delight. "Now, that makes me even happier."

Not able to resist her another moment, he claimed her mouth. There was time enough to join their parents.

He also had to find time to send a message to Hawksworth, as the Throughgoods and the Hillers would attend Lady Bellamny's Christmas drum this evening. But that could wait as well. His immediate need to kiss his betrothed took priority over everything and everyone else.

The weather was just cold enough to be pleasant. A light dusting of snow softened the crunch of the frost on the ground. After Lady Smithson had murmured a proposition for him to meet her later, Damon made sure to keep Meg by his side.

The thought that Smithson might attempt to do the same to Meg started Damon's temper rising. He shook it off. Surely the man was not stupid enough to ignore his warning, and she was an innocent from a powerful family. If he didn't destroy Smithson, Lord Featherton would.

After finally realizing that breakfast would not be forthcoming,

Lady Darby had joined the group as well, declaring that fresh air might be what she required.

"Not too cold?" Damon asked Meg as they strolled down the trail that the groom with a cart, who had been sent with him, pointed out.

"Not at all. I find the temperature pleasant. When do you wish to stop so that we can get to work?"

He signaled the groom. "Will here do?"

"If you go just a little bit along, you'll find a better spot."

Someone gave a frustrated sigh, which Damon chose to ignore. "Thank you. We'll take your advice."

A few minutes later, Meg exclaimed, "Oh look, hellebores! And here is some holly. I am sure this must be the best place."

He glanced back at the groom, who winked. "Then this is where we shall gather the greenery."

Much to Damon's surprise, the ladies all gravitated to different plants.

After about half an hour, Meg returned to his side. "We must also cut some pine and fir."

He raised a brow, more for effect than anything else. He was surprised that she had asked for his help. Yet he was beginning to think he might interest her more if he was a little less accommodating. "And I suppose you expect me to tell them."

Her gaze was drawn to a clump of hellebores, which was being rapidly denuded. "I think they will take the suggestion better from you. After all, you are a gentleman." The inflection in her voice had risen, making the statement seem almost like a question.

"Miss Featherton, I pray that you are not doubting my status."

Her pale cheeks flushed. "I certainly am not! I merely think it will appear as a suggestion coming from you. Whereas coming from me, it might be seen as an order."

She was clearly uncomfortable. Drat all this bloody game playing. It was getting him nowhere. He bowed as if they were at a ball and not in the middle of the woods. "I would be delighted to be of assistance."

"Thank you, my lord." She turned, marched to the nearest fir, and began attacking it with a pair of garden shears not nearly sufficient to cut the branch.

He walked to the cart, grabbed a short saw, and strode back to her. "May I help you?"

"I am perfectly capable of..." She looked at the branch and shook her head. "Thank you for the offer."

"Don't mention it." Within a few minutes, they had several small branches of fir. "Ladies, if you can help gather some of the pine and fir, we will be done here."

That, apparently, did the trick. The groom was enlisted to help cut, and in less than an hour they were well on their way back to the house.

Meg strode alongside Hawksworth. Even though she was sure he was trying to hold back for the ladies, she was having trouble keeping up with his long legs.

Finally she tugged his jacket sleeve, and he stopped. "Yes?"

"Could you please slow down?"

"Sorry." He gave a contrite grimace. "I must have forgot where I was."

"You were rather marching along." He had mentioned his war memories once before, and she wondered if that might have something to do with his pace.

"Old habits die hard." He smiled and his face changed, so that she could see the boy he once had been. "However, you should know the Rifles do not march in the regular fashion. We have two speeds: dawdle and quick march."

"Rifles? I would have thought you in the House Guard."

His devilish grin made her catch her breath. "I was for a short time. Then I was given an opportunity to join the Rifles."

"Was it more exciting?" She seemed on the cusp of understanding this man and had to know more.

"For me it was. The relations between officers and the enlisted men were different, as were our duties. Someday, if we have a chance, I'll tell you about it."

Gentlemen so rarely spoke about military matters around ladies. Meg had gleaned as much as she could by reading the newspapers, but still felt woefully ignorant. "I would enjoy that."

"I'm going with the groom to help unload the greens. Save me a cup of cider, will you?"

Meg nodded and watched as he did a sort of run. She would have to ask him if that was a quick march. Goodness knows, she had never seen him dawdle.

She and the other ladies entered through the main door.

Lady Culpepper came up beside Meg as they were taking off their outer garments. "I hope you and Lord Hawksworth will be happy."

Meg sucked in a sharp breath. "I do not understand you."

"Oh dear. I suppose I should mind my words. It is just that the two of you seem so pleased in one another's company." The lady removed her gloves and bonnet as if she had not said anything unusual. "I thought you had an understanding."

"Not at all." She groped for something else to say. "We barely know each other." And he was not the type of gentleman she wished to marry.

Lady Culpepper gave Meg a sharp, searching look. "Perhaps you should learn to know him better."

Fortunately, before Meg had to find a response, Lady Bellamny bid them warm themselves with hot chocolate and mulled cider.

Hawksworth appeared a few moments later, and she handed him a cup of cider. After finishing it, he said, "I shall see you at luncheon."

For reasons she did not understand, Meg was reluctant to let him go. "Naturally, unless you plan to miss a meal."

"Me?" He placed his hand over his heart. "Never. Always eat when you have a chance." He strode away, then stopped and turned. "Save me a place, will you?"

"I will." Meg could not, would not, allow herself to feel anything but friendship for Hawksworth. He was too handsome, too—too everything, and he had secrets.

Damon entered his chambers in a more buoyant mood than he had left them. Meg had been intrigued by his military time. And although he did not usually discuss it with anyone but former soldiers, or others who had played a role, he would talk to her about it. After all, if she was to be his wife, there should be no secrets between them, and she would have to know about his bad dreams as well.

"My lord." Hartwell handed him a letter. "This came from Lord Throughgood."

"Thank you." Damon opened the missive.

Hawksworth,
I don't have time to write more, but Miss Hiller and I will be at Lady Bellamny's drum this evening.
Throughgood

Not at dinner, which was a blessing. If he knew his godmother, she would have the evening filled with games. All he had to do was keep Meg away from Throughgood and pray she did not hear about the betrothal from anyone else. Quite frankly, he'd rather be back in Spain fighting the French than see her disappointed.

As soon as he had washed the morning's dirt off, he went in search of Lady Bellamny, and found her in the hall directing the decorations. Fir garlands studded with flowers and red bows already adorned the pillars and staircase. Swags were being mounted above the doors, each with a gold angel in the center.

He sidled up to her. "I thought you were going to make the guests do that."

"Are you offering?" She tilted her head and gazed at him. "We can always make use of tall men."

As he was expected to, he inclined his head. "I am yours to command. I did have a question, though."

"And what might that be?"

"In what order are this evening's games to be played?" If the fates were with him, he might be able to get Meg away from the others.

"Snap Dragon will come first. After which we will play Charades. You should find someone to make up the riddles with." She raised one brow. "Before luncheon."

Before someone else partnered with Meg was what his godmother meant. "I shall take your advice." Yet not quite in the way Lady Bellamny meant. He detested word games and would do his best to avoid them.

He strode out of the hall, down the corridor toward the breakfast room, then stopped. If Meg came down to the meal early, as she had this morning, he might have an opportunity to speak with her before anyone else arrived. But he did not like those odds. A better idea would be to send her a note. Yet, would she even accept it? At times she seemed happy to be in his company, then she would hide behind her mask. It was hard to know what mood she would be in when his missive reached her.

He continued down the corridor to the back stairs. He would have his valet relay a message to her lady's maid to partner him for Charades. A perfectly unexceptional method of solving his first problem of the evening. Even his father couldn't complain about Damon's behavior. Although that had never stopped the duke before. When had he ever been pleased with his heir? He probably wished Damon had not returned from the war.

Thinking of his father reminded Damon about the party his stepmother was being made to plan, to introduce him to marriageable young ladies. He did not mind at all embarrassing the old man by failing to appear, but he would not hurt Catherine's feelings or disappoint her.

His feelings for Meg had grown to the point where he had no doubt he loved her. She, on the other hand, was not only hard to read but still very afraid of being betrayed again. He was certain that, given time, he could earn her trust and her love. The difficulty was in convincing Meg to commit to him in such a short period of time. Yet it had to be done. Otherwise he would quite probably find himself betrothed to another woman, and that would not suit his plans at all.

He could weather the consequences of his outright defiance of his father. The question was, could the rest of his family? For if Damon did not attend the party, and he had no doubt he would be banished if that were the case, the duke would take out his ire on the rest of his children, perhaps even Catherine. Even though Damon was only the heir, he still had a responsibility to his family and future dependents.

There was nothing for it. Miss Margaret Featherton must be conquered rapidly, and held.

CHAPTER THIRTEEN

Meg held Hawksworth's note in her hand, but did not understand why he would want her as a partner for Charades. She was not at all clever with words in that fashion, although he could not know that. Nevertheless, she supposed the other guests had already picked their partners. Even Amanda would have her mother. Meg prayed Hawksworth was not counting on her. On the other hand, he had many talents. Perhaps one of them was riddles.

"Miss, have you decided?" Hendricks stood by the open door.

"I will be happy to partner with his lordship." Meg fought down the panic as she said the words.

Normally, she would find somewhere else to be, but she could not see her hostess allowing that sort of escape. Directly after luncheon, she would repair to the library in search of a book of riddles. There must be at least one. Perhaps she should forget the meal and search now. Her stomach growled, but fear of embarrassment overcame her hunger, and she strode rapidly down the corridor to the back stairs, and thence to the library.

She opened the door and halted. Meg was used to large homes, castles, abbeys, and all sorts of grand houses, but this took her breath away. Other than the ballroom, it was easily the largest room in the house. The library was paneled with book cases. Three spiral staircases rose three levels up. Each level required ladders to reach the highest shelves. Long, narrow windows broke the line of books, providing light to each floor. The roof appeared to be a glass dome. She had never seen such a wonderful room, but how was she supposed to find one book of riddles amidst such a collection? Yet find it she must.

After a few moments it became clear that the books were in order by type, author, and year of publication. If only she knew which classification a book of riddles would be in. Her stomach complained again as Meg began to search. This could take all day.

"May I help you find something?"

She whipped around, tripping over a stool. Before she hit the floor, a pair of strong arms pulled her up and held her against Hawksworth's hard chest. Her heart thudded almost painfully. He should not be holding her so closely, or at all. Yet his scent, pure male with a hint of lavender, captured Meg's senses.

Lavender? She had never liked the fragrance on a man, yet on him it was intriguing. She forced herself to take one step back, then another, until there was a proper distance between them.

"Are you all right?" His voice wove its way around her, while his deep brown eyes reflected concern.

"Yes, thank you. I was simply startled. I did not expect to see anyone else here." Meg felt like a complete fool. She should have told him that she was not good with Charades. Her stomach made itself known again.

"I brought food." He waved his arm in the direction of a long wood table. "And I am happy to share."

Against her will, her lips curved into a smile and she laughed. "Of course you did."

He took hold of her elbow and led her to the dishes that covered a large silver tray. "You did not answer my question."

Well, drat. There was no reason to prevaricate, other than her pride. She may as well admit her failing. He would discover it soon enough in any event. "I was looking for help with the riddles for this evening. It is not one of my talents."

Hawksworth began filling a plate with cheese, boiled eggs, chicken, and ham. "Neither is it one of mine. I had hoped you could save me. Perhaps we shall have to find an excuse not to join the others."

She harrumphed. "Good luck convincing Lady Bellamny we should be excused."

"You may have a point. Here." He placed the plate in front of a chair, and began loading another one. "If you don't eat, your stomach will not allow us any peace."

She wanted to make a clever retort, but was too hungry to think of one. After gobbling down a piece of cheese, she asked, "Where would a book of riddles be?"

"Under games, or maybe comedy." He ate quickly and efficiently, but gave every impression of enjoyment. As if he was determined to savor the meal. "Now that both of us are searching, we should find something."

As she glanced around the massive room, the enormity of the task finally sank in. It could take days. "What if it eludes us?"

"In that eventuality"—he wiped his lips and fingers on a large white serviette—"we call for reinforcements. I'm not one for a Forlorn Hope."

Meg set her plate on the tray. "What does that mean?"

He leaned back in his chair with his hands crossed over his stomach. "During a siege there comes a time when a group of soldiers, enlisted men and officers, volunteer to lead the attack to breach the city walls. The casualty rate is exceedingly high, and the chances of success can be low. They are the Forlorn Hope."

That made no sense at all. She frowned, trying to comprehend the impossible. "Why would anyone volunteer to be killed?"

Damon gave a short, derisive chuckle. Some would say that by simply entering the military, one was volunteering to die. Still, it was important to him that she understand. "Because if they do succeed, the rewards are promotions. Not every officer has the funds or family willing to buy a promotion. In the enlisted ranks, it is hard to move up."

Her brow cleared a bit. "An act of desperation?"

"For some. For others it is a way to achieve recognition."

She shook her head slowly. "I cannot even think of a situation in regular life that would compare."

"Can you not?"

She had ambled back toward the first of the rows of bookcases taking up the center of the room.

"What of women and men who marry for status, or money, or both?" *Or one beautiful, passionate lady who is too afraid to love.* "They are, in their ways, acts of desperation."

"I suppose you are correct. Many people, particularly women, do things that could cause them harm."

"Then there are the merely foolhardy. Young men who take risks because they cannot foresee the possible consequences."

"Such as when a couple elopes."

"Or believes they know the other person, but has been fooled by the face he or she shows the world." Damon prayed she would finally understand that she was meant to have been a dupe.

"We should search for the riddles."

He wondered if the conversation had pricked at her enough that she wished to end it. They still had hours until it was time to dress for dinner. "Indeed. Our time is running short."

He and Meg took separate sections, looking for classifications that might include riddles. After about an hour her shout echoed from above. "I found them."

Thank fate for favors. "I'll be right there." Taking the steps by twos, he was quickly beside her. "That's it?"

"Just the two books, but surely that will be enough. We don't need many."

He began to flip through one of the books. "Here is one from David Garrick. I had no idea he was such a wit.

"Say, by what title, or what name,
Must I this youth address?
Cupid and he are not the same—
Tho' both can raise, or quench a flame—
I'll kiss you if you guess."

She screwed her face up. "I have no idea."

"Chimney sweep."

"Good God." She sank gracefully onto the floor. "I am never going to guess any of them."

He felt the exact same way. "There might be enough time to have someone search the rooms for the other guests' riddles."

"It will not help." She held up a letter. "This was stuck in the book. A Mrs. Littleton sent it to Lady Bellamny. She had it from another friend.

"When my first is a task to a young girl of spirit,
And my second confines her to finish the piece,

*How hard is her fate! but how great is her merit
If by taking my whole she effects her release.*

"The answer is hem-lock."

"I'll be dam—a dunderhead."

"Precisely." Her fallen face reminded him of someone who had lost her dearest friend.

Every sinew and nerve in his body needed him to come to her rescue. "We will find the ones we wish to use, and trust I shall find a way out of the game."

"If only you could." Clearly she had a low opinion of his abilities. "I do not know why they call it a game when it is pure torture."

"Here is our last one.

*"My first, tho' water, cures no thirst,
My next alone has soul,
And when he lives upon my first,
He then is called my whole.*

"The answer is a sea-man." He rose and held out his hand. "You should have more trust in me."

She placed her hand in his. "Why?"

Damon pulled her up so that there were only inches between them. "Because I never promise what I cannot make happen."

Her ocean-deep-blue eyes searched his. "We shall see."

Meg's skepticism pricked his pride. Only one other person doubted him, and that was his father. By the end of this evening, Damon would make bloody sure she would have no reason to distrust his word.

Austin Smithson gazed at his wife before pulling out a piece of pressed paper from the desk drawer. "Why so glum, my pet? I thought at least one of us would be having some fun."

"There is no one here," she uttered in tragic tones as she flopped on the bed.

"Hawksworth is unattached." He dipped the pen in the standish twice, composing the letter in his head.

"He has made it quite clear that he is not interested. Apparently, Lady Bellamny is his godmother."

"Ah, expectations. Mustn't ruin them."

My dear Tarlington,

"I suppose that is it," Carola said, interrupting Austin. "She is such a rigid old lady." Her normally melodic tone had become whiny.

"We will not be here too much longer." He smiled at her. "I give you my word."

She pouted. "You gave me your word that we would have an enjoyable visit."

"Darling, is it my fault that I mistook the situation?" If he didn't get her out of here soon, she'd be throwing tantrums. "Allow me to finish this letter, and I will see what I can do to make you feel better. Perhaps Paris. I understand the men there are quite ardent."

"You could come here now." Her voice had suddenly become sultry, and he turned. The front buttons of her gown were undone, and she was pulling it off.

His cock jumped, even though her blatant sensuality had long ago ceased to excite him. By the time she had given birth to two sons, one after the other, Carola had worn him out with her incessant demands to be swived, and he set her free. However, it had been too long for him as well. "I need to finish this missive."

"Who is that important?"

"Tarlington. Apparently he couldn't bring his American heiress up to scratch."

"He and his mistress are bores."

As was anyone who would not bed her. "He is a friend, and I will do what I can to assist him." Austin glanced over his shoulder. Carola was naked and touching herself. *Hell!* His hand trembled as he dipped it in the inkwell again. "This won't take long."

As you thought, Miss Featherton is present. I have heard comments suggesting that she thinks love is not essential for marriage. I suppose that has to do with you. However, since she has given up her childish longings, you may as well have a go. I stand ready to help if you require assistance.
Yr. Servant,
Smithson

CHAPTER FOURTEEN

Meg wanted to bite her tongue. She had meant her words to be teasing, yet she knew her tone had not lightened as it should have done. She had never seen Hawksworth's countenance as hard and determined as it was now. She should apologize. It was the only polite course to take. But she was tired of men making promises and not living up to them.

And once again, they were far too close to each other, and her breathing was shallow. His fine lips were pressed tightly together, but she saw hurt lurking deep in his eyes. Surely she was being fanciful. Nothing she said could injure him. In any event, it was time to dress for dinner.

She dipped a shallow curtsey. "I shall see you this evening, my lord."

"Indeed you shall, Miss Featherton," he said in a voice as hard as his face.

Keeping her spine straight and her chin held high, Meg made her way as quickly as possible down the stairs and out of the room. She did not stop until she reached her bedchamber.

Once in her room, she held on to the bedpost, trying to breathe deeply, but her heart was pounding as if she had been running. That man should not affect her the way he did. She was not going to lose her heart again, and if she did, it could not be to *him*.

God, she was a goose! He had not even given her a reason to think he was interested. Hawksworth was simply being friendly. After all, they were the only single people here, other than Amanda.

If not for the fact that Amanda's parents were with her, Meg would have been worried that she had not seen her friend in so long, and that didn't make any more sense than thinking Hawksworth was interested in her. Most likely the Hillers had gone to visit relatives or friends in the area or perhaps Mrs. Hiller was keeping her daughter away from Hawksworth... but why had no one said anything? The only thing to do was to speak with Amanda. There would be a simple explanation for her absence.

Meg removed her boots. She was probably tired. Otherwise she would not be overreacting as she was. She climbed into the bed, sinking into the soft mattress.

Hawksworth began to smile. Their lips were so close she could feel his warm breath. Then she reached up and stroked one lean cheek, and his lips descended to hers.

"Miss, wake up. It's time to dress."

His kiss had seemed so real, she touched her lips. But there was nothing unusual about them at all. She could not fall in love with him. Even if her heart wished it. She would not betray Amanda.

She rose from the bed, and allowed Hendricks to unlace her gown. "I don't know how I'll get all these wrinkles out. You should have called for me."

"I didn't intend to fall asleep."

Hendricks snorted. "Fagged to death, that's what you are."

Meg could not disagree. She rarely slept during the day.

After she washed and donned an evening gown, she sat at the dressing table.

A few minutes later, her maid was pinning her hair up into a knot. "Miss, you're fidgeting."

"I never fidget."

"Well, you are now," Hendricks said in a tone that finished their short exchange.

Meg took a breath and attempted to calm her disordered self. Maybe her maid was right. She had not been herself lately. Hawksworth was not helping. That dream had not helped.

She smiled to herself. Lavender. She did not know another man who could carry it off. She hoped Amanda liked it.

"There you are." Hendricks placed a ruby-trimmed comb in Meg's hair.

Meg put on a ruby and diamond necklace that her parents had given her for her twenty-first birthday and fastened the matching earrings.

A sudden longing for home struck her. Her family would just now be finishing the Christmas decorating. Dinner would have been served early, and a choral group from the church would come and sing carols. All their neighbors would join them for games, and she would be allowed to make herself scarce while Charades was being played. At midnight they would attend church services, and afterward open presents.

Willing away her tears, she gave herself a shake. She was only making herself miserable by thinking of dear and familiar customs. Attending the house party had been a mistake. After this year, she would never leave home at Christmas again.

Almeria opened the door to the terrace of her private morning room. "Come in and warm yourselves."

Lucinda Featherton paused to kiss Almeria's cheek. "It is chilly."

Constance Bridgewater entered on Lucinda's heels. "Lovely decorations in the front of the house. I had not thought of putting up a fir wreath with fruit and ribbons."

"I am pleased you like it. Are you sure you would not rather stay here?"

"Naturally," Lucinda smiled, "we would love to visit with you, but we do not want Meg to know we are in the area unless it is necessary."

"Your daughter-in-law?" Almeria asked.

"Indeed. After her reaction to our matching Kit and Mary, it is better that she not think I am involved."

"Very well." Almeria tugged the bell-pull, and not long after her butler arrived with a tray. "I did not know what you would be in the mood for, so there is tea and spiced wine." Lucinda's nose wrinkled. "Not English mulled wine, but in the French style."

"Wonderful! I remember now that you prefer the *vin brulé*. Do you recall when we were young ladies and traveled to France with our parents for Christmas?"

"How could I forget? We had to sneak out to the *marché de Noël* in Strasbourg," Almeria said.

"All because our parents had gone elsewhere, and we could not convince our governesses it was safe."

Constance frowned. "I have no memory of anything such as that. The only one I visited was in Paris."

"That was because you were busy bringing Bridgewater to heel in Paris," Lucinda said.

"Did he not almost betroth himself to some Austrian duke's daughter?" Almeria queried.

"Not after he got fleas from her wig," Constance retorted as she picked up a cup of hot wine.

"Fleas." Lucinda's shoulders shook with amusement. "However did you manage that?"

"Her maid was not well paid, and my groom was." Constance grinned. "I must say, Bridgewater was worth it. Now, how are Hawksworth and Meg getting on?"

Almeria wished she had better news for her friends. "I must confess, I do not think it is going well. Meg is still extremely wary. I have hopes that Damon will get her alone this evening. We are playing Christmas games and will begin with Snap Dragon. After which we'll play Charades, a game he hates." She looked at Lucinda. "You told me that Meg does not like to play it either."

"Very true. She will absent herself if possible," her friend replied.

"I will ensure they have the opportunity." Almeria selected a biscuit, with dried fruit and wine. "Also, the new Lady Grantville has offered to bring over kissing balls with mistletoe. Perhaps that will assist our efforts as well."

Almeria had hoped that the two would fall in love during the holiday. "The only problem is that I have heard from Catherine Somerset. Damon's father is planning a house party for him to meet eligible ladies. He is not pleased that the boy decided to come here. I have a feeling it may upset our timing."

"The old fool." Constance twisted her lips. "There must be something we can do to give them more time together. Whenever I have seen Meg and Hawksworth together, the air practically snaps with the attraction between them."

"I do not think she trusts herself," Lucinda said thoughtfully. "Would you if you had made two such terrible choices in a matter of months?"

"*And* fancied yourself in love." Almeria nodded. "I am open to any suggestions."

"Let us see how it goes this evening." Lucinda held her cup out for more of the wine. "We have always been able to come up with the answer."

Damon sucked in a breath as Meg emerged from the corridor wearing a deep-red velvet gown that accentuated her curves as she glided toward the stairs. Her dark curls picked up the candlelight and danced around her face. Sweet Jesus, she was the most beautiful woman he had ever seen, and she would be his.

Pretending that she was walking to him, he held out his hand. "Good evening."

She lifted her eyes to his, but they were shuttered, as if she was attempting to deny even the friendship that was growing between them. "Are you always before times, my lord?"

"I like to scout out the area before others arrive." He waited until she placed her hand on his arm before asking, "What is your reason?"

"I merely enjoy being timely."

"A virtue, to be sure. After you left, I found another riddle."

"Were you able to figure out the answer?"

"This one was not difficult. Shall I recite it to you?" Without waiting for her to answer, he began. " 'My first doth affliction denote, which my second is destined to feel; and my whole is the best antidote that affliction to soften and heal.' "

She wrinkled her brow, then after a moment shook her head. "No. You will have to tell me."

"The answer is a woman." Meg opened her lips, but he continued before she could speak. "It appears that many men think of women as the remedy to any affliction."

"I am positive I do not wish to be anyone's cure."

"Perhaps it is better that one has experienced love, even if one then loses that love."

"Why would you think that?" Meg made a derogatory snort. "I am quite sure that is only true in your imagination. Normal people are perfectly capable of living their lives in calm contentment. Mad love is not necessary to happiness and can be detrimental to it."

Perhaps now he would have the conversation he had wanted to

have with her. "Marriage without passion seems to be a rather boring proposition."

"Not at all. It is perfectly reasonable. Neither party need be injured by the other's actions."

"No need to be upset if the husband looks too long at another lady. No need to—"

"I did not say that." Her chin firmed as if she was ready to do verbal battle. "After all, it would be a matter of respect for the husband not to leer at other women in his wife's presence."

He fought to keep his lips from quivering with a smile. "I understand you. He may act as he pleases as long as his wife is not around."

"You are being unreasonable."

"Not at all. I am merely trying to understand your point. You do not wish for passion in marriage, yet you would forbid passion altogether."

"One may have passion for one's family and children."

"Do you plan to—"

"Hawksworth." Lady Bellamny led a footman carrying a box of greenery. "I have received these from Lady Grantville. Since you and Miss Featherton are early, you may direct their hanging."

He carefully picked up one of the red ribbons and grinned. Hanging from it was a kissing ball, complete with mistletoe. "It would be our pleasure. Although, I must confess, I know little about hanging kissing balls, but I am certain Miss Featherton will know."

She turned bright red then gasped. After a few moments' struggle, she retorted, "I can only tell you where my mother hangs them, my lord. She must know best, as they are denuded of berries before Twelfth Night."

"Get to it then." Lady Bellamny waved her hand. "I want them up before the other guests come down."

"That should teach us. While we are here we are better served being late," Meg grumbled as she scanned the room. "Let us begin here. My lord, you must help as you are taller."

"I have a ladder," the footman offered.

Damon took the box. "I'm tall enough to reach most of the doorways, but bring it along. We may need it."

He and the servant followed her around the main parts of the house, placing the kissing balls where she directed. After about a half hour, there were only two left. "Where do you want these to go?"

"One in the servants' hall, but I cannot think of anywhere for the last one."

He gave one of the decorations to the footman. "Hang this where you think it will do the most good." After the young man left, he took the last one. "I shall be in charge of this one." Voices filtered down from above. "You should go into the drawing room."

She glanced at him as if she wished to say something, but instead she turned into the drawing room, where they all met before dinner.

Now to decide where to hang the kissing ball. Another way to ask the question was where would he take Meg to avoid Charades. It would be cold outside. He smiled to himself, but not for long.

Striding through the music room, he opened the doors to the terrace. To the right was an old torch holder. He quickly affixed the decoration to the holder and went back into the house the same way he went out, almost colliding with Lord Bellamny in the process.

"Sorry, sir."

"There was no harm done. I take it you were hanging the last kissing ball."

Damon felt his jaw drop and snapped it shut. "Was that a lucky supposition, or do you know something I don't?"

"Oh, I imagine I know a great deal you do not." Lord Bellamny chuckled. "I haven't lived all these years for nothing. Lady Bellamny does it every year to the only uncommitted couple present. Most young men have the sense to grab a kissing ball for their own use. The old sconce on the terrace is perfect."

And here Damon had thought he was the first, or at least one of the few, and clever at that. "Any advice on spiriting the lady outside?"

"During the last part of Snap Dragon. No one wants to miss it, but then the game becomes too competitive for most, and they will drift away."

He turned to stroll down the corridor with the older gentleman. "Thank you."

"Happy to help, my boy," Lord Bellamny replied warmly. "We have missed having you visit. Please come anytime you wish."

When Damon had been at school, the Bellamny house had been his salvation. It had taken some doing, but he had managed to spend most of his holidays here, without the duke's knowledge. During those years, he had learned more at his lordship's knee about being a man than from all the punishments he had endured from his father.

"Thank you, sir. I will plan to visit more often."

After dinner, Meg sought out Daphne, yet Meg's gaze strayed to the door each time she heard a sound that could be the gentlemen joining them. At first she attempted to tell herself she was waiting for Amanda, who had not joined them for dinner. Yet the truth was Meg could not be still until Hawksworth arrived.

She encouraged Daphne to talk about her new house, the baby she was sure would be a boy, and, of course, her husband, who was perfect in every way. Several times she started to say something, then blushed and changed the subject. It was then that Meg remembered, with more than a little irritation, that her friend would be holding back some information because she was still unwed. When she was eighteen, and even nineteen, she had accepted the idea that maidens should be kept in the dark when it came to relations between men and women. But the past year had made her impatient with that way of thinking. Although to be fair, it was her miserable experience with Swindon and Tarlington that caused her change of mind.

The door opened, and all their heads turned toward it. Preceding the gentlemen were the Hillers and the Grantvilles. Then all her attention was riveted on Hawksworth. He and Fotheringale headed directly to her and Daphne.

Fotheringale took his wife's hand. "Forgive us for being so long. Sir Randolph received a letter about more riots that have taken place."

Meg looked at Hawksworth. "Where?"

"In the north. With the laws the government has, it is no wonder, but Lady Bellamny will not appreciate our bringing that debate into her drawing room on Christmas Eve."

As far as Meg was concerned, it was this type of discussion that ought to dominate the conversation, but he was right. It would not be welcome.

Footmen started snuffing the candles, and a huge, shallow silver bowl filled with brandy and raisins was set on a round table that had been placed in the middle of the room. The purpose of the game was to pick out the raisins and not get burned as one ate them.

She placed her fingers in Hawksworth's hand, and rose. "It is time for Snap Dragon."

"That bowl is large enough to accommodate everyone." He wasted no time in finding a place at the table. The Fotheringales were on one side of them and the Culpeppers on the other side. Across the table, Amanda wiggled her fingers at Meg, and mouthed, "I will tell you soon."

Soon the only light in the long room came from the fireplaces at either end. Then the brandy was lit, creating an eerie blue blaze.

Meg gave a shiver of delight as she reached out and plucked a burning raisin from the bowl. Hawksworth got two of them, handing one to her. Then she did the same.

"You're very good at this." His voice was warm with praise.

"So are you." Even though the fire burned off most of the alcohol in the brandy, the flavor was still strong.

Shrieks of laughter filled the room, as he leaned close to her. "A passionate game."

Oooh, she was going to murder him right here. Not wanting anyone else listening, she kept her voice low. "We have already had this discussion." Easing herself out of the circle, she murmured, "I need some air."

Hawksworth caught up to Meg at the end of the long terrace. "What is it about passion you do not like?"

She closed her eyes and counted to ten before turning to face him. "What has passion to do with anything?"

He prowled slowly toward her. The torches reflected the fire lurking in his eyes, making him more dangerous than ever before. She took a step back toward the wall, and before she knew it her back had hit the cold stone.

"If you do not want love, you must at least have passion." Bracing his hand on the wall next to her cheek, he leaned forward until his breath caressed her face. It was sweet with raisins and brandy.

Nervously, she licked her lips. Would her breath smell the same? "I want . . . I want . . ." Oh God! Why was it so difficult to articulate what she desired and that it did not include him? "I do not need passion. I want respect from a man who will never betray me." Not someone who made her head spin and stirred strange feelings in her body and heart. "I want a calm life and children."

"Children." He spoke the word as if it had made his argument. "And how do you plan on getting children?"

How dare he mention what went on between a man and a woman? Her sister-in-law had given Meg some information. Still, an uncomfortable heat rose in her neck and face as she realized that he probably knew much more about the subject than she ever would.

Unable to stop the threadiness in her voice, she forced the words out. "In the usual way."

Before she knew it, his lips were next to hers. "You have no idea." The tip of his tongue trailed languidly along her bottom lip, and her knees began to turn to marmalade. "Will you lie in your cold bed with your nightgown on while your husband ruts?"

She should be shocked. No one had ever talked to her like this. The image Damon brought up held no appeal. Mary had said when a man and woman loved one another... But that was not something Meg would have.

His wicked tongue moved from her mouth to her ear, as he whispered, "Or do you want to scream as he takes you to heaven and back?"

How weak did he think she was? Despite her shock, she managed to answer. "I never scream."

Damon chuckled, a low, sinful sound. "I'd make you scream and enjoy doing it."

She was sinking, and she had to find a way to fight back before she lost the argument and herself. "You will never have the opportunity."

He smiled, his teeth flashing white. "Afraid of what you might feel?"

"Do not be ridiculous. I feel nothing for you, or any other man. I refuse to."

"Poor Meg." His finger caressed her jaw. The palm of his hand cupped her cheek, as she had dreamed about doing to him, and he pressed his lips to hers.

His mouth was open and hot, but not wet. She opened her lips to tell him that she had not given him permission to use her name, but his tongue invaded, and conquered, and she was lost in the heat that speared through her from her breasts to her thighs as he explored her mouth.

She should pull away. She should slap him. Instead she slid her arms up over his shoulders, allowing her fingers to play with his soft, waving hair as she pressed her body to his.

He slanted his head, and Meg moaned. Even through the layers of muslin and velvet, she felt the hard warmth of his chest. His arms wrapped around her, and his legs pressed against hers. Then his tongue stroked hers, insisting she return the caress. An urgent throbbing started low in her belly. She should stop, but she didn't want to.

This was what she would be giving up by marrying Lord Throughgood. He would never hold her like this, kiss her like this. No one had ever kissed her as Hawksworth did. Other than on her hand, Tarlington had not even attempted a kiss.

She gave a small sob, and he lifted his head, capturing her gaze with his fathomless dark eyes. "That is passion."

Before she could formulate any sort of coherent answer, soft voices drifted from the stairs down to the garden. She glanced over. Amanda and Lord Throughgood were locked in an embrace.

A chill ran through her, sobering her as quickly as if she had been doused with snow. "You knew."

"Yes. Miss Hiller would not tell you because she did not wish to hurt your feelings."

Hawksworth's arms had not dropped, nor had he moved away.

"How could I not have seen it? She is my dearest friend. We have known one another forever."

"Sometimes when we have decided on a course of action, we become blind to all else."

CHAPTER FIFTEEN

In Damon's arms, Meg struggled to break away, but he held her fast. If he let go of her now, he might never have a chance to tell her how he felt.

"What have I done?" Her tone echoed the despair she must have been experiencing since she learned of Tarlington's betrayal. "You and Lord Throughgood must think me an absolute fool."

"No." He kissed the top of her head, attempting to calm her. "We did everything we could to ensure that you were not embarrassed. It was clear that you were hurting, and attempting to find a way forward." Damon pressed his lips to her forehead. Determined to solidify his gains. "But not, I think, as Lady Throughgood."

"No." The word was hollow, reminding him of a child lost in the woods.

He would like to drop to one knee and propose, but that would give her an opportunity not only to take his proposal the wrong way, but stalk off, wrapped in her dignity. "Perhaps there is another gentleman who would like to marry you."

She shook her head slowly. "No."

Damon swallowed his frustration. "Have you never even considered being the Marchioness of Hawksworth, and future Duchess of Somerset?"

Her head jerked up, her eyes as wide and wary as a startled deer. "Marry you?"

"Why not?" He captured her lips, and this time she opened her mouth, allowing him to plunder. A few moments later, he grinned. "We at least have passion. I'll wait for you to fall in love with me."

"Fall in love?" Her jaw dropped, but she quickly recovered. "Are you telling me that you love me?"

"Almost from the first moment I saw you last spring, but it was clear that you were already committed. I arrived in Town this past autumn to find you taken once again."

"You..."

"Still, there is something you must know. I have sworn not to marry unless the lady loves me in return."

Once more she attempted to break loose, but apparently settled for glaring at him. "You *cannot* be serious."

"Why?" Raising one brow, he challenged her. "Because I am a man?"

Meg winced. "I just never thought it was that important to gentlemen."

"I think your brother might disagree. As for me, I need the type of loyalty that only love will bring. If you agree to marry me, we would have to remain betrothed until you return my affections."

"I cannot. I mean, what if I never do?"

Damon kissed Meg again, slowly, until she moaned. Even through his clothing he could feel her soft breasts touching, pressing into him. Feel when her nipples became tight buds. This time when he broke the kiss her eyes were glazed and her lips parted. "We will."

A few moments later she took a breath. "I will not wed a man with secrets."

"Secrets?" He barked a laugh. "The only secret I have is that my father dislikes me as much as he did my mother."

"Impossible." She shook her head, rejecting his truth. "Look at you. For one thing, you dress like a Dandy, but you do not act like one."

Damon wanted to rake his fingers through his hair, but he didn't dare let go of her. "Merely the product of being bored. I came back from the war and had nothing to do except be on the Town. I would much rather be learning the business of being a duke, but my father is not at all interested in allowing me to do so. That was when I hit upon the idea of being an Original. Dressing like a Dandy, to an extent, but pursuing sports as well. I must admit the temptation to be able to make a lot of idiotic men follow my whims was one I could not resist." Meg still looked unconvinced. "I can promise you that I am neither a sadist nor rolled up. Even without the allowance I receive from my father, I am wealthy."

"Tarlington?"

"Indeed. I hear there is an extremely rich American heiress in Paris who is looking for a title."

Her shoulders straightened, and beneath his fingers her spine stiffened. That was his brave lady love. "I wish him good luck in his endeavors."

"You are magnanimous."

"I am sick of being tricked." A sob broke through. "I saw him with another woman."

That he had not known or suspected. With his thumb, Damon wiped away the one tear that had leaked from her eye. What he did understand was that she needed to speak about it, and that she had probably not been able to tell anyone. "How did that come about?"

Meg rested her head against his shoulder, slumping into him. "I received a note, as I had with Swindon."

Surely she . . . "Tell me about Swindon first."

"I had a missive. It told me that he—that he was cruel to women, beyond the type of beatings one sometimes sees. I had never heard of such a thing and did not believe it." She took a breath, and he was afraid of what he would hear next. "Then another letter came telling me to go to a certain address. It gave the time." She stared into his eyes. "A woman was waiting there. She—she showed me the scars he had made when he whipped her. There was also a letter from him asking her to forgive him for leaving marks. The next day I sent him a missive telling him I no longer wished to see him."

Damon held her closer. Willing all the hurt she had felt out of her. "What happened with Tarlington?"

"The same thing. This time the letter included an address and time. I saw him with a woman and two children. He was so in love with them." When she ended, her voice was strained. "I—I cannot go through that again."

He wanted to roar at the injuries she had received at the hands of the scoundrels and kill them. He wanted to hold her until she healed. Yet most of all, he wanted to show her that she did not need to fear love any longer. "You have good reason to be wary, but I can promise you, I will never give you any cause to doubt me."

Tears coursed down her cheeks. "I don't know if I can ever trust a man again."

He decided to press his suit. Perhaps his surprise attack would work better than attempting to talk her around. After all, the passion they shared was a start. "Accept my offer of marriage. We will work on the rest."

She was shaking her head again, but at least she had stopped weeping. "That is not fair to you. You cannot jilt me, and what if I can never bring myself to love you?"

At this moment, he could have told her it did not matter, but at the end of the day, it would—to them both. She had to know she could love and be loved in return. "Give us until just before Twelfth Night. If your feelings have not changed by then, you may jilt me." She opened her lovely lips, but he placed one finger on them, stilling her. "However, if you feel anything for me, we will continue the betrothal until you are certain."

"I think you are mad."

Despite her words, he thought she was coming around. "What do you have to lose? One way or another, it will be settled long before the next Season begins."

She drew her brows together, studying him. Trying to find an ulterior motive for his proposal. Then again, if he was right and their passion meant something, what did she have to lose? The sound of steps coming toward her and Hawksworth made any further conversation difficult. "Very well. We shall try it your way."

His arm snaked around her waist, just as the other couple joined them. "Miss Hiller, Throughgood. I wish you a Happy Christmas."

Amanda glanced from Meg to Hawksworth, her smile growing wider by the moment. "Happy Christmas to you as well." Amanda's arm was tucked securely in Throughgood's. "May we assume that you being out here means . . . Oh dear." The joyful look on her face faded. "Have I got ahead of myself? Meg, you are my dearest friend, and I only want your happiness."

"True enough," Throughgood said. "She even thought about giving me up, but I wouldn't let her."

Meg forced a smile and covered the few feet to hug her friend. "Amanda, you should have told me not to even think about Lord Throughgood. If only I had known, I would never have—"

"Thought to save her from me." Hawksworth cut in, saving Meg from embarrassing herself. "And giving me an opportunity to discover that my estimation of Meg was correct." He pulled her back into the warmth of his arm. "You may wish us happy. Obviously, I must speak with her father before an announcement is made."

She sucked in a breath. That was well done of him. "Indeed. If it is at all possible, we will leave after Boxing Day. I would like to be home for the rest of the holiday."

"I agree." He held her even tighter against his side. "As pleasant as this party has been, nothing more can be accomplished until we can speak with her parents."

"I understand." Amanda glanced at Lord Throughgood. "We have been spending time with Chuffy's parents."

"M'mother and father have taken a liking to Amanda and her parents." He focused his gaze on Meg. "Please call me Chuffy. All my friends but Hawksworth here do. Maybe next year we can attend the fair together. It was deuced uncomfortable having to play least in sight with you and Hawksworth." So that was what all the strange turning down other rows at the fair had been about. "We wanted to give him time to bring you up to scratch before we made the announcement. Amanda wouldn't even allow me to propose properly until to-day. We mean to marry as soon as I can procure a special license."

All three of them were silent, waiting for her to say something. "Thank you. Your kindness means a great deal to me." Even if Hawksworth never became her husband, she now knew how good a man he was, and a true friend. "I think we should go back in before we are missed."

"Throughgood, Miss Hiller," Hawksworth said. "We shall follow you."

They were several feet away when he drew her into another kiss. "I have already made use of your name. Please call me Damon. No one else does, and it would mean a great deal to me."

Sensing a vulnerability she had not expected, Meg clung to him for a few moments longer. There was so much about this man she wished to know, must know now that she needed to see if she could fall in love with him. "I am pleased that you want me to use your given name."

"You honor me." He glanced at the drawing room doors. "Let us see how well our friends can hide our absence."

They need not have worried. When Meg and Damon entered the

room, it was filled with loud laughter as most of the guests were deeply involved in a game of Charades. She shuddered, and he squeezed her hand. One thing was certain; if they did wed, they would not require anyone to join riddle games.

He led her straight to Lady Bellamny, who was talking to the Hillers and Grantvilles.

"We shall make the announcement before the service," Lady Grantville was saying when they strolled up.

"Perfect," Lady Bellamny agreed. "And what about the two of you?"

She had not turned her head toward Meg and Damon, but they both knew to whom she was speaking.

Damon grinned and kissed her on the cheek. "If you have no objection, we are off as soon as possible to speak with Miss Featherton's parents."

"Much good it would do if I did object," Lady Bellamny said in a wry tone. "Who will be your chaperone?"

"I thought that my maid might be enough." Meg hoped against hope that either Mrs. Hiller or Lady Bellamny would agree.

"Not when your betrothal has not been announced. However, I have had a letter from your grandmother Featherton. She is passing through this area and wished to stop to visit. There is no reason why you cannot ask her if she is willing to play gooseberry."

"Grandmamma? I thought she was in Bath or somewhere."

"I have known her since she was a girl, and there is no counting on her being where she says she will be. However, she always is where she is needed." Lady Bellamny bussed Meg's cheek. "Send a message to your dresser to start packing. Your grandmother is traveling with the Dowager Duchess of Bridgewater."

Meg wanted to roll her eyes. "When is she not? My sister-in-law, Mary, says they are as thick as thieves."

"There you are. Old ladies need to have some fun, or where would we be?"

On the heels of that cryptic remark, Lady Grantville glanced at the clock. "I think it time for the announcement, and the champagne has arrived."

Indeed, it was already a quarter after eleven. This would give them just enough time to congratulate Amanda and Chuffy before donning their warm clothing for the trip to the town for services.

"We have an announcement to make." Lord Grantville motioned to Amanda and Chuffy. "Miss Hiller has graciously agreed to marry my son, Throughgood. Please join me in wishing them happy."

The newly betrothed couple was wreathed in smiles as they were congratulated and champagne was passed around.

Meg was sorry she would miss Amanda's wedding, but Damon was right. She must discover if their friendship could blossom into something more. After the past few days, she was convinced that she would be more comfortable exploring her feelings at home.

A footman handed her a glass of champagne, and she took the time to study Amanda and Chuffy. He gazed at her as if she was the most important thing in the world, and she gave him the same look.

"It is almost as if they were made for one another." Damon's arm brushed Meg's shoulder.

"It is." They already appeared so comfortable together.

"We should congratulate them again." He placed his palm on the small of her back and together they wished Amanda and Chuffy happy.

Soon she was garbed in warm boots, gloves, a cloak with a large matching muff, and a bonnet. Damon remained beside her as they walked down the drive toward town. "What shall we tell my grandmother?"

"Why not the truth? There is nothing wrong in what we are doing. You have been deeply hurt, and I love you enough to wait."

"You make me sound tragic." And she was not sure she liked thinking of herself in that way.

"On the contrary."

She could feel him glance down at her.

"I think you are brave to risk your heart again."

"I do not know what you see in me to want to wait." That was the truth. Ever since he had been introduced to her, she had been sullen more often than not. Her only recent joy was when they had sung together and visited the fair. Perhaps that should tell her something. She just did not know what.

"You have a certain *joie de vivre* I have not seen in most well-bred ladies. You are also intelligent and not afraid to show it. Again unusual. And you are a good friend. The thought that you would sacrifice yourself to protect Miss Hiller humbles me."

"Protect her from *you*, and you turned out to be no threat at all."

Every time she thought of it, she cringed. How could she have been so blind?

"But you did not know that. I could have been as evil as Swindon."

"Or as broke as Tarlington." He still could be, and she would have no way of discovering it. Except for her guardian angel. Whoever that was. Well, probably not in dun territory. Lady Bellamny would not have been happy about their plans if that were the case. She knew Meg's family too well to deceive them.

"Exactly. However, I am friends with your brother Kit and his circle. If there was something smoky about me, they would have cut the connection."

CHAPTER SIXTEEN

If only Kit was around to ask, Meg would feel immensely more secure.

For the present, she enjoyed the warmth of Damon's large body next to her. Despite her doubts, something about him made her feel safe and protected. "I suppose they would have." As they entered the town, the moon seemed to shine directly on the old Norman church spire. Candles were placed in the long windows, and sconces holding torches lit the front, illuminating the evergreen swag over the door. "It is lovely."

"Yes." His voice was soft and filled with wonder. "I wonder if the inside is as impressive as the outside."

Eager to see the rest of the church, they picked up their pace, entering immediately after Lord and Lady Bellamny. The stone floors were covered with small pine branches that gave off a wonderful aroma as they trod upon them. Fir swags decorated each pew and were topped by a candle. Framing the sanctuary was a wooden rood screen full of greenery.

Even at home, she had never seen a church so beautifully or lovingly decorated. "The townspeople must have worked all day on this."

Although the church was rapidly filling, the hush in the air had not broken, until one lone voice began to sing "Oh Come, All Ye Faithful." Meg's throat tightened and tears of joy started in her eyes.

Next to her, Damon asked, "Are you all right?"

She nodded, unable to speak for a moment. "It is my favorite."

After the first verse, the rest of the choir joined the soloist. Damon led them to places next to the Bellamnys at the front of the church.

When the song was finished, men carrying candles walked down the aisle, greeting those present and belting out "We Wish You a Merry Christmas."

Damon began to chuckle. "That is something I have never heard in church."

"Nor I." She grinned.

Suddenly the church was quiet again, and the vicar stood in the front, arms wide as if to enfold the entire congregation. "Welcome to all of you." His voice echoed through the church. "We are here this night to celebrate the birth of our Savior, Christ Jesus."

"He is magnificent." Damon was overcome with an urge to cheer. Before entering the army, he had attended hundreds, if not thousands, of church services. Even at Christmas, church was a place where jollity was left outside. He whispered to his godmother, "Where did you find him?"

"Grand, is he not?" She beamed toward the sanctuary. "My husband discovered him. He spent many years in the Holy Land before returning to England. You would not believe how happy he has made the town."

Damon thought he had a very good idea of what a difference the rector must have made. "You are fortunate that it will still be many years before I have a living to fill. I would steal him away from you in an instant."

She grinned. "I doubt you could. Unless you could prove you had a greater need for him. Fortunately for you, he is training a young clergyman."

Another carol had begun as he turned from his godmother, who had joined in the singing, to Meg, who was still staring around the nave. "How would you like a clergyman like this one?"

Her eyes were bright as she smiled. "I doubt there is another like him."

As usual, the readings consisted of the gospel versions of Christ's birth. The sermon was a short reminder of Jesus's love for mankind, and mankind's responsibility to love one another. After communion, the congregation rose while singing "While Shepherds Watched," and everyone filed out the door, then headed toward the Bellamnys' house.

Miss Hiller and Throughgood walked beside Meg and Damon.

"Why are they going to Lady Bellamny's house and not to Grantville?" Miss Hiller asked.

"The earldom does not own the living," Throughgood said. "Which as far as I can see was an excellent happen-so. I can't see my uncle choosing a rector like that one. Best sermon I've heard in years."

"I agree," Damon said. Short but poignant. A model for all sermons. "What did you think, Meg?"

"I enjoyed it very much indeed. Did you notice that there was a feeling of peace as well as the celebration of the birth?"

"I did." This was how Christmas should be. As she strolled beside him, he did not sense the tension that had been present in her before. Whether it was their kisses, the like of which he had never before experienced, or finding out about her friend's betrothal, or, perhaps, his offer of marriage, she was more relaxed and happier than he had seen her in a while. He would not delude himself into thinking he had won her heart, but the path had just become clearer.

Men carried torches, lighting the way to Lady Bellamny's house. Children ran back and forth, catching candy and coins that were thrown to them. He took out his purse and tossed coins to the children as well. It truly was like they were celebrating a birthday.

Even with the torches, the path was dark. Damon had already kept Meg from stumbling several times. On her other side, Amanda linked her arm with Meg's so that the four of them were connected. If she married Damon, there would be frequent opportunities for her to spend time with her friend. If only he did not require her to love him.

"If he hasn't done so already," Amanda whispered, "make sure Lord Hawksworth gives you kissing lessons." She giggled happily. "They are quite enjoyable."

"Kissing lessons?" Meg was at a loss. She and Damon had already kissed.

"Mm-hmm. Ask him. He will know." Amanda dropped Meg's arm and turned to give Chuffy her complete attention.

She supposed there would be no harm in asking him. They were betrothed, after a fashion, and she agreed, kissing had been quite enjoyable. Yet would he take that as a sign she was falling in love with him?

They climbed the shallow steps and entered the house. The relative quiet of the night gave way to the din of at least a hundred people piling into the hall. Large wooden half-barrels had been set up with apples floating in them, and the wassail bowl was steaming. Long tables covered with snowy-white linen were groaning under platters of food. In the massive fireplace, the Yule log was burning, and the scent of fresh pine competed with the scents of apples, Christmas baking, and food.

Under one of the kissing balls, a young couple embraced. The woman's blush was as red as the silk ribbon holding the ball.

Footmen stood at the ready to help the houseguests with their outer garments, but Damon insisted on removing Meg's cloak. A tantalizing shiver raced down her spine as he pressed his lips lightly to her neck. "I filched one of the kissing balls," he said.

She must be going mad to even think of wanting to know. "Where did you put it?"

He stuck his hand into his waistcoat pocket and pulled out several berries that were definitely the worse for wear. "Guess."

"Devil." She tried and failed to sound stern; however, she did manage arch. "Are there any left?"

"Come with me and we'll find out." No man had ever sounded so seductive.

She should not allow him to steer her out of the crowd of people playing bob apple, singing carols, and drinking wassail. She should not want him to do it. But the thought of his warm mouth on hers caused her lips to tingle, and there might be kissing lessons. "We cannot simply disappear."

"Can we not?" He made a point of glancing around the hall and into the drawing room, whose doors had been thrown wide open. "Even Throughgood and Miss Hiller have made themselves scarce."

Probably for more kissing lessons.

Damon had a point. There were so many people milling around, their disappearance would hardly be noticed. And she *had* promised to give him a chance. "I believe I need kissing lessons."

He cocked his head at her for a moment, then the corners of his lips curled up in a wicked smile. "And I would be happy to oblige you."

Meg took his hand and led him down the corridor past the music room, where the piano was already in use, to a parlor next to it where no one would see them leave. When they had reached the terrace, she turned to face him, and his arms closed around her. She breathed in, entranced by the scent of fresh air, lavender, and his own musk. His scent.

She leaned her head back and caught his gaze. "Where do we start?"

"Lesson one." He bent his head, pressing his lips to the corner of her mouth. "Savor."

As if he had nothing else to do in this lifetime or the next, he moved his hot lips slowly along hers, stopping every so often to nibble her bottom lip. She wrapped her arms around his neck and pressed against him, returning his caresses.

He groaned, and she wanted to crow with satisfaction. "I take it that means I'm learning."

"You are an amazingly adept pupil." He cupped her face. "Lesson two. Unite."

The tip of his tongue trailed lazily along the seam of her lips, urging them open. Meg sighed with pleasure and did as he requested. Damon's tongue slid sinuously into her mouth, tangling with hers. Although the thinnest thread would not fit between them, she tried to get closer. Then remembered that she could enter his mouth as well, and it was wonderfully pleasurable. Languorously, she stroked his tongue with hers, savoring his taste.

Unity.

It would almost be worth it to marry him for his kisses alone. But he wanted love. Perhaps passion could lead to love. Or did passion spring from love?

He broke their kiss, leaving her bereft. "You are a fast learner."

Not ready to stop, she asked, "What is next?"

"That is for your subsequent lesson. Someone is coming." He reached up, plucked berries from the kissing ball, and handed two to her. "This is a joint endeavor. You should be rewarded, as well."

"Hawksworth, Miss Featherton." Smithson leered drunkenly at Meg. Damon drew her next to his side. If the lecher wasn't careful, he would find himself on the ground.

"Let's have a Christmas kiss." Smithson reached out for Meg. The second before he touched her, Damon rammed his fist into the cur's jaw, and the man crumpled on the stone pavers.

He waited for Meg to scream or try to break away from him; instead, in a matter-of-fact tone she said, "He is thoroughly in his cups. Excellent flush hit."

Bringing her with him, he leaned against the wall and started to laugh. "That was the one reaction I did not expect."

"I have brothers," she said, chagrined. "Kit would, of course, never have engaged in pugilism around me, but my younger brothers are not so circumspect. A few times I was called to witness their prowess. What they really wanted to do was impress me with their knowledge of the sport."

He could not imagine her elder brother allowing that for long. Until he married, he was known as Mr. Perfect. "What did Kit have to say about that?"

She shrugged. "The boys were given a strict lecture and some punishment I was not privy to."

Smithson groaned, but didn't move.

"I suggest we take our leave before he comes around." Damon pressed his lips to hers, urging her to practice what she had just learned. After a few moments, Smithson moaned, and Damon lifted his head. "You should know I am not fond of the idea of another man kissing you."

She stared up at him, widening her eyes, and teased, "Not even Lord Bellamny or Sir Randolph?"

He lowered his brows at her. "Even them, but I will make allowances."

"Hmm, I'm not sure I care for your possessiveness." This time her tone was serious.

"What I meant was"—he did not want to argue with her now—"unlike Smithson and many men in the *ton*, I will not share my wife."

She tucked her arm in his, turning them toward the door. "If I *do* marry, I would not share my husband. I suppose that makes me no better than you."

Before entering the house, he wrapped his arms around her again, wanting to simply say *I love you*. However, that indulgence would leave her without a response, which would make for an unnecessary awkwardness between them. And leave him scrambling to come about.

Instead, he kissed her deeply, wishing they could remain here, or better yet, repair to his chamber. "Merry Christmas, Meg."

She pulled his head down so that their lips touched once more. "Merry Christmas, Damon."

He wanted her. If he were not at his godmother's home, if she were not an innocent, and if the damned house were not filled to the brim with people, he would drag her upstairs to his room and ravish her. But for now he would have to settle for plundering her warm mouth. Through their clothing he could feel the tattoo her heart was beating, keeping time with his. Damon wanted to taste every bit of her. He traced her ear with his tongue as he stroked the long line of her back, taking care to stop just above her tempting bottom. She leaned her head to one side, giving him access to her neck. It would be the work of a moment to free her breasts. Instead he dipped his tongue between her ivory slopes, taking care not to disturb the neckline of her gown. Her fingers tangled in his hair, as she moaned and made all the little sounds that drove a man mad. She was beautiful and passionate, and not yet in love with him.

Her breathing was ragged as he slowly lifted his head. "We had better stop."

Meg blinked slowly as she stared at him, her eyes glazed with passion. "I need a moment."

"We should stroll to the end of the terrace and back." By then the cold air would have made both of them more presentable. Fortunately the terrace was long.

Meg wanted Damon. She had never been as attuned to her body and its desires as she was now. Her breasts ached for him to touch them. Even without touching her lips, she knew they would be puffy. If only passion were love, she would marry him. For the first time, she understood how a lady could allow herself to be led to ruin, and even encourage it. Yet somehow she knew Damon would not harm her in any way. His honor was every bit as strong as her father's or Kit's. Unfortunately, that was not enough.

By the time she and Damon returned to the parlor door, she felt as if she could enter the house and no one would know what had gone on between them. Normally, she loved the Christmas revels, but tonight she wished Damon and she could have remained on the terrace, where the music and laughter were not so loud. More than anything, she wanted time to know him better. Learn what his views were, and if she could trust him enough to allow herself to fall in love again. That, she was sure, could only come by spending time alone with him.

She had met and been courted by her other two suitors during the Season. Spent time with them only during social events and walks or rides in the Park. Perhaps that was the reason she had not seen how false they were. She would not make the same mistake again. Yet how to find the time? Even at one and twenty, she was closely chaperoned. Sneaking out for kisses was one thing, but she would require much more time with Damon than that. Somehow she would find a way.

As they entered the house, he twined his arm with hers. A clock chimed one, and they slipped into the music room, joining in the last two verses of "Good King Wenceslas" before making their way into the hall.

"Are you hungry?" Damon asked as they passed one of the younger maids trying to catch an apple stem between her teeth.

"Famished. Dinner seems so long ago." Even with the crowd, there was still a great amount of food still on the tables. "Look, there is plum pudding with sauce. Now I know why it was not served at dinner."

He picked up two plates. He filled one with mince pie, plum pudding, and candied fruits. The other he used for the savory dishes. Meg hailed a footman, who found them a place to sit and gave them a bottle of wine and glasses.

She took a bite of the pudding, savoring the combination of fruit, wine, and spices. "How does your family celebrate Christmas?"

"With great pomp and very little frivolity." Damon's tone was dry as tinder. "My father believes that it is a holy day and not to be sullied."

"Oh dear." That sounded horrible. Fortunately, he did not seem to agree with his father. "How do you like to spend it?"

His crooked grin gave him such a boyish look, Meg wanted to kiss him again. "As far away from my father as possible."

She cast her gaze to the ceiling. "I should have asked, how *would* you like to spend the holiday?"

"This"—he waved his hand—"has a great deal to recommend it."

"My family does something in the same vein, but not nearly as lavishly. I think our vicar would faint in horror if he saw the church service. This time of year he is very fond of reminding the congregation of their Christian duty."

"My father would have apoplexy if anyone suggested servants partake in a fest."

Sir Randolph and Lady Culpepper strolled by, arm in arm, stopping under a nearby kissing ball to share an embrace. Meg thought back to the day at the inn when she had rejected the idea of love and passion in a marriage.

"I think the Culpeppers are collecting berries," Damon said. "This is the second one I've seen them under. It's a lucky thing we have our own."

She could feel the heat in her cheeks and ate a piece of mince pie rather than answer. Yet the fact that he had saved one out warmed her in a way she would not have thought possible only a few hours ago.

Just as they had finished eating, Lord Bellamny came over to them. "Hawksworth, I am claiming a host's right to kiss this lovely lady under the mistletoe."

Damon held her chair. "I suppose I cannot object?"

"Not at all." The older man grinned.

He pecked her lightly on the cheek, then Sir Randolph wanted a kiss as well, and Lady Culpepper coaxed Damon under the kissing ball.

The next thing Meg knew, Damon twirled Lady Bellamny under the kissing ball and gave her a loud smack on the lips. "Thank you."

Tears filled the lady's eyes as she patted him on the cheek. "You were always a good boy. It is a sin that stubborn old goat cannot see it."

He hugged her briefly but said nothing.

There was definitely a great deal Meg must discover about Lord Hawksworth, yet his godmother's real affection for him made her breathe a little easier.

An hour later, Damon escorted Meg to her chamber. "Will you meet me for breakfast before anyone else comes down?"

"Gladly, but will there be any food?"

He glanced around as if he did not want anyone to hear him, then bent his head. "I'll have you know, I am held to be an extremely charming gentleman."

"And how is that going to get us fed before everyone else?"

"Meet me and you'll see."

"Very well. I shall see you at nine o'clock." She waited, wanting him to kiss her once more. Even if it was in an ill-advised place.

He stepped back. "Pleasant dreams."

Apparently he was more circumspect than she had thought. If only she knew how she felt about that. "Good night, Damon."

CHAPTER SEVENTEEN

Christmas Day dawned clear and cold. Damon stood at the window, breathing in the crisp air. The sun was just coming up, promising another lovely day. Yet a ridge of clouds appeared to be gathering in the west, which would need watching. He hoped snow would not delay to-morrow's journey to Meg's home.

At eight thirty, Damon went down the servants' stairs to the kitchen. An older woman wearing an apron stood in front of the closed stove, issuing orders like a sergeant as she stirred a pot.

Two maids ran around setting bowls and plates on the massive, thick wooden table set in the middle of the room. He had almost reached the cook when one of them looked up. Shaking his head, he placed one finger on his lips.

A second later, he slid his arms around the woman who had befriended an angry and confused boy. "Happy Christmas, Millie."

A spoon wacked his fingers and he jumped back. "That hurt!"

"So it should have, my lord. How many times do I have to tell you that gentlemen don't come down to the kitchen?" She turned and a broad smile shone on her cheery, round face. "But since you're here, Merry Christmas to you. I heard you were, and made your favorite apple bread."

He handed her a bag of candied almonds. The first time he'd given them to her, he had been on leave from Spain. "I brought these just for you."

She took the package, placing them in a capacious pocket in her apron. "I haven't had these since the last time you were here, and much too long it's been." She raised her spoon as if to hit him again. "Now what are you doing down here in my kitchen?"

"Aside from seeing one of my favorite people?" He grinned, remaining out of spoon's reach. "I have a favor to ask. There is a lady whom I have invited to join me for breakfast at nine. Would you mind finding us something to eat?"

"Suky," she called to the girl cutting bread, "let one of the footmen know he'll be needed early." Once the girl had gone off, Millie turned to him. "I'll send up your apple bread, toast, baked eggs won't take long, and ham, unless you prefer beef."

"Ham is wonderful. Thank you."

"Be off with you now, or I'll smack the other hand."

Damon bowed, retraced the steps to his chamber, then to the main staircase, and lounged against the wall, waiting for Meg. After what seemed like a lifetime, she emerged from the corridor. "Merry Christmas." Not daring to kiss her in such a public setting, he settled for caressing her with his gaze. "You look beautiful. Green becomes you."

She blushed, making her appear as if she had just come in from outside. "Happy Christmas to you, sir. Thank you. Your red waistcoat is very festive."

He escorted her to the breakfast room. "I fully intend to celebrate all twelve days of Christmas. Alas, I failed to bring gifts for each day."

She paused and frowned for a moment, then smiled. "Just as well. I did not come prepared."

They entered the breakfast room to find the dishes Millie had promised already on the sideboard.

A footman stood from where he was tending the fire. "Happy Christmas, miss, my lord. May I get you coffee, tea, or hot chocolate?"

"Tea," Meg said at the same time Damon replied, "Coffee."

She laughed. "It seems a pot of each is in order." Moving to the sideboard, she surveyed the offerings. "Very impressive, my lord. How did you manage this?"

"I bribed the cook with candied almonds."

"She must like them a great deal."

"Try some of this. It is apple bread." He leaned over and whispered, "She makes it just for me."

"I did not know you had spent so much time here."

"Not as much as I wanted to. My father decided Lady Bellamny was a bad influence and curtailed my visits . . . when he could. There was more than one school holiday when I told him I was off on a trip and came here instead."

"Is your father so very bad?"

Absently, he filled their plates, setting them on the table. "I told you he doesn't like me. For a long time I tried to find a way to make him love me, but it was useless. He lavished all his attention on my half-brothers and -sisters. Lord Bellamny became the father to me my own was not."

"I'm glad to see you did not take your disappointment out on the other children."

The coffee had come, and he stopped in the middle of pouring a cup. "How did you know?"

She grinned. "You bought Christmas presents for them. You also seem fond of your step-mother."

He watched as Meg put two lumps of sugar and milk in her tea. "Catherine. As I said, she has always treated me as one of her own."

"Could she not have spoken to your father about his treatment of you?"

"Catherine is a warm, kind, gentle lady, not a tigress. She was there to dry my tears, but she would never gainsay my father."

Meg had never heard Damon speak in such a forlorn tone. And how horrible for a boy to have been rejected by his father. She could not imagine for an instant her father treating any of her brothers and sisters badly. If he had, Mama would have had a great deal to say about it. That must be the reason Damon was so intent on a love match. "What was your mother like?"

"I was only seven years old when she died. Other than that she had dark hair and eyes and was beautiful, I don't remember much about her. Mostly an impression of laughter and movement. With me she was always happy and laughing, but she was never still. I don't think my parents got along well. I remember her arguing with my father a great deal." He gave a slight grin. "She was a tigress. She was also a Greek princess."

"A princess? How fantastical." Meg had thought that it was due to being a duke's heir that he carried himself with a haughtiness that had been bred into him. Yet he had not been treated like any duke's firstborn she had ever known. Having royal blood was most likely the reason he had such an air of command.

His eyes twinkled with mirth. "I even have a title through her. Unfortunately, a vast number of my perfectly amiable cousins would have to die before I would be eligible to become the king."

She was glad to see him happy again, and decided this was a better subject for the present than his father. She was about to ask another question when two fashionably dressed elderly ladies swept into the breakfast room, bringing the scent of winter air with them.

"Grandmamma! I did not expect you until later." Meg jumped up from her chair and rushed to hug both ladies. "Your Grace. I'm so glad to see you. I must introduce you to Lord Hawksworth. Damon, my grandmother, the Dowager Viscountess Featherton, and Her Grace, the Dowager Duchess of Bridgewater. We are..." She glanced back at him.

He had already risen and was bowing. "Unofficially betrothed. We agreed I should speak to Meg's father first. A pleasure to meet you."

Her grandmother curtseyed, beaming at Meg and Damon. "What an excellent Christmas present."

Now she was going to have to spoil the announcement. "It is a bit more complicated than that."

The duchess grunted. "You love him, he loves you. You are both eligible *partis*. What can be the matter?"

"Well..." Feeling like a little girl attempting to explain something she had done wrong, Meg rubbed a damp hand down her skirts. What she had agreed to was unusual, but not wrong. After all, she did like him, and she truly adored his kisses. "I'm not sure if I can fall in love again, so Lord Hawksworth is giving me time to find out."

"Oh." Her grandmother's lips formed a perfect O. "In that case, you should spend more time together."

Meg wanted to roll her eyes and tell Grandmamma that was what they had been trying to do when she arrived. "Our thoughts exactly."

"We shall depart after dinner," the duchess announced, thumping her silver-headed malacca cane. "Hawksworth, you will leave a few minutes before and meet us at the end of the drive. For the present, we shall break our fast."

She turned to the footman. "More tea and fresh toast, please."

So much for having time alone with Damon.

He held her chair for her as she resumed her seat, and whispered, "Do you have any idea what they are up to?"

She wished she knew which direction his thoughts were going. The older ladies, who had taken places at the opposite end of the long table were in close conversation and unlikely to hear her hushed discussion with Damon. "Joining us for breakfast?"

"But is that all?"

"What else could they be about?" She was astonished at the thought that her grandmother could have any scheming purpose in mind. "Grandmamma is the sweetest person I know. Everyone loves her. Mama is the only one who sometimes is out of patience with her, but that is because she thinks Grandmamma should do more charity work." Which Meg did not quite understand, but she had heard her mother tell Grandmamma that, last spring around the time they discovered Kit had wed Mary. "The duchess may give the impression of being gruff, but she is really very nice. My grandmother and the duchesss have been dearest friends since they were girls." Damon still looked unconvinced, so she continued. "They are two elderly ladies. What could they possibly have to scheme about?"

He grunted, but did not otherwise respond.

During the meal, Lucinda, with Constance's occasional assistance, ferreted as much information as she could from Meg and Hawksworth. They appeared to be extremely comfortable in one another's company. He hovered over her, looking completely besotted. For Meg's part, she appeared to be learning as much about him as she could. A friendship had definitely formed, and with just a little help, Lucinda was certain that her granddaughter could fall in love with him.

Less than an hour later, Lucinda and Constance were ensconced in a cozy parlor situated between their bedchambers, listening to Almeria tell them what had been occurring.

"... And I am quite sure they were taking advantage of a kissing ball I found hanging from one of the torch sconces on the terrace." She gave them a knowing look. "Very few of the berries were left."

"Passion and friendship," Lucinda remarked. "How much time have they spent together?"

"Hawksworth has made a point of always being where she is. At times he reminds me of a large, dangerous beast, ready to strike out at anyone who would offend her. According to my cook, he planned a breakfast for two this morning."

"And we interrupted." Constance's lips formed a *moue*. "I thought that might be the case. I have a plan that will allow them to spend a great deal more time together."

Constance and Lucinda had been her friends for so long, Almeria knew what her friend was thinking. "Broken traces near the Cross and Shield Inn. Perfect."

* * *

"Did you find the handkerchiefs?" Meg tied the bow of her bonnet beneath her ear.

Hendricks handed Meg her gloves. "I tied them up with a bit of red ribbon and put them in your reticule."

She had bought them as a present for Kit, but could always buy more. She would not have liked for Damon to give her a Christmas gift, as he had hinted earlier, and not have one for him. She only wished she'd had time to embroider something on them. A little frisson of excitement passed through her as she wondered what his present to her would be and when he would choose to give it to her.

"Better hurry or you'll be late."

Once again, Lady Bellamny had decided they would all walk to church. Yet even if she was tardy, she knew Damon would be waiting for her. Come to think of it, he had been, ever since he had arrived. He'd even protected her from Smithson—not a difficult task, but proof that Damon would not allow anyone to harm her. She was beginning to get the feeling that he was more warrior than sophisticated gentleman of the *ton*.

Fortunately, she was not quite the last guest to arrive in the hall. Neither of the Smithsons were present yet.

Lord Bellamny held his arm out to his lady. "We may depart now."

Damon had already tucked Meg's hand in the crook of his arm. "To keep it warm."

"Naturally." She smiled to herself, clutching the inside of her large muff with her other hand. "Where are Lord and Lady Smithson?"

"Confined to their quarters until the gentleman, a term one must apply loosely to him, is well enough to travel."

"Surely, you did not tell Lady Bellamny what happened last night?"

"I?" He raised one black brow in surprise. "Let me assure you, I do not need to seek my godmother's protection."

Chastened, Meg replied, "Of course not. If not that, what did occur?"

"I really don't know. However, I do not think they will be missed."

She still did not understand why the Smithsons had been invited. "I am excited about the service. I wonder what he will do to-day."

"I appear to be bereft of information this morning. I can only say that I was warned to bring coins."

They had reached the outskirts of the town and were not far from the church, when the party came to a halt. Slowly, the crowd attempting to enter the church allowed them through.

Fresh candles had been lit on the pews, and even though Meg could see her breath, the atmosphere was warm. Lord and Lady Bellamny led them to the manger at the front of the church, which now held a couple and an infant. He placed a purse in the basket set off to the side, and the other gentlemen followed suit.

When they reached their pew, Lady Bellamny whispered, "The money will go to the needy families in the area and to the school. We have found that when the townspeople contribute to the school, they are more likely to send their children."

"Where did the idea of the figures in the manger come from?"

She shrugged. "Southern Europe, I believe."

"It is common in Spain and Portugal," Damon added. "As well as Greece."

Meg watched as even the youngest boy placed a coin in the basket. "I wish my father would find a rector like this one."

"Lady Bellamny told me that he is taking on a cleric. Someday I'll be in a position to grant a living to one of his acolytes." Frustration infused his voice. "However, that is not likely to be soon."

Meg could well understand his annoyance. Not that she thought he wished for his father's death, but having no occupation was unhealthy, and led to dissipation. She did not know how peers and other gentlemen of property could waste so much of it on gambling and other pursuits. "What will you do until you come into the title?"

"That depends." His lips twisted wryly.

Heat rose up her neck. Naturally, what he would do if he were single was not the same as if he wed. Yet surely if she could not love him, he would marry some other lady. He moved his hand over hers, engulfing it, and the sudden thought that she might lose his attentions disturbed her more than she liked.

CHAPTER EIGHTEEN

Damon held Meg's hand throughout the service, and began to feel as if the tide was turning in his favor. To a man used to action, his slow progress with her had been excruciating. This was the very reason soldiers hated sieges.

After the service, an icy breeze quickened their steps back to the house. He scanned the horizon, studying the cloud formation that appeared to have strengthened and darkened the sky. If they departed immediately after dinner, as the duchess had said they would, the worsening weather might miss them.

Until then, he would remain by Meg's side and make as much progress as he could.

By the time they reached the staircase, they had outstripped the rest of their party. "Meet me back here after you have shed your outer garments. I have something I wish to give you."

To his astonishment, she went up on tiptoe and kissed him lightly on the lips. "I won't be long."

He rounded the corner into the corridor where his bedroom was located and bumped into Smithson. "Still here?"

The other man scowled. "We shall depart after dinner, which we have been instructed to take in our chamber. I take it everyone knows?"

"It is a small house party," Damon said, not wanting to be drawn into a discussion.

"It's all that stupid bitch's fault," Smithson said, slurring his words.

Damon's hands clenched. The cur had damn well better not be talking about Meg. Keeping a tight rein on his temper, he raised his brows. "Excuse me?"

"My wife." The man raked a hand through his already disordered hair. "Tried to pay a groom to swive her, and Lady Bellamny found out."

Bloody hell. Damon was just glad he was not around when his godmother had been told. He said the only thing that came to mind. "Indeed."

"I'll never get my great-aunt's money now." Smithson looked up at Damon, hope in his eyes, and Damon prayed he wasn't going to be asked to do what the groom would not. "Don't happen to have a bottle of something in your room, do you?"

"I believe I do." He shook out one fist, almost feeling sorry for the man.

"Thank you." Smithson trotted after him down the corridor. "Word of advice, be careful which family you marry into. Thought because she was a virgin when I had her that she could be trusted. In the blood though."

"Bad luck." When they reached his room, Damon gave a bottle of brandy to the man. "I must leave you now. I am due to depart myself."

Smithson wobbled a bit. "Must write to Tarlington. Promised him my help."

What the devil? "Tarlington? I did not know you were friends."

"Since Cambridge." The man's overly bright eyes fixed on Damon's face. "In dun territory, you know."

"I thought he had his eye on some American heiress."

"Fool took his mistress and brats with him to Paris, and the girl found him out. Back here now." Smithson held up the bottle. "Thank you for this. Any time I can do you a turn, let me know." He stumbled down the corridor and Damon heard a door open and shut.

He was not at all pleased to hear Meg's last suitor was back in England. Fortunately, by the time she saw Tarlington again, she would be Damon's wife.

He stripped off his gloves and greatcoat, took Meg's gift out of the desk drawer, and arrived at the stairs as she emerged from her wing.

He held his breath as he gave her the package of green paper tied with silver ribbon. "I thought you might like these."

She carefully untied the ribbon and laid open the wrapping. "Damon, thank you. The combs are beautiful."

"Garnets." Even to him his voice sounded gruff. He had never bought a woman such a trumpery gift. Then again, he had never bought a gift for a lady. Soon, if fate was kind, he would buy her rubies fit for a duchess, and emeralds to match the gown she wore.

Meg smiled, and he let the breath out. "I know. Wait here. I'm going to have my maid put them in my hair." She took three steps, stopped, and turned. "Perhaps you would like to do it?"

As much as he wanted to, he had never done anything with a woman's hair except take it down. "I'm not much of a hand at dressing a lady's hair."

She walked back to him. "There are pins in it as well. Simply take out one of the combs and replace it with one of yours. Then do the same with the other one. I will help hold my hair."

To touch her shiny tresses was heaven. He couldn't stop himself from twisting one of her thick, silky curls around his finger as he removed the comb. He half expected the mass of hair to fall down around her shoulders, where he would like to see it. "Exquisite."

When he trailed the back of his hand down her long, swanlike neck, she sucked in a breath. Meg's reaction was all he could have wished for. He toyed with the idea of kissing her neck, but he would not have her trapped into marriage with him.

She turned and reached into her reticule. "I have something for you as well. It is not nearly as fine as your gift."

He took the handkerchiefs that had been meant for her brother, doing his best to appear happy to receive them. Then again, that wasn't really fair to her. At the time of the fair, she had no idea he was interested in her, and she was trying to protect her friend from him. Next year she would select a gift just for him. "Thank you. I am always in need of more handkerchiefs."

Something in his voice must have called to her. She lifted her eyes, searching his face. Her fine dark brows drew together for a few moments and he wished he knew what she saw.

The front door opened. A rush of cold air rose up the steps, causing her to shiver. If only he could take her in his arms, but Lady Bellamny's voice from below put paid to any amorous desires.

"Will you wait here while I put your gift in my room?"

She gave a curt nod. "Gladly."

"I won't be long." He strode off.

Before turning the corner to his chambers, he glanced behind him to make sure she was still there. She grinned, and Damon knew he could never let her leave him.

There was a way to make Meg love him, and he would find it.

Meg wanted to kick herself. Damon knew she had bought the handkerchiefs for her brother. He had been there when she made the purchase. Unfortunately, she had nothing else suitable for a gentleman, and what would she have got him? It had been a large fair; if she had been thinking of him at all, she could have found something. She remembered when they were at the stall where she had admired the combs. He must have bought them for her while she had been looking at the ribbons for her sister.

Devious man. A pleasant glow started to spread through her breast as she touched the combs. But devious in a good way.

"You must be having a *very* good Christmas," Daphne said as she and her husband climbed the stairs.

Meg started, not understanding.

"Your smile," her friend said. "It is radiant."

Lord Bellamny winked at her as he passed. She had never been winked at in her life. "Merry Christmas, Miss Featherton."

Damon joined her as Lady Culpepper reached the landing. She said nothing, but gave them another knowing look.

Once the rest of the guests had passed, Damon took her hand. "Shall we repair to the drawing room until their return?"

"Yes." Meg curled her fingers around his large palm. "I hope they do not take too long."

"Why is that?" His tone was soft but guarded.

"We cannot depart until we have had dinner."

"Ah." He raised her hand to his lips, and tingles raced along her fingers. "Very true."

How had she been so dense not to have seen his attentions for what they were? If only Chuffy had not sent the flowers, she might have been more aware of Damon. Yet, if she had known his intent, she would not have spent so much time with him. After all, the only reason she had done that was to save Amanda.

In the drawing room, Damon handed Meg a glass of wine, and she took a sip.

Still, she did not understand why Chuffy would have sent her flowers. It was clear Amanda had been his interest from the start. Some piece of the puzzle was missing. If only Meg knew what it was.

"You are deep in thought." Damon took her wineglass from her hand, setting it on a nearby table. "Come with me for a moment."

Without waiting for her to reply, he opened the door and led her to where he had placed the kissing ball. There were only a few berries left.

"Not many, but enough," he said, drawing her into his arms.

His mouth touched hers, nibbling and licking his way from one corner to the other. Meg wrapped her arms around his neck, winding her fingers in his fine wavy hair, then opened her lips, inviting him in. Despite the cold, heat curled through her body as he continued to play, ignoring her craving. Finally she cupped both his cheeks, angled her head, and possessed his mouth, stroking his tongue with hers until their breaths were ragged.

He clutched her to him, his fingers kneading her back from nape to waist. If this continued, her legs were going to give out, and she would melt into him. To her surprise, she found she didn't care.

Voices broke through her haze of desire. If she continued to kiss him, they would be discovered and would have to marry, and she could have this all the time. But he needed to be loved.

Before she could act, he broke their kiss. "We should go back in."

"I suppose we must." Meg reached up, picking the rest of the berries. "I believe these are mine."

Damon barked a laugh. "I believe they are."

His eyes seemed darker, like the rich earth, as he gazed at her. Slowly, as if he did not wish to do it, he removed one hand from his cheek, then the other, kissing the center of her palms and closing her fingers around them. "Until we can be alone again."

Who knew when that would be? Not soon enough. They would have to wait until they were at her home, and probably another day or so after that.

She did not want to leave, but new voices joined the first ones she had heard. She took his palms and kissed them, curling her fingers around them. "I will count the minutes."

And she would. But was it for the right reasons?

Once again, Austin Smithson pulled a piece of Lady Bellamny's elegant pressed paper out of the drawer. He used a penknife to sharpen the tip of a quill. The familiar process calmed his agitated nerves. He really needn't have sharpened the pen. Like everything in the rest of the house, all the quill tips were in perfect condition and ready to be used. The knife slipped and blood welled from the shallow cut. He should know better than to use a knife when he was in his cups. He wrapped a handkerchief around his thumb, tied it off, and began to write.

> *My dear Tarlington,*
> *Sorry, old chap, but I've cocked it up. Lady Bellamny has politely, but firmly, asked us to take our leave.*
> *You might be interested to know that Miss Featherton will depart as well. She is traveling home with her grandmother.*
> *Yr servant,*
> *Smithson*

He poured too much sand on the paper, shook it off, and sealed it. He would send it by special messenger from the next coaching house he came across.

"Come, Carola." He shrugged into his greatcoat. "The coach is waiting."

"Are we going to Paris?" She perched a fashionable bonnet on her head.

"I did promise you that treat." Once they had arrived in London, he would make arrangements for her to live comfortably in France. After which he would travel to his estate and work on a way to get back in his great-aunt's good graces. With Carola not in England to create talk, that should be easy enough.

Almeria stepped into the overly warm parlor she had given to her friends. "You missed a stirring sermon."

"I have no doubt, but you know how the cold affects Constance. Even hot bricks in the pews cannot keep her warm enough. If only there was a way to heat churches." Lucinda glanced at the duchess, who was talking with her lady's maid. "We shall visit next summer."

"Trust me, it is not much warmer."

"I hear you are getting rid of the Smithsons." Constance had finished her discussion with her servant. "Not surprising. They are bad *ton*. Why did you invite them and what did they do?"

That same question had probably been on the tip of everyone's tongue, but Constance was the only one who would ask. Almeria sighed. "I did it as a favor to his great-aunt, Lady Bollingworth. She is quite elderly now and thought to leave her money to him, but she heard rumors about the way he and Lady Smithson conducted themselves. Well, mostly Lady Smithson. In any event, Lady Bollingworth knows that I will not put up with anyone bothering my servants, or anyone else, and asked if I would invite the couple." She pulled a face. "My master of stables went to my husband yesterday and told him Lady Smithson was attempting to pay a young groom to bed her. They will be leaving shortly."

"Such a shame," Lucinda said.

Almeria stared at her friend. She could not imagine why Lucinda would feel sorry for the couple. "In what way?"

"It is not as if she can help herself," Lucinda said in a patient tone. "Have you not noticed that there are some who suffer from uncontrollable lust? We turn our heads in the case of gentlemen, but ladies are made to suffer."

"Very true." Constance nodded. "Do you not remember Lady Elizabeth Wallingstone? Her parents had to ensure that some family member stayed close to her even when she was dancing. If not, she would whisper lewd invitations to her dance partner and attempt to make an assignation."

Almeria cast her mind back. There was something. "She was barred from Almack's."

"Of course she was," Constance said. "But not before she was betrothed to a Prussian duke."

"And her brother was allowed to chase everything in skirts." Lucinda pressed her lips together in disgust.

"Yes, yes, my dear," Almeria said soothingly. "It's unfair, but it is the way of the world and will never change. Now, what about Hawksworth and Meg?"

"I told him to pull up at the end of the drive," Constance said. "However, I have no opinion of young men in love doing what they are told. Perverse creatures that they are, they will do the exact opposite of what they should do. Therefore, I have instructed my maid to depart first, and block the drive."

Lucinda smiled smugly. "It appears the weather is on our side. I have been assured there will be snow. That will be even better than broken traces."

Almeria rose. "Before this scheme can take place, we must dine."

"Now that you mention it"—Lucinda followed suit—"I am quite peckish."

"Onward." Constance thumped her cane. "We'll have a wedding before the Season is out."

CHAPTER NINETEEN

Damon's palms burned with Meg's kisses. She had shocked him when she took his face in her hands and kissed him. With each exploration of her tongue, desire, lust, and love had speared through him. He doubted his cock had ever been as hard as it was now. And he had to stroll back into the drawing room with her on his arm, acting as if nothing had occurred. As long as the older ladies were not down yet, his problem might go away without notice. He didn't give himself a chance in hell of escaping either Lady Culpepper's or his godmother's sharp eyes.

What the devil had he been thinking, letting a kiss get so out of control? Again. On the other hand, kisses had never before incited such a hunger for a woman. He had certainly never wanted to lay another female on the cold flagstones and take her then and there.

Just thinking about Meg beneath him made him harder.

Down!

If only he could come up with an excuse to remain out in the cold, without Meg, for a few minutes, or figure out a way to hide his state. He glanced in the music room. It was empty. "Do you play the piano as well as you sing?"

She lifted her long, sooty lashes. "Why?"

"I thought we could sing a duet." That would give him an opportunity to sit behind something larger than his erection.

"Another Christmas carol?" Meg asked, making her way toward the door.

"Let's see what we find."

A few moments later they were looking over the sheet music.

"What about 'Scarborough Fair'? It is not a carol, but . . ." But he had wanted to sing it with her that first night and had been afraid he would scare her off.

"We will have a great deal of time to sing Christmas songs at my family's house. Besides, this is one of my favorites." She slid onto the bench, and he sat down next to her, setting the music where he could easily turn the pages.

"You start and I will come in on the second verse."

Meg slid a glance at him. The corners of her lips tipped up, making him want to kiss them again. She played the first chords, then began to sing.

> *"Are you going to Scarborough Fair?*
> *Parsley, sage, rosemary and thyme;*
> *Remember me to the one who lives there,*
> *For once she was a true love of mine."*

Damon was lost. Lost in the lovely sound of her voice. Lost in her eyes as she gazed at him. He forgot to turn the pages, but she did not need them. She played from her heart, and he prayed she was giving that organ to him.

> *"Love imposes impossible tasks,*
> *Parsley, sage, rosemary and thyme;*
> *Though not more than any heart asks,*
> *And I must know she's a true love of mine.*
>
> *"Dear, when thou has finished thy task,*
> *Parsley, sage, rosemary and thyme;*
> *Come to me, my hand for to ask,*
> *For thou then art a true love of mine."*

If they had not been interrupted by clapping, he would have proposed then and there. Yet her forehead wrinkled, as if a thought she had not had before came into her mind. Meg was either not in love with him yet, or she was not ready to admit it to herself, and either way she would have refused.

He stood, helping her rise. "Is it time to eat?"

Lady Bellamny's dark eyes studied them for a moment. "I believe it is."

As they strolled into the dining room, the scent of roasted goose made his mouth water. He bent his head to Meg's. "One year on Christmas Eve my unit was in the mountains on the border between Spain and France. We came across a French troop who looked almost as miserable as we were. One of their soldiers was leading a fat white goose. Their commander requested a truce. Since it was Christmas and our provisions were so low as to be almost nonexistent, I agreed."

Meg's eyes began to twinkle. "You wanted the goose."

"I would have laid myself bare for that goose. The French officer and I decided to pool our resources. It was quite generous of him, considering all we had were some dried beans and a few bottles of wine and brandy. It turned out that the soldier leading the goose had been a cook in training before being swept up into the army. We all went scrounging about and found nuts, some wild garlic, and a few other things. The cook made stuffing with the nuts and some bread. It was the best goose I've ever had."

"What happened afterward?"

"We went our separate ways. I was always thankful we never came across them again. It would have been a shame to have had to kill them."

Damon expected her to ask how he could have fought men who had shared their food, but that was the way of war. Instead she said, "War demands a great deal."

"Soldiers expect it. It is the innocents who suffer the most."

Lord Bellamny called them to attention, and the vicar rose. "Come let us bow our heads and give praise to the Lord for this bounty."

Damon held on to Meg's hand, praying not only for this dinner, but for the French soldiers who had shared theirs with the enemy.

After the vicar had finished, Meg shook out her serviette. "Do you ever wish you knew where they were?"

"Only if they are alive." He lifted his wineglass. "I very much hope the cook survived and is putting his talents to good use."

She shook her head, grinning. "Every time we speak of the war, you end the conversation with a jest."

"That, my love, is the only way to survive it." He touched his goblet to hers. "One must remember the good times. The best stories come from moments that were not funny at the time."

"That must be the reason most soldiers do not speak often of the war with those who were not there." Giving him a blinding smile, she toasted him as well. "To roast goose at Christmas. I am glad you are here now."

So was he. Glad he had survived and that he was here with such an extraordinary woman.

Their private toast prompted others at the table to begin toasting as well. Cries of "Merry Christmas!" filled the room, and Damon was happier than he had been in a very long time.

Meg was falling in love. Or she thought she might be. The feelings she had for Damon were unlike anything she had experienced with the other suitors. Frissons of pleasure raced through her when he touched her hand, or his shoulder brushed against her arm. She enjoyed being in his company. Even when she spoke to Lady Culpepper on his other side, he made some gesture, such as stroking her fingers, which let Meg know his focus was on her.

She had spent hours listening to her father and eldest brother discuss the needs of war veterans, but she had met very few. Only the officers who came from families who were part of the *haut ton*. Even then, a lady did not ask about the war, just as a gentleman would not speak of such things to a lady. Yet Damon did, because he wanted her to know who he was. That was more honesty than she had experienced from any gentleman lately. Especially one who was courting her. The need to know everything about him became more than a practicality. She was fascinated by his experiences, and simply by him, as a man.

Still, there was his restless energy that must be addressed. Damon had said boredom had led him to become a leader with the Dandy set, when he was nothing of the sort. Now he was pursuing her with the same determination, but what next? She was not so naïve to think she could occupy him completely until he came into his title. He needed an avocation. If only his father cared enough about Damon to train him and give him responsibilities, as her father was doing with Kit.

"Roast goose with chestnut stuffing. Which part do you like best?" Damon's question wrenched her from her thoughts.

"A bit of the thigh, if you would, please."

"Gladly." He placed two slices of goose meat on her plate and a spoon of stuffing. "That is my favorite as well."

Next came Brussels sprouts, potato puree, cod in a wine sauce, and small portions of various other dishes.

"Enough." She laughed. "I will never eat all of this, and we still have several courses to go."

His lips twisted, giving him a perplexed look. "I should have asked. Except it all smells so good I was sure you would like to taste it."

"It has a wonderful aroma, and I would love to partake of a small bit of each dish." Her stomach would burst if she ate everything he put on her plate. "Unfortunately, I am not that big an eater."

"I shall ask the cook to pack in a basket what you cannot eat. Then you can sample them later."

She wondered when she would have the time to eat the enormous amount of food he was sure to think necessary. It must stem from his experiences with hunger. Meg kept her tone light. "I can see you stealing lobster patties from a supper."

"If they were good." His eyes twinkled mischievously.

Even after all the meals they had taken together and the hints he had dropped, until to-day she'd had no idea how much sustenance meant to him. When he told her his Christmas story, she finally understood how close he and his men had been to starving. It was hard to imagine that English soldiers could have gone hungry, particularly when peers in the House of Lords complained about the amount of money being spent on the war, while at the same time giving money to Prinny to build his houses. A man of Damon's size would require a great deal to sustain his large frame.

She wondered how often he had gone without victuals. That, however, was a conversation for later, when they were alone. She applied herself to the dishes on her plate with more appetite than she'd had for months.

After dinner, Damon escorted her to the landing between the two wings. "I will probably not see you again until we are at your parents' house."

She had not thought of that before. Naturally, he would take his own coach, and she would ride with her grandmother and the duchess. Even if they were properly betrothed, she would not be allowed to make a journey of several hours alone with him in a closed carriage.

Suddenly, she did not want to leave. "I believe I will miss your company."

"I know I'll miss yours." Warmth lurked in his dark eyes, and he lifted her hands, placing them on either side of his face.

She wanted to close the distance between them. Slide her hands behind his neck. Kiss him until their breathing was ragged. Before she could do any of that, he drew her to him, and pressed his firm lips to hers, then stepped back. "Until we meet again."

He left, his long legs taking him away from her.

"Until we meet again," she murmured to herself.

By the time Meg reached her chamber, only one small trunk remained. Her traveling gown hung over the wardrobe door, waiting for her maid to return to help her change. Meg removed her slippers, one of the few items of clothing she could manage by herself. Padding to the dressing table, she lowered herself to the cushioned bench.

The kiss lingered in her mind. Damon had not even given her an opportunity to return his embrace. She had never met a gentleman like him before. Long before he had declared himself, he'd brashly intruded into her thoughts, where she had not wanted him.

Swindon and Tarlington paled in comparison. Tarlington did not even have the courage to claim the family he obviously loved, and Swindon, he was simply a coward, preying on women and hurting them for his own disgusting pleasure. Hawksworth had the courage to have fought in the war and still be able to laugh about some of his experiences. No. Damon was strong in ways none of her other suitors could have dreamed about.

The problem was not him, it was her. She was the one who had fallen in love with a monster like Swindon. Once more, dread crept up her spine at what might have been her fate with him.

Tarlington was much easier to understand. He was handsome, charming, and an excellent dancer. He had showered her with extravagant compliments and the attention she had craved so badly at the time. He spoke lovingly of his home, and mother, and sisters. Assuring her that she would love them as he loved her.

No. He never actually said that he loved me.

He'd loved many things *about* her. Her beauty, her wit, her courage, her determination. Although how he could have admired the last two traits was a mystery. They had never spoken of anything of substance. Not like she did with Damon. It was her fault she had mistaken what the man had meant. How pathetic of her. How easy he must have thought it was, making her fall in love with him.

And now she was falling in love again. Three men in less than one year. Was that even possible? Or was there something in her that desperately needed a gentleman to love and marry?

Meg gazed sternly at her reflection in the mirror as she removed first one of her earrings then the other.

You must be careful. Damon will wish to wed as soon as you declare your love for him. This time, you must be certain. He needs true love, not a silly girl's infatuation with love.

Unhooking her necklace, she placed it on the dressing table with the earrings. Perhaps she had not really been in love before. She had been horrified to find out about Swindon, and her heart had felt as if it was being torn into pieces when she had discovered about Tarlington's mistress. At the same time, she had given both of them up readily enough.

Would a woman in love behave in such a manner? Even after Lord Byron had repudiated her, Lady Caroline Lamb continued to love him, and her husband loved her though she loved another. Then again, her mother and grandmother had very little good to say about the three of them.

Perhaps Meg simply did not know what love was, and if that was the case, how would she recognize if she truly loved Damon?

Damon's coach came to an abrupt halt near the end of the Bellamnys' drive. What in the bloody hell was going on? He had already been delayed by dinner taking so long, then by farewells and promises to visit more often. He'd had to wait for Millie to send up another loaf of apple bread as well as a basket filled with food. That he truly appreciated. One never knew when the provisions would run short, or run out. There was a reason officers in the Peninsula went hare coursing, and it wasn't only for sport. There had been many a day when the supply wagons had failed to keep up with the troops.

He banged on the roof of his carriage. "Why have we stopped?"

"There's a coach in the road," his coachman replied in a laconic tone. "It ain't movin'."

"Devil a bit." Damon slammed open the door and jumped down. He would never make it to Meg's house at this rate. Lady Bellamny told him the duchess traveled as if Beelzebub himself were after her. Not to mention that she had a team, and he had only a pair. He would be lucky to arrive before the snow started.

He took in the conveyance that covered most of the drive. Large, black, and stacked with luggage. Three women and a man occupied the interior. He quickly strode the short distance between the two carriages.

"My lord."

He couldn't believe his ears. Damnation. "Hartwell." Without even trying, his voice was dangerously calm. "What are you doing in that coach?"

"I beg your pardon, my lord," an older woman said, pushing the window down. "Her grace said to remind you that she instructed you to remain here until she arrived."

For several seconds Damon was speechless. "That does not explain the presence of my valet."

The woman shrugged. "I just carry out my orders, sir. If you wish to know why her grace gave them, you will have to ask her."

He ignored her and focused on his valet. "Hartwell?"

The man flushed. "I—I was told the order came from you, my lord."

Damon counted to ten, then to twenty. He couldn't very well take his ire out on his servant when it was clear the dowager was at fault. Both dowagers he'd go bail and his godmother. They had most likely been the reason he had been delayed leaving the house. They were up to something. The question was what.

The duchess's dresser might not tell him anything, but one of the others might. He glanced up. The coach windows closed, the shades lowered, and he was left standing in the road. Bloody Lucifer. Obviously, he wasn't going to get any more information, and it was almost colder than the Spanish mountains in the dead of winter, and his freezing to death waiting for her grace to appear wouldn't help anyone. He climbed back in his carriage, grateful for the warmth of the hot bricks and his greatcoat. He hoped she had a care for the horses.

Not long later, the sound of horses roused him from a doze. Now he would find out what the hell was going on.

CHAPTER TWENTY

"Hawksworth," the Duchess of Bridgewater barked out as her massive traveling carriage came to a halt beside his much smaller conveyance. "Come get Meg. She will ride with you. There is not enough room for three in my coach."

Damon did not believe that for a moment, but was not about to argue. Having Meg with him for hours was more than he could have hoped for. More than he had dreamed possible.

He'd jumped down from his carriage and opened the door of the duchess's coach before the footman had stepped down from his perch. Lifting Meg out, he carried her to his carriage. The feel of her in his arms was all it took for lust to slam into him. Hours alone with her. No one would be around them. He could kiss her until . . . *Hell!*

"My lord, if you get in, I'll put the stairs away," his groom said.

"Thank you." Damon climbed into his coach and sat next to Meg on the forward-facing seat instead of opposite her, as he probably should have. He would simply control his urges. She would never know that all he wanted to do was extend the seat and lay her down on it. Although that would necessarily involve the removal of some of their clothing.

"Follow us," the duchess commanded as her conveyance started forward.

Her carriage moved forward, followed by his, then the baggage coach.

Meg removed her bonnet, and he put it on the overhead shelf next to his beaver hat. As much as he wanted her here, he did not trust the dowagers' motives. "I find it hard to believe that her grace's coach was too small for three."

"Would you rather I rode with them?" She widened her eyes and stared at him.

"No. God no." Damon wrapped his arms around Meg and kissed her. "I simply do not understand why she could not have told me her plans."

She settled herself against him. A warm bundle of female wrapped in fur. "I do not think either her grace or my grandmother believe it is necessary to advise anyone of their stratagems."

"Are there more?" he asked, almost afraid of the answer.

"I have no idea." One gloved hand fluttered airily. "The answer is either yes or no, and we have no control over it. I suggest we put their largess to good use."

It occurred to Damon he was being perverse. Here he had his beloved with him alone in a closed coach, and he was concerning himself with the schemes of two old ladies who obviously wished to assist him to the altar. "In that case, how do you wish to spend our time?"

Her lips curved. "You could give me more kissing lessons."

His gut clenched. That was exactly what he was afraid of. If they began kissing, he would be hard-pressed to stop with kisses. He already wanted her more than he had any other woman. He breathed, his nostrils filling with lavender, bergamot, and woman. Meg's scent. He could already imagine what she would smell like with the musk of arousal added to her already enticing mélange.

He would have to try to leave her hair untouched, but he could unfasten her gown and stays. He could kiss her neck and breasts. Discover if her nipples were pink, or rose, or brown. He could taste her and make her come in his arms.

He could damn well behave himself.

Grabbing a blanket from the bench across from him, he threw it over his lap.

"Or we could talk."

"Talk." His voice sounded rusty. He was lucky to be able to speak at all. Anything that kept his mouth off her was the best for now. "We can eat as well."

She let out a peal of unfettered laughter. "I take it the cook packed it for you?"

"Did I tell you I am one of her favorite people?" As long as he did not enter her kitchen, that is. "What would you like to discuss?"

"You."

"Me?" Damon sounded dubious and perhaps a little worried. "There is not much to know about me that you do not already know."

Meg seriously doubted that was true. He may think it, but that was only because he was not puffed up in his own consequence. "Yes, you. However, you may ask me any questions you like as well."

"I have one." He glanced down at her. His brown eyes probing as if he wished to know a great secret. "Why Throughgood?"

She twisted around so she could look Damon in the face without straining her neck. "I met him one evening. He was very nice. He struck me as uncomplicated, and I thought he might be easy to get along with. Then he sent me flowers."

"Sent you flowers?" Damon's black brows shot up.

"What is so surprising about that?" She tried not to be offended, but it was hard. Did he think gentlemen never sent her flowers or other trifles?

He was quiet for a few moments, as if his thoughts needed organizing. "They would not have been roses, would they?"

"Yes. How did you know?" She wondered if Chuffy had told Damon.

"Too clever by half," he mumbled. "The note was unsigned. What made you think they came from him?"

He had definitely been told. Yet if that was the case, why was he surprised? "The color of the livery. Blue and green. The Grantville livery was the only one that made sense."

"Blue and red." Damon's jaw ticked. "The livery was blue and red. Who told you otherwise?"

"One of our younger footmen. Why are you so upset?"

He raked his fingers through his hair, causing a curl to fall on his forehead. "Do you know if he has difficulty distinguishing between red and green?"

Meg thought back to that day when her mother had come into the library and Mama's strange comment. "He might have."

"Sweetheart, I sent you the flowers." He grimaced. "I wanted to pique your interest so that you would wish to discover the sender yourself. I knew you would not be able to resist the challenge. What I did not count on was your footman suffering from an eye disorder."

"Eye disorder? I do not understand."

"A man by the name of John Dalton documented a condition

where a man could not tell the difference between red and green. Two men in my first company, brothers, had the same problem."

She tried to speak, but nothing came out. After several moments, she managed to say faintly, "You wrote that lovely note."

He nodded. "Would it have made any difference between us if you had known?"

What would she have done? For one thing, she would not have focused on poor Chuffy. Amanda would not have had to hide her attraction for him. But Meg was already trying not to like Damon. If she had known... "I would never have allowed you near me." Damon scowled. "You do not understand."

He crossed his arms over his chest. "Why don't you tell me?"

His jaw firmed, and he had lost the warmth in his gaze. Oh dear. This was not a conversation she wanted to have, but he deserved to know the truth. "I was so hurt, betrayed if you will, and, as I told you before, I knew you were hiding something. If I had known of your interest, I would have thought that you would deceive me."

A moment later her huge muff was tossed to the floor, and she was enveloped in his strong, safe arms. "I did not know then what you had gone through. I knew Tarlington had left for France, but I thought you had merely tired of him."

She need not bother to ask who had told him. It had to have been Lady Bellamny. Pressing her cheek against Damon's muscular chest, she sighed, feeling that he would always protect her. No matter what threatened her, he would be there. But could she say the same?

He pressed a kiss to her head. "What do you wish to know about me?"

Even though she was loath to leave his embrace, she simply could not have a conversation talking into his chest. Meg moved back, reaching up to kiss him before regaining her original position. "You've told me about your family." She did wonder if his father was truly as horrible as he thought him to be. "What do you wish to do until you are a duke?"

His countenance told her nothing. "I told you before, that depends."

And at that time, she had agreed with him, but it wasn't true. "Very well, if we wed, what would you do?" His hot, sinful gaze caressed her, and she wanted to melt into him and lose herself in his kisses. "One cannot do that all the time."

His lips kicked up. "Do what?"

Oooh, she was going to make him pay for causing her to turn as red as a pickled beet. He had not even pretended it was an innocent question. "I am not entirely naïve. My sister-in-law told me some of what goes on between a man and a woman. She said that she had known nothing, and it had been extremely awkward and embarrassing."

Damon fought his grin. Meg was adorable when she was on her dignity. Not to mention that her heightened color made her even more beautiful than she already was. He would have to think of more ways to make her blush.

She was also intelligent and perceptive. Even if she loved him, she would not marry a wastrel. He did need something useful to occupy himself. His father was in good health, so it might be years before he was a duke. "What does your brother do?"

"I suppose you mean Kit."

Damon nodded. "It is an heir-in-waiting dilemma."

"He manages most of my father's estates, and he has one of his own as well. He and Papa discuss politics, and I know Kit has written at least two of my father's speeches for the Lords."

Damon was gobsmacked. Except for the times he spent with Lord Bellamny, when he caught glimpses of what it would have been like to have a man such as he for a father, Damon had a hard time imagining what it would be like to have a father who appreciated one's talents and encouraged them. "My father has never discussed anything with me, much less politics. That, however, might be a blessing. I do not think we would agree."

She drew her brows down as she considered his problem. "I am sure my father, or perhaps Lord Bellamny, would be happy to instruct you."

"As much as I care about his lordship, he is vastly more interested in his scientific endeavors than in estate management. As for your father, I'm not sure that your brother would like me intruding."

"He probably wouldn't mind at the moment." Her countenance lightened. "He is enjoying married life a great deal."

Damon would like to be enjoying married life as well, with Meg. "What do you think I should do?"

"Find a cause." Her answer was swift and sure. "There must be something you are passionate about."

"Other than pink silk neck-cloths?" He had meant it as a joke, but she cast him a gimlet look.

"Yes. What would you like to change?"

As much as he enjoyed being in the coach with Meg and would not trade places for the world, his frustration was growing. "The difficulty with that is that the things I do care about, I cannot do anything about. I am not a peer. My father would never consent to my running for the Commons. I don't even have my own house." That was it in a nutshell. The real reason for his dissatisfaction. He had no place he could call his own home. No servants that were not his father's. Recently he had felt like a piece on a chessboard, to be played at his father's will. Which was the reason he had not opened the letter he'd received from Catherine this morning. "The only property I own is in Greece."

Meg canted her head to one side, considering him for several moments. "Other than the allowance you receive from your father, do you have any money?"

He did. Quite a lot of it, actually. It had amused him to spend his allowance on things his father would not approve of. The majority of his funds were invested. But what that had to do with anything, he did not understand. "Yes."

She lifted one shoulder in an elegant shrug. "Then buy a house, or a small estate, or both, if you have the funds for it."

His mouth gaped open. He became aware of it when she placed one gloved finger under his chin and shut it for him. The idea had never occurred to him. "What would I do with more property? You would not believe the extent of the dukedom's holdings."

"Oh"—she smiled slowly, a knowing look on her face—"I think I might have a relatively good idea."

He remembered then that despite Viscount Featherton's rank, he was extremely well-off, and she had been raised around the duchess.

She gazed up at Damon, her earnest sapphire-blue eyes mesmerizing him, and took his hands in hers. "You need a place to call your own. To be able to do with what you wish. After you become a duke, you may sell the property or, oh, I don't know, do any number of things with it. You do not need a plan for that now. It is the present and immediate future you should look to."

He allowed the idea to sink into his brain. Houses of his own *would* solve many of his concerns. If his father would not allow him to take charge of any of the dukedom's estates, having one of his own was the perfect way for him to learn how to manage his holdings once he came into them. He did have ideas about farming and estate management and wished to experiment with new methods. On his own estate, he would not be required to have his father's or the steward's permission to implement them.

A town house of his own would enable him to hold political entertainments with people who held the same beliefs he did. He would have his own servants. Ones whose loyalties would be to him and not his father. He had no doubt at all that, with the exceptions of Hartwell and his groom, the other servants sent regular reports to the duke. It would be necessary for Damon to set up his own stables, but that was no hardship.

The solution was so utterly simple that he didn't understand why the devil he had never thought of it before. Had he been on his way to becoming nothing more than a worthless fribble?

"I'll do it," he said. "I shall write to—" Not his father's man of business. He would ask for a recommendation from a friend or perhaps Lord Featherton. Damon should do it soon before all the houses in Mayfair had been snapped up for the Season. He also should buy an estate at the same time so that he'd have time to make plans for spring planting and animal husbandry. "A land agent as soon as I find one and have him send me listings."

"I think my grandmother might know someone. She has begun searching for a house for one of her charities." Meg had never seen Damon so excited, and she became as eager for him to begin his plans as he seemed to be.

"I suppose anywhere in Mayfair would do for a town house."

She stared at him, unable to believe what he had just said. On the other hand, he had been away from England for a long time, and had never spent much time on the Town until recently. She brought up a mental image of Mayfair, which she knew as well as she knew her family's estate. They discussed streets that were suitable for the house of a future duke and those that were not.

He mentioned a street where one of his army friends leased a house, and Meg shook her head. "While that street may do very well for someone who is just up for the Season, it will not do for the heir to a dukedom."

In the end, he agreed that focusing his search in the areas of the squares was the best idea.

It turned out that he had a great many interests, most of them, unsurprisingly, having to do with the plight of the returned soldiers and their families. She was pleased that he agreed with her when it came to political, social, and estate issues. Never once did he make a comment that led her to believe he thought women were not intelligent or that he wanted anything less than a partnership with his wife.

Meg was involved in some charities that aided widows and orphans. "We always require more funds. The officers' widows are gently born, and the children must attend school."

"Is anything being done for the families of severely wounded officers and regular soldiers?" he asked, an idea clearly coming to him.

"Not that I know of. However, we could ask Lady Worthington. She began one of the charities I am a member of."

Damon turned his hands so that he was now holding Meg's. "Thank you."

A new, stronger rush of affection for him almost took her breath away. This was the type of feeling she should be having with a gentleman she might wed. She had learned more about him in the short time they had been traveling, than she ever would have attending balls and riding in the Park. More importantly, she liked what she was discovering, and the way he considered her opinions and accepted them or engaged in a reasonable debate when he disagreed.

They had closed the curtains against the cold, and she was surprised when the coach started to slow.

He glanced outside. "Just as I thought. The weather has caught us."

Snow was coming down in fat flakes so large she could almost see their patterns. And that was the only thing she could see from her side of the carriage. She turned, trying to look over his shoulder, but he was just too large. "Where are we?"

"Coming into an inn yard. It appears that the duchess has already sent someone inside."

She picked up her muff from where it had fallen. They would not be the only travelers stranded in the storm. "I hope they have room for us."

He gave one of his wry smiles. "I would not wager against her grace. She is more than a match for anyone of my acquaintance."

Meg had to agree. The only one she knew who had ever been able to change the duchess's mind was the former duke and Grandmamma. "She is a formidable woman."

"I would have said Tartar, but never to her face." He went back to his view out the window. A few moments later, he said, "She has prevailed."

He opened the door, and freezing air filled the space. He lifted her down, and soon they were in the entry-way of the well-kept and unexpectedly spacious inn.

She had missed the first part of the landlord's conversation, but heard him say, "Yes, Your Grace. With the exception of the common room, the entire inn is yours. But that shouldn't bother you, as it has a different entrance."

"What an interesting idea," Grandmamma said approvingly.

The landlord preened under Grandmamma's praise. "It was my wife's idea. It gives the ladies in our town a place for tea and luncheon." After giving directions to two young men who resembled the landlord greatly, he continued. "Dinner will be served at five o'clock, unless you'd like it at a different time."

"Five is perfect." Grandmamma graced the man with one of her charming smiles.

The duchess nodded, and they were shown to their chambers.

Behind her, Damon's warm breath touched her ear. "Don't you find it a bit odd that the entire inn was empty?"

"Are you this suspicious of everyone?"

"Not you."

He might be better off if he did not trust her so much. She couldn't even depend on herself to know her own heart. A chamber door opened, and Hendricks beckoned. "I shall see you at dinner," Meg said, as she entered her room.

Her maid had already unpacked most of the items Meg would require for the night. "I have your gown out, and wash water."

Meg walked over to the fireplace and removed her cloak, intending to warm herself, but the chamber was already comfortable. That *was* strange. Not that she had been in many hotels or inn rooms, but they generally took longer to heat than a few minutes. "Hendricks, how long have you been here?"

She looked at the watch pinned to her bodice. "About a half hour or so."

Which meant at some point the coach carrying the servants had passed them, but Meg did not remember that at all. She might have been so engrossed in the conversation with Damon that she hadn't noticed, but she doubted he would have missed it.

"We took a short cut the driver knew." Her maid seemed completely unaware that the original plan was to arrive at home this evening.

To be fair, servants were not expected to question travel arrangements, and by the time they had departed Lady Bellamny's house, they would not have arrived until very late in the day. Yet why had Grandmamma not said anything to Meg about stopping?

She gave herself a shake. Even if Damon was correct, and her grandmother and the duchess were scheming, what harm could they possibly be up to? Her grandmother would never wish to see her injured.

CHAPTER TWENTY-ONE

Damon waited until the door to Meg's bed chamber had closed before turning to make his way farther down the corridor. He had expected the dowagers' rooms to separate her from him, but it appeared the road noise disturbed the older ladies' sleep.

The door across from Meg's opened, and his valet stood waiting. Devil a bit. First the unchaperoned coach, now his room across the corridor from hers. It was almost as if the dowagers were encouraging him to compromise her. Unless, of course, they had decided he could be trusted to protect her from himself.

Hartwell bowed. "My lord?"

Damon entered the spacious chamber, trying to think of a way to have his room moved to a different floor. Perhaps he should sleep in the stables. He would just have to keep his hands off her. He'd done a good job today of not giving in to his need to kiss her. How much more temptation was he expected to resist?

Glancing around the room, he noticed one trunk was tucked against the wall next to a wardrobe. "Where is the rest of my baggage?"

His valet cleared his throat. "Gone to Granby Abbey with the duchess's and Lady Featherton's baggage, my lord. I was told it would be a night or two before we arrived."

In that case, you should spend more time together. Lady Featherton's words came rushing back to him.

Had it been only this morning the ladies had arrived? So much had happened, it seemed longer. It would have taken more than half a day to arrange the inn. Anger rose up and threatened to spill out. Walking to the bank of windows overlooking the street, he placed his clenched fists on the sill. He detested manipulation. Even, it appeared, if it was to his benefit. Still, he could not very well confront the old ladies. They would pretend not to know what he was talking about. He blew out a breath, watching as it fogged the windowpane. It was up to him to ensure that Meg left here with the same freedom of choice with which she had arrived. And with the way the flames ignited whenever they touched one another... Holy hell. He could not even trust himself to kiss her.

Every other time he'd had one ear out for a guest approaching. Here there was no fear of being caught. He would be able to focus solely on Meg, her soft curves, the way she gave herself over to him and to pleasure. He might very well take a trip to the water pump he'd seen in the yard this evening. A good dousing with frigid water would do wonders.

"My lord, if I had known..."

It would not have changed anything. Given the opportunity, Damon might have argued with the dowagers, but it was unlikely he'd have prevailed. They had obviously already set their plans in motion. "It's no matter, Hartwell. How much time do I have before dinner?"

"An hour, my lord, but you will need to wash and dress."

"Bring me my travel desk." Damon had sufficient time to read the letter from his step-mother and send her a response telling her where he was going. Though God only knew when they would arrive. He wouldn't put it past the old ladies to keep Meg and him together until she had either fallen in love or decided she never would.

He pulled the letter from his pocket and tore off the seal.

> *My dearest Hawksworth,*
> *I have the best news. Well, not for the twins, but for you. The poor things have come down with the measles and are full of them. Cook has been making them their favorite dishes, including ice cream, so that they are, fortunately, not too uncomfortable.*
> *Of course we cannot have guests while they have spots. Therefore, the house party your father was planning has had to be postponed. Now you may enjoy your house party without worrying about leaving before it is over.*
> *Your loving step-mama,*
> *Catherine*
> *Duchess of Somerset*

A weight seemed to lift from his shoulders. If he remembered correctly, his bout with measles had lasted a good two weeks. It would be at least another month before his father could assemble another group of guests.

He pulled a piece of paper from his desk, then wrote Catherine telling her that he was *en route* to Lord Featherton's principal estate for the remainder of the Christmas holiday and to thank the twins for him. He was now in their debt.

As he sanded the letter he grinned. One never knew what the children would ask for in repayment. He sent a prayer to the Deity that he would not be subjected to a parade of eligible young ladies. He'd had more than enough of that during the Season. He was also thankful that, once again, he would be allowed to skirt his father's wishes without causing harm to anyone else.

He was certain that Meg Featherton as a suitable mate for him had not even entered his father's head. Her family, after all, were known for their liberal politics. The duke would wish to avoid any union that held no material or political benefit. Yet after Damon's conversation with Meg in the coach, he was more convinced than ever that she was meant for him. She was caring, brilliant, and would never be afraid to challenge him if she believed his decisions were in error. She was also the most beautiful woman he had ever met. That was what he required in a wife. A wife he would choose without his father's interference.

Damon placed two half-crown pieces on the letter, then dripped a large dab of wax over them. Catherine would know they were for the twins. The poor lads would tease him if they knew they were giving him more time to woo Meg Featherton.

The butler Lucinda and Constance traveled with stood to the side as an inn servant, most likely the landlord's daughter, set up the dining table in a parlor she and Constance would share. Immediately after the girl left, one of Lucinda's footmen arranged the silver and plate to her liking, then set out her own scented waxed candles, which were far superior to the inn's. Earlier, Constance's lady's maid had supervised the airing of the bed linens—their own, naturally. Even in an establishment such as this, one could never trust the sheets.

The arrangement had developed over the years and had served them well.

"Davies Street," Constance said as she perused the information on town houses they had received from Jones and Son, Land Agents.

"Too busy," Lucinda responded.

"Mount Street." Her friend glanced up. "I believe this address belonged to old Lady Busby."

Lucinda raised her brows. "*Old* lady?"

"She could give us fifteen years, if not more." Constance harrumphed.

After her granddaughter Mary's marriage to Lucinda's grandson Kit, and the promise of a new addition to the Featherton family, she and Constance had decided to set up house together. Lucinda because Kit and his wife would require the additional room in the Featherton town house, and Constance because her nephew, the Duke of Bridgewater, had finally decided to take his place in society. They had been searching for months for the right location. Unfortunately, Lucinda was unable to enter into the search with more enthusiasm. She was more concerned about the two young people down the corridor than houses.

Nevertheless, a response was expected. "She did not entertain much in her later years, but I remember attending a card party there once. It would probably require a great deal of refurbishing, but it is certainly large enough to accommodate us."

"Are you concerned about Hawksworth and Meg?" Constance gazed at Lucinda over her reading glasses.

There was no hiding anything from her oldest and dearest friend. "Perhaps a bit. After all, I would not want her to feel as if she was being forced to wed Hawksworth. I have been thinking that leaving them alone this evening might be a little too much time together."

Constance placed the documents in her lap. "We did discuss this and we both agreed that Hawksworth is honorable and Meg has a great deal of good sense."

"Yes, we did," Lucinda said slowly, unable to keep a frown from her face.

"If something were to happen, it would be because she is in love with him, and if that is the case, they will wed in any event."

She pursed her lips. "True."

"Then let nature take its course. It has always worked before."

Inwardly, Lucinda cringed. If her daughter-in-law found out, she hoped she would not take umbrage as she had with Kit and Mary. In the course of arranging that match, Constance and Lucinda had been forced to take more drastic measures than they were doing now. With poor Mary's cousin harassing her and Featherton, demanding that Kit wed, they were left with very little choice in the matter. Lucinda still winced at her daughter-in-law's pithy suggestion that she take up charity work instead of meddling in the children's lives. Still, how were her grandchildren to find suitable matches if she did not help them? And the fact remained that she and Constance were here as chaperones, albeit not very good ones.

"We shall see how this evening goes."

Meg dressed in her favorite silk rose-colored evening gown, and a warm cashmere paisley shawl. Her maid had used the garnet combs Damon had given her as well as some pearls in her hair. She stared at the combs for a moment. He really was very kind and thoughtful.

Damon had just finished pouring a glass of wine when she entered the private parlor on the ground floor. "Good evening."

"Merry Christmas." Straight white teeth flashed as he handed her his glass and poured another.

"Thank you." Sipping her wine, she studied him.

There was something different about the way he looked. She had seen him in evening dress many times before, but to-night he appeared even more handsome. His broad forehead and the lean planes of his cheeks had not changed. His lips were still sharply defined, his bottom lip slightly fuller than the top one. His jaw was still strong, punctuated by a chin that just missed being square. And he still smelled of his curious blend of lavender and male. But now as she gazed at him, there was something more. A tightly controlled strength and force she had never before noticed exuded from him. This was a man who had the power to influence the world around him, even if he had not been the heir to a dukedom.

What had changed? Or was she simply finally seeing him as he was? And how did that affect how she felt? It bothered Meg that she had only questions and no answers. She took a sip of wine. "They have a good cellar here."

"I would not expect less from a place to which your grandmother and her grace give their custom."

His statement refocused her thoughts onto the incongruity of their being here alone. "I think you were correct when you said they were scheming. I do not understand for what cause." She took another sip of wine. "When they come down, I shall ask."

"I do not think we'll see them again to-day."

She started to disagree when a knock came on the door, and the duchess's maid entered. "Miss, my lord. I was sent to tell you that her grace and Lady Featherton will sup in their rooms. They wish you a pleasant evening."

Meg stared at the woman, unable to think of anything to say. Then the door shut, and she and Damon were alone. "I never thought . . ." For several moments she couldn't find the words to finish her sentence, then she blurted out the first thought that came into her head. "My mother would not approve."

Damon gave a short laugh. "Which is probably the reason we are here and not at your home."

"Evidently." She was still stunned that her grandmother would be so lost to propriety, and the duchess as well.

He escorted her to the table, then tugged the bell-pull. "I want you to know that you have nothing to fear from me."

At first she did not understand his meaning. Finally a light dawned. "You mean you will do nothing to further compromise me?"

"We are the only ones here. They made sure of that." He sat at the table across from her. His deep brown eyes were grave. "You are not compromised, nor will you be."

Her heartbeat increased from a trot to a full gallop. Until he had spoken, the fact that he might take advantage of the situation had not occurred to her. Which made no sense. She had kissed him far more than she had kissed her other suitors, who had received nothing more than a peck. Yet trepidation about what he might have done was not the reason her breath had become shallow. It was the realization that she would have allowed . . . no, *wanted* him to kiss her, and more. She wanted his hands on her body and his mouth on hers. Just the thought made her shiver with expectation.

It was not solely he who must resist temptation, but she as well. At least until she was sure of her feelings.

Damon watched as Meg began to comprehend what he was saying. He had never wished for a chaperone more than he did now. He wanted her more than he could have imagined a man could want a woman, and here they were. His self-control was stretched almost to breaking. Being alone in the coach with her all day had been bad enough, and there had been many more layers of clothing between them. She had been encased in fur up to her neck.

He'd put the width of the table between them. Yet now, in the darkened room, the candlelight played softly over her luminous skin. Her evening gown enhanced the soft swell of her breasts, and his fingers wanted nothing more than to caress every inch of her. If she touched him, he would go up in cinders.

She licked her lips, and his groin twitched with hot desire as he remembered her taste and the feel of his lips on hers. The taste of her. They did not have to remain here long. Dinner would be light. After the feast at his godmother's house, the meal would be more of a late-night supper.

The pupils of Meg's eyes dilated, leaving only a rim of blue. "Damon, I—"

"Miss? My lord?"

Hell!

I what? I love you, Damon? I should flee because you look as though you might eat me? If only he had waited to summon their dinner.

A knock sounded on the door before it opened. A tall, slender young man entered carrying a covered tray. He set the table, placing a soup tureen off to one side. Fruit and cheese were next. "Lady Featherton said this would be fine, but if you'd like anything else, just ask."

"Thank you," Meg replied evenly, as if they had not been looking at each other with naked lust. "I am sure this will be sufficient."

As the lad left the parlor, Damon ladled soup into bowls. "I shall retire after we eat."

She flashed him a weak smile. "I shall do the same."

The air sizzled between them as they quickly finished the meal. He glanced at the bottle of wine and decided he'd had enough. He cursed her grandmother and the duchess for placing them in this position. There would be no flirting this evening, no light conversation, not even serious discussions. His control was hanging by a thin thread. One touch from her and he would explode and take her with him.

The moment she placed her serviette on the table, he jumped to his feet. "I'll escort you to your chamber."

And leave her there, untouched, not even a good-night kiss.

She must have been feeling the same. Meg did not place her fingers on his arm, or attempt to hold his hand. As they climbed the stairs, her lush bottom swayed before him, begging to be caressed. He clenched his jaw until it ached, and when they reached the next floor, breathed a sigh of relief. A few more steps and Meg would be safely in her room, and he in his.

Before retiring he would have a glass or two of the brandy his valet would have left out, then go to bed and dream of nothing but her, dark hair fanned out covering his pillows, naked and crying out with pleasure.

She stopped at her door, turned, and placed her palm on his cheek. "Damon?"

Then, because fate laughs at men, Meg rose onto her tiptoes and pressed her lips to his. He gathered her into his arms, her mouth opened, and he claimed her. Soon her fingers were at the back of his neck, holding on as the rest of her soft form pressed against him. He cupped her derrière, holding her tightly against his already raging erection. One of her slippered feet hooked around his leg, and he stumbled back against the door to his room, reaching behind for the latch. She could be his, would be his.

"Meg." He breathed against her lips.

He was the experienced one and should be the one to stop them. Instead, he placed soft kisses on her jaw, and brushed his thumb across an already hard nipple. He knew precisely how to lift a breast, freeing it from stays and gown. One taste and he would stop.

"Damon," she moaned, as her fingers clutched his bottom, sending flames straight to his groin. "Do that again."

Through the fabric of her gown, he rolled the tight bud, she deepened the kiss, and her tongue stroked his with a frenzy of frustrated desire. He inched down her bodice and almost reached the tender flesh it was hiding, when the door opened.

Damon grabbed at the door, trying to stop their fall. Then his rear hit the hardwood floor, and she fell on top of him in a flurry of silk and soft breasts, staring right at him. If they could remain here forever, he would be a happy man.

"My lord!" Hartwell stood back, snapping his mouth shut and standing stock-still.

"Miss!" A woman who could only be Meg's maid rushed into the room.

Damon jumped up, bringing Meg with him. He should apologize, but damn if he would. The only thing he was sorry for was that they'd been caught.

"I—I," she said, giving him a warning look. "Thank you for catching me when I tripped."

God, she was magnificent. "My pleasure. I hope you are not injured."

"Not at all." She slew him with a slow smile as she tugged her bodice up a fraction of an inch. "Falling on you saved me."

So much for wanting chaperones. He now had two, and wished them to perdition. "I shall bid you a good night."

"Sleep well." She walked across the corridor, pausing before she entered her chamber. "I shall see you in the morning."

Meg's maid gave him a stern look before closing the door behind her.

Brandy. He needed brandy now.

An hour later, Damon was still awake. As long as they were here, neither of them could be trusted. If she decided to marry him, it would be because she loved him, not because they couldn't keep their hands off each other. To-morrow he would tell Meg he was leaving and would meet her at her parents' home.

CHAPTER TWENTY-TWO

Despite having lain awake long into the night reliving the pleasure Damon's touches and kisses had given her, Meg woke early the next morning. Lying still for several moments, she listened for any sign Hendricks was in the room. Once she knew she was alone, she rose, slipping her feet into her slippers and donning a robe. She would ask Damon's forgiveness for practically attacking him last night. No other man had ever incited her to do anything half as rash.

She opened the door to the corridor, poked her head out, looked both ways, and listened.

No one. Not even one of the servants seemed to be around.

Creeping across to his chamber, she knocked lightly on his door, praying his valet was not there. The poor man had been shocked to silence. Hendricks, fortunately, took the entire incident as an accident.

The door swung open. "Meg!" Damon's tone was gruff as he glanced down the corridor. "You should not be here."

Oh dear. He was angry. This was going to be much worse than she'd thought. "I simply wished to say I was sorry for my behavior last evening."

He blinked once and stared. "*Your* behavior? I was the one to blame."

"No. I started it. I should not have kissed you, then I . . . well, I kissed you harder."

His eyes began to twinkle. "Did you enjoy it?"

"Could you not tell?" Had she kissed that badly?

"Then you have nothing to apologize for." A lazy grin appeared on his face. "I am certainly not going to ask *your* forgiveness."

She took one step, closing the short distance between them. "There is no reason you should. I greatly enjoyed your kisses." She should be backing up and going through her open door. Instead, she reached up and brought his head to her, brushing her lips lightly against his.

As if she'd struck flint, he pulled her to him, and his mouth came down hard on hers. She opened her lips to him, allowing him to take what he wished, as she did the same. His palm covered one breast, squeezing softly, as he teased her nipple. Her breathing grew ragged and she leaned into his hand, encouraging him as she had last night. Every nerve was alive and wanting more. Then his hand was on her derrière, and the throbbing deep in her mons began again. She rubbed against the hard ridge that had formed between them, and he groaned.

Suddenly, Damon broke their kiss and set her away from him. Loss speared through her, then mortification. She had done it again. "Please, for—"

"Don't." He reached out, then stopped. "Meg, I want you more than I have ever wanted a woman in my life. If we keep this up, I will lose what little control I have, and we will make love. I cannot allow either of us to be dishonored." He raked his fingers through his hair. "I shall take my coach and depart this morning for your father's house." He gazed at her, pleading with his soft brown eyes. "Please understand."

Oh God. She wanted to touch him again, but she dare not. Clasping her hands in front of her, she nodded. "After you have gone, I shall tell my grandmother." Not wanting to look away from him, she backed into her chamber. "I shall see you later to-day." She closed the door, then leaned her forehead against it. A moment later, she heard the sound of his door closing.

Meg waited until Damon left the inn before going to the parlor her grandmother shared with the duchess. A footman standing next to the door bowed. "I wish to see Lady Featherton."

"Yes, miss." He opened the door, then stood aside.

"Meg, dearest." Grandmamma rose and soon Meg was enveloped in a warm embrace. "I thought you would be with Hawksworth."

Her cheeks warmed. She would turn into an inferno if she thought much more about their kisses and caresses. She was almost sure she had fallen in love with him. Now she required more information. One married not only the man, but the family, and if anyone knew about Damon's father, it would be the two ladies in this room. "What do you know of the Duke of Somerset?"

Grandmamma's eyes took on a hard glitter. "More than I wish to."

"The man never listens to sense," the duchess added.

"Not that Damon said anything that was improper about his father"—Meg glanced from her grandmother to the duchess—"but he appears to avoid the duke as much as possible." Which was putting it mildly.

"As well he should." Her grandmother drew her into the parlor. "You are right to come to us. What do you already know?"

She recited what Damon had told her about never going to his home if the duke was in residence. While she had been talking, Grandmamma poured glasses of wine for all of them and interrupted to say, "We will all need this."

Meg took the glass. "How could he not love a son such as Hawksworth? He leads a life far less debauched than many men in his situation. He loves his step-mother and half-brothers and -sisters. Even though he did not want to be a soldier, he excelled at it." Meg threw her hands up in defeat. "I do not understand."

"Well, my dear." Her grandmother settled them comfortably on a small sofa. "Most of what I know came from Almeria Bellamny. She and Somerset are connections and do not get on at all well. According to her, the duke was madly in love with his first wife, Hawksworth's mother. When she died, he changed. I do not think he was ever a doting father, but from that point on, Hawksworth could never live up to his expectations. Many heirs are not sent to school, but his father thought it would toughen him up and teach him discipline. Fortunately, in my opinion, that meant he was able to spend many of his school holidays with Almeria and her husband. Then the duke found out and stopped the visits. You see, she had been a good friend to his mother and was never reticent about criticizing the duke about the way he was raising Hawksworth. She was the one who kept up a steady correspondence with him during the war. I do not think the duke wrote at all. Although I believe his step-mother did."

"I am glad he had a champion, but I do not understand how the duke could take out his grief on a child."

Her grandmother's lips tightened into a thin line. "It is sometimes difficult to understand the workings of the mind and heart. The end result is that Hawksworth wants nothing to do with his father, and the duke appears to still believe that his son is not good enough."

"Not good enough! I'll give him not good enough." Her hands curled into fists as anger at the duke coursed through her veins for the little boy who had lost his mother, for the man who felt no connection to his father, who only received care and understanding from his godmother. "He is obviously not willing to be pleased by anything Hawksworth does."

"The worst thing that Somerset did was not tell Hawksworth about his inheritance from his mother," the duchess said. "He also refused to allow her family to see the child or let him know anything about his mother's family."

Meg opened her mouth and shut it again. "How—how cruel." No wonder Damon avoided his father. "To treat her memory as if she had not even existed."

"I believe the entirety of the duke's behavior toward Hawksworth is not to be borne." Grandmamma's normally sweet voice had taken on a hard edge. "I am surprised the boy has turned out as well as he has."

Meg wholeheartedly agreed. "Grandmamma, Duchess. I wish to go home now."

Home. Where Damon would be waiting for her. Where she would finally sort out her heart.

Sometime during the night, the snow had stopped, and several hours later, Damon was on the final road to Granby Abbey. He had spent most of the trip alternately thinking of Meg, and how he would explain his presence to her father. Although, if Damon's baggage coach had arrived, he would be expected.

The feeling of rightness he had whenever he was with Meg, especially when they embraced, was unlike anything he had ever imagined. It was as if he had found the missing half to himself. A half he'd never known existed. As for her father, the man would more than likely treat any new suitor with caution. Kit could vouch for him, if he was not in the north.

A few minutes later, one of his concerns was resolved as he approached the drive to the abbey and heard the thunder of horses' hooves behind him. How the devil had they caught up with him? The ladies could not possibly have departed the inn less than an hour after he'd left. Then again, his godmother had told him the duchess traveled as if the hounds of hell were chasing her. She was probably traveling a little slower to-day.

As if anticipating Damon's order, his coachman pulled to the side, allowing the duchess's coach to precede him. Much better, in any event, to let the ladies explain how he had come to follow them home like a lost puppy. He mulled the puppy analogy over and decided he liked it. In many ways it suited him. With luck, he had finally found a home in Meg.

By the time he came to a halt in the drive, her grace's coach was being led away. A great number of people were hugging one another, and even the duchess could not escape the exuberant welcome. Although to be fair, she did not appear to be trying.

Even in the best of times, when his father wasn't around, his brothers and sisters were more cautious in their displays of affection. It was always best not to get into the habit of doing something the duke considered to be ill-bred. He remembered his mother hugging him and placing kisses on both cheeks. Her spontaneous affection was what he had missed most after she died. Catherine's hugs were always gentle, as if she was afraid she would hurt him. He could very easily become used to hugs and kisses.

He opened the door and jumped down to the gravel drive. Not able to bring himself to intrude on the family scene, he stood aside. Much like a schoolboy who had been invited but was unsure of his welcome until someone deigned to notice him. To his amazement, it did not take long.

Meg finished hugging a young lady and turned. "Hawksworth." Walking toward him, she held out her hands. "Come meet my family."

As he had suspected would happen, the only adult male, a gentleman with dark hair sporting a few silver threads at his temples, lost his smile. Meg's grandmother drew the man aside and began speaking in his ear.

Before Damon could take in anyone else's reaction, Meg was with him, smiling. "I am so glad we got here before you. I cannot imagine how awkward it would have been for you to arrive first."

"I did not think of that until after I'd departed." He gave her a rueful smile. "I am very glad to see you."

"I'm glad to see you as well." She took his arm in both her hands and led him to her group of people.

Unable to remain silent, he continued. "I rather thought I would explain I was a lost soul you had decided to bring home for Christmas." Blast him for being a blithering idiot.

"Hmm. Why do I have a vision of a puppy in my mind?" She glanced up at him, her eyes full of laughter. "Perhaps I should tie a red bow around your neck. You might look less threatening."

"I wish I would have brought my red and white striped silk neckcloth. If my godmother had not forbidden any of my more outré garb, I would have."

Meg gave a thrill of laughter. "*That*, I can assure you, would not have recommended you to my father." Increasing her pace, she gave him a slight tug. "Come meet my family. Mama just told me Kit and Mary will be here in a few days. Then we shall all be together."

By the time he and Meg had reached her parents, Lord Featherton had lost some of his forbidding look.

"Papa," Meg said, "I would like you to meet the Marquis of Hawksworth. Hawksworth, my father, Viscount Featherton."

Her mode of introduction gave Damon all the information he required about his position at present. Normally, as the higher ranking gentleman, her father would have been introduced to him. Yet, due in large part to the failings of others, Damon was in the position of supplicant. He bowed, then held out his hand. "Sir, I have been looking forward to meeting you. Your son, Kit, is a friend of mine."

A sense of power radiated around the older man as his blue eyes, the same color as Meg's, appraised Damon before shaking his hand. "Welcome to our home. I trust you will enjoy the rest of the holiday. Come to think of it, the children have just started to get up our yearly Pantomime. Perhaps you will take part."

"I would like nothing better." He slowly let out the breath he'd been holding. Here was a man who would not give a damn about appeasing his father, or him for that matter.

A lady who looked a great deal like Meg came up and stood beside Lord Featherton. "Mama," Meg said, "may I introduce you to the Marquis of Hawksworth. Hawksworth, my mother, Lady Featherton."

The woman's smile was guarded, but kind. "Welcome, my lord, and Merry Christmas."

Meg kept hold of his arm as they all entered the round hall. Built in the Georgian style with arches and pillars, it was light and airy, but with strong colors. The blue-gray of the hall was bathed in light by a glass dome that made up the main part of the ceiling. The floor was marble with small, dark blue insets, and statuary was tucked into niches. Charcoal drawings and watercolors of Greek and Roman historical sites punctuated the walls, and swags of fir and pine decorated with gold bows were affixed to each niche. Even with the relative formality, it had a homey feeling. Unlike his father's house, which reminded him more of a mausoleum.

"Where is the abbey part?"

"Not far," Meg said. "The original house that had been built amid the abbey ruins was destroyed about fifty years ago. My grandfather moved the location so that the ruins could be explored and someday excavated. You will see we are very modern here. We even have water pumped into the bathing chambers."

Accompanied by her brothers and sisters, they walked along a wide corridor to a parlor in the back of the house. Two sides of the room were covered with long casement windows. The third consisted of French windows leading on to a terrace, and the fourth wall was covered in bookshelves. "It's lovely."

"It is one of my favorite parlors. We call it the morning room, but the original name was the Lady's Room."

The space was large enough for three game tables, two large sofas with low tables between them, and several chairs. Under the two banks of windows were cushioned window seats. Then he noticed there were no fireplaces. "I can see why. How is it heated?"

"Under the floor, hot water runs through pipes. I think my grandfather got the idea from something he saw in Rome."

The children had gone over to a table already set with a game of fox and geese that appeared to have been interrupted.

He was still an outsider, and he needed to find his way into this family where love and caring were given freely. "What is the Pantomime?"

"*Twelfth Night*," one of the girls answered.

"Oh, Da—Hawksworth, please forgive me. I completely forgot to introduce you to my brothers and sisters." Meg wrinkled her nose. "Georgiana and Sarah." The girls rose. "I would like to introduce you to Lord Hawksworth. Hawksworth, Miss Georgiana and Miss Sarah Featherton."

He made his bow as the girls curtseyed. The older one giggled, and he understood why Meg thought she was not ready to come out.

Before Meg could go on to her brothers, the lads introduced themselves.

"Gideon Featherton, sir," a young man of about eighteen said. He also had dark hair and resembled his father. "I'm pleased to meet you. I read your name in a number of dispatches."

Damon shook the young man's hand. "I am happy to meet you as well. There were many men who ought to have been mentioned more than I."

"I'm Alan, sir." The younger brother stuck his hand out. "I suppose by now you know we are all Feathertons."

"Pleased to meet you, Alan." Damon grinned. This then was the bookish one. "I had noticed a similarity in the names."

Sarah poked her brother and said, "I think you and Meg should play Orsino and Viola. At least then Georgie will not have to kiss Gideon."

Next to him Meg choked, which made it more difficult for Damon to keep from laughing. "I cannot imagine kissing one's brother would be pleasant. I am happy to take the part as long as your sister agrees."

She held her hand over her lips and nodded. "Of course. I absolutely agree that kissing one's brother is not to be desired. Georgie, you have been rescued."

"What about me?" Gideon asked in an injured tone. "As much as I like my sister, I don't wish to kiss her."

"You have been saved as well," Damon assured the lad.

His stomach grumbled, and Meg glanced up at him. "Did you not stop for luncheon, or are you always hungry? I seem to remember you ate a great deal at the fair."

He had not eaten since early this morning, when he finished the basket Millie had sent. Right now a whole roasted ox wouldn't go amiss. Well, there was no point in roundaboutation. "I am famished."

She tugged the bell-pull, and a footman appeared. "Please bring some sandwiches and tea." After the servant left, she turned back to him. "There, that should take the edge off your hunger until dinner."

She glanced around the room as if just noticing something or someone was missing. "Where are my parents?"

He shrugged, but Gideon, who had just taken his turn in the game, replied, "They went with Grandmamma and the duchess down toward Papa's study."

Meg looked at Damon, her brows raised and drawn together.

The only question Damon had was whether that tête-à-tête would turn out well for him.

CHAPTER TWENTY-THREE

Lucinda led the way to her son's, formerly her husband's, study. Since the house had been built, that was where the serious family discussions had always taken place.

As was proper, Featherton escorted Constance. Helena walked on her husband's other side. He had not been as pleased as he could have been about poor Hawksworth's appearance. Still, after Swindon and Tarlington, Lucinda could not blame her son for being overly protective of Meg. It had appeared as if her granddaughter had developed an unfortunate penchant for falling in love with curs and scoundrels. Until Hawksworth, that is. He was everything she could have wished for Meg. Lucinda was willing to admit that they might have given the couple too much time alone. However, Constance was correct. Hawksworth and Meg had done what was right and chosen to continue on to the abbey before their passions overcame them. That said, Lucinda was exceedingly pleased that they were passionate about each other.

The only thing for her to do now was to convince her son that Hawksworth was a worthy man and that it was safe for Meg to follow her heart with him.

Featherton led Constance to one of the chairs flanking the fireplace, taking his seat next to his wife on the small sofa facing the fireplace. Lucinda sat in the other chair. All quite *convenable*. Although why the French word rather than a suitable English word had formed in her mind, she could not say. Perhaps it was because most treaties were written in French, and this conversation must end in a treaty of sorts.

"I am going to assume that Hawksworth was at Lady Bellamny's house party," Featherton said, firing the first round.

"He was." Lucinda always believed in not giving any more information than requested.

"Meg met him in Town," Helena added. "He was very kind to her after she broke it off with *that man*."

"Hawksworth is Almeria Bellamny's godson," Constance added.

Lucinda could tell by the way Constance focused on Featherton that she had decided to actively champion the boy. Not that a man in his early thirties could truly be called a boy, unless one was on the shady side of seventy.

Her son's lips compressed, forming a thin line. "The sole fact of which makes him acceptable in your eyes?"

"Not at all," Constance replied, unperturbed. "What makes him acceptable is that, other than a lamentable tendency toward levity, I have found nothing untoward in his doings. He was an excellent student, and an exceptional officer. He earned his last two promotions on his own merit. I will admit, his deciding to see if he could convince the Dandy set to follow him was not well done. However, if that is the worst thing a young man gets up to when he has been left at loose ends, I am willing to overlook it."

Helena's eyes began to sparkle. "Was that what it was? I did wonder. Although I must say, I adored the jeweled heels on his evening shoes. They reminded me of a pair my father had."

"Oh yes." Lucinda grinned. "Before we married, my husband had a pair embedded with rubies made to match a pair of mine. We were quite the thing when we were younger."

"I am not an admirer of Somerset." Featherton cut in on what was becoming a pleasant conversation.

Really, there were times when he was like a dog with a bone.

"Who is?" Constance's tone was as dry as dust and just as haughty. "I think you will find yourself in accord with Hawksworth."

"In any event"—Lucinda smiled at her son and daughter-in-law— "Meg has not yet made up her mind whether to marry him or not. To his credit, he has told her he will not marry a woman who does not love him, and she has yet to decide if she does. However, to my mind, I think she is very close. She and Hawksworth chose to come here so that he could come to know her family and be in a setting that was more comfortable for her."

Helena nodded thoughtfully. "I must say, I am impressed that he cares enough about Meg that he would assist her to be in a position where she will not feel pressured to accept him." She glanced at her husband. "I think we should allow this matter to take its own course."

He shifted, clearly uncomfortable with allowing yet another man to court his daughter at the moment. "Very well. However, if any of us discover anything about him that makes the man ineligible, I shall ask him to leave."

In other words, if he did not receive another letter from "a friend." Lucinda let out a breath, careful not to show how happy she was about her son's decision. There was no need to appear smug. "A prudent decision."

"In the meantime, I shall write to my man of business and have him look into Hawksworth's finances. One cannot be too careful."

Over the past few months, Lucinda and Constance had used all their resources and had found nothing to Hawksworth's discredit, other than the pink and white silk neck-cloths.

Hearing footsteps, Meg glanced at the door once again. Ever since her brother had said the four of them had disappeared into Papa's study, she had focused on every noise in the corridor, waiting for them to appear. With every fiber of her being, she knew that her parents, grandmother, and the duchess were discussing Hawksworth. No matter if she loved him or not, she would not allow them to make him leave. Not at Christmas. Not when he was so in need of a family. If her father tried, she would convince Grandmamma and the duchess to take them elsewhere. Unlike the duke, Papa would not be so cruel.

During the time Meg had known Damon, she had never seen him so ill at ease as when he was standing off to the side, waiting to be invited in. She had seen the longing in his wonderful brown eyes for the closeness she and her family enjoyed, and it broke her heart that he had never truly known that type of love. Even now, sitting next to her, his jaw was tight and the muscle in his cheek twitched.

If she ever met the Duke of Somerset, she would have to exercise all the control and manners she had learned over the years, and force herself to bite her tongue to keep from telling him what she thought of his child-rearing methods. If anyone had been unjust to a son, it was he. It might be best if she never met the man. Yet, if she really was in love with Damon and married him, there would be no avoiding it.

How much longer are they going to take?

Meg looked at the door again and, as if answering her plea, it opened. Her grandmother and the duchess entered, followed by her parents. Grandmamma glanced at Meg and grinned.

She covered Damon's hand with hers, and the feeling that he might be her future seeped into her bones. It was almost as if she had known him forever. Was he what she had been searching for all along? If so, she had lost a great deal of time and spent a lot of tears over men who should not have mattered. Yet was she the right lady for him?

"Children," her mother said, addressing the game table. "You should be dressing for dinner."

The children left the game intact until the next time and began to file out of the room. Then Gideon said, "Meg and Lord Hawksworth are going to play Orsino and Viola."

"Are they?" her father slanted a curious glance at them.

"They don't mind kissing each other," Alan added as he walked out of the door.

Unbidden, Meg's face heated until she was sure she was bright red. "It is just that Gideon and Georgie did not wish to..." She stopped before she made a fool of herself.

"You should dress for dinner as well," her mother said in a calm tone.

"I shall escort you up the stairs." Damon rose and held his hand out to her.

She placed her fingers in his palm. "Thank you. I'll ask one of the footmen to show you to your chambers."

Once in the corridor, he whispered, "I take it that I passed?"

She took in the concern in his face. "Yes. I just wish I knew what was said."

"As do I. No, on second thought, I do not want to know." They had reached the landing, and he kissed her. "I am merely happy that they took pity on me."

"You may not feel the same when we begin rehearsing for the play. The children are far ahead of us."

"Ah, yes. Kissing." He had a wicked glint in his eyes, and she knew he was thinking of the last time they had kissed. "At least we have practiced that part."

She wanted to slide her arms over his shoulders, press her body to his, and touch her lips to his. Yet no matter how she—or they—felt, what had occurred at the inn could not be allowed to happen here. At least not until she was sure they should wed. She released his arm. "Meet me here in an hour."

He raised her fingers, and she waited breathlessly for his warm, firm lips to touch her hand. He pressed his mouth lightly to each digit. She curled her fingers around his hand as desire swamped her, making her nipples hard and achy. How easy it would be to pull his head to hers and take what she wanted. Then the familiar sounds of her parents came from the hall below.

Damon lifted his head, and for a moment she thought he would take her in his arms, but instead he grinned ruefully. "I'll be waiting."

Sweeping him a curtsey, she strode to her chamber before she gave in to temptation. If only she knew that her attraction to him was not solely due to his kisses, or the way his arms felt around her, or his hands. Oh God, the way he touched her sent lovely shivers down to her toes.

He needed her to be sure. Damon was much more vulnerable than she would have thought, but for all that he was one of the strongest men she knew. He deserved a woman who would love only him for the rest of her life. But was she that woman? An image rose in Meg's mind of him with other ladies, and she wanted to drag him away.

Perhaps she was worrying about it too much. If only her sister-in-law were here. Mary would help Meg sort out her feelings. She did not dare ask her mother again. Mama would assume that once more Meg didn't know her own mind. And Grandmamma was actively promoting the match, so she would be no help.

"You look like you have the weight of the world on your shoulders," Hendricks commented as Meg turned to have her gown untied.

That was exactly how she felt. "I am merely a little tired."

"Not surprising, with all that's been going on."

She had to cease worrying about it. Something would happen. Fate would take control. It had to.

Damon checked his watch as he waited for Meg to appear from the other wing. He should not have been in such a rush to see her. He still had at least ten more minutes to wait. Unless she was early. That was why he was here. He wanted more time alone with her. Every minute apart from her felt like hours. He would not even consider that she was not falling in love. That way would lead to madness.

"Waiting for Meg?"

Damon wanted to groan. He had been so lost in his thoughts, he'd not even heard Lord Featherton approach. Damon stood a little straighter. He had never cared about impressing anyone before, but this man had the power to make him leave, and interfere with courting Meg. "Yes, sir."

"She is not usually late."

"I am early." He resisted the urge to look at his watch again, or down the corridor where the family apartments were located.

"You may come with me. We can wait for the ladies and children in the drawing room."

Hell. It wasn't even a suggestion. He stood his ground. If it came to a choice of disappointing Meg or her father, she won. "I told her I would wait for her here."

"I shall send her a message." Lord Featherton's countenance relaxed and a humorous glint appeared in his eyes. "Then she will know you did not desert your post."

Fortunately, the decision was taken out of Damon's hands. Meg strode out from the other corridor. Her gaze captured his, and he started forward. If her father ordered him from the house, he'd find a nearby inn.

As she held out her hands to him, her father coughed. "Your mother will be a few minutes longer."

"I hope nothing is wrong," Meg said.

"No, nothing like that."

It was clear that her father had wanted to speak with him alone, and Damon was not particularly looking forward to the conversation. He had a feeling he would be made to feel six again. Yet if that was what it took to convince her father that he loved Meg and would never harm her, so be it.

The three of them went to the drawing room. Once Lord Featherton had poured them glasses of wine, and they had disposed themselves near the fireplace, he focused on Damon. "I understand you have been in need of an occupation recently."

That was one way to put it. "Yes, sir. However, after discussing the matter with Miss Featherton, I believe I have found a way forward."

"Indeed?" He raised his dark brows.

"I had been waiting for my father to find something for me to do, but she made me understand that it was up to me to take charge of my life..." He told her father about their discussion, but not where it took place. "As soon as I am able, I shall ask her grace for the name of a land agent. Better to do it now than wait. I will also begin the process of starting a charitable endeavor I am interested in."

The man sipped his wine and said nothing for several moments. Meg glanced quickly at Damon, but did not break the silence.

Finally Lord Featherton nodded. "I approve of your plans. If you would like, I shall introduce you to some gentlemen who might be interested in supporting your charity." A slight smile appeared on his lips. "After all, we should not leave good works solely to the ladies."

What came next was an invitation for Damon to give his lordship a shortened version of his life. He was certain that if Meg had not been there, her father would have asked about his mistresses as well. They often knew a man better than his family, or knew more about his foibles. He assured his lordship that other than for entertainment, he did not gamble. Nor did he frequent the hells. By the time Lady Featherton entered the room, Damon knew what it was like to be thoroughly interrogated. The questions about women would necessarily be asked at a later time, when Lord Featherton was sure none of the ladies were around.

By the time the dowagers arrived, Damon hoped to hell they planned to rescue him.

"Mama, Your Grace." His lordship poured them glasses of wine. "You will be distraught to know that the jewels on Hawksworth's shoes were paste. He is apparently not devoted enough to fashion to waste money on such fripperies."

"I, for one, think there is nothing wrong with that," Meg said loyally.

Her father considered her for a moment. "What if he wished you to wear paste?"

Her chin rose. "I dare say that if finances did not allow jewels, I would simply do without."

"There is absolutely nothing wrong with my finances"—Damon had to stop himself from growling—"and although I do not have access to the Somerset jewels, I have my mother's, if Me—Miss Featherton should desire them."

Damn. He had almost given away that the two of them had been using their first names.. Her father was sure to disapprove of that. That he was being goaded Damon realized, but for what purpose? He had given his lordship all the information he had asked for.

"Even if the duke cuts you off for marrying a lady of whom he did not approve?"

No matter the provocation, he would not give in to his frustration. He could not keep his jaw from clenching. "Even then, I have sufficient income to support my wife and a family as well as command the elegancies of life."

"Excellent." Lord Featherton sipped his wine and turned the conversation as if he had not asked a question that had come just short of insulting Damon.

Yet the more he thought about it, the stronger the feeling that the question had not been about his ability to provide for his family.

Even if the duke cuts you off.

That had been the real issue. Not the money. *Hell!* Did Meg's father know something he did not? He had been counting on presenting Meg to his father as a fait accompli.

"Damon?" she whispered.

His gut twisted. Taking her hand, he held it in a tight grip. What *would* he do if his father discovered his intent and tried to stop the marriage?

CHAPTER TWENTY-FOUR

Meg squeezed Damon's fingers. The moment she had heard her father's voice, she'd dashed down the corridor to save him from what was bound to be an uncomfortable discussion.

His face had briefly lost its mask, and the stern expression he had shown when answering her father's questions changed to a look closer to despair. Whatever was wrong had to do with Papa's queries. She glanced around the room. If she could draw him to the other side, near the windows where they could be alone, she could ask him what was troubling him.

A second later, Benson announced dinner. Damon was summoned to escort her grandmother to the table. Perhaps unsurprisingly, the children did not appear. Her father must have decided the conversation would not appeal to them. Well, it didn't appeal to her either. She had returned home in order to get to know him better, and so that he could meet her family, not for her father to upset him.

Although the hours alone in the coach, where they had done nothing but talk, had given her almost all the knowledge of him she needed. The rest would come with time. She scoffed at herself. She had spent eons more time conversing with Damon than she had done with Swindon and Tarlington combined. If they had remained at the inn, she would have given herself to him, made him hers, as she would have been his. Then none of the discussions that had occurred to-day would have mattered. Grandmamma would have already sent for a special license.

Since their numbers were uneven and the table had been shortened, she was able to sit next to Damon. As at Lady Bellamny's house, he selected dishes for her. Not as many as he had before, but there was still an ample amount of food on her plate. His eyes smiled down at her, and she wanted nothing more than to wrap her arms around him and kiss him until their breathing was ragged.

Oh dear God. She must be in love with him. Nothing else could explain her feelings toward him. She had never before wanted to protect a gentleman, or throw herself into his arms. Now she would just have to find the right time to tell him.

After tea had been served she pleaded fatigue, hoping he would escort her to the first-floor landing. Although she had caught his eye, he was unable to escape her mother. She climbed the stairs more slowly than she ever had before, trusting he would be able to join her. Yet by the time she turned into the family wing, he had still not appeared. Why had she ever thought being home would be better?

Damon almost missed what Lady Featherton was saying as he watched Meg leave the drawing room. Granted, he and Meg had only been here a short while, but he'd had barely one moment alone with her since they had arrived. Truthfully, they had not been by themselves since he had decided to flee the inn and his overwhelming desire to make Meg his.

"Have you made plans for the Season, my lord?"

He jerked his head around. *Marry your daughter and dance every waltz with her at every entertainment we attend.* Starting a family was actually higher on his list, but if he thought about Meg naked in his bed, his cock was sure to stiffen. Damon shifted in his seat and wished frock coats had not gone out of fashion. "I would like to find a place to live before too long."

"Good for you, my boy," the duchess said. "The Dowager Lady Featherton and I have an excellent land agent. As a matter of fact, you may have a look at some of the documents he sent us. No time like the present to begin your search."

He thought he had been dismissed, and was about to rise when Lady Featherton again commanded his attention. "A house in Town?" she said, as if no one else had spoken. "Or an estate?"

From the corner of his eye, he saw the Dowager Lady Featherton grimace slightly. So the duchess had attempted to rescue him.

"Both. There is much I must learn and accomplish." And the sooner Meg decided she would wed him, the sooner he could begin the life he wanted.

Lady Featherton asked another question, and he felt like he was repeating himself, until he remembered she had not been present when her husband had interrogated him earlier. Or was she merely calculating the time it would take for her daughter to climb the steps, tire of waiting for him—assuming Meg did wait for him—and go to her room?

He took a surreptitious glance around the room. Lord Featherton had left as well. Was he speaking with Meg? As far as Damon knew, neither of her parents had consulted Meg about her wishes. Of course, he would dearly love to know that as well.

Damon took a sip of tea.

"What exactly is your income, my lord?" Lady Featherton asked.

He swallowed and must have inhaled more, because it went down his throat like a painful lump.

"Or do you not know?" This was accompanied by a raised eyebrow.

The gauntlet had been cast down, and it was for him to either pick it up or attempt to avoid the battle. He set the cup down and met her gaze. "To a farthing, my lady. Would you like the amount in actual figures and holdings?"

She waved her hand airily. "An approximation will suffice."

"I am not quite as wealthy as Mr. Ball is said to be, but neither do I have his extravagant habits."

"Which is the reason your shoe heels were paste."

Damon inclined his head. "Precisely. None of my personal wealth derives from my father, although I do receive an allowance from him."

That should satisfy her that he could easily support a family. He had said as much at dinner. Still, once again he was left wondering what the real question was that had been asked, and what the lady was deriving from his answer.

She studied Damon for several moments, and he forced himself not to fidget under her appraising gaze.

Finally, she nodded slowly and rose. "I shall bid you a good evening."

He'd stood the moment he had seen her start to rise, and bowed. "Good night, my lady."

After the door closed behind her, one of the dowagers let out a breath.

"My daughter-in-law is usually more direct."

The duchess harrumphed. "I will send you the list of houses, Hawksworth. I am going to seek my couch."

"I shall join you." Meg's grandmother stood. "As you are aware, Meg breaks her fast early. Unfortunately, it won't do you a bit of good in this house; they all do. A pity it is not summer."

On that perplexing remark, the old ladies left the drawing room. He waited several minutes, mulling what Lady Featherton had asked. Then it struck him. She wanted to know how well he took care of what he owned, or if he left it all to others. Which many gentlemen did, and as far as he was concerned, that was a recipe for disaster.

Nevertheless, he prayed Meg's parents were satisfied with what they had learned from him. For starting in the morning, he planned to find a place in this huge house where he could be alone with Meg, and discover how receptive she was to a proposal of marriage.

Meg had waited for at least a half hour before giving up hope that Damon would be allowed to leave the drawing room. Around midnight she awoke, and toyed with the idea of finding his chamber. Yet before she could make up her mind whether to go or remain, she had fallen asleep. The next time she opened her eyes, her curtains had been opened and a weak ray of sunshine greeted her. She would not arrive in the breakfast room before the rest of her family, but she could spend time with Damon.

Perhaps they could steal away for a few minutes, or even longer, and she would tell him she loved him. He was the kindest, most honorable man she had ever met, and she trusted him as she had no other. No matter what happened, he would never hurt or betray her. Then there was their passion. How had she thought she could live without desire for her husband? Thankfully, now she would not have to.

A mere forty-five minutes later she strolled into the breakfast room to find her father and beloved deep in a discussion. "Good morning."

Both men stood, but Papa resumed his seat, while Damon came to her and took her hands. "Good morning. Did you sleep well?"

If only she could tell him that she had wanted to go to him last night. "Well enough. You?"

"Yes, the room is very comfortable. Your brothers and sisters have eaten and gone. We are commanded to appear in the morning room for the Pantomime practice."

He began to fill her plate with the selections she indicated. "That is hardly fair. We have not even read our parts yet."

"What do you think of our chances of finding a quiet place to learn our lines? If I recall correctly, most of our scenes are together."

She glanced at her father, who had abandoned his newspaper and was watching them.

"Not good."

"Then we may as well join the children." He sighed.

"I have a better idea. We can take a ride into the village."

An hour later, they were in the stables. He did not have his own horse with him, but Lord Featherton kept a well-stocked stable.

"Grimes," Meg said to the master of the stable. "What do you think about Lightning for his lordship?"

The old man looked Damon up and down. "Aye, he'll do."

Her horse turned out to be a large bay gelding with four white socks. Not what he would have thought appropriate for a lady's horse, but the beast nuzzled her, looking for affection. After feeding the bay an apple, she started toward the mounting block. He stopped her. "Allow me." He cupped his hand, and she placed one booted foot into it, then he tossed her up on to her saddle. "He is very fond of you."

It had been years since anyone had helped her mount a horse, and she enjoyed the attention a great deal. "Thank you. He is. Almost like a dog."

Damon grinned at her. "You're welcome." In one fluid motion he was up on his hack. She did not think she had ever seen a gentleman move with such power and ease. "Down the drive?"

She nodded and led the way, bringing her horse to a trot once they had cleared the front of the house. By the time they reached the road, she glanced over to him. "I'll race you to the first cottage."

He looked at his horse. "Will he run?"

"He is one of the fastest horses in the stable. In fact, Galahad and Lightning are well matched." What she did not tell him was that the beasts were rivals, and her horse never allowed Lightning to win.

"In that case, I would enjoy a race."

"Very well, on the count of three."

The moment she said "Go," they flew down the lane, side by side for a few minutes until Galahad began to pull ahead. A few moments later, as she was rounding a bend in the road, she couldn't resist the urge to glance back, but the curve hid him from sight.

A shout rent the air.

"Watch where you're goin'!" a coachman called.

A carriage driven by a pair came to a halt. She wondered who it could be. The abbey was the only house large enough to warrant a visit from someone in a private carriage. Galahad danced around as she rode up to the carriage.

A gloved hand shot out, grabbing her reins. "Miss Featherton," Lord Tarlington said. "How very accommodating of you."

Fury and fear clashed within her. If only she had not got so far ahead of Damon. "Release my horse."

"That would not suit my purposes at all," Tarlington drawled. "I believe we can come to an accommodation."

Galahad tossed his head, but the fiend's grip tightened. "As I stated in my letter, I have nothing to say to you." She wanted to reach out and smack the man's hand away, but that would give him the opportunity to grab her instead of her horse. For the first time she wished she used a riding crop. That would have made short work of this situation. Whatever happened, she must remain mounted until Damon arrived.

"Grab her!"

Before she knew what had happened, she'd been pulled off her horse. Galahad's head turned, and she heard clothing tearing.

"That beast ought to be put down," a man screamed. "He got me arm."

She was shoved onto the carriage floor and the door closed. Fear for herself was replaced by fear for Galahad. "He'd better not harm my horse."

"No one has to be hurt. I merely need to make sure you'll marry me."

The coach had turned and it started again. "You may as well let me go. No matter what you do, I will not wed you."

"Oh, but I think you will. It really is a much better option than ruin."

He reached down, yanking her up. "You will be much more comfortable up here."

The shades were open, which did not help her cause. Anyone could see her in the carriage. Which was probably part of his plan. Closing her eyes, she pressed back against the squabs. She had to find a way to escape before they arrived at their destination.

* * *

Galahad was prancing nervously and riderless when Damon found him. He glanced around, but there was no sign of her on the ground. "Meg! Where are you?" Straining his ears for any sound, he waited for a few moments. What the hell had happened to her? Lightning had moved them close to her horse. *The horse that loved her like a dog.* And he knew she had been abducted, and the only person desperate enough to do it was Tarlington. What was strange was that the beast had not made immediately for the stables. What if . . . Damon was out of his mind. Still, he had nothing to lose. "Galahad. Come, boy. Let's find Meg." Damon started forward and the horse trotted along with him a few moments, then he took off galloping. Damon followed. No matter how long it took, he would find Meg and make her his forever.

Just as the town came in sight, Galahad veered off onto a smaller road. A few minutes later, a coach came into sight, and the horse sped up. That was it. Damon breathed a sigh of relief, then reached for his riding crop that had a long whip on the end. "Stay with me now." If only he had Mentor with him, this would be easy. "I'm going to do something you may not like."

Hoping that the driver would be on the left side, he urged the horse to the right side of the carriage. Two men were on the box, but the one on the left held the reins. Standing in his stirrups, he struck out with the whip, curling it around the other blackguard's neck. "Stop now, or he'll die, and you'll be next."

As he knew it would, the coach came to an abrupt halt.

A loud shout came from inside. The door slammed open, and Meg burst out. True to his name, Galahad lost no time in placing himself between her and the coach.

Damon reached inside his hunting jacket, brought out his Manton-made pistol, and approached the coach. Inside, Tarlington, the coward, was howling in pain, holding his hand.

"Meg, are you all right?"

"Yes. When the coach stopped he grabbed me and I bit him."

Of course she did. He almost laughed, but Tarlington had meant to hurt her, and Damon could not allow that to stand.

From the corner of his eye, he saw Galahad kneel. Meg scrambled onto his back, fixed her skirts, and nodded. Damon's heart swelled with pride and love. He really had not known how brave she was.

"I just wanted to speak with Miss Featherton," Tarlington squeaked.
Bloody liar!

Damon handed Meg the pistol. "Do you know how to shoot?"

She nodded.

"Point it at them." He motioned to the men on the box, then reached into the coach and dragged Tarlington out.

The worthless fribble landed on the ground, covering his face.

"Get up." Reaching down, Damon pulled the man to his feet. He slammed his fist into Tarlington's jaw, and Tarlington went down.

How the devil was Damon supposed to beat the man senseless when he wouldn't defend himself? Damnation! Did the scoundrel have no pride?

Tarlington whimpered and looked as if he was about to weep. Damon wanted to roll his eyes. "You may consider yourself fortunate that I have not beaten you senseless. Which is what I will do if you ever bother Miss Featherton again."

"I would not have harmed her," the cur screeched.

Damon reached down, pulled Tarlington up by his cravat, and shook him. "Never. Touch. Her. Never. Speak to her. Again. Have I made myself clear?"

Tarlington nodded several times before Damon flung him away like the vermin he was.

"Get back in the coach before I change my mind."

Damon doubted the scoundrel had ever moved so quickly in his life. He slammed the door shut, then stepped back, glancing at the two men on the box seat. The coachman had already freed his companion from Damon's whip. Damon grabbed the end that was still dangling down the side, retrieving his weapon. "His lordship is leaving."

The carriage jolted forward and in a few moments, it was gone from sight. He turned to Meg, seeking any sign of distress or injury. "I will always protect you."

She searched his eyes for several moments, then handed him his gun. "I know you will."

When Damon had spoken to her former suitor, his face had been dark with rage, his words clipped. For the first time Meg could see the warrior in him. Her heart beat faster. The romantic in her, that she had thought was dead, could easily imagine him in a suit of armor. She wanted to tell him she loved him, but was afraid he would think she was simply thankful for his rescuing her. Although she was shaken—

who would not be?—she wanted time alone with him. "Would you like to see the abbey?"

"I would, but later. I think we need to go back to the house. In case you have not noticed, your clothing is rather worse for wear."

"Oh?" She glanced down, and grimaced as she tried to slap off the dirt. She did not even want to know what her hair or bonnet looked like. "Perhaps you are right."

Not long after they left the spot of her rescue, Damon and Meg entered the family dining room.

"Did you enjoy your ride?" her mother asked, then glanced up. "What on earth happened to you?"

"We saw Tarlington. Actually, he abducted me."

Her father, who had been reading some correspondence, looked up. "Did he?"

"Hawksworth saved me and sent him away." She slid Damon a sidelong look. "I do not think he will return."

After a few moments of studying them, her father said, "I agree with your assessment."

Perhaps now Papa would be receptive to speaking with Damon about marrying her—after she told him she loved him, that is. If only she could find some time to be alone with him.

Late the next morning, Meg had still not been able to be private with Damon. Last night, she was about to go to him when her youngest sister woke from a bad dream, causing everyone in the family wing to awaken. She had decided that after their Pantomime practice, she would tell her mother what she wished to do.

She and Damon sat on the sofa reading the script, while Georgiana, Sarah, and Alan were practicing their roles for *Twelfth Night*, when Benson appeared. "Miss Featherton, my lord, the Duke of—"

"Stand aside, man. I told you I don't need to be announced." A tall gentleman, who looked to be in his late sixties, pushed the butler out of the way.

The man's high-handed rudeness and lack of good breeding was inexcusable. She clamped her lips together to stop herself from engaging in a similar display of incivility. Even without the beginning of the title, Meg would have known exactly who he was. His resemblance to his son was unmistakable.

His Grace of Somerset had just thoroughly aroused her fury, and he was about to be taken down a notch or two.

The children lapsed into what had to be stunned silence. They had probably never heard anyone speak to Benson with such disdain.

Damon stood, his countenance a mask. If not for the tick in his jaw, she would not have known how angry he was, and she fought to keep her temper under control. A fight she might very well lose.

Meg took the hand Damon held out, rose, curtseyed, and raised a brow just as she had seen the dowager duchess do. No one could suppress pretentions and bad behavior better or more quickly than her grace. She glanced at Benson. "I shall apologize for his grace's conduct, as it is clear he will not. You may leave us now."

"You—you!" The duke's complexion darkened. "No one, especially some young chit, takes that tone with me."

Maintaining a chilly haughtiness, she directed her attention back to the older man. "I was not addressing you." Damon's fingers tightened around hers. His other hand was almost certainly clenched. "I am Miss Featherton. You, sir, are in my family's home uninvited. I do not particularly care how you behave with your own servants, but I will not tolerate the mistreatment of our staff by anyone."

Damon cut her a warning glance, perhaps to restrain her, but after everything she had heard from her grandmother and him, she had had a surfeit of the Duke of Somerset. And personal acquaintance had not improved him.

She kept her voice stern but calm. "If you cannot behave like a gentleman, I shall have you removed."

The duke narrowed his eyes. "I came to get my son. After that, I shall be delighted to depart."

Meg raised the other brow. "Have you not noticed that Hawksworth is a grown man long past his majority, a decorated war veteran, and well able to run his own life?"

The duke pointed a finger at her, stabbing the air for effect. "*You* are an impertinent girl. He is my heir and will do as I say." He turned his head toward Damon, as if to cut Meg out of the conversation. "Hawksworth, your valet may follow us. I have decided on a wife for you. You have an appointment to meet her and propose. I do not wish to arrive after dinner."

Meg's free hand curled into a fist. What she would not give to be able to punch the old brute in his nose for making Damon's life a misery. She tamped down the anger that threatened to boil over. His grace was about to feel the sharp side of her tongue. A little plain speaking, giving the man a taste of his own medicine, would probably do the trick. If not, then she might just hit him. "I am vastly sorry to be the one to disabuse you," she said with specious sweetness, "but Lord Hawksworth is already betrothed to me." Damon squeezed her fingers again and the tension seemed to leave him. She turned to him and gazed into his eyes, hoping he would be able to see how much she loved him and that she would fight for them to be together, and protect him as he had protected her.

After a moment his gaze warmed, and he nodded. Turning back to his father, she lied. "The settlement agreements have already been signed, and the wedding will be on the morning of Twelfth Night." To Alan she said, "Summon Benson and tell him to bring two footmen. His grace is leaving now."

The duke sputtered and flushed red. "I will not be thwarted by you! Hawksworth, come immediately."

"No." Damon's tone was soft but firm. "I will choose my own wife. Indeed, I have chosen her already. She is Miss Featherton."

The duke's brows drew together. "I will cut you off. You'll not receive another penny from the estate until I am dead. And you will never see your brothers and sisters again."

Damon glanced at a woman standing next to the duke, whom Meg had not even noticed. She could only be the Duchess of Somerset.

"I'm sorry, Catherine. As much as I love them, I will not marry another woman. I will not give up the love of my life to dance to his tune."

Damon's tone was so full of regret, Meg almost gave in to the duke's demands. What would it be like for him to be completely cut off from his family? She could not imagine being barred from seeing her mother, brothers, and sisters. Then again, she could no longer envision a life without Damon.

"Somerset," Her grace said in a soft voice, "I have tried to tell you that taking this tack with Hawksworth will not work. Calm yourself or you will have apoplexy." She laid her hand on his arm. "He did as you told him and found a lady to marry. He cannot, as you are well aware, jilt Miss Featherton, who is a perfectly acceptable *parti*."

"Then she shall cry off."

If Meg had not clamped her lips together, her mouth would have gaped open. Of all the misbegotten, despotic, here-and-therians!

One fist went to her hip, and she jutted her chin out. "I most certainly will not jilt Hawksworth, and you belong in Bedlam for suggesting I do. I am terribly sorry that our love for each other got in the way of your plans, but since you did not see the point in telling Hawksworth of your scheme, you must live with the results."

"Love?" The Duke of Somerset glared at her as if he would like to spit. "Love has never done anyone any good. It turns one's brains to mush. It almost killed me, and I will not have it for him. I shall speak to your father immediately and demand that he force you to end it." He cut his gaze back to Damon. "Hawksworth?"

"I have already given you my answer, sir. I shall marry no one but Miss Featherton."

For a moment, Meg truly believed the duke would have a stroke right in the middle of the morning room.

Her grace patted her husband's arm. "Perhaps it is time you explained yourself to Hawksworth. I have done my best to understand and do as you have asked. Still, the fact remains that your behavior has only served to alienate him."

Damon still clung to Meg's hand, squeezing it almost painfully. The rest of his body was again rigid. She made a shooing motion to her brother and sisters. Once the door had closed behind the children, she turned her attention to Damon's step-mother. "I believe it might be time for a talk."

The duchess smiled softly. "I think you are correct. A pot of tea might help."

In Meg's opinion something stronger might be needed, but she tugged the bell-pull. Benson appeared immediately, two footmen standing behind him. "Yes, miss."

"Tea, please, Benson."

He bowed. "As you wish."

She steered Damon to one of the small sofas, while the duchess prodded the duke to the other one. Once they were seated, Meg focused on his step-mother. "Your Grace, I wish we had met under more pleasant circumstances."

"I as well. However, I believe once everything has been made clear, the situation will change for the better."

When the tea tray arrived, Meg busied herself pouring, then braced for whatever revelation was about to be made.

Damon sat as close to Meg as propriety allowed. He was still having trouble believing she'd finally told him that she loved him. For the past two days, he had been praying she could admit it to herself. The passion they shared could not exist if it were not for love. It was too special. Like nothing he had ever experienced before.

If it wasn't for the presence of his father, he would have grabbed her up and whirled her around the room. On the other hand, listening to her give the duke his own was an experience he would not have missed for the world. He only wished his brothers and sisters were present to hear her. She was magnificent.

He sipped his tea. Fortunately, her assertion about the settlement agreements was not a complete lie, not that she knew it. Before Meg had come down to breakfast, he had told Lord Featherton the whole of their story. At that point, his lordship had suggested they discuss the settlements. Wanting to marry as soon as Meg agreed, Damon had readily assented. Lord Featherton's secretary had studied law, and the documents could already have been drafted. Not that it would matter for the betrothal to be valid.

Damon selected one of the biscuits, intrigued to hear what Catherine had been talking about. Fortunately, he did not have to wait long.

"Somerset," she said in her gentle way.

His father drained his cup, set it down, and focused on Damon. "Everything I have done has been for your own good."

Typical of him to make excuses for his behavior. This conversation was going to be exceedingly short and would not go as his father wished. "I am aware, sir, that you care no more for me than you did for my mother. If I were not your heir, you would have nothing to do with me—"

"Is that what you think?" his father cut in. For the briefest seconds, the duke's jaw had dropped. "Nothing could be further from the truth. I loved her to distraction. When she died, I thought I would die as well. But she was willful and would never listen to reason. That's what comes of having been spoilt and never learning discipline. She knew that horse was only half-broken. Yet she insisted on riding him, no matter what I said."

Damon couldn't believe what he was hearing. He had been old

enough to know she was killed while riding, but all he had seen was his father's anger.

"I love you, son. Yet you look so much like her that I knew you would carry her wild streak. I had to make sure that you learned restraint. Too many people would depend upon you."

"By beating me?"

His father's mien hardened. "I got rid of that tutor as soon as I discovered what he was doing. No one thrashes a child of mine without my permission."

"You sent me into the army, when I wanted to stay home and learn what I needed to."

"I sent you to learn leadership. You needed the ability to command men." Father hit the arm of the sofa, and tears appeared in his eyes. "You were supposed to go into the House Guard, where I could keep you safe. Instead you finagled your way into the Ninety-Fifth."

Damon's chest began to ache, but anger filled him as well. "*Keep me safe!* How the deuce did you imagine that you could keep me safe in the middle of a war? Do you think you are omnipotent?"

"Do not be impertinent. That is obviously something you learned from Miss Featherton."

"Hawksworth does have a point. Not even you could ensure his well-being during a war," Catherine said calmly. "Can you not seek a compromise with him?"

He wasn't about to let the old man off that easily. "That also does not explain why you kept from me the knowledge of my inheritance from my mother."

"Blasted lawyer," his father grumbled. "Your loyalty has to be to England. If you knew how many times your mother's relatives asked to have you sent to them . . . Well, I was not about to let them spoil you as they did her." The duke's shoulders slumped, something Damon had never seen happen before. "You are the only thing I have left of your mother. I will not lose you as well."

"Do you not understand, Your Grace?" Meg gave his father a look he imagined she would give to a misbehaving child. "Your actions have been driving Hawksworth away. How you cannot see that he is almost the image of you is beyond me. He is everything you wanted him to be, and so much more."

"He is a damned Dandy!"

"Somerset, watch your language," Catherine snapped. "I will not tolerate swearing."

"Nor will I," Meg said in a haughty tone. "Aside from that, it was all an act. Because he was bored, and that I lay at your feet. What did you expect to happen after he sold out? For the first time in years, he had no occupation. You, sir, should be glad that he did not engage in all the low forms of entertainment in which many other gentlemen partake."

His father opened his mouth and closed it again. Damon had never seen the duke flummoxed before. Finally, he said, "What about the match I planned? Aylesbury—"

"You wanted to betroth Hawksworth to Lady Pamela Anvers?" Meg said in an incredulous tone. Then she began to laugh.

"I do not know what is wrong with her. She appeared to be a perfectly behaved young lady. Pretty as well."

"And prone to throw temper tantrums when she doesn't get her way," Meg said in a tone as dry as the Spanish dust. "You do not want her for a daughter-in-law."

"Well, I'm not sure I want you either," Damon's father retorted.

Damon had had enough. Even if it meant he would not be allowed to visit Catherine and his brothers and sisters, this time his father demanded too much. "Nevertheless, she is the one you will have." He slid his arm around his beloved. Now that he knew she loved him, he wasn't going to let her go for anyone. "It is, perhaps, fortunate that I am being banished. For I will not allow my betrothed to be abused by anyone, even you."

"Enough of this nonsense. If he doesn't behave, Miss Featherton can box his ears."

The duke's head swung around so quickly Damon thought it might snap. "You! What are you doing here?"

CHAPTER TWENTY-FIVE

Lady Bellamny entered the morning room with the Dowager Viscountess Featherton, the Dowager Duchess of Bridgewater, and Lord and Lady Featherton.

"We have come to make sure you do your duty by Hawksworth and his betrothed," the Duchess of Bridgewater said.

Lord Featherton and his wife stood back as the older ladies found chairs.

Once the Duchess of Bridgewater was settled, she thumped her cane on the floor. "They will require one of your larger estates and an allowance suitable for their circumstances."

"And he must be responsible for the management of the estate. They will also require use of the town house," the Dowager Lady Featherton added, "or one purchased for them."

"I shall buy my own," Damon said, with no hope of being listened to.

The list grew, until Father finally roared, "I am well aware of what my son and his wife require." He glanced at Lord Featherton. "If you are ready, now would be an excellent time to discuss the real marriage settlements. Hawksworth can do what he wishes with his own property, and probably did, but we will take care of the rest." He stood, lowering his brows at Damon and Meg. "I want a lot of grandsons. It never pays to put the succession in jeopardy."

Once the door shut, Damon let out a shaky breath. "I had no idea how he felt."

Yet it did not assuage his hurt and anger. He had been made to feel as if his father did not care at all for him. That type of pain did not go away upon a pronouncement. The fact remained that if he had not had his godmother and her husband, he would have been completely lost.

And he was quite sure that the duke was not going to let the matter of Damon's marriage rest. Yet there was no reason to distress his stepmother. She had tried to make his life better, and he would not destroy her hope of a reconciliation, even if he had no hope at all.

"It is a shame he was unable to tell you before," Catherine said. "However, I would not expect him to ever admit he was wrong in the least."

"I suppose if I'd got myself killed during the war, it would have been my fault."

Her lips twitched. "Naturally. Only because you joined the Ninety-Fifth. You had no way of knowing. Even though he was livid—you scared him to death, you know—he did nothing to try to change your decision. From that day, he had his secretary read every dispatch. He could not do it himself."

Lady Featherton reached out and patted Meg's hand. "I was very proud of the way you handled him, my dear."

She gave her grandmother a saucy grin. "How long had you, Papa, and the others been listening?"

"When you sent Alan to have the duke thrown out, he came to us. Except for the beginning, which he told us about, we heard most of it."

"You sounded like a duchess, my dear," the Duchess of Bridgewater said.

"I agree." The Duchess of Somerset looked at Damon, tears misting her eyes. "I like your Miss Featherton, and I am very glad you found love. I have known for years that was what you needed."

"I wish you both happy." Lady Featherton stood. "We shall leave you alone now that you are properly betrothed."

The ladies filed out, making plans for the wedding; Lady Bellamny included, even though she had to travel back to her house.

Damon lost no time pulling Meg onto his lap. "We have some unfinished business."

She gazed at him, her blue eyes sparkling. "Do we?"

"Indeed we do." He bent his head down, and kissed her. "My darling Meg, will you do me the honor of being my wife?"

"My beloved Damon." Her lashes lowered for a moment. When she raised them, he could see all the love he had ever wanted. "I would be delighted."

She reached up, threading her fingers through his hair. "Right now, I would like more kissing lessons."

He nibbled her ear, then pressed hot kisses down her neck. "I think you've got most of it down. All you require is practice."

When he tilted his head, she opened her mouth, meeting him caress for caress, tangling their tongues together. He wanted her naked, her dark hair spread around her on the pillow. He cupped her breast, and she arched against him, pressing into his hand. If only he could make her his now. Yet they were in her parents' house, and he could not betray their trust.

On the other hand, he could finally say what he had been wanting to. "Meg, I love you."

"I love you too. When your father started to attack you, I knew I could not allow him to continue." She pressed her lips to his. "I had already planned to tell you that I wished to marry you. Yet it was not until then that I was completely certain that I could never let you marry anyone else, and I am the right lady for you."

"After coming to know you, I could not have wed another. I was counting on the spirit of Christmas and kissing balls to bring you around."

"Kissing balls were helpful."

"I have seen some here as well."

She grinned. "I can show you where all of them are."

He kissed her again. "Twelfth Night. Do you really wish to marry then?"

"If it can be arranged." She nibbled his bottom lip.

"It most certainly can be arranged." And he did not even have to dash somewhere to procure a special license. He wondered if he should tell her about the one in his traveling desk. The army had taught him to always be prepared.

His fingers found the laces at the back of her gown and he itched to untie them. They *were* betrothed and the wedding was in a few days.

"Meg," one of her sisters called. "May we come in? Grandmamma said we had to ask."

"In a moment."

Damon helped her up. In no time her gown was straightened, but nothing was going to help his cravat.

"Come in."

Alan rushed into the room, followed by Sarah. "Papa says you and Damon are to come now."

"They are in his study," Sarah added.

"That was fast." Damon glanced at Meg. "I hope this isn't bad news."

"We have both reached our majority. It might be aggravating, but nothing we cannot overcome."

"You don't know my father," he mumbled in an undertone.

Lucinda, Constance, and Almeria had repaired to Lucinda's parlor. She raised her flute of champagne. "To another successful match."

"Here, here." Constance thumped her cane. "I knew they would be perfect for one another."

Almeria sipped her wine. "I must say, I did not think Somerset would go along so easily."

"Easily?" Constance's eyes widened. "The blasted man argued about everything."

"Very true." Lucinda suddenly experienced a sense of foreboding. She said, "Featherton made sure there was no room in the agreements for him to renege on any of the provisions."

"I still think Somerset gave in too soon." Almeria glanced at Lucinda. "Normally, if he has a plan, he's like a dog with a bone."

"Perhaps he is happy that Hawksworth now understands his reasoning for the way he was treated," Constance said.

"Perhaps." Almeria sighed. "In any event, Meg and Hawksworth are safe here, and I depend on you to see them properly wed before they depart."

"Of course. If the old goat is scheming, we will foil his plan." Lucinda took another sip of champagne, raising her glass again. "To a long and happy life for them."

This time Almeria raised her flute as well. "To defeating Somerset."

Meg and Damon stood just outside the study, listening as her father and his conversed while drinking brandy. She had a good view of her father, but could not see the duke at all.

"I don't like you, Featherton," the duke said affably.

"I would say the feeling is mutual," her father responded in the same tone.

"Your daughter is willful."

"Like her mother, she knows her own mind. I have never found that to be a fault in a lady."

"If she hurts my son . . ."

"If he hurts my daughter . . ."

The duke chuckled. "I never could intimidate you."

"No." Papa smiled. "And I sincerely doubt that you will be able to bully Meg. I suggest you do not attempt it."

"Did you send for them?" the duke growled. "I won't be kept waiting."

"On a willful chit?" Papa asked, although it was not a question.

"On anyone, damn you. I understand now why she practically laughed in my face when I told her I'd demand you make her jilt Hawksworth."

"And having a long acquaintance with me, I would have thought that you'd have had better sense than to make the threat."

"I don't like allying myself with you, Featherton. You do me no good at all," the duke grumbled. "You don't require either my money or my influence. Aylesbury needed both."

"Neither do you need mine." Her father sipped his champagne. "What you do need is a strong woman to marry your heir, and I need an honorable man to wed my daughter."

"I don't like her. She will never do what I ask, but she'll make a fine duchess. Not that I approve of the match, mind you."

"I would be astonished if you did," her father agreed. The shuffling of papers could be heard. "Despite that, you made a fair settlement."

"I did not really have a choice," the duke said with chagrin. "I am surrounded by enemies, and Almeria Bellamny is the worst."

Her father nodded. "She is a force to be reckoned with, as are my mother and the Duchess of Bridgewater."

"I'd never know any peace if I did not do right by your daughter and my son."

"I believe you are correct in your assessment."

That appeared to be the end of the conversation. Meg had never known Papa thought she was so like her mother, but she was glad that he did. The duke was nothing but an old curmudgeon who deserved to be taken down a bit. At the same time, she did not want to have bad relations with Damon's father and step-mother.

"I do not trust him," Damon whispered in her ear. "He is being far too pleasant."

"Most likely he has realized he must have civil relations with my family." She tightened her hold on Damon's hand as they stepped into the room. "We are here, Papa."

Damon inclined his head. "Father."

"Meg, Hawksworth, please sit at the table."

A few moments later, her father had given them the documents, saying, "You will notice that these include the settlement we decided upon earlier." Thank God, Papa was maintaining the fiction that their settlement contract had been signed. "In addition, there is the portion that his grace has deemed suitable."

She and Damon read them together. Occasionally, a question would arise, but in a relatively short time, they had settled the matter. As she reviewed the part concerning Damon's property, she was surprised. How would her father have known what to put in the settlement? Unless he'd had a plan already in the making. That must be it. Kit always said that Papa was awake on every suit. She had simply never seen it until now. She had the strange feeling that he knew all about Damon before they arrived.

Once the papers were signed, the duke leaned back in his chair, arms folded across his chest. "The wedding will take place shortly after Easter at Saint George's. That will insure the greatest number of guests for the wedding breakfast. Catherine will arrange a ball as well."

Necessitating a delay of several months. The old devil. Damon sucked in a breath, let it out, and glanced at Meg, who shook her head. "We will wed on Twelfth Night as we have planned."

His father raised his chin. "Very well, but do not blame me when people ask why you had to be in an unseemly rush."

"We know what we want, and there is no reason to wait."

"There is also the matter of a honeymoon," Meg said. "Hawksworth and I have a great deal to do once the Season begins, and we will not wish to cut our wedding trip short."

The duke glared at her. "Let me tell you something, young lady. Having an answer for everything is an extremely irritating habit of yours."

"I see nothing wrong with the morning of Twelfth Night," her father said. "Although the children will not be happy that the Pantomime shall be cancelled."

"Why cancel it, sir?" Damon flashed a grin at Meg. "My understanding is that it takes place in the late afternoon, before dinner."

"We do not need a separate wedding breakfast." In fact, she would rather not have one. They would have time to change from their costumes. "We shall celebrate our nuptials at the ball."

"If that is what you wish." Her father gave them a dubious look.

"You may as well give in, Featherton." The duke's scowl almost made her laugh. "There is no telling them anything."

Papa tugged on the bell pull and a moment later Benson arrived. "Please ask the others to join us, and bring more champagne. Lord Hawksworth and Meg are going to be married."

The butler bowed, but she thought she saw the slightest smile on his lips. "May I wish you both happy?"

"Thank you, Benson." She smiled at Damon and for the first time since his father arrived, he smiled as well.

"Yes, thank you for your good wishes."

A few minutes later, the dowagers, Mama, and the Duchess of Somerset entered, followed by the children.

Once the champagne flutes had been filled, her father raised his. "To Meg and Hawksworth."

Damon took a sip. "To the joining of two great houses."

The discussion turned to the wedding, and Papa sat down at his desk. "I shall send for a special license."

"Oh." Grandmamma gave him a sheepish look. "I have one."

"You told me you were not match-making again." Mama pressed her lips together in disapproval.

"I do not think you could call it match-making," Grandmamma protested. "I simply believe in being prepared. It was clear as day they were meant to be together."

Damon had opened his mouth, but shut it. Then he grimaced. "I have one as well. Just in case I was able to convince Meg to marry me."

After her grandmother's confession, he needn't have said anything, yet she was glad he had. After all, he had promised there would be no secrets between them. "I am relieved to know we will not run out." She rose, giving Damon a little tug. "We have some things we should discuss alone."

When they reached the corridor, she turned left.

"Where are we going?"

"You'll see." She opened a door, pulled him inside, and shut it. "We are going to make a tour of the kissing balls."

He glanced up and grinned. "What a wonderful idea."

CHAPTER TWENTY-SIX

Later that night, Damon sat in a chair next to the fireplace, an untasted glass of brandy in his hand. He still had trouble believing his luck. The only thing that could make this day better was if he had Meg with him now. More than anything, he wanted to make her truly his. He wanted to wake up next to her as he would be doing for the rest of their lives. There would be no separate bedchambers for them, and he didn't care how unfashionable they would be seen to be when they spent most of their time together.

The door to the corridor opened, and a wraith dressed in white and rose slipped into his room. Meg's thick sable hair tumbled in waves down over her shoulders almost to her waist. He had never dared hope it was that long. He was afraid to move, or even to breathe, lest she disappear.

"Damon." Her voice, a low whisper, caressed him. "I want more than kissing lessons."

He set the glass on a small table and rose. God, she was going to be the death of him. "Anything." His mouth was suddenly dry. "Anything you want."

"That is excellent." She sauntered forward. Where had she learned to be such a siren? "For I found that I want quite a lot."

He stood stock-still, watching her hips sway under her rose-colored wrapper. A moment later she reached him. One hand slid slowly up over his silk banyan, grasping the back of his head. The other caressed his exposed chest. "I have been wanting to know what you felt like under your clothing." She rubbed her thumb over his nipple, and his cock immediately stood at attention. Still he waited, wanting her to begin the seduction.

Her tongue trailed lightly over his lips, and he opened his mouth, inviting her in. Meg moaned as she slipped her tongue between his teeth. Kissing lessons. She had learned them well. His resolve hung by a thread. Finally, she wrapped her arms around his waist and stroked. Her fingers lightly skated over his bottom, and he groaned.

"Damon, I want you." Her sultry voice wrapped around his senses, making it hard for him to think. "Hold me."

The thread snapped and he gathered her into his arms. "Are you sure? There is no going back after this."

"Very sure."

He untied the cloth belt of her wrapper, allowing it to hang open as he cupped her breasts, reveling in the feel of her silky skin. "Were you not afraid of being caught in nothing but your robe?"

"No." She pushed his banyan over his shoulders. "Everyone is asleep or, at least, in their rooms." The robe fell to the floor, pooling around his feet. "Kiss me."

He tilted his head and pressed his lips to her as he removed her wrapper. "This will be much nicer in bed."

"Will it?"

"I'll show you." He swept her into his arms. A few long strides had them to the bed, where he had dreamed of her being. Carefully, he placed her in the center, and just as he had fantasized, her hair covered the pillows. He should have lit more candles. Damon feasted on the sight of her as he climbed into the bed. "Beautiful."

Smiling, Meg propped herself on her elbows, causing her perfectly rounded breasts to push out. "So are you."

He reached out, touching her with one finger, tracing the line of her jaw and neck before taking one dusky-rose nipple in his mouth, licking it. "I have dreamed of this."

"If I had known about it, I would have too." She shuddered and made little mewing noises. "That feels so good."

Damon switched to the other breast, sucking it lightly as he moved to straddle Meg, coaxing her legs apart. "I want to kiss every inch of you."

"I think I'm about ready to explode." Her breath was rough.

Soon she would be panting with need. He caressed her rounded stomach, down to the soft curls of her mons. Then he dipped his finger into the wet heat. With a cry of pleasure, she arched up to meet him.

Frissons of heat and need speared through Meg as she clung to

Damon. Her body seemed to know what she wanted and what to do to get it. Her breasts had become instruments of bliss that Damon knew how to play; her tightly budded nipples ached for his attention, and she had wantonly pressed them into his mouth.

She should be doing something for him, but she'd discovered how greedy she could be, taking his caresses as her due. Tension wound through her as he stroked between her legs, and her hips moved with him, encouraging him to continue. He slipped his finger into her, and her legs fell open, wanting. Her breath came in short bursts as he stroked harder and deeper. Then she began to tremble and felt as if she would explode. She did, and every nerve, every sensation in her body, coalesced in one place and took her up in flames. Damon swallowed her cry with a kiss. Yet that was not all. There was more. Meg wanted it, wanted him and his love.

She wiggled down, touching the tip of her tongue to his flat nipples. He groaned, and his body went rigid. Smiling to herself, she rubbed the other one, copying what he had done, stroking her fingers over his taut belly, reaching lower until she reached his shaft, surprised to find the skin so soft.

"Meg, my love." Damon gasped as if in pain. "I need you."

Once again, he bent his head to her breasts. The desire rose again even stronger than before, and his shaft rubbed between her legs. "Now. Take me now."

He entered her, moving in and out, each time going deeper. As before, her hips rose to meet each stroke. Then he stopped. "Wrap your legs around me, sweetheart. I hope that will make it hurt less."

She did as he said, and he made one hard thrust. The pain was sharp but less than she thought it would be. Damon stilled, waiting. "I'm all right."

"Are you sure?"

She smiled at him. "Yes."

He moved in her again, using the same short strokes he had before. The tension and heat returned, but this time he was with her. Kissing her as he plunged deep into her body. She rose up to welcome him, until she was once again consumed by the flames. A moment later, Damon's mouth covered hers, taking her in a searing kiss as he thrust one last time.

He cupped her face and stared down at her, his dark eyes telling her everything he was feeling. "I love you, Meg Featherton, soon to be Hawksworth."

"And I love you, Damon Hawksworth, soon to be my husband in the eyes of the world."

"Not soon enough." If Damon had had any idea of how different and how wonderful being with Meg would be, he would have insisted they marry to-morrow. As it was, they would have to wait for over a week.

The sweat on their bodies was cooling, and he lifted Meg, tucking them under the warm bedding. Her head was on his chest, and he held her securely next to him. "If your father and step-mother had remained here, we could have been married sooner."

His father and Catherine had gone to tell Lord Aylesbury that Damon would not be marrying the man's daughter after all. "He will not return until just before the wedding. I am not sure we could have tolerated him if they had remained."

"True. He would not have been happy about our wanting to marry before Twelfth Night, in any event."

"He would have cut up stiff over that."

"At least your brothers and sisters will be able to be here."

"That is a blessing. You'll like them." Damon kissed her hair.

Meg yawned and snuggled into him. "We should get some rest."

Before he could answer, her breathing deepened and she was asleep. But a thought that all was not as it should be kept Damon awake long into the night.

Austin Smithson had just returned from putting a delighted Carola on a ship to France. He was in his study at his house on Mount Street when his butler announced Tarlington. "Come in, come in." Austin poured two brandies, handing Tarlington one of them. The man's face was bruised as if he'd been in a fight. "I did not expect to see anyone. Please, sit. How have you been?"

His friend took a large drink of brandy, and focused his gaze on the fireplace. "You know I told you that the Duke of Somerset paid me to abduct Miss Featherton?"

Austin had not been pleased about that. "I regret I was even a part of giving you information about her. You said you merely wished to speak with her."

"Yes, well." Tarlington had a sheepish look on his face. "I didn't have a choice, really. He'd bought up enough of my debts that I could not refuse. After failing to accomplish the task, I was fortunate that he gave them to me. In any event, it all worked out for the best. Meg has found a gentleman who truly loves her, and I shall be able to move into my town house by next Season." He touched his mouth and winced. "Not only that, but I have wonderful news. I am married."

Who the devil had he found to wed him in such a short period of time? "Congratulations. Who is the lucky lady?"

His smile grew. "Maria."

Maria? Who the hell was Maria? Austin had to exert his tired brain before he came up with the answer. "Your mistress?"

"Yes, but, well, after the first six months, she was not actually my mistress."

Smithson tossed back the rest of the brandy in his glass and poured another. "I've had a long few days. Perhaps you had better explain it to me."

Tarlington set his tumbler down and leaned forward. "To my shame, I married her in a sham wedding. She is half Scottish, and even though she was gently bred, I knew my father would never approve. But I had to have her, and she would not be with me unless we were wed. A few months later, we traveled to Scotland and lived as a married couple. Under Scottish law, we are married and have been since before my son's birth."

"I thought you had to say vows of some sort."

"No. If one lives as a married couple and holds themselves out as a married couple, then under Scottish law they are married just as if they had said vows over an anvil or in a church."

Sitting back against the chair, Austin shook his head. "I do not understand. You need to marry money, but you are happy that you are wed to Maria?"

"Yes, it was really the only thing I ever wanted. Now I no longer have to try to find a rich wife."

Austin was more confused than ever. Tarlington wasn't making any sense at all. "I fail to see how that settles your financial problems. Not only that, but how did you not know you had wed?"

Tarlington laughed. "I'm not explaining this well at all. After I botched the thing with the heiress in France, I was in my cups and bemoaning that I would never be able to survive. That I had failed Maria and the children. That was the first Maria knew anything about my trying to marry money. You see, I had hidden it all from her. I didn't want her to worry." He took another sip of brandy. "She called me daft, and said she had an uncle who could help us if we needed it. Then she explained about the marriage." His smile belonged on a church figure. "She knew the original wedding wasn't legal, but when we lived as man and wife in Scotland, we would be legally married. She knew I was strapped for funds, and never complained about not having fine clothing, or entering Polite Society, or having sufficient servants. She was trying to protect my pride." Tarlington ended on a note of wonder.

"Well, that is a jolly Christmas present." It wasn't exactly what Austin should have said, but he'd been having a bloody horrible holiday.

Tarlington stood. "It is a wonderful present. I must be getting back home, but I wanted to thank you for your help, and tell you that it has all worked out for the best. I believe I have truly experienced a Christmas miracle."

Austin shook his friend's hand. "Merry Christmas to you and your family."

The silly smile was still on Tarlington's face. "There was one other thing I forgot to mention. Swindon is dead."

"I can't say he will be missed. How did he die?"

"He was whipped to death by a woman he had relations with."

"That makes me think there is justice in the world after all."

Tarlington nodded. "Well, Merry Christmas to you. Maria and the children are waiting for me."

"I smell a rat." Constance took another sip of tea.

"A large, stinky one." Lucinda nodded. After due reflection, she had come to the conclusion that the duke had given in much too easily. When she, Constance, and Almeria had met for breakfast in Lucinda's apartments, she had voiced her concern. "One might say that Somerset had been thoroughly routed."

"And one might be wrong." Almeria stirred another lump of sugar in her tea. "If we were dealing with a reasonable man"—she sighed—"but we are not."

Lucinda dipped her piece of well-toasted bread into a baked egg. "What are we going to do? We cannot act on a feeling. We must have an idea of what we are up against." She turned to Constance. "When did you begin to form a suspicion that he was up to something?"

"When he said he was going to see Aylesbury to smooth things over. It would not occur to Somerset that he should even bother. What about you?"

"When he said he would take care of his guest list himself. That was when I knew he would invite someone we would object to. Almeria?"

"When he sent Catherine back home by herself. He hates to travel, and he does not like her traveling alone."

Chewing slowly, Lucinda let her thoughts flow until they coalesced around an idea. "He must plan to somehow disrupt the wedding by making it impossible for either Meg or Hawksworth to marry the other."

"Or both," Almeria said. "That would suit his plans perfectly."

The next several days passed quickly. Meg was kept busy with invitations to the wedding ball, and she pressed Damon into service as well. Although there was no snow, it was cold enough for the ornamental lake to freeze, allowing them all to skate.

They moved their practice for the Pantomime to a room with a raised platform that had been built for the play. Trunks had been brought down from the attic, and they selected their costumes. As Viola, Meg had to wear breeches. It was now only three days before their wedding and the performance.

That morning, was their first dress rehearsal. The children had already gone down for luncheon, leaving her and Damon alone.

"I must say, I have never seen breeches worn so well." He ran his hand over her derrière and a look of pure lust entered his eyes. "I'm not happy about other men looking at you and thinking what I am."

She looped her arms around his neck. Pressing against him, she wantonly rubbed against his member. "No? And what exactly are you thinking?"

He turned her around. "Lean over the table and you'll soon find out."

They had spent every night together since she had first gone to him, but this was the first time they would make love during the day.

In short order, he had locked the door and had her breeches down around her knees. He lifted the shirt, exposing her bottom. Meg had never before felt so wicked. Damon rubbed between her legs, and she throbbed with need. "Please, now."

"When we have our own house, we can make love in every room." Reaching a hand under the shirt, he played with her nipples. "If we go to Greece for our honeymoon, we can make love on the roof of the house."

She frantically rubbed against him, trying to gain some relief. "Damon!"

"Patience, my love."

One hand skated down over her stomach, stopping when it covered her mons, where he found the small nub and circled it lightly. Finally, just when she thought she would scream, he entered her with one thrust, and she convulsed around him harder than ever before. Meg buried her head in her arms to keep from crying out. Damon brought her to completion again before he sought his release.

Damon collapsed into a large chair, holding Meg on his lap. "I cannot resist you."

She placed her palm against his cheek. "I cannot resist you either, and I don't want to. I hope it is always like this between us."

"It will be," he promised her. He would love and cherish Meg until he died; nothing would rip them apart. Nevertheless, he could not rid himself of the feeling that something bad was about to happen. "We should find something to eat."

Meg laughed. "Naturally. You must keep up your strength."

"Minx." He nuzzled her neck, breathing in her scent. "I love you." He glanced at the breeches. "We had better change."

An hour later as they left the family dining room, he heard the sound of horses. "Someone has arrived."

"I hope it is Mary and Kit."

"Shall we have a look?" He pulled her into a parlor overlooking the entrance. He glanced out to see three baggage coaches being taken around to the side of the house.

She looked up at him. "One is Kit's. I don't know who the other two belong to."

"My father and, unless I miss my guess, Aylesbury."

"That old scoundrel." Meg's eyes had grown angry and hard. "He has not given up after all."

"Oh, there you are." Her grandmother rushed into the room. "Come quickly."

He and Meg exchanged a glance, but did not argue. They followed the dowager to a part of the house he had not been in previously. Before long, they were seated with the duchess while Meg's grandmother paced the room.

"I will murder him."

"Calm yourself, Lucinda," the duchess said. "Hawksworth, there is wine on the sideboard. Please pour everyone a glass."

"Yes, ma'am." He needed one himself. If Aylesbury was coming, he'd bring his daughter. Which meant that Damon needed to stay as far away from the lady as possible.

"I will protect you," Meg said, her tone fierce.

Apparently she had come to the same conclusion he had. "He will not have just one scheme in motion. I shall protect you as well."

"You will both sleep in my apartment," the Dowager Lady Featherton pronounced. "There is only one way he can attempt to stop your marriage, and that is by compromising one or both of you with someone else."

The duchess thumped her cane. "You will be ruthless about remaining together during the day and evening. After you retire to your chambers, you will come here."

"Use the servants' stairs and back corridors," Meg's grandmother added.

"Grandmamma, will you leave our rooms empty?"

"No. Whoever decides to make a midnight visit will have quite a surprise." The dowager's lips kicked up in a wicked smile. "The duke may be a wily old fox, but he has met his match. Tell no one about this. I do not want word getting out."

Meg's brother Kit and his wife were the first to arrive. He thumped Damon on the back. "Congratulations. I am happy for you. Though I cannot say I'm surprised."

"I don't understand." He bowed to Mary and waited until Meg hugged her brother.

"Our grandmothers were talking about a match between the two of you last spring."

Now, that was a revelation. "I had no idea. I really did not even have an opportunity to talk with her until Beresford's wedding."

Kit grinned. "Don't feel bad. They decided Mary and I should wed as well."

"Apparently"—Mary grinned—"they have quite a habit of it. I must admit, though, they seem to do a good job."

Damon looked at Meg. "Shall we?"

She nodded. "I know what Grandmamma said, but I think Kit and Mary can help us."

"I have not a clue what you're talking about, but meet us in our apartment in a half hour." Kit placed his hand on Mary's waist. "That will give us sufficient time to wash the dust off."

By the time the duke and Aylesbury arrived, Kit and Mary had agreed to help Damon and Meg.

CHAPTER TWENTY-SEVEN

Meg and Damon had decided to play least in sight until they could not avoid meeting his father, Aylesbury, and whoever he brought with him. The rest of the wedding guests would arrive tomorrow. She was not looking forward to seeing Lady Pamela again. The young woman had been mean to Amanda, teasing her about having to wear eyeglasses.

Meg dressed in the red silk gown she'd worn at Lady Bellamny's and had her maid put Damon's combs as well as a pair of pearl combs in her hair. As was their habit, they met early on the landing separating their wings.

When they got to the drawing room, he pulled her under the kissing ball. "You are beautiful. I am happy to see you wearing the combs I gave you."

Meg felt the heat rush into her face. "I still feel bad that I did not have a present for you." She pulled a package from her reticule. "But I have one now."

He took it from her, slipped off the ribbon, and opened the paper, revealing a small box.

She bit her bottom lip, praying he would like it.

"Thank you." He lifted the garnet tie-pin from the box. "Help me put it on."

She removed the ruby one he had worn and replaced it. "Shall I keep the box in my reticule?"

He walked to the bell-pull. "I'll send it up to my valet."

A footman arrived and was dispatched with the jewel worth far more than the one she had given him.

They were half-way through their glasses of wine when her parents entered the room. The look on Papa's face was grim. "Did you see who your father brought with him?"

Damon took a sip of wine. "I did. Which is the reason we have not been in the main parts of the house this afternoon."

Papa nodded. "Give them a wide berth. I'll look forward to being given a reason to ask them to leave."

Kit and Mary were the next to arrive, then the dowagers. By the time the duke and company got to the drawing room, there was a tacit agreement that Meg and Damon would remain together, and that the others would draw off anyone attempting to separate them.

The duke entered, and she gave him what she hoped was a sweet smile, and curtseyed. "Your Grace, how lovely to see you again."

"And you, my dear." His smile did not reach his pale blue eyes. "Hawksworth, good evening." He made a motion with his hand and Aylesbury and his daughter appeared beside the duke. Lady Pamela's pale blond hair was dressed in ringlets. She wore a white gown with a beaded bodice. "Miss Featherton, I believe you are already acquainted with Lady Pamela?"

"I am indeed." Meg smiled and watched the girl as his grace introduced her to Damon.

"My lord," Lady Pamela simpered. "I have long wished to meet you."

Not straying from Meg's side, he bowed, then raised a black brow. "Indeed, my lady. I cannot imagine why."

Grandmamma turned her chuckle into a cough, and Papa's eyes began to twinkle.

A moment later, Benson announced another guest. "Viscount Anvers."

"Miss Featherton," the duke said smoothly. "Has Lord Anvers been introduced to you?"

She took in the man's hard eyes. Although he was lean, there was a look of dissipation about him. Meg knew immediately the reason she had never met him. He most likely spent his time in gaming hells.

Damon took her hand and placed it proprietarily on his arm. "He has not, Your Grace. And he will not be." Damon's low, dangerous tone drew everyone's attention from the newcomers to him. "If you knew who he was, you would not have brought him to this house." He turned to Papa. "My lord, is there a tavern in the village?"

"There is."

"What is the meaning of this, Hawksworth?" The duke flushed angrily. "You have no right to insult a guest of mine."

Damon took a breath, focusing on Anvers. "He is a coward and a deserter. His actions caused the death of an entire platoon. He was fortunate to have been allowed to sell out."

Papa glanced at the duke. "Did you know about this?"

His grace's jaw ticked for a moment before he spoke. "I did not. Naturally, my son is overly sensitive to matters that occurred in the army. Other than that, do you have an objection to him, my lord?"

"He is known to frequent haunts I would not wish my sons to visit. Based on what I have heard, I cannot think he is a proper *parti* to be introduced to my daughter—any of my daughters."

Anvers's glare had never left Damon's face, nor had Damon's focus moved from Anvers.

He inclined his head. "I shall go."

"Benson." Papa looked at the door. "Have one of the grooms escort Lord Anvers to the Crow. I am sure Lord Aylesbury will be happy to lend his coach. My lord, one of my footmen will help with your bags."

"Hopefully, we got rid of one," Damon whispered to Meg.

The silence was broken by a titter coming from Lady Pamela. "I had no idea Anvers was such bad *ton*. Really, Papa, you should have known better than to bring him here. There was no way that Lord Hawksworth could possibly have countenanced his presence."

"Yes, of course, you are correct, my love. Hawksworth, I beg your apology. I must not have been thinking. Lord Featherton, my apologies to you as well. I did not know that my heir was not welcome in Polite circles. Don't get around much anymore, you know."

The duke was rigid with fury, but he nodded to Damon. "I am sure Aylesbury and Lady Pamela would appreciate a glass of wine. I know I would."

Kit smiled, and handed the duke a glass. "To your health, sir."

Papa poured glasses for Lady Pamela and her father.

"Come," Mama said. "Let us not allow a misunderstanding to ruin the joyous occasion of Christmas and the marriage of our children."

"Indeed." Damon raised his glass. "To Christmas, my betrothed, and our life together."

Lady Pamela cut a glance at Meg, and smirked. "To a joyous occasion."

"Lord Hawksworth." Lady Pamela came forward placing her hand on his other arm. "Please tell me about the war. I am so interested in what you did."

Damon smiled politely and said in a perfectly calm tone, "I killed Frenchies and they tried to kill me."

Lady Pamela's eyes widened in horror, and Meg bit off a laugh. She could not even find it in her heart to chastise Damon.

Fortunately, Mary joined them. "My lady, we have not been introduced. I am Lady Mary Featherton, Mr. Featherton's wife." Mary linked her arm with Lady Pamela's. "I adore your gown..."

Thank God for Lady Mary. Damon was exceedingly happy to be aligned with a family who loved and cared for one another. He tightened his grip on Meg, bending his head so that only she could hear him. "I should not have been so rude."

"I don't know about that." She glanced at her sister and Lady Pamela. "She may give you up now."

"And miss out on an opportunity to become the next Duchess of Somerset?"

"No, I suppose not." Meg sighed. "What a bother this is. I have quite lost my Christmas spirit."

"We cannot have that. After dinner we may sing some carols if you would like. Speaking of dinner, Benson had better announce it soon. I am hungry enough to eat a goat."

Meg grinned up at him and his heart beat painfully against his chest. This really was true love. "That must be very hungry indeed."

"Not really. Goat is very good." Lady Featherton joined them. "My lady. I came to tell you that I have ordered your bags moved to the family wing. We will be bursting at the seams by to-morrow evening." She started to turn away and stopped. "I do not know what you said to Lady Pamela, but she has been giving you horrified looks ever since."

"Thank you, my lady." His lips tilted up. "Then I have achieved my goal."

Lady Featherton cast her eyes at the ceiling. "You have chosen to join the right family. All of my children have wicked senses of humor."

Damon's stomach had just started to growl when Benson announced dinner.

"Hawksworth," his father said. "You shall escort Lady Pamela."

Before he could answer, Lord Featherton was next to them. "Hawksworth will escort my daughter. It is their right as a betrothed couple."

Damon had no idea if his lordship was stating preference or actual etiquette, but it didn't matter. His father inclined his head and left to escort Lady Featherton in to dinner.

"Have I told you how much I like your family?" He wanted to wrap his arms around Meg and kiss her.

"They are wonderful." She sighed happily. "Except for the day we arrived, and I was not allowed a moment with you."

"Yes, but they did it out of love and concern for you. Not to advance themselves."

She stopped their slow stroll toward the dining room. "I love you, and they do as well."

He turned to face her. "That is the second most wonderful gift you have given me."

"Meg, Hawksworth, come along." Her grandmother stood smiling at them. "In fact, I believe I shall claim your other arm, Hawksworth. We do not have enough gentlemen present."

"Gladly, my lady."

After the gentlemen joined the ladies and tea had been served, the duchess set her cup down. "Hawksworth. You may escort me to my chamber. I am not as young as I used to be."

"None of us is, Your Grace."

"Impertinent boy. I can give you thirty years at least." She placed her hand on his arm. "When you get to be my age, you tell me how you're feeling. I won't be here, but I'll be listening."

A moment later, Meg's grandmother claimed her attention. "Meg, my dear. I have something I wish to show you. Do come with me."

Meg and Damon bid her family and the duke's company good night. When they reached the landing, Damon said, "Well done, Your Grace."

"Thank you. You'll make a good duke one day. We just need to get you leg-shackled to Meg. She'll keep you from making the mistakes your father made."

"You've known him for a long time, haven't you?"

"He was still a boy when I came out, but I knew his family. They sent him on his Grand Tour, and he fell in love with your mother. The story is that they defied both her family and his to marry. She knew how to handle him, though. He never would have become such a despot if she'd lived. But we all die. He took it hard, and married Catherine less than a year later. She would have been better off with a vicar. She is a kind woman, but hasn't enough backbone for your father."

Damon's throat closed. He had never even known that much about his parents. But then again, he had never asked his godmother, the only other person who might have known. "Thank you."

"You do well by Meg and that will be thanks enough. I love her as if she were my own granddaughter."

"I will." He loved Meg to distraction, and if anything did happen to her, he would hold their children close, and tell them what a wonderful woman their mother was.

His valet stood outside his room. "I did not know if you knew exactly where we have been moved to, my lord."

"I did not. Thank you. As soon as I am ready for bed, you may retire. Wait until I call for you before you come up in the morning."

Hartwell frowned slightly. "Yes, my lord."

A half hour later, Damon stood in the corridor, waiting for Meg. The only problem was that he did not know which chamber was hers. A door opened and she walked out, heading toward the back of the house. "Meg."

She startled. "Damon. I did not know you would be here."

"Your mother changed my room." He took her hand in his. "Let's go before anyone sees us."

When they reached her grandmother's apartments, one of the footmen guided them to two rooms next to one another. It did not take long to discover that the chambers connected.

How was it that he continued to fall into the dowagers' traps? "They planned this."

Meg shook her head and grinned. "They are shameless. But, as my grandmother said earlier, we are in love, betrothed, and hot for one another."

"I can see you will be just like them when you are older." He wrapped his arms around her.

Laying her head on his chest, she replied, "I sincerely hope so."

* * *

Sometime in the middle of the night, screams rent the peaceful quiet. Next to him Meg stirred.

"What is it?" she asked in a sleep-filled voice.

"A trap being sprung."

"They really did it." Her arm slid across his chest.

"Apparently. Part of me wants to go and find out what's going on, but the other part demands I stay here with you."

"I know what you mean, but we cannot both go."

"No." Damon acknowledged the truth in that. "It looks as if our curiosity will not be satisfied until morning."

He thought they would both have trouble going to sleep, but Meg pulled him down, kissing him until they made love again and drifted off in each other's arms.

Lord Featherton was in the breakfast room when Meg and Damon entered. He went immediately to the sideboard. By now he knew what she liked and would make plates for both of them.

Meg took a seat at the table and ordered more tea. "Papa, what happened last night?"

He lowered his newspaper. "Anvers was let into the house, and he entered your room. One of your grandmother's footmen, a former pugilist, was there. It did not turn out well for his lordship."

She busied herself fixing the tea. "Was that all?"

"No. Lady Pamela was found in Hawksworth's former room in the arms of the duchess's lady's maid. Not quite what she expected. I informed Aylesbury that he was no longer welcome. He and his daughter departed at dawn. The duke has not yet appeared."

"How interesting." Meg handed Damon his cup as he placed her plate in front of her, and sat. "All's well that ends well?"

"I do wish my mother would apprise me of her plans before she executes them," her father said.

She saw his point. It could not have been comfortable to be dealing with all the difficulties and not have any notice. "What would you have done differently?"

"Nothing at all." He took a piece of toast that she offered. "Other than have been dressed."

"But then the duke would have known you had set the trap."

"Contrary to what you and your grandmother believe," he said dryly, "that would not have been all bad."

Damon sipped his tea. Normally he drank coffee, but this was very good. "You may know better, sir, but I have come to the conclusion that elderly ladies are a force to be reckoned with. I think I shall leave them to their own devices."

Her father rolled his eyes. "Which is most likely the only choice I have. God knows I have not been successful keeping up with them."

A few minutes later the duke came down to breakfast, a fierce scowl on his face. "What is this I hear about my guests being evicted from your house, Featherton?"

Her father drained his cup, and she poured him another.

"I regret to be the one to inform Your Grace, but Lady Pamela was found climbing into bed with my mother's lady's maid. Her scream woke me from a dead sleep. I am truly in awe of your ability to have slept through the racket." Papa took a sip. "Someone allowed Lord Anvers into the house, and he was found attempting to seduce a footman. Naturally, he was removed immediately."

The duke's countenance remained unreadable, and for once he seemed to have nothing to say.

Damon set his cup down. "Father, your attempt to separate me from my betrothed not only failed dramatically, but you have embarrassed our house." He waited for a response that did not come. "If you are intent on ruining my wedding, you may go. If you can support my marriage to Meg, you may stay. I am weary of constantly fighting you, but that does not mean I will allow you to dictate my life."

For several moments, the duke said nothing, and Damon prayed that he would see reason.

"I shall depart as soon as I have packed. Catherine and the others will arrive later to-day." He rose. "I do not and will never agree with your choice, but I shall bid you a happy life."

No one called him back. There was no reason to do so.

Meg's eyes filled with tears. "My love, I am so sorry."

"Don't be. He was never a father to me." Not after his mother died. He had hoped and prayed his father would change. But perhaps even God had tired of the man and was willing to let him go his own way to hell.

"I want you to know you will be treated as a son here. If that is what you want." Her father waited for his response.

"I appreciate that more than I can say." His throat ached with unshed tears. "Meg."

She stood and folded her arms around him. "I cannot say that I know how you feel. I can only offer you my love."

He held on to her as if she was an anchor in a storm. "Thanks to you, I have found my home."

She chuckled wetly. "I think you may have to thank my grandmother and the duchess for that."

"And my godmother."

CHAPTER TWENTY-EIGHT

Meg woke next to Damon with a start. Then she remembered they were in her grandmother's apartments, and it was their wedding day. Yesterday guests had poured in, and the house was full. She had met her new brothers and sisters, and liked them all. The hour was early, but she had to dress for her wedding.

Not wanting to wake him, she slipped quietly out of the bed and opened the door to the adjoining room.

Hendricks was waiting. "I just filled the tub."

"You are a treasure."

"Don't know about that, but it's that glad I am you're going to marry his lordship."

And so was Meg. Breakfast had been brought up, but she was too excited to eat. Damon had been ushered out to bathe and dress.

Meg had decided on a dark green cashmere, which would be warmer than silk, and she did not fancy shivering during her wedding ceremony. Pearls had been threaded through her hair, and she wore one of the combs Damon had given her.

Her sisters, followed by Mama and Amanda, entered the room.

"You are so beautiful." Georgiana leaned forward carefully and kissed Meg's cheek. "I would hug you, but I'm afraid I'd mess something up." She held out a handkerchief. "This is for you. I just finished it last night. Mama said you needed something new."

Tears started in Meg's eyes. "Well, I am going to hug you." She embraced Georgiana, then turned to Sarah.

Sarah held out a small gold brooch. "I thought you might like to borrow this for the day." Once Meg pinned it to her bodice, Sarah threw herself into Meg's arms. "I'm happy for you, and I like Damon, but I'm going to miss you."

She hugged her youngest sister for several moments. "We'll visit often, and you shall visit us."

"This," Mama said, "has been handed down to the eldest daughter on her wedding day." She clasped an ancient pearl and ruby necklace around Meg's neck. "Now it is yours."

"And blue." Amanda brushed a tear from her eye before handing Meg a sapphire ring.

"Now, girls, we must go." Mama opened the door. "We will see Meg at the church."

A few minutes later she met her father in the hall. "Hawksworth?"

"He should be arriving at the church now."

Their wedding would be held before the service began. It was unusual to have a wedding on Sunday morning, but Papa had prevailed, as she knew he would. He did own the living.

When they arrived, Mr. Richardson, the rector who had known Meg all her life, stood under the rood screen filled with greenery and smiled. The scent of pine filled the air. Less than an hour after she and Damon wed, the townspeople would file in, and the church would be overflowing.

Damon turned as she appeared on her father's arm. Chuffy, who had arrived yesterday with Amanda, stood up next to Damon.

He caught her gaze and his smile grew.

"I am happier for you than I was at my own wedding," Amanda whispered.

"I do not think I have ever been so joyful." Meg gave thanks to the Deity that Damon had not given up on her.

To think she would have been willing to settle for mere contentment. She glanced around the old Norman church. Damon's brothers and sisters seemed to fill half of it. The duke sat next to Catherine. He had been furious that he had not succeeded and was here only so that his absence would not reflect badly on him.

In strong, steady voices Meg and Damon said their vows.

He held her hand, slipping a ring of rubies and diamonds on her finger, and promised to, among other things, worship her with his body. She had never before understood that, but she did now.

After they were pronounced man and wife, they signed the register.

Gideon pointed toward the ceiling. "You have to kiss her."

She and Damon glanced up. Someone had hung a kissing ball directly over them.

He took her in his arms. "We cannot disappoint whoever was enterprising enough to provide us with our own kissing ball."

Despite all they had done together, she blushed. "No, we cannot." She slid her arms around his neck, and his mouth came down on hers.

He ended the kiss and pressed his forehead to hers. "Merry Christmas, my lady wife."

Meg grinned and Damon wanted to kiss her again. "Merry Christmas, my lord husband."

Lady Bellamny came up to them. "Hawksworth, Meg, you have my best wishes. I would not have missed your wedding for the world, but I must go home now."

He hugged his godmother. "Have a safe journey."

Catherine joined them. "I am glad the two of you married. I would love to remain for the ball this evening, but I must return to Somerset. You do understand?"

Damon embraced her. "Yes."

Suddenly they were surrounded by their brothers and sisters wishing them happy. A few minutes later, Mr. Richardson called them to take their places in the pews.

Later, the townspeople came to wish everyone good health with wassail, and the group from the church sang carols. When they left, Amanda sat down at the piano.

Damon took Meg's hands in his, and when Amanda had finished playing the first notes, he began to sing.

> *"Come live with me and be my love,*
> *And we will all the pleasures prove*
> *That hill and valley, dale and field,*
> *And all the craggy mountains yield.*
>
> *"There we will sit upon the rocks,*
> *And see the shepherds feed their flocks,*
> *By shallow rivers to whose falls*
> *Melodious birds sing madrigals.*

> "There I will make thee beds of roses
> And a thousand fragrant posies,
> A cap of flowers, and a kirtle
> Embroidered all with leaves of myrtle;
>
> "A gown made of the finest wool
> Which from our pretty lambs we pull;
> Fair lined slippers for the cold,
> With buckles of the purest gold;
>
> "A belt of straw and ivy buds,
> With coral clasps and amber studs:
> And if these pleasures may thee move,
> Come live with me and be my love.
>
> "Thy silver dishes for thy meat,
> As precious as the gods do eat,
> Shall on an ivory table be
> Prepared each day for thee and me.
>
> "The shepherds' swains shall dance and sing
> For thy delight each May morning:
> If these delights thy mind may move,
> Then live with me and be my love."

Meg's eyes filled with tears, and Damon held her tenderly.

It would have been perfect if his brothers and sisters as well as hers had not thumped their collective feet on the floor, making so much noise one could not hear oneself think. "Cease. You make enough racket to wake the dead."

"I will warn you right now," Meg said tartly, "I shall not have fifteen children."

"Not even to secure the succession?" he teased.

"Not even then."

"What about"—he placed his lips close to her ear—"if we cannot keep our hands off each other?" Ignoring their brothers and sisters, he twirled her under a kissing ball, and pressed his lips to hers. "I can assure you, my lady, I will never get tired of this."

She wrapped her arms around his neck. "Neither will I."

* * *

Hawksworth House, London, late May 1818

Meg held Amanda's letter in one hand while she rubbed her growing stomach with the other. "They are traveling to Vienna."

"Vienna is lovely in the summer." Damon glanced at his wife. "Are you sorry that we did not decide to go with them?"

"No. Well, maybe a little. If we had not received the letter telling you to return immediately due to your father's stroke, I would have been happy to have remained overseas a bit longer."

"The completely false letter about the duke's stroke, you mean."

"Yes, but then he did have that bad fall from his horse and has not been in good health since."

"True." At least Damon was now taking charge of much of the estate's management. Frank, his oldest half-brother's decision to marry the American heiress, Jenny, had not helped their father's health either. "Have you heard from Jenny?"

"Yes, she wrote to say your father will still not acknowledge their marriage, but that Frank is taking to her father's business like he was born to it."

"I don't doubt that." Damon rose. "We had best be going."

Meg placed the letters on a side table next to her. "Indeed. It would not do to be late."

Several minutes later, they entered Featherton House.

Benson bowed. "My lady, how good it is to see you and his lordship again."

"Thank you. Are they in the drawing room?"

"Yes. Allow me to announce you."

"Of course." She thought she would be allowed to simply enter, but obviously her father's butler was enjoying her new status too much to allow that to occur.

Once the door had closed behind them, Mary greeted Meg. "You have no idea how nervous I am. Your mother glanced over the final lists and deserted me."

"I recall that she said this would be your ball."

"Yes, she did." Mary pulled a face. "I just did not realize what she meant." Linking her arm with Meg's, she said, "I believe you know most everyone here."

Naturally, all of Kit's and Mary's friends, and now Meg's and

Damon's, were present for dinner. Phoebe Evesham and Serena Beaumont got to Meg first and hugged her. Anna Rutherford waved from across the room where she was in a discussion with Caro Huntley and her husband, the Earl of Huntley. Eugénie Wivenly, who was standing with them, laughed. Her husband, Will, smiled at his wife with the besotted gaze he always gave her.

Vivian Stanstead kissed Meg's cheek. "You look wonderful."

She took in Vivian's large stomach. She would give birth about two months before Meg did. "As do you."

Her brother handed her a glass of champagne. "I think Huntley wishes to say something."

"Not quite three years ago, a wager was made at Robert and Serena's wedding. At the time, we thought Rupert Stanstead was the last of us to marry, but then an old friend returned from the war, and found his mate."

"And they could not wait to wed until the rest of us arrived," Will said.

Damon's arm snaked around her waist. "I seem to recall hearing that you were in a hurry as well."

Laughter filled the room, and Huntley raised his glass. "A toast to finding the right mate."

Damon whispered in her ear. "Have I told you how much I love you?"

"I never tire of hearing it. I love you as well."

Meg remembered wishing for a man to look at her the way her friends' husbands looked at their wives, and now she had Damon.

AUTHOR'S NOTE

I wanted to end The Marriage Game with the whole group together again. However, as Huntley said, Meg and Damon made that impossible to do at the wedding, as I normally do. Winter is not the best time to travel quickly. Then I came up with the idea to have them all together in London, where it all began. If you are not acquainted with everyone present in the last scene, I hope you'll read the books and get to know them.

The series will be in hiatus until my characters' children are old enough to start thinking about love and marriage. In the meantime, a new series, The Worthingtons, begins in spring of 2016. Please join me and a new set of characters and stories.

Ella Quinn

In the first book in her dazzling new series, bestselling author Ella Quinn introduces the soon-to-be Earl and Countess of Worthington—lovers who have more in common than they yet know. The future promises to be far from boring...

Lady Grace Carpenter is ready to seize the day—or rather, the night—with the most compelling man she's ever known. Marriage would mean losing guardianship of her beloved siblings, and surely no sane gentleman will take on seven children not his own. But if she can have one anonymous tryst with Mattheus, Earl of Worthington, Grace will be content to live out the rest of her life as a spinster.

Matt had almost given up hope of finding a wife who could engage his mind as well as his body. And now this sensual, intelligent woman is offering herself to *him*. What could be more perfect? Except that after one wanton night, the mysterious Grace refuses to have anything to do with him. Amid the distractions of the Season he must convince her, one delicious encounter at a time, that no obstacle—or family—is too much for a man who's discovered his heart's desire…

Please turn the page for an exciting sneak peek at

Ella Quinn's

THREE WEEKS TO WED

coming in April 2016 wherever print and e-books are sold!

CHAPTER ONE

End of February 1815, Leicestershire, England

The sky had darkened and wind rocked the carriage, causing at least one wheel to leave the road. Hail mixed with freezing rain battered the windows. Lady Grace Carpenter pounded on the roof of her coach, trying to make herself heard over the storm. "How close are we to the Crow and Hound?"

"Not far, my lady," her coachman bellowed over the wind. "I'm thinkin' we should stop."

"Yes, indeed. Make it so." She huddled deeper into her warm sable cloak. When they'd started out this morning, the weather had been dry and sunny, giving no indication a storm of this magnitude would come on.

She was only an hour or so from her home, Stanwood Hall, but they wouldn't make it. It was better to trust in the discretion of the innkeeper at the Crow and Hound than risk her servants and cattle to this weather.

A few minutes later, they turned off the road, and her coachman bellowed for an ostler. Moments later, her coach's door was quickly opened and the steps let down. Her groom, Neep, hustled her from the carriage to the open entrance of the inn.

The innkeeper, Mr. Brown, was there to greet her. Saxon blond, with blue eyes and of middling height and age, he shut the heavy wooden door against the weather. "My lady," he said in a surprised tone, "didn't expect to see you this evenin'."

"For good reason." Grace whipped off her damp cloak and shook it. "I didn't expect to be here. I was visiting an elderly cousin, and the storm blew up on our way back."

"It's as they say, my lady," he said, nodding. "No good deed goes unpunished."

"Well, it certainly seems like that at times. Thank God, we were close to you. I have my coachman, groom, and two outriders"—Grace grimaced—"but not my maid." She prayed no one would discover she was there without her lady's maid, Bolton, who was sure to give Grace her *I told you so* look when she finally made it home. "I shall require the use of one of your girls. It should go without saying, you have not seen me here."

"Yes, my lady." He nodded, tapping the side of his nose. "Ye were never here. Don't expect to see anyone else in this weather. Ye and yer servants will sleep warm and dry tonight." He pointed to the door next to the stairs and within easy reach of the common room. "I'll put ye in this parlor for dinner."

She gave him a grateful smile. "Thank you. That will be perfect."

Susan, one of Brown's daughters, showed Grace to the large chamber at the back of the inn on the first floor. She handed the girl her cloak to dry, then shook out her skirts. "I'll call for you when I am ready to retire."

"Yes, my lady. Anything you need, just pull the bell." Susan bobbed a curtsey and left.

Grace glanced around. Although she had stopped here any number of times on family outings, she'd never spent the night. The inn had been in the Brown family for several generations. The building was old, but it was clean and well maintained.

She took a book and Norwich shawl from her large muff before descending the stairs to the parlor. Although it was early, not much past two o'clock, Mr. Brown had closed the shutters, and a fire was lit, as well as sufficient candles to brighten the room.

An hour later, warm and dry, she was engrossed in *Madelina*, the latest romance from the Minerva Press. Over the storm, sounds of another carriage arriving could be heard. Grace lowered the book, wondering who the newcomer could be.

The inn door slammed open. Moments later, Mr. Brown's agitated tone and that of another man, a gentleman by his speech, reached her.

Her heart skipped a beat. *Worthington?* Could it really be him? She hadn't heard his voice for four years, but she'd never forget it.

Opening the door slightly, she peeked out. It was him. The man she'd wanted to marry her whole first Season and had never seen again. His dark brown, almost black hair was wet at the ends where his tall beaver hat had failed to keep it dry. If he turned, she knew she would see his startling lapis eyes and long lashes.

"Could you not ask the traveler in the parlor if I might share it with him?" Worthington asked the landlord, his tone strained but still polite. He was probably already cold and wet, and the common room would be chilly at best.

The kernel of an idea began to form. Swallowing her trepidation, Grace stepped boldly into the hall. "Mr. Brown, his lordship is welcome to dine with me."

"If you're sure, my . . ."

She flashed him a quelling glance. If he said "my lady," there'd be too many questions from Worthington. Whatever happened, he could not know her identity.

"Ma'am."

She tried not to show her relief. "Yes. You may serve us after his lordship has had time to change." Grace dipped a slight curtsey to Worthington and returned to the parlor.

Closing the door, she leaned back against it. This was her opportunity, maybe her only one, and she was going to take it.

What are you doing, my girl? Are you out of your mind? her conscience berated her.

"No one will know. Brown will deny I was here."

How do you expect to preach propriety to the children when you are—

"Oh, do be quiet," Grace muttered. "When will I have another chance? Answer me that. All I want is to spend some time with him. What is the harm in that?"

Water dripped off Mattheus, Earl of Worthington's greatcoat, as it had dripped off his hat earlier. A puddle had to be forming at his feet. He was not particularly impressed with the small inn. Although he'd passed it every time he made the trip to Town, he'd never stopped here before. If it weren't for the weather, he wouldn't have done so now.

"I can add more wood to the fire in the common room, my lord," the landlord said. "But me parlor's already got a guest."

He glanced over at the fairly large space. Even with the shutters closed, the windows rattled. Cold and drafty. "Would you please ask your guest if he will share the parlor for a short time?"

"Couldn't do that, my lord." The older man shook his head. "I could send the meal to yer room, but I ain't got an extra table. Once it warms up, you'll be right comfortable in the common room."

He sincerely doubted that would be the case.

"Mr. Brown..."

Matt turned at the sound of the low, well-bred, no-nonsense female voice. He suspected it would belong to an older lady, perhaps a governess, most definitely not the vision of loveliness standing before him. Before he could even thank her, she gave a curt nod and closed the door.

"I'll show ye to yer room, my lord." The landlord grumbled as he picked up Matt's bag.

"Thank you. It will be nice to be dry again." Half-way up the stairs, he stopped as a memory played hide-and-seek with him. He knew her, but from where? London. During the Season. He shook his head, trying to knock the memory loose, but nothing more came to him.

"This way, my lord."

"Coming." It was her hair that stuck in his mind. It shone like a new guinea coin. The landlord held a door open at the end of the corridor. "Thank you."

"I'll send one of me boys up with warm water."

"I would appreciate that."

Brown set about lighting the fire.

Matt didn't know many ladies who would offer to share their parlor with a complete stranger. The feeling that they had met before grew stronger. Who the hell was she?

"There ye be, my lord."

Once the door closed behind the landlord, Matt began shedding his damp clothing. The sooner he got back downstairs, the sooner he'd know who his mystery woman was.

Less than a half hour later, Matt made his way downstairs and knocked on the parlor door before entering. He bowed. "Thank you for agreeing to share your parlor and your meal. Permit me to introduce myself. Worthington, at your service."

Nothing like sounding pompous.

He was almost surprised when she smiled and rose instead of

turning her pretty nose up at him. "How could I refuse to assist a fellow traveler and in such dreadful weather as we are having?"

Graceful.

That was the first word that sprang to mind as Matt watched her glide to the bell-pull. When he entered the parlor, the table had already been set up for tea. She took a seat, motioning him to the chair opposite her. "Please. There is no need to stand on formality."

She handed him a plate, and in a few moments a young girl brought in a pot covered in a brightly colored cloth, set it down, then left.

"Do you take sugar?" the lady asked, glancing from beneath her long gold-tipped lashes.

It was clear that the lady, for she was certainly gently bred, had no intention of telling Matt her name. "I do, Miss—"

"Milk or cream?" she responded hastily.

"Two lumps of sugar and a splash of milk, if you would."

The corners of her lush lips tilted up slightly.

He made a point of looking around the room, as if searching for something. "Are you traveling alone?"

A deep rose crept up into her face. Though, under the circumstances, that wasn't surprising.

"Sometimes one cannot order the weather to suit one's convenience." Her voice was tight, as if she did not approve of either his question or the weather.

Her long, slender fingers showed no indication of a wedding ring. A fleeting memory niggled at him once more. How could any red-blooded man forget that glorious hair, gold glinting with burnished copper in the candlelight? On the other hand, the hair he remembered. It was her name he'd forgot. Her brows, a little darker than her golden curls, arched perfectly over eyes that tilted slightly upwards at the outer corners. He'd never seen a more beautiful woman.

He wished he could make out the exact color of her expressive eyes, but the light was too dim.

Blue. That was encouraging. Now if he could only recall the rest. Damn the devil. He had seen her before, but where, when, and why, he couldn't remember. His gaze was drawn to her mouth, deep rose and a little wider than what was considered fashionable. What would it be like to taste her, to feel her soft lips on his, and where had that desire sprung from?

Grace's heart was in her throat by the time Worthington joined her. In the short time he had been gone to his room, she had changed her mind a dozen times, at least about inviting him to join her.

Mattheus, Earl of Worthington.

Grace allowed her eyes to trail over his perfect form, adding to her still clear memories of him. He was tall and broad shouldered, his jacket was cut to perfection. His cravat perfectly tied. He had always been so well dressed. She never thought she'd see him again, or if she did, he would probably be married with several children. Come to think of it, even though he wasn't wearing a ring, he could still be married... Oh, he was speaking.

"Miss...?"

When she did not give him her name, he looked at her curiously. Grace walked over to the bell-pull, giving a sigh of relief when a few moments later Mr. Brown's other daughter entered the room.

She'd have to do better than that if she wanted him to... well... She fought the blush rising in her cheeks. "Please take a seat. I shall enjoy the company."

There, that was much better. Remember you are five and twenty, not eighteen.

This was not going to be as easy as Grace had thought it would be.

Worthington took a sip and his almost black brows drew together. "This is extraordinarily good tea for an inn."

"It is my blend. I travel with it." She only had it this time as a treat for her elderly cousin, who professed to love Grace's tea but would never allow her to leave the canister.

Now what was she to say? With the exception of her vicar, it had been so long since she had spoken with any male who was not a family member, and those had not been pleasant discussions. "Have you family that will worry about you?"

"Only my sisters and step-mother, and they do not know when I plan to return home." He took another sip of tea. "I imagine your family will be anxious."

They would be frightened to death. She should have been home long before now, but her cousin was lonely and had needed the company. "A bit."

"Do you have far to travel?"

Grace studied him over the rim of her cup. She had thought there'd been a spark of recognition in his eyes, but it was clear he did not know who she was. It had been several years since they had seen each other. He had probably danced with thousands of ladies since her one dance with him. In any event, she did not want him to know. It would only complicate her already overly complicated life.

"Not more than a day," she finally answered. True, but misleading. She had to turn the course of this conversation to a safer subject. "What do you think about the progress of the peace treaty?"

A small smile formed on his well-molded lips. "That the process has gone on far too long and that the new French government is not as strong as it needs to be."

Mr. Brown tapped on the door, then entered with another of his many daughters. "Come to clear the tea away, if you're ready."

Grace tore her gaze from Worthington's mouth. Oh my. If she'd thought he was mesmerizing before, it was nothing to what he was doing to her insides now. She had to pull herself together. "Yes, please. We shall dine at six."

Mr. Brown bowed. "That's perfect, my—"

She gave the man a sharp look.

"Ma'am."

Enough was enough. Just being around Worthington was turning her mind into a bowl of jelly. The landlord and his daughter left, leaving the door slightly ajar. She met Worthington's steady gaze. She would probably never see him again and might as well talk about what she wanted to. "I do not mind discussing politics, though you should know that I'm a Whig."

CHAPTER TWO

That was certainly throwing down the gauntlet. Matt had a feeling this was going to become an interesting conversation. If only he could either remember or discover who she was, it would be even better. "My party, as well. On the left side."

The lady's eyes sparkled with pleasure. "Then we should have much to discuss..."

During the meal and afterward, their conversation ranged over politics, philosophy, and estate management. In fact, any topic that came into their heads, except the weather. Hours later they had not even had to search for subject matter to discuss. He had not had such an interesting conversation in months, maybe years, and never with a woman. She was as well or better informed than any lady he had ever met. He'd never been so taken by a woman. Suddenly Matt wanted to know everything about her.

"Are you an adherent of Wollstonecraft?" she asked.

He leaned forward, placing his elbows on the table. "Completely. I find her views on the rights of women interesting in the extreme, and I am pleased to see that the numbers of Wollstonecraft and Bentham followers have grown in political circles."

A far-off expression crossed the lady's face. "I've not been in London much of late, though I do keep up a lively correspondence with my friends."

Perhaps this was his opportunity. "Do your friends hold the same ideas as you do?"

"Most of them." A note of caution entered her tone.

"We might know some of the same people."

"Have you joined the group attempting to help the war veterans?"

That hadn't worked. "I have."

They discussed some of the proposals being batted around. She was certainly knowledgeable. He peered at the large armchair near the fireplace. A book with a marbled cloth cover lay on the seat. "Is that one of the Minerva romances you have there?"

"Yes, it is." She lifted her chin a little. "I find them excessively diverting."

Based on their conversation, no one could accuse her of muddling her mind with romances. She was as well-informed as any bluestocking, but she didn't have the acerbic tone of one. "My step-mother reads them. She tries to hide them from my sisters." Matt grinned. "I'm not sure she always succeeds."

A smile played around her lips, and she tilted her head a little to the side. Much like an inquisitive bird. "And you, my lord?"

He wondered, not for the first time this evening, what it would be like to kiss those lips. To tug lightly with his teeth on her full lower lip. She was beautiful, intelligent, and he had to answer her question. Damn, now he wished he had read the books. "Not yet."

"You might enjoy them. Some gentlemen do."

"On your recommendation, I shall most definitely read at least one."

She colored prettily, as if pleased that she had made a potential convert.

Before he knew it, the clock struck half-six.

He came to his feet as she rose. "I must tidy up for dinner."

"Of course. I'll meet you here shortly."

She left the room, and he poured a brandy from the decanter on the sideboard. Never in all his years had he been as drawn to a woman as he was to his mystery lady. They agreed on almost everything, and when they disagreed, she stated her opinions clearly and intelligently.

Yet how the devil was he to discover her name and direction? The only idea he could come up with was to offer to escort her to her home to-morrow, provided the weather cleared. But what if she refused? He could follow her. He tossed off the brandy. Somehow, someway, Matt was determined to court her.

Grace shut the door of her chamber behind her and leaned against it. For years Matt Worthington had been nothing more than an infatuation, but now he was rapidly becoming so much more. It had been years since she had allowed herself to feel angry at the hand fate had dealt her. Yet now, now she could do something just for herself. She would not leave here, leave him, without knowing what it would be like to know joy with a man.

What if someone finds out? Everything you've worked for will be for naught. Her conscience popped up, just when Grace had thought it had given up.

Even with her family around, there were still times when she was so lonely. Not being able to marry was the one thing she had never got over. "Am I to have no joy of my own? I just want one night. One night to last me the rest of my life, that's all I'm asking."

Wanton!

"So be it." Her hands trembled and her stomach lurched. If only she wasn't so ignorant.

So much for your grand plans, her conscience sneered. *You don't have any idea how to go about this.*

"I am sure he'll help. How hard can it be, after all?"

He'll recognize you. Then where will you be?

"He won't. Other than that one dance, when Lady Bellamny made him ask me, I am sure he never took a second look at me. I was just one of many girls who came out that year." He certainly did not remember her now.

So you say. What if you get with child?

"Would you cease! It must be fate. After all, what were the odds that we would both be here at the very same time, with no one else in the inn?"

Wishing she had something nicer to wear, Grace gave up arguing with herself and washed her hands.

When she returned to the parlor, she called for wine. By the time Worthington arrived, she'd calmed her jangled nerves, and her conscience had decided to leave her to go to perdition in her own way.

He had changed his linen, but not his suit. "I apologize for dining in boots."

"I do not mind at all." She handed him a glass of claret. "As you see, I have no other clothes with me. This was only supposed to be a day trip."

"I expected to be home as well, and sent my valet ahead with the rest of my kit." He gave a rueful grin. "A lesson to me to keep a bag with me." He took a sip. "This claret is excellent."

"Yes, Mr. Brown keeps a well-stocked cellar."

She had wanted to confide in Worthington. Tell him that her father used to bring them all here because of the quality of the wine. Confide the difficulties she was experiencing now. Fortunately, before she revealed too much, the door opened and Mr. Brown entered followed by one of his sons, both carrying covered trays.

The savory aroma made Matt's stomach rumble.

"My missus thought ye might like a nice cream of mushroom soup to begin. Then we have a haunch of venison, with frenched beans . . ." By the time the man finished, the dishes covered the table and sideboard. "And here is a trifle for dessert."

Matt offered the lady selections from the offerings before filling his plate. They were silent for a few minutes as they ate. He, because he was ravenous. She simply appeared a bit shy. That was no wonder. She most likely had never dined alone with a man before.

"I must tell you that at first I was not impressed by this inn, but the food and wine make up for it being a bit shabby."

"I have always found the place to be cozy."

He gazed at her, mesmerized by the dainty way she licked the cream from the trifle off her spoon. "I think I agree."

He asked her what she thought of the experimental farm in Norfolk and was surprised to find she knew as much as he did. The hours flew by as they had earlier. Soon the clock chimed ten, and she rose.

Matt stood as well, expecting her to make a hasty retreat. Yet rather than curtseying and heading for the door, she stood before him, searching his face, waiting. That was all the invitation he needed.

Tentatively, he reached out and with the back of his hand slowly caressed her cheek. He had never wanted a lady as much as he did her. *What would she do if I kissed her?*

Suddenly, where she was from or who she was didn't matter any longer. She was his. He knew it in his bones. Fate had created a storm and placed her here for him to find and claim.

She took a small step toward him as with one finger he traced her jaw. She closed the distance between them again.

This is like tickling a trout, but with a much greater reward.

Worthington had proven to be everything Grace thought he would be, and now . . . now, even if she wished to resist him, she could not. She shoved down her rising anxiety. Her plan was coming to fruition, and now was not the time to be frightened. After all, what good would her virginity do her in her spinsterhood?

His eyes mesmerized her, and she wanted him. To feel his mouth on hers, his arms around her. How much else there was, she wasn't sure, but she wanted him to show her. Then he wrapped one arm around her waist, drawing her the few inches to him. He placed his hand on her cheek, and brushed his slightly callused thumb over her lips. This was going just as she'd wanted it to. It would be the most perfect night of her life.

"You are exquisite." His voice was low and sultry.

A pleasurable shiver ran down her spine. She'd never thought to hear a man say that to her. She or fate had chosen well.

He bent his head and moved his lips softly against hers.

She rested one hand lightly on his shoulder. He took the other, encouraging her to wrap her arms around his neck. When he trailed his tongue over the seam of her mouth, she did not know what to do, so she puckered them a little. He smiled against her lips. Had she done something wrong? She could not allow him to stop.

As bold as the lady had been when she had invited Matt to join her in the parlor and in their conversation, he had expected her to be experienced. She was not, and, for no reason he could understand, he wanted to crow. It was as if she had been waiting just for him.

Matt lifted his head and gazed down at her. "You've never been kissed before?"

A blush infused her cheeks. "Is it—is it that obvious?"

"No." Yes, but he wouldn't tell her that.

She lowered her long, thick lashes, and her unexpected shyness captivated him. "You are perfect."

Once again she raised her face to him. He leaned forward, breathing in her light, spicy scent. So different from the flowery perfumes other women used. Cupping both her cheeks with his hands, he kissed her again, nibbling her lush bottom lip, teaching her, urging her to open her mouth to him.

Her tentativeness gave way, and she held on to him tightly, returning his kisses with more vigor. As he stroked her back, he itched to untie the laces his fingers traveled over, and he paused for a moment. Too much, too soon. This lady was the most remarkable woman he had ever known, and he needed to ensure he did not scare her away.

She sighed, sinking, boneless, against him.

Two of his good friends had recently married, and it was time he did so as well. He hadn't believed his friend Marcus all those years ago when he'd claimed to have fallen in love with Phoebe at first sight. Matt did now.

He had no brothers, and it was past time he wed. The idea to look seriously for a wife had been pestering him more and more over the past few months. Matt wanted to laugh. It never occurred to him that he would meet his future wife when they were stranded together in a small inn. He held her closer. Whoever she was, she was his. If only she would tell him her name. He considered ignoring all the manners he had learned and asking her for it. But he was afraid she'd flee. What did it matter, though, when he would spend the rest of his life getting to know her?

He supposed he'd have to wait until to-morrow to propose or to ask whom he should go to for permission to address her. Yet her countenance, conversation, and the mature curves of her body told him she was not a young lady. So much the better if she could answer for herself.

A knock sounded on the door. He broke the kiss and set her away from him. "Yes?"

Brown opened the door and poked his head in. "My lord, my—um, I mean ma'am. Your chambers are ready. I had one of my girls run a heating pan between the sheets and put hot bricks in them."

When Matt had released her, his lady had turned from the door to face the fireplace, leaving him to deal with the innkeeper. "Thank you, Brown."

"Ring if you need anything, and someone will answer straight away."

"Thank you, again." Matt closed the door.

In two steps he was with her again. He placed a finger under her chin, tilting her head up. "I shall escort you to your room."

She nodded. Even in the candlelight, he could see the desire lurking in her eyes. He wished he could take her to his chamber, but there was time enough for that after they were betrothed.

Leaving her at her bedroom door, he went to the chamber he'd been given at the opposite end of the hall.

Matt was pleased to find a decanter of brandy on the bedside table. He stripped off his clothes and donned a serviceable dark green wool dressing gown the landlord had left for him. He stood staring into the fire, twirling the glass and trying to decide what he would say when he proposed. Finding out her name might be a good idea as well.

Grace could not believe he had kissed her like that and then left her at her chamber door. Good Lord, she had practically thrown herself at him.

You see, he didn't want you, her conscience mocked.

"He did, I—I could tell by his—by his kiss."

Why did Worthington have to be such a *gentleman*? It was not the most helpful thing he could have done at the moment. He could have made it easier for her. After what he had said and the way he had kissed her, how could he have just left her here? Obviously if she was going to have her night, she'd have to do something. There was nothing for it. She would have to go to him.

She called the maid and undressed. It had taken another glass of wine and several minutes to gather her courage. Then she threw a blanket around her shoulders and stepped out into the corridor to find him.

Fortunately, a light shone under the door at the other end of the hallway. Except for her servants, sleeping on the floor above and in the stable, she and Worthington were the only two guests in the inn.

The old, worn floorboards were cold under her feet as she walked the short distance to his chamber. Taking a breath, Grace fought down the fear threatening to overtake her. Surely he would not turn her away. She knocked on the door and entered.

The pleased expression on his face told her she had not been mistaken. He did want her. Every bit as much as she had prayed he would.

Lightning Source UK Ltd.
Milton Keynes UK
UKOW04f1040031117
312116UK00001B/87/P